Here's the Thing...

A novel by Laura Rudacille

for Julia
laugh!
Laura Rudacille
6/05

ISBN 0-7414-4687-1

Published by:

INFIﾍﾉITY
PUBLISHING.COM

1094 New DeHaven Street, Suite 100
West Conshohocken, PA 19428-2713
Info@buybooksontheweb.com
www.buybooksontheweb.com
Toll-free (877) BUY BOOK
Local Phone (610) 941-9999
Fax (610) 941-9959

Printed in the United States of America

Printed on Recycled Paper

Published April 2008

Acknowledgments

When I began the project of writing this book, I didn't type or even own a computer. Armed with a three-ring binder and a great deal of notebook paper I began. I wrote whenever and wherever I could; doctor appointments, oil changes, waiting for the kids' soccer practices or guitar lessons to finish. Countless times I was asked if I had returned to school. I would just laugh and say, "Nope, I'm writing my first novel!"

The only thing worse than writing part time was having people who love you know you're writing. "When is that book coming?" "Are you still working on that book?"

Early in the process I read a book by Nicholas Sparks who noted that a simple plot had taken five drafts and countless re-writes to create. I decided at that moment to set mini goals and expect at least five drafts. It took many more than that, but what an exhilarating feeling to finish!

In addition to the tremendous friends who served as full time sounding boards, I wish to thank:

Amy Anderson, Ann Shoemaker, Kristen Warner, Sherry Keen, and Carin Kohlbus, for reading and editing my various manuscripts.

Paige Mundy for genuine Spanish, and Britt Mundy for counterfeit Spanish.

Garrett Hartman for collaborating to create a fun and fabulous cover.

Carol, Christine, and especially Keith for laughter, encouragement and celebratory frozen strawberry margaritas in twelve inches of snow!

My Mom, Gene Dyke, for 'generational eliminates' as well as valuable advice along the way.

My husband, Adam and my boys, Mason and Teague who tolerated as I monopolized the brand new computer.

For Kristen Kline, 'thanks' is too small a word. Kristen walked each tedious step of the four year process with me, and wouldn't allow my lack of typing skills to derail the vision of the book to come. She selflessly gave her time and transferred my notes and midnight scribbling to disk. My biggest cheerleader, Kristen soothed my doubts, bolstered my ego and ultimately helped me grasp my dream. For those things and countless more, my gratitude to you is immeasurable.

To the numerous people who said to me over the years, "I have always wanted to write a book." I say start! Carry a journal record your ideas and discover your voice!

Dedication

For Mom: You are more than a mother
            You are an inspiration

Una Profesora desinteresada, una guardiana,
Una defensora compasiva, una apoya,
Una madre de corazón tierno, una amiga

Mi campeona… mi madre

Here's the Thing...

Ella (bride)

Meg (daughter)

Sylvia & Arthur (parents)

Anya & Warren (sister and her husband)

Mitch & Somi (brother and his girlfriend)

Thea & Honeysuckle (friends)

HawHaw & Julien (relatives)

Jewel (friend of Sylvia)

Phil (groom)

Hontie (Mother) aka Charlotte, Lottie

Gavin & Jade (brother and his wife) Davis (son)

Nathan & Barb (father and wife)

Isabella (aunt, Hontie's sister)

Clare (cousin)

Heath & Catheryn (cousin and his wife)

Georgia (cousin) Brennan & Payton (sons)

Tom & Sueanne (friends) Drew (son)

Joe (friend)

Prologue

August 18, 2007 3:40 pm

My white knuckles clutched the seat as the truck raced wildly on the narrow road, making me grateful I hadn't taken the time for French tips. My exhausted brother Heath was at the wheel. His hands responded as if on auto pilot, as his vacant eyes transferred the information needed to navigate the pavement's twists and turns. His wife Catheryn, seated shotgun, attempted to gloss her lips. The applicator, loaded with color, skipped as the vehicle pitched without warning. The vanity mirror closed with a snap. Catheryn dug a tissue from her purse and scrubbed at the apricot streak that now accented her chin. A peek over my shoulder in third-row seating revealed Payton, my four-year old snoozing quietly, while he clung to his toy airplane. On my right with a death grip on the door handle, sat my older sister, Clare. Absently she scrunched her still drying hair and muttered to herself while the woodland scenery blurred past the window.

With furrowed brow Clare turned to me and shook her head with disgust, "The wedding started forty minutes ago; we will never make it."

The truck careened dangerously close to the gravel shoulder. I held my breath and tried to talk myself out of becoming car sick. The tires squealed as Heath whipped the truck into a tight u-turn.

Clare's arms flailed out in search of stability. "Good grief," her breath heaved. Slowly, we began to climb a steep one-lane dirt road. I glanced again to the rear seat. Payton, now horizontal, was still fast asleep with the plane securely tucked in his tiny fist. "Georgia," Clare asked me. "Tell me why are we endangering our lives exactly?"

1

"Family?" I answered weakly.

Yeah... family...

More precisely the wedding of my cousin Phil and his fiancée Ella. They had been my bloodline's out-of-state entertainment for several years. Both Phil and Ella were blessed with extreme intelligence blended with that oh so common, **lack** of common sense. I'd never known two individuals so scarily similar who didn't repel like same-sided magnets.

They had mastered a lifestyle which could only be described as 'gypsy'. We would enjoy their energy when we visited, always coming away feeling 'oh, to have such a free-spirit go-with-it attitude'. Wouldn't that be nice?

Nice from time to time, sure, but to make a life out of it... Was that possible?

Not only was it possible for Phil and Ella, but I had discovered it was truly an art to be mastered.

The truck had come to a halt and moments later I stood in front of a quaint one-room school house styled chapel. Perched high on a mountaintop in upstate New York, the panoramic view that encircled me was a visual masterpiece. Fields abloom with August's wild flowers added dashes of vibrant color to the multiple depths of green the surrounding farm fields and forests offered. The endless clear blue sky was dressed with an occasional cloud, which appeared placed by an artist's hand. In the distance a long abandoned threshing barn stood in a grain field. Its roof sagged deeply from obvious age and having endured many heavy winter snowfalls. I breathed in the pure mountain air and absorbed the unblemished scene. I closed my eyes and committed the snapshot to memory.

Heath, Catheryn, and Clare hustled inside the chapel leaving me little choice but to follow with a sleepy Payton on my hip. We discreetly shuffled in and found a pew toward the back. I sat with the grace of an eighty-year old lady and landed with a not so gentle thud on the solid pine pew bench. Off loading Payton, I watched as he curled into a ball with his head cushioned on my lap. His gentle breathing and peaceful expression combined with the quiet atmosphere allowed the fatigue of the last three days to root and roll through my entire body. I stroked Payton's blond hair and wondered for a moment if anyone would notice if I stretched out along beside him. Deciding against it, I rolled my neck, stifled a yawn, and scanned the numerous unfamiliar faces throughout the chapel. Everyone else, oblivious to the fact the wedding should have begun an hour ago, appeared alert and joyful while they awaited the union of Phil and Ella.

So why was it I found myself seated, exhausted, hurriedly dressed, and not looking forward to the ceremony of my loved ones?

Here's the thing…

For years the female members of my family had traveled to my Aunt's home in upstate New York for Estrogen Weekend. For five glorious days we would wander the neighboring counties for antique and flea market treasures. No children, no husbands, no itinerary, nothing was looked forward to more.

Two years ago, my cousin Phil, a thirty-three year old a jack-of-almost-everything, announced he and Ella intended to take the plunge and tie their nuptials in with our weekend.

Hey, thanks for saving me an extra trip to New York, but don't screw with my weekend!

Compromise was called for and my vision of an idyllic Estrogen Weekend vanished. Hours of precious flea marketing would have to be sacrificed for the greater good of families merging. *Cripes.*

Phil and Ella's vision of their wedding was a shabby chic affair for about one hundred family and friends. Honestly, despite the mentioning of the potential wedding, I wasn't holding my breath. The odds were this bohemian pair would elope or possibly forego the whole idea as quickly as they had verbalized the thought.

Unfortunately, they hadn't forgotten.

Seventy-two hours ago I pulled into my Aunt's property as an invited wedding guest. To my horror I discovered two years was merely enough time for an implosion of Phil's ADD to occur.

Just a thought, when entrenched in a free-spirited lifestyle combined with severe ADD, one should not attempt to plan an affair for one hundred people. Then again, if you were afflicted with such ailments you were probably blissfully ignorant to the basic organizational tasks of preparing for everyday life.

The mastered gypsy lifestyle of Phil and Ella did not follow the template of main stream American living; growing up, schooling, employment, car payments, rent, eventual mortgage, marriage, and babies. Not in any particular order mind you, but a check list nonetheless.

Phil and Ella's lifestyle was more of a 'create as you go', 'roll with it' design. They would move from place to place on a whim, find somewhere to squat and auspiciously fall into "meaningful" employment. Their last cross country trip was in a vintage Land Rover that had a bean bag chair for a back seat and no safety belts to secure Meg, Ella's six-year old daughter, to the vehicle. I had inquired once about the lack of seat belts in their car. The response I received was "Georgia, are you one of those seat belt people?" To which I replied, "No I am one of those keep your child's arms, legs, and head attached to their body people."

Call social services, cripes!

Acquiring a rent-free place to live was another Phil and Ella bohemian talent. Their current squatter's residence was a friend of a friend's vacant lake front property. Phil and Ella moved in under the guise of exchanging home improvements for rent. They had been living there a year and a half now and no improvements had yet to occur. In fact the hot water heater which was to be the first repair, Phil and Ella deemed unnecessary. "Georgia," Phil had told me, "There is a perfectly good lake just fifteen feet from our door which works just fine, three seasons a year, for bathing."

On impulse Phil and Ella would pull up stakes and leave promises unfulfilled and debts outstanding. Yet along the way good people had befriended and supported them, looked out for them, and nurtured them.

It was truly an obscure way of surging through life.

But really, ***here's the thing...*** ; we're at the marriage. With a sleeping child on my lap in a quaint countryside chapel surrounded by one hundred family and friends, it was happening. Phil and Ella were about to take the plunge.

But oh, how had we arrived at this moment?

How much insanity could a body wade through on adrenaline, sweat and self preservation?

Grab a life jacket folks... after surviving those six seemingly infinite days...

... I will tell you.

Chapter 1

When orchestrating a family trip involving a five hour road trip, multiple vehicles, and a wedding, some prearrangement may be required.

"Is the wedding still a go?" I asked Mom. I had received an invitation, two weeks ago. A black and white photo of Phil and Ella fully clothed amidst a mid-air leap off a lakeside dock. The image caught the two of them suspended inches from the water drenched in the long shadows of the afternoon sun. Across the top of the cleverly handmade invite were the words "Phil and Ella Jump In!" Striking in its black and white simplicity, I scanned the underlying details which read:

August 18, 2007, Solidarity Chapel

RSVP regrets only.

That was it. No time and no phone number to regrettably reply to. That was classic Phil and Ella. My cousin was probably the only person on the planet who could plan an event for two years and had yet to have permanent arrangements made.

"Yes, Georgia, the wedding is on," Mom said with an undercurrent of impatience.

"Well you never know with those two."

The journey north for *Estrogen Weekend* had become tradition for the females in my family. Aunt Charlotte, whom we call Hontie, invited us each August to use her modest home as our bed and breakfast for the trip. I coveted the sedate pace that pulsed within Hontie's town. Estrogen weekend offered the break from my hectic life and the perfect excuse for antiquing and flea marketing in another nearby town called Bouckville.

For one week each year, the remote one street town of Bouckville would explode with more then two thousand antique and flea market vendors. They poured in from all over the U.S. to display wares of ultimate variety and price point for countless patrons to peruse.

Each day at sunrise my family would drive forty minutes from Aunt Charlotte's home to Bouckville. Endless hours would be spent combing the acres, fields, groves, alleys, and streets in search of treasure. Rain, shine, scorching hot, or freeze blasted, we would head out and not return until late in the afternoon. In the evening with a cold Corona in hand, we'd arrange that day's flea market loot on the benches of the deck for all to view and enjoy. At the completion of the trip the collection would be recorded in a traditional photograph, "Bouckville Bounty". We'd end up broke, exhausted, rich and revived, having shared laughter and camaraderie as well as rubbing each other the wrong way, occasionally. We'd return home to our husbands and children with grand tales, fond memories, and no permanent scarring.

My Mom had been picturing this year's Estrogen weekend/wedding as a family reunion of sorts. The vision included her three children Heath, Clare and me, our spouses, and all eight grandchildren frolicking in the lake, stoking camp fires, and devouring s'mores. Several times over the last year Mom had been heard reciting those forbidden words, "Let's all go! Vamanos! Husbands, kids, total familia!"

Mom had recently decided to teach herself Spanish. Wonderful goal, except it meant she would randomly toss out words and offer no translation.

Husbands? Children? *Hello...* **Estrogen** weekend, *not* testosterone. Kids and husbands don't come to

Bouckville. *Ever.* Just a little side note that has not changed, not even when the wedding plans were mentioned, but this fell on deaf ears. Mom's plan making was understated yet clever. Her goal would be to subtly sculpt her adult children's plans back into the original and only acceptable plan. *Mom's plan.*

Today's conversation with Mom was proving to be more of the same. "Georgia, the kids would love to have lake fun and maybe the men could rent a boat for the day or a kayak, and take them fishing, canoeing, whatever, while we are at Bouckville. That would be mucho fun!"

"Mom, they are not coming," I patiently responded again while applying pressure to the top of my head and gently pushing my protruding devil horns back under my scalp. *I distinctly remember we covered this at Thanksgiving, Christmas, and again at Easter.* "And I'm pretty sure Clare's not bringing family either."

I endured Mom's eight second moment of silence, followed by a sharp inhalation of breath. "Well Georgia, I have never heard this before," Mom said in that *tone.* The hair on the back of my neck was straining to new heights. *What is that tone anyway, and will I inherit it to use on my own children?* That almighty power that no matter what your age, your mother could utter a tone or pass you a look and instantly you'd be reverted back to childhood and rendered powerless.

"Anyway," I carefully shifted topics. It was one week until departure and, not unusual for my family, we had no firm travel plans. I was all for spontaneity, but by this point I needed at the least a sketch of the proposed trip. "Departure time," I said to Mom. "I'm off work Wednesday and Clare is off work Wednesday, so we'll be able to head north easily, early in the day." The trip would take five hours, traffic not withstanding, and I planned to be in New York before dark.

"Oh… Wednesday… Georgia… I'm not sure if Hontie wants us to arrive that early," Mom answered. We had multiple family members, and several vehicles tackling a five hour road trip to a home that will be housing more bodies then beds for six days. Food, clothing, air mattresses, extra pillows, and blankets… *Fore thought? Planning?*

As a beauty salon owner, my life revolved around an appointment book. With each day broken down in quarter hour increments, punctuality and planning were a must. After scheduling the trip and juggling my clientele around the days off, I found it impossible to ignore travel details.

"Well Mom, that's my plan. I want three days at Bouckville before the wedding events happen."

"There's still a lot that needs to come together," Mom said, "you will be able to pitch in when you get there."

Great.

Two years ago Hontie had given the bride and groom two stipulations if they were to have a backyard reception at her home. Phil and Ella were to paint the exterior of her house and help with her extensive gardens: weeding, pruning, mulching, the works. Two years, do-able. Right? Well, not quite. The first year's procrastination pushed the painting to the next summer and this year New York State's unusually rainy season had made painting virtually impossible, and the gardens had the nerve to grow, so maintenance was constant.

Mom had just returned from a "work" weekend at my aunt's home, the proposed sight of the reception. She and my sister Clare's eleven-year-old son, Colton, journeyed to Hontie's to help with outdoor chores and yard work for three days. Mom had boasted that Colton had worked like an adult. He had gotten up at 7:00 A.M. and worked for hours barely stopping to eat. Colton had come back seventy-five dollars richer and Mom returned with the makings for one hundred pin wheel favors and raw fabric for tablecloths.

"Ella still needs to call me about tables and sizes," Mom told me, "and Clare and I will start work on pin wheels this week in the evenings."

Translation – after working full days and caring for their families, Clare and Mom would embark on projects that should have been done months ago. I didn't offer any comment because doing so would only involve me in ventures I don't support.

I ended the conversation with Mom, since it clearly wasn't resolving anything. Then being the youngest, I quickly dialed my big sister Clare. "Hey, are you aware that Mom thinks your entire family is attending the wedding weekend?" My youngest son Payton had appeared and was tugging on my pants.

Clare's exasperated sigh came through loud and clear. "She's just not hearing me. Georgia, have I ever said that any of them were going?"

"Juicy, mommy?" Payton said. I patted his head to pacify him.

"No Clare, but you've also never said they weren't…"

"Drinky drink?" I held up a finger to Payton signaling to give me one minute.

"…this leaves quite a loophole in the world of Mom, Clare."

She groaned.

Brennan, my nine-year old, had now joined Payton and me in the kitchen. "Who's on the phone, Mom?" Brennan asked as Clare's ramblings buzzed in my ear. I waved him off, trying to focus on the conversation. Brennan pulled the goldfish crackers from the cupboard. "Can you hand me a bowl please, Mom?" I rolled my eyes and pointed to the phone at my ear.

Has there ever been any documented proof of the magnetism between kids and phones? Why is it as soon as you touch it your offspring magically appear and command your undivided attention?

"Travel plans," I redirected Clare's tirade.

"I just can't look that far ahead, Georgia. I'm just not in the right frame of mind to discuss this now." Clare answered. Older than me by four years, Clare could be quite a procrastination queen.

"I'll be ready to roll by noon on Wednesday." I said as I punched the straw through into a juice pouch and sent Payton on his way.

"Oh… well I was thinking more like four o'clock, That way Catheryn can ride with us too." Catheryn, my sister-in-law, needed a ride because my brother, Heath, was headed to New York on Monday. Some large item inventory for Hontie's antique shop needed to be transported; a wardrobe, a blanket chest, and a bedroom suite. Heath borrowed a metal trailer and had been nominated to haul the load. He also needed to handle some projects Mom had discovered during her work weekend that needed 'Man Hands'. *Whatever that meant.* Anyway, leaving late in the day for a five hour trip was not an option for me.

Clare launched into her need to firm up baby sitter times and had begun to recite the activities her kids had for the week. *For cryin' out loud.*

"Well Clare," I interrupted, "I may drive up myself then. That way I'll have my own car and I can get in and get settled before dark."

"I don't think that's necessary." *Big sister override.* "Why take an extra car?"

I could think of several reasons why, in addition to the one I just gave, but I know it's better to back down than debate. "Check on your babysitter times and we'll confirm everything later. Bye"

I sat at the table with my head in my hands. I was tired and we hadn't even left yet. "Mom, why can't we go to the wedding?" Brennan asked while munching on his snack.

"Because, honey, this is my vacation. And it is really an antique trip more than a wedding. The wedding is only one afternoon."

"I want to go on BACATION!" Four-year old Payton appeared with his ever present blankie draped over his head. He climbed into my lap and I felt the double team coming on.

"You just don't want us there, and that's okay," Brennan stated knowingly as he rose and put his dish in the dishwasher. *The wisdom a nine-year old with a thirty-year old soul could fling at you.* I scooped up Payton, draped my arm around Brennan's shoulder and together we walked into the living room to the couch.

"Really, Brennan," I tried to word carefully, "you don't understand. It's just that if it rains, we go to Bouckville; if it's cold, we go to Bouckville; if it's 1000 degrees, we go to Bouckville. Then we walk and walk and look and look. When we look, we look at 'mom' stuff, not 'kid' stuff. When you think you are so tired and hungry, so hot or cold, that you can't go one more step – that's when we walk and look some more… all day from breakfast until dinner… sun up to sun down." OK, I think I got my point across.

"I get it Mom, your day, your stuff, your trip." Pause. Tilt of the head, earnest eyes. "Really, I can do it." Brennan really, *really* wanted to go.

"It's *not* fun, honey," I asserted firmly.

"Really, I get it," said Brennan with the expression of understanding on his face that belonged on a D.A. just before his final trick question. "Your trip," his bottom lip was showing signs of a pout.

I was wavering. "No whining, I mean it." My solid stand was deteriorating, fast. "If I hear ANY fussing, bickering, or ANYTHING, I am fining you BIG bucks." Fining had become my latest revelation in discipline.

"I just want to see Hontie's home; I've never been there before... and the wedding of course, never been to one of those either." Brennan's head rapidly bobbed up and down in an effort to close the deal. "I'll be good, too. No whining, I promise. I think I can be a big help, too," – here it comes, the kill shot – "But it's your trip so really, it's up to you Mom."

I was completely dead. I had no defense against rational child thinking. "The deal, Bren, is this. We'll go and you *will* behave and we will have a trip together. I'm not so sure about..." I jerked my head toward Payton, careful not to say his name out loud. "I need to check with Daddy."

"Thanks, Mom," came Brennan's calm reply, even though I could see through to the internal happy dance he was doing.

Deciding on a firm plan and sticking to it was the only true source of survival as a youngest child. After I discussed it with my husband, we weighed the pros and cons of my taking the boys, *Yes, Plural*. Both boys were going along. *Won't Mom be pleased!*

Departure from Pennsylvania was set for noon Wednesday, in my own vehicle. That gave me two flea market days, one wedding/reception day, one antiques filled day, one return trip day. I invested in a child hiker backpack to haul Payton's forty-three pounds around the endless acres of flea market when he got tired. We wouldn't be able to move as fast, but I could cut our days short if needed. It sounded nearly perfect to me. Whenever the rest of the family got there, fine. Best of all, if I needed an early exit from family bonding, I had my own car.

So everything was settled, or so you would think. Two days before departure, Mom stopped in and examined my pile of luggage. After a brief mental wrestling match she actually said, "Are you really sure you want to take the boys along?" *Come on.* For two years I had heard nothing but family trip, fun on the lake, blah blah blah. And now that I'm actually dragging my offspring – the only one of her three children who'd folded – I get the 'are you sure want to do this?'

With an exasperated huff, I replied just loudly enough to be heard, "I can't win for trying," which left Mom momentarily speechless.

Thankfully she stayed quiet long enough for my band aid sentence. "Mom, after the last two weeks of back and forth plans, this is what I have decided. I'm choosing to travel with my kids. I'm choosing to carry Payton and compromise my flea market experience, and I'm driving to maintain some micro-morsel of control over our daily schedule. I'm choosing, I've decided, and that's my plan."

Resignation, and I was pretty sure a measure of respect, crossed her face and she left wishing us a safe travel!

Well done youngest child, a true grown-up moment.

Chapter 2

**They say that getting there is half the fun...
however, in this journey getting there was not
only half the fun, it was the *only* fun.**

The boys were tucked securely in the back seat of the Jeep with all of our gear around them. Payton's blankie, snugglers and toys he could not live without for six days, a stroller, a piggy back chair, and of course the wedding gift, were all in the cargo area.

"I think we have it all." I pulled out of the drive. "Everything but the kitchen sink, as they say."

"Why would we bring the sink mommy?" Brennan asked curiously.

"That's just silly," Payton agreed.

"It's just a figure of speech. It means I feel as if we packed the whole house."

"The whole house?" Payton giggled again, "That's just silly."

We settled in for the lengthy journey. I called my husband and Mom to let them know we were off and assured them I'd call again when we crossed the New York State line.

Five hours; one McDonald's lunch and bathroom break later, we exited Rt. 81 to the remote back hills of upstate New York. Perfect journey.

The majestic mountains were covered in a variety of trees. The thick foliage and depth of color was extraordinary. "Isn't this the most beautiful countryside you've ever seen?" I asked the boys.

"Mmm Hmm," Brennan responded with awe. Payton was too involved in the latest Game Boy game to bother raising his gaze.

The forty-five minute trip from the interstate to Hontie's small town fooled your mind into believing you had been transported back in time to simpler days. In contrast to my home town where a seven mile trip to the store involved six traffic lights and countless vehicles in a rush to nowhere. This village offered a church, a funeral home, a flower shop, a single school, and one fire company. Located in a region of natural and man made lakes, the beautiful area was paradise three-quarters of the year, yet each winter promised a severe test of the elements.

Ahead one of my favorite roadside accents filled my sight. "Look at that barn – gorgeous!" The architecture was so different from the barns in Pennsylvania. The barn had a short sloping metal roof, tall grain silo, and a long forgotten out-building with partially collapsing rafters. The main difference, however, was back home the barn and farm house usually shared the same parcel of land. Here it seemed barns were erected for convenience wherever the land manager felt best.

"Ooo, look at that one!" Created with the stones from the field it sat upon, the aged barn stood sturdy. Over several years vines had grown thick and heavy claiming the structure from ground to roof top. "Beautiful!! Do you see it?"

"Yes, Mom, you said that about the last one, too," Brennan chuckled.

"I just love it here."

Wriggling as far forward as his seat belt would allow, Brennan asked, "How far to Hontie's?"

"A few minutes, I better call your dad before we lose cell phone service and let him know we're here."

"No service?" Brennan asked. "How will we call Daddy the rest of the time?"

"Hontie has a phone."

"Yeah, that's right," he was relieved.

"Does she have a potty?" Payton asked.

"Of course!" I laughed. "It's not like we are traveling to a different planet!" After the call had been made, the boys and I went back to enjoying the countryside.

"Mom, where's the town?" Brennan zipped up his Game Boy gear.

"Well honey, out here you drive along for miles and miles and see nothing. Then a few homes, a gas station, bank, post office and mini mart, that's the town. Only about two streets and forty or fifty buildings, it's remote and wonderfully peaceful. I love coming here. It's so relaxing. We'll visit and flea market, sit on the deck and visit some more." I sighed blissfully, "Total serenity."

"*Senity*?" Payton questioned.

"Quiet time," I explained.

"Oh, like nap," Payton said seriously.

"Yep, like nap."

Brennan shook his head, "But you're awake."

Hontie's town, settled before the Depression, exuded a quaint understated confidence. Her house, like most of the homes in the area, had wooden siding. The maintenance of scraping and painting was an incessant process. Her home had a large shaded deck perfect for lazy mornings or unwinding after a long day. The deck's twenty- five foot planks were wrapped with deep bench seating capped with a heavy twelve inch railings. I felt it was one of the dwelling's best features. Every year flower boxes straight out of *Martha Stewart Living* balanced on the railing tops. Each box boasted variegated foliage, herbs, nasturtium, and lobelia. All of which thrived under Hontie's patient care. A retro aluminum legged table with a white enameled top trimmed in red served many practical functions as well as just looking awesome. Randomly placed mismatched wooden chairs were the only other deck furnishings. In the lone sunny corner of the deck, Hontie's passion for the mid-west was evident. Native American clay pots hand carried from her trips to the Grand Canyon boasted a dozen or more different types of cacti. Small and large with and without thorns, flowering, ground covering, also meticulously cared for. I could envision how beautiful the deck would look for Phil and Ella's reception.

In the distance I could see the pizzeria on the corner. Every small town's got to have a pizza joint. "We're here!" We turned right, fourth house on the left. "That's it! There it is! We're here!" I shouted excitedly and was joined by a chorus of hoorays from the back seat.

Chapter 3

Mother of all madness... what happened here?

"Unbuckle your brother Bren, get your shoes on, hop out, and stretch your legs." I shouted orders to the boys. With the Jeep securely parked, I stared through the windshield dumbfounded as my mind made an effort to digest the scene in front of me.

Maybe we had taken a trip to another planet after all.

I understood the bride's idea for the wedding was 'shabby chic'; however, the carnage that met my eyes surpassed shabby in a big way.

My much sought after deck haven was lost. Buried under unspeakable towering piles of... I wasn't sure what. A waste land of trash bags, plastic totes, and cardboard boxes positioned on top of one another with the contents spilling over to the deck planks below. Used dishes sat forgotten. Utensils and drinking glasses were stacked carelessly on the ledge that normally boasted Hontie's beautiful flowering window boxes. Beside the glass doors to the home, tool boxes, power equipment, and electrical cords were lying in a tangled heap. Galvanized sap buckets nested inside one another resembled a towering sand castle. On top of one pile a trio of oversized hand-blown wine glasses teetered on narrow blue stems. Hontie's enamel top table's only visible leg had dropped into a crevice near the back edge of the deck. The railing and bench from the far side of the deck had been removed completely, and Amazon sized house plants served as a barricade preventing a three foot tumble into the overgrown flowerbed below.

I blinked slowly. Surely this had to be an elaborate trick of my mind. *Were there really one hundred guests arriving here in three days for a wedding reception?*

The roar of a table saw startled me back to my surreal reality. My brother Heath was operating the deafening saw. Engrossed in his work Heath hadn't heard us pull in. A well worn ball cap shielded his eyes. All I could see was the pencil gripped in his teeth as he leaned over the spinning blade. Heath flipped off the saw and abruptly looked up. I inhaled sharply, as the saw whined slowly to a stop. Fatigue captivated his face. Deep circles under his eyes made them appear sunken, as he stared blindly at me through heavily lined eyes. His complexion normally ruddy and healthy was pale. He offered nothing by way of greeting. He just fixed his eyes eerily on mine. *Cripes, not good.* Without breaking eye contact, Heath collected the pieces of cut lumber and strode up the steps. His long legs disappeared into unseen foot holes within the debris filled deck.

My attention was pulled from Heath, as my cousin's fiancée Ella burst from the house. She zigzagged under Heath's lumber and maneuvered through the obstacle filled deck with practiced grace. "Georgia!" Ella threw her arms wide. "Welcome!"

The blue handkerchief tied over Ella's wild naturally curly hair tended to be a summer staple as well as a fashion statement. A unique genetic blend had yielded beautifully bronzed skin and a stunningly huge smile. She was currently sporting multiple tank tops and low slung cargo pants torn off at the ankles. Despite the welcoming smile Ella wore on her face, the underscore of fatigue was evident. "How was the trip?" she asked me. Brennan and Payton had joined me at some point during my visit to the twilight zone and were standing unsure beside me. "Hey Brennan, Payton, glad you came!"

"I'm on BACATION," Payton offered.

"You sure are." Ella ruffled his hair and then turned to Brennan. "And look at you, all tall and grown up!"

"Thanks for having us to your wedding," Brennan said.

"It's going to be great!" She gave him a warm hug.

"Cats Mommy!" Payton took off after them.

"Bren, honey…"

"On it Mom," He trailed after Payton, always the protective big brother.

"It appears you have a lot of work to do." I looked around; my stomach clenched the more my eyes absorbed.

"It's coming," Ella leaned on my bumper obviously exhausted. "I'm just cleaning the bathroom. Then I'm done for today."

Done? Done for the day? The sun was still hours away from setting.

"Phil and I have errands to do before the rest of my family gets in," Ella said calmly. "My parents should arrive in an hour, and my brother and sister are over at the lake house settling in with their families. The lake…."

Don't panic. I tuned her out. *I'm sure there's a plan. There has to be a plan, right? I mean, there is a wedding reception here in three days. Don't say anything; don't say anything, I began to mantra in my head. Done for the day, surely she's kidding.*

I closed my eyes and took a cleansing breath. I exhaled and peeked out from under my lids. *Nope not a hallucination.* Two well worn tire paths beside the house served as Hontie's secondary driveway. For convenience she used the drive to unload groceries when entering the house through the deck. Currently the drive was occupied by the fifteen foot metal trailer Heath had pulled from Pennsylvania. The furniture he had brought had been unloaded and the trailer was acting as worksite dumpster. The trailer was heaped with discarded lumber, drywall, two by fours, and

PVC piping. On closer inspection I realized the trailer also held the remains of Hontie's bright yellow kitchen cupboards; nails protruding, edges splintered.

Ella had stopped talking. Patiently she stood smiling at me. "Just wait until you see Meg," her six year old daughter. "She's really looking forward to seeing Brennan and Payton. Maybe you can bring them to the house for a swim later."

"Yeah, they were hoping we could fit that in." I gnawed my lip nervously. "Ella, what is going on here?'"

"Huh?" her head angled, honestly confused by my question.

I gestured to the deck astounded by the amount of crap that was occupying the normally spacious planks. I figured the deck was under there somewhere and the load of jagged wood on the trailer? Unless we were having a bonfire, it couldn't possibly be needed for the reception. I hadn't touched a toe inside the dwelling and I could see there was plenty to do before I called it a day.

Ella just laughed. Movement on the deck drew our attention.

"Hey Georgia," Phil emerged and gazed adoringly at his bride to be. "Sweetie are you done in here?'"

"Just about," Ella pushed from the Jeep. I watched her go. On the top step of three, Ella tangled herself around Phil in a not so PG display. He gave an affectionate pat on the rear, as she passed through the garbage maze and slipped back into the house.

Phil looked calm. So I'll be calm. *Why get frantic? Worry is a useless emotion after all.* "Where are the boys?" he asked.

"Under the canopy." I nodded toward the only thing in sight that gave any inkling that some type of outdoor function was pending. Stark white, it stood in the shaded yard, hastily assembled, its dark canvas carrying tote dangling from the aluminum eaves. Three heaps of earth about four feet apart sat next to the canopy like giant ant hills. A shovel jutted from the top of one pile and the handle from another was all that was visible from where it had disappeared into the ground.

"Hey Brennan, hi Payton, watch those holes okay guys?'" Phil called across the yard. Striding towards me in battered leather boots, I was astonished how he, like Ella, appeared casually fashionable. Trendy and urban, as if they had walked from the pages of a hip magazine. Phil's once blond hair had darkened over his thirty-three years, adding more contrast to his green eyes and strong-featured face. His jeans hung loosely around his narrow waist, frayed at the ankles, holes in the knees and seat. The faded denim showed more wear than most teenagers and was met by a ragged concert t-shirt which clung to his ultra long torso. At 6'3", Phil towered over the boys, as they rushed over and shared a fierce bear hug with him. Moving quickly, Phil caught Payton under the knees and flipped him upside down. Payton's squeals of delight rang out as he hung two feet off the ground. Comfortable with the child's play, Phil asked easily, "So Georgia how was the trip?"

"Good, great – no problems."

Phil returned Payton to his feet and sent him after Trivet, Hontie's three-legged cat. "How's your Mom? Clare? When are they coming?"

"Clare and Catheryn should be here by 7:00 tonight and Mom tomorrow mid- day."

"Cool." Phil shoved his hand deep into the pocket of his pants and pulled out a pack of cigarettes and a lighter. With a flick he ignited the tip and inhaled deeply, as he leaned comfortably on the Jeep. The haze of fragrant smoke surrounded us casting a hue of illusion over the carnage in my view.

Hontie's incredible gardens had thrived during the unusually rainy summer. Ferns nearly three feet tall were mixed with large variegated leaf Hosta. The garden followed the line of the house from the road to the deck. Beside the deck steps dozens of unplanted annuals sat in plastic containers straight from the nursery. Leggy, wilting, and left for dead, their sad yet colorful faces bowed toward the ground beseeching some good soul for a sip of water.

Unwilling to look any further I turned toward the front of the house. The two story home had a simple design. Five eight-foot paned glass windows shared the home's front face with a solid wooden door. Decorative wooden corbels lined the roof as well as the eave above the front door. The wooden landing and steps had rotted long ago and been removed from the base of the door for safety, which left the door suspended three and a half feet above the flower bed. Seven feet of incredible color and variety welcomed you to the unusable front door. Crimson and colonial blue Bee Balm mixed with Black Eyed Susan's, periwinkle Phlox, and fuchsia Cleome. An artfully arranged trellis assisted Morning Glory and Fire Cracker Vine to lofty heights. Completing the horticultural masterpiece were the cheerful whimsical faces of garden angels. Smiling, they beckoned butterflies and hummingbirds to the fragrant blossoms.

The view of the garden had just begun to soothe my internal war, until I noticed a mass of mulch heaped on the sidewalk. It had been delivered but had yet to be spread. Hontie's mailbox had nearly missed being buried by the pile. The mailbox stood like a candle on a birthday cake, with a full bottle of water perched on top. Off the front walk at the edge of the flowerbed too conspicuous to be a lawn ornament, was a crib. Yes, a fully assembled crib. *A crib?* Overwrought again with the apparent dysfunction, I looked up to heaven for a burst of divine intervention.

What I received, however, was more horror. Rain spouting dangled from the corner of the second story's sloped roof. Multiple ladders abandoned after a paint scraping session leaned against the side of the house like a bizarre scaffold. Perched on a second floor windowsill a large gray tabby cat surveyed the scene below with blatant disinterest.

Sasha, Hontie's 100 pound Bernese Mountain dog, lumbered into the side yard. At the bottom of the deck steps, she slowly turned her massive head from side to side in search of an opening. From where I stood, I couldn't imagine her immense body squeezing through the web of wreckage successfully without inflicting harm to herself. She rapidly arrived at the same conclusion and retreated. Tongue lolling from the side of her mouth, Sasha flopped in the side yard beneath the erected white canopy.

"You just missed Dad." Phil's voice broke into my nightmare.

"Oh, I'm really looking forward to seeing him." Uncle Nathan, my ex-uncle via divorce, had vanished following a rousing game of family football on Thanksgiving Day when I was about ten years old. A renowned photo journalist, he had spent more time away from Hontie and their two boys during their marriage than he had with them. Uncle Nathan had remarried and now resided in California with the new wife and *perfect* children. Anyway, I was ten, the football game was great and for me it was a good last memory of him. The adult in me, however, knew anyone who left his family to create another family had committed a HUGE no-no.

Violation of Value #101, clear cut, right and wrong.

My eyes glazed over as Phil rattled on about his dad's latest photo expedition to the South Pole. Uncle Nathan had captured never before seen images of the frozen eco-system which were featured in a worldwide documentary to raise awareness about global warming. Eventually silence seeped through my haze as Phil stopped mid-sentence. Clearly detached from his words, I found his grinning face monopolizing my field of view. My mouth closed with an audible snap.

Phil gave me a chummy shoulder punch. "Georgia," he said with a laugh and dropped his cigarette nub to the ground and drove it into the earth with the heel of his work boot. "Come see what we're working on." Phil turned and walked toward the house. His long legs took the deck steps in two easy strides.

Having no choice I followed across the buried deck and walked through the door into the kitchen. All I could think of was Bill Paxton in 'Twister', *"We're goin' in."*

Mother of all madness!

Sheets of dry wall leaned against the far wall waiting to be placed over exposed horsehair plaster. In the corner Heath lay on his back focused as he delivered a final hammering whack to the kitchen sink, which was supported by a two by four frame creation. Beneath the sink, pipes jutted from the wall but joined nothing. *Cripes! This just was getting better and better.*

All in all, the entire "project", as Phil put it, looked like an episode of While You Were Out. *Apparently that just applied to the bride and groom's mental status.*

Phil's voice had become a buzz in my ears. He rattled on about a sandblasted antique refrigerator and a new lighting fixture that was on order for the kitchen. His cheerful chatter faded as he left the kitchen. My feet stuttered after him into the dining room, and my breath left my lungs. The calamity continued. This room was normally a showcase of antique furniture and displayed collectibles. Today, however, the room was covered in grime. Every removable item from the kitchen had been transferred to the small dining room. Furniture, appliances, dishes, pots and pans, cookbooks, in addition to mounds on top of mounds of used mugs, cups and plates, and the guts contained in every household kitchen. Remarkably the utensils, measuring cups and spoons were still in the drawers where they had been housed. Countless drawers sat perilously on every visible surface.

The gorgeous Hoosier cupboard, oak heirloom table, and three-tiered wooden ice chest had been safe guarded with bed sheets, *thankfully*. The valuable antiques had been rolled to what I could only assume was the unwarlike safety of the dining room. The Hoosier cupboard was wedged between the dining room table and the kitchen table leaving a narrow walkway into the heart of the room. Powdery dust from dry wall coated the sheets and relocated appliances. Mercifully the glass paned pocket doors that separated the dining room from the living room had been pulled closed. Although the white trim was nearly black with construction dirt, it appeared as if the living room had been protected.

Phil leaned against the door jam by the bathroom where Ella's tush was all that could be seen as she furiously cleaned the bath tub. It took a moment for me to realize, after the brief tour of the kitchen, that the bathroom was the only source of running water in the house. Cold water, Phil told me nonchalantly during his rambling, but that would be rectified tomorrow by three o'clock.

"All finished in here." Ella stepped into the dining room and sat her empty bucket on top of an already teetering pile. "We need to get going."

"Right-o!" Phil scooped Ella into his arms and spun her in a circle. "We are down to hours now sweet'ums."

I watched the pair as they floated out the door discussing some errands that needed done before the out of town guests arrived at the lake house.

I walked back to the kitchen and tried to absorb my rather unfortunate reality. Shaking my head I turned and found Heath, all 6' 4" of him, leaning over me. Wearing a please-put-me-out-of-my-misery expression he said. "If I tell you this is ninety percent better than when I landed here on Monday, I know you won't believe me." He lifted his ball cap and raked a hand through his hair. "Did you bring any liquor?"

"Wow, sorry, packed for kids… not for grown-ups." *Disappointment noted.* "But I'll go get some." I turned and took in the devastation and sighed. "What's the plan? Is there a goal of any kind?"

"***Their*** goal includes deck renovation, light fixtures, and a restored metal antique refrigerator that is currently at the auto repair shop." Heath looked intently at me daring to question that last remark. *I'm no fool.* "***My*** goal, he continued, "is to get the walls and ceiling completed enough for primer in time for the wedding."

Hike up the pants, we're wading in. "Where should I start?"

"Trash," Heath directed, "if you're up for it."

Chapter 4

Recycling efforts save the planet but can make even the most sane of people lose their minds.

Trash in New York, as it should be all over the country, was quite the big deal. Let's just say that EVERYTHING gets recycled. Cans with clear glass, plastic bottles cleaned without lids, colored glass, foil, paper, card board and even food had its place on the compost pile. *Even on a daily basis wouldn't a few trash cans for the different items make sense?* Now remember, 100 guests were expected for the celebration. Most coming from out of state and like me won't know the recycling rules. *But hey! It's only Wednesday, all the time in the world.*

In the dining room I collected numerous used dishes and piled them on the floor. More than a few day's worth of coffee mugs, a heavy pottery bowl with popcorn seeds in the bottom, plates and silverware. Gathering trash as I went, I had filled two bags, one with paper one with cans and bottles. The dining room less these items still appeared as if I hadn't begun. *Thank-less.* Frustrated, I walked to the kitchen. My hands were full with more dirty dishes that I'd unearthed from the dining room. "Heath, can I stack these here until we have water?"

"Water, we now have. It's just not hot." Heath's long body contorted to adjust the pipes under the sink.

"This is insane.*"*

"Yep."

"Now that I have the dishes under control my problem is the piles of recyclables." I fetched the bags from the dining room. "I can't keep straight which goes where."

"I have simplified the process."

Simple sounded good.

"I designated my trailer as trash." He rose on his elbow, "Anyone who feels the need to sort it can. If not I'll haul it back to Pennsylvania and pay the landfill to take it."

"Excellent." I walked outside and asked Brennan to pitch any debris that had fallen from the deck on the trailer. I tied three trash bags to the deck railing and sorted garbage as I went. For the next hour and a half I moved garbage, plates, cans, bottles and construction debris to the metal trailer. Believe it or not, I found the deck. Progress! I grabbed a warm bottle of water and admired my accomplishments. I felt like I could kneel down and kiss the moss covered planks that were now visible. *Maybe not.*

Water rushed down my throat and spilled over my lip. I wiped the drip and noticed the dying annuals on the lawn by the steps. Taking pity I decided to soak the droopy blooms. Underneath the steps I found a scrub bucket and another dozen or so recyclables. Squatting down I filled the bucket with cans and bottles. I shifted to my sorting bags and stood holding a glass bottle in one hand and a can in the other. Once again I found myself confused by the rules of recycling.

I heard some puffing and looked up. Chugging toward me was a woman neck deep in the clean up efforts. Flushed, her heavy set freckled face was dressed with auburn pig tails, and her mouth was set in an impressive pout. Her plump body had been jammed into a pair of denim overalls. Rolled to the knee, the denim showed pink Converse high-tops that were severely grass stained on the toes. A matching pink bandana secured over her brow, completed the woman's ensemble.

"Hey New Yorker," I called out to the new stranger. "Could you tell me one more time – cans with glass or cans with plastic?"

The overstressed face moved to a more pronounced pout. "I am not a New Yorker," she nearly whined. "I'm from California." She rolled her eyes and sighed heavily. She climbed the deck steps and plopped on a bench. I watched as she removed her bandana and began to mop her face.

Well, Ms. California came with an attitude. "Sorry – I'm Phil's cousin, Georgia from Pennsylvania," I added the state as part of my ID.

"Thea… Thea Norton. I'm an artist." *Explained the get-up.* Thea chuckled, "A starving one at that."

The straining denim did not agree.

"I need water, desperately." Thea said as she balanced a grass stained heel across her knee. "I am just killing time until Ella comes back for me." I handed her a bottle of water and apologized for it not being cold. She sucked it down without complaint.

Brennan stepped on the deck, arms loaded with tools and wooden debris. "This is my oldest son Brennan. He's carrying non-essentials to the barn."

Thea nodded a hello to Brennan. "I'll help you out." She grabbed a cooler in one hand and set out for the barn with Brennan trailing behind her looking like a pack mule.

A familiar Subaru eased across the sidewalk and parked in the yard beside my Jeep. Hontie had arrived! Bursting with plants, her car resembled a greenhouse on wheels. She climbed from the car grinning, "Hey Georgia, you made it!" An avid outdoors woman she usually had a bike or kayak strapped to her roof just waiting for someone to point her in the direction of adventure. Hontie was more at home in a sleeping bag under the stars than a five star hotel. Despite her love of adventure, I would bet this wedding was becoming more urban adventure then she had ever dreamed.

I crossed the lawn to greet her. "Yes, it was a great trip. Payton has been excited all week to come on BACATION to Hontie's!"

Hontie's forever youthful face smiled fully, as she popped open the trunk. "Look at all these great plants the nursery gave me." I peered inside astounded by the amount of end of season ferns and colorful annuals that crammed the Subaru's interior. "The nursery called me and said they were going to toss them in the trash. Can you imagine?" My head shook slowly as I tried to envision when we would find time to plant them. Hontie hefted a large fern from the car. "I've been such a great customer this year, they gave them to me! Gave!" She beamed. "Let's just spread them through the beds in their boxes. They'll blend and just add color."

Super idea! Keep the focus on the flower beds, and then no one will notice that there are no walls in the kitchen and a trailer full of trash in the driveway!

This garden was kidney shaped, nearly twenty feet long with two gigantic boulders in the center. Lush ferns thrived among soft pink and white flowers. An architectural harvested porch pillar stood above the foliage with a hand painted bird house mounted on top. Following Hontie's instructions I placed the leggy red petunias and purple inpatients throughout the flowerbed. *Thank goodness there was no plan for the planting.*

"This is the last of them, Georgia." Hontie laid another flat of pink and white begonias at the garden edge. She walked toward me checking out my progress. "Um… Georgia…," caution coated her voice. "My thought was to maintain the color scheme of pink and white only in this bed. The reds and purples will go on the other side of the house." I raised my gaze to meet hers, and found her serious.

She must be on crack.

I pasted on my best anything-for-you smile. "Oh sure, Hontie I'll fix it."

Hontie dashed into the house to check on the advancements in chaos. I finished spreading the flowers throughout the beds on both sides of the house. I stood and absorbed the plethora of blooms. What do you know? They actually looked great!

Hontie returned. "One more favor Georgia – could you run down to the shop with me to move some furniture back inside? I need to close down. It shouldn't take us but fifteen minutes."

"No problem Hontie – let me check with Heath and see if the kids can stay here."

Hontie's shop harbored the coolest combination of all things I love and those things I could never quite pull off. It had been a longtime wish of Hontie's to combine her framing talents with unique pieces of history. The old wooden sided building had been tediously restored to the original store front and color scheme. Tinted photo glass protected the sampling of fabulous wares showcased in the front windows. An oak washstand with a pottery bowl and water pitcher, a red flyer tricycle, vintage prints, and current artists' work all framed with the utmost skill and care teased potential shoppers.

The lawn in front of the shop was cleverly littered with antique trunks, an Amish buggy seat, factory carts and even a four piece bedroom suite from 1910. I climbed the two concrete steps and pushed open the heavy wooden door. The inside of the shop always stole my breath. The décor here also had been restored to period. The walls and moldings had been painted with pumpkin, eggplant, and teal, a color combination which had to be seen to be appreciated. Hontie's work area was separated from the shop by an original post office wall. She had acquired the solid wooden wall at an auction. It stretched the width of the shop complete with tiny locked mail boxes and barred teller windows.

The eclectic inventory was displayed cleverly in clusters. One area held old photographs and post cards. In another, metal factory carts held matted artwork and a display of framing samples. In my favorite corner, a porcelain lined baby bath, an infant scale with wicker basket mounted on the top, and some old children's toys created a unique curio. Hand made blankets and old quilts added a sweet charm, and on the walls a trio of paper dolls from 1950 created a clever nursery theme. Each precious doll was framed with their specific clothes. Wooden blocks teetered on the frame edge spelling "PAPER DOLLS". *Fabulous!*

"Hontie, you should be so proud. Your shop is lovely!"

"Thanks Georgia, just not enough hours, you know?" She tidied her work area and we got busy carrying in the inventory from the lawn. We lifted the dressing table and moved up the steps. With our arms full with furniture, Hontie whispered, "Oh dear this always happens." I followed her sight line and saw customers unloading at the curb. Caught halfway in and out of the shop, Hontie called, "Come on in! We're just closing, but feel free to browse!"

During the attempt-to-close process several more cars of enthusiastic shoppers, most of who were in the area from Bouckville, stopped in for a 'quick' look. At the counter Hontie chatted with a woman from Maine who was looking through the extensive post card selection. Another lady hopped out of her still moving van while shouting over her shoulder to her not-so-happy family, "I just need to check it!" I watched as she dashed into the storefront window, measured the wash stand 'hip to hands' (classic flea market measuring mentality) and dashed back out again leaving my permanently pleasant aunt chuckling in her wake.

Might as well get comfortable. I settled out front on the factory bench. I loved this town! Area businesses had begun to refurbish the old homes and store fronts based on recorded history. It was like a slice of hidden treasure. The lone traffic light cycled slowly in response to low traffic volume. I recognized Phil's car at the intersection and waved as Ella and Thea rolled up to the front of the shop.

"Hey," I said to Ella as she hopped out of the car. "I hope you're not here to buy. We can't get out of here."

"No shopping, I just need to switch cars with Lottie." Ella stormed into the shop. "Hey Lottie!" she called. Lottie was another conversion of Hontie's name. At one time Phil and Hontie worked for the same framing company. Phil didn't feel it was professional to call his mom 'Mom' at work, so he changed Charlotte to Lottie. "I need your car for a quick Coli run." I heard Ella say. Coli, was short for Colinotia, the neighboring town. Stunned, but still smiling, Hontie reached into her pocket and came up with her keys.

"What's in Coli?" I asked Thea as she joined me on the bench.

"Booze," she said with a quick double raise of her brow.

Ella jogged down the front steps. "Ready, Thea?"

"Why the vehicle swap?" I asked Ella.

"Our car isn't street legal." *Not legal? Of course it wasn't. For cryin' out loud.* Ella slid behind the wheel of Hontie's Subaru. "Phil and I just figured we'd wait for his Dad's wedding gift to get the tags and stuff."

Uncle Nathan had given a big fat check for a wedding gift to his other son, Gavin. So counting their chickens so to speak, Phil and Ella were pre-spending their anticipated bucks.

I made sure Ella added Jim Beam to her booze list for Heath. With a toot of the horn the girls were off. A forty-five minutes road trip seemed frivolous, but after only being here a few hours, and despite of the massive amount of work to be done... I had to agree that this was a necessary run.

Finally, Hontie and I hefted the last of the large items into the shop. We threw the bolt, hopped in the not-street-legal car, and trudged back to the homestead.

"Sorry Heath, that took longer than I expected."

Grunt.

"Were the kids okay?"

Grumble, grunt.

Glad we could have this talk.

Time I got back to the multitude of tasks at hand. The dining room void of dishes and garbage now boasted numerous piles of kitchen guts stacked on top of every available surface. I was again unsure where to begin. A quarter inch of drywall dust blanketed everything in sight. Every movement I made sent up smoke signals. I lifted a stainless steel box and gently blew across the top. The toaster. *Lovely.*

What on earth were Phil and Ella thinking? I needed to emotionally prepare before venturing any farther into this seemingly endless chaos. I watched Heath as he sealed the seams in the sheet rock. The motion made its own hypnotic rhythm like lulling music, scooping and swiping... scooping and swiping. The air was heavy with humidity, so much so, Heath had to run large fans and work lights, in an effort to cure the joint compound.

"Shoot! I forgot I needed to call home and leave Hontie's phone number." I looked at the empty walls. "Heath where's the phone?"

"No phone." Heath's robotic voice was void of all inflection. *A little unnerving, really.* Older than me by two years Heath and I were tight as kids and fortunately still were as adults. An officer in the Coast Guard and a devoted father of three, Heath's demeanor tended to vary. *Officer* Heath required the facts only. He tended to respond with, 'I'm understanding that' instead of 'yes', or 'okay'. *Daddy* Heath engaged in nature walks with his three kids and trained for marathons for fun. I thought I had pretty much seen all phases of Heath, but what I had observed today was alarmingly new.

"Of course there's no phone," I mumbled into the din of the humming fans. "How silly of me."

I took a good look at Heath. The fatigue weighed heavy on his filthy face, "Have you eaten?" I shouted over the fans. "I was planning on walking the boys to the pizza shop." Hunger filled his eyes. "What would you like?"

He flipped off the fan. "Mom sent all kinds of stuff. It's in the fridge." He turned on the faucet and splashed water on his face, "Needs to be eaten." Not a paper towel in sight, the water ran off his chin and dampened his filthy shirt.

Our Mom had this need to pre-bake large quantities of meat for family gatherings. 'For slicing' she'd say, 'perfect for sandwiches.' *Efficient and cost effective but it was one of those things that would never cross my mind.* However, when I'm sixty, I'll probably do it for my boys and they'll think *I'm* nuts.

I looked at my filthy hands and decided to visit the cold water facilities and attempt to wash some grime off. Hontie's bathroom was practical but small by today's standards. The room was the width of the tub with a pedestal sink and mirror in the center. The bathroom essentials were contained inside three unique factory bins. The galvanized bins were shaped to stack on top of one another. Off to the left, the toilet was tucked beside an old milk bottle carrier filled with glass bottles from different dairy farms in New York State. Much to my surprise I discovered the toilet seat was not attached to the commode and I nearly landed in a heap on the floor.

I regrouped and stepped to the mirror. The damage the day had inflicted was apparent. My naturally curly hair had gone wild, and grime streaked across my face like war paint. *Lovely.* My hands shivered at the first contact with the water. Cold wasn't cold it was freezing! I sucked in a deep breath and doused my face. Shivering, I pulled a towel from the factory bin and noticed there was no shower curtain. Not a problem until the hot water was back on, I realized. The tub did however give me concern. Ella's cold water cleaned bathroom would definitely require hot water sanitation.

The fact that these mounting obstacles were beginning *not* to surprise me, was certainly not a good sign. *Folks, we're in way over our heads here.*

In the kitchen I discovered all food had been placed inside the fridge for protection. I gathered bread, mayo, lettuce, tomato, and one of Mom's cooked turkey breasts and headed out to the deck. Hontie's retro table, unearthed in the deck recovery process, was transformed into deli central. Ella and Thea had returned with the much needed liquor and were sipping dirty martinis. Phil and Hontie were discussing plans for the evening in the corner surrounded by mammoth house plants. Brennan and Payton sat on the steps brushing Sasha's long black fur.

Gang's all here. Tired and hungry, they watched as I prepared the fixins. I decided my priority was to Heath who was dead on his feet. "Heath, how do you want your sandwich?"

"Any way you make it is great," he said as he collapsed into a chair, cocktail in hand.

"Hontie?"

"Same as Heath, anyway you make it Georgia. I haven't eaten all day."

"Mommy?" Brennan looked up at the roof, puzzled. "There's a cat up there."

I turned and looked up, "Oh, that's Skitz." The large gray and white tabby was stretched out on the peaked dormer. "Hontie leaves the window open because he likes to stretch out in the sun."

"Cool."

By the time I had settled the boys into their dinner picnic, I noticed Heath had all but inhaled his sandwich. "You want another one?"

"Mmm hmm," was his reply. I hurriedly fixed him a second.

"Looks great Georgia." Ella was seated on the railing of the deck with her feet on the bench. With her eyes closed and face tipped to the sky she stretched yoga-esque. "I'll take everything on mine, Georgia." Swinging her arms in a large circle, Ella lowered her head and rotated her neck loudly popping each vertebra. *Gross.* "And didn't I see some bologna and cheese blocks in the fridge?"

That would be the after-antiquing-on-the-deck-with-beer snacks that I brought from home.

"Yeah, I'll grab them," Phil hopped to action.

Phil and Ella had mastered the many facetted gypsy lifestyle. In addition to living rent free, their ability to sniff out a meal was incredible. Show up and be fed. Much to my dismay, I watched my after antiquing snacks be transferred from the safety of the refrigerator to this evening's fare.

When all sandwiches were made and being enjoyed, I turned to Hontie. "What's up for the evening?"

She held up a finger and swallowed. "We need to move the crib up to the middle bedroom."

"The crib in the flower bed?" Hontie nodded. "I thought for a moment that was just a garden accessory."

She laughed lightly. "No, no, Gavin, Jade and Davis arrive at the airport tonight at 11:30. I am going to pick them up." Gavin was Hontie's oldest son and Phil's brother. He and Jade lived in Indiana, and Davis was their little boy.

41

They had taken a week's vacation for the wedding and would be joining the household for the duration. "I can't wait to get my hands on Davis," Hontie said with affection. "I am also picking up Phil and Gavin's Uncle Adam. His plane is due an hour after Gavin and Jade's."

My brows shot up. *More people?*

"Don't worry; Uncle Adam is not staying here." She laughed. *Thank heaven for small miracles.*

Yes, that's right... for all those playing along. Tonight's room and board total in Hontie's home would be seven adults, three children, an enormous canine and three cats. No hot water, no phone, no kitchen... For cryin' out loud.

"We have a meeting with the minister," Ella said. I watched as she balled up her napkin and tossed it on her plate. Chugging the last of her martini, she stacked it on top of her plate, then sat the pile on the bench. *Consume what you see, crap where you stand.* "Phil, we need to get going." Ella stood. "Thea we'll drop you at the lake." Thea nodded and she and Ella walked to the steps and off the deck.

Your trash! I screamed in my head. After spending three hours immersed in trash collection and the rules of recycling, *Cripes*! The trailer was right there! My internal Tourette's syndrome was fighting to kick in.

Phil grabbed a handful of bologna and cheese. "Minister, right-o sweet'ums," He tossed a wedge into his mouth. "We should swing by the hardware store, too, check our account. More people should be making deposits by now."

Instead of traditional gift registration, Phil and Ella had asked for deposits to be made into their account at the hardware store. They had grand plans of renovating the second floor of Hontie's shop for their home.

"More people?" Hontie asked.

Phil chomped on his bologna, "Yeah, I needed some stuff for the lake house on Monday. You know like fireworks, rafts, and lawn torches... so we ran down to the store and the clerk told me we had a twenty-five dollar credit." Phil raised his shoulder, "So, I just put the stuff on account. Why pay, right? I mean *here's the thing...* more money will be coming everyday." Heath and Hontie just stared blankly at Phil. I had to stifle a chuckle. *Finances, according to Phil. Cripes.*

Phil turned to Hontie and held out his hand. "I need your car." Fingers wiggling he waited for Hontie's keys. I watched the effortless exchange. Like an old familiar dance one moment her keys dangled from her fingertips, the next, whoosh, Phil and Ella were gone taking Thea with 'em.

Alright, I took a moment to gather myself. We had a toddler, a son and daughter-in-law, plus Clare and Catheryn, all arriving tonight. We had a crib in the flower bed... maybe regrouping was not the best plan. *One task at a time might be a better idea.*

Ever since I had pulled up at Hontie's, I had been swept into the madness and hadn't even made it to the upstairs of the house. The main staircase led from the entry way to the center of the second floor. Hontie's master bedroom was in the front of the house, the middle bedroom had a double bed and a large fish tank and a door off the middle room led to two steps that lowered into a back bedroom, and storage area. From the storage space you could access the perilous ladder like staircase which led back down to the first floor laundry room off the kitchen.

Hontie and I tidied up the quick dinner and got out of Heath's way, so he could continue construction. "Where are you putting everyone, Hontie?"

"I let Heath take the front room, and I would like to set up Gavin and Jade in the middle room with Davis. I plan to bunk in with you guys in the back room. You brought air mattresses right?"

"Yeah," *Cozy.*

Even for normal Bouckville trips, sleeping arrangements were low on the list of priorities. Treasures were the goal, and searching for them until exhaustion, made bed assignments unimportant. "Time to set up our bedroom boys," I called to the kids on the deck. "Grab your stuff from the Jeep." Eager to help, Brennan and Payton scrambled to get their bags. We hauled all of our trip necessities up the back steps to one of my favorite parts of Hontie's house. The stairs, narrow and steep, brought you to a small storage type room which led to the back bedroom. Wide exposed plank floors, angled ceilings and a huge window overlooking the gardens added to the charm of the small space.

The bedroom had a double mattress and box spring on the floor and a folded up army cot propped by the door. The boys raced through the room, leapt the two steps into the middle bedroom, then on to the main staircase. Their feet pounded on the plank floor and echoed throughout the upstairs. I listened to Payton's delightful squeal as he discovered the fish tank. "Mom," Brennan called out, "you've got to see this." I followed his voice. In the main staircase he leaned out over the railing. "Look Mom." Here, another of Hontie's talents. Photographs of the Grand Canyon were displayed as well as in any gallery. Breathtaking images of the Grand Canyon, some from the rim, others from the rapids, all stunningly raw. "Have you ever seen these?" Brennan said with wonder.

"Yes, pretty incredible huh?"

"I want to go there."

"Someday, buddy, someday." I left him to enjoy the pictures and got back to work in our room. Using a hair dryer I inflated, *poorly,* the double mattress. I've never slept on an inflate-a-bed before let alone with two kids. *An adventure for sure.*

"This house is so cool," Brennan said. "Awesome bed, Mom."

"Can I bounce?" Payton asked playfully.

"I'm not sure *cool* covers it, and bouncing on a wood planked floor is probably not a great idea." The looks of devastation fell across their faces. *Mom just sucked all fun out of this experience.*

I retrieved the only TV in the house and placed it on a chair by the air mattress. I popped in <u>Pirates of the Caribbean</u> and gave the boys their Game Boys. "Sorry to abandon you guys," I ruffled Payton's hair. "I need to work downstairs at least until Aunt Clare and Aunt Catheryn get here. There is just so much that needs to be done."

"Will you play cards with me later Mom?" Brennan asked.

"You bet, buddy."

"Mom, can I ask you a question?"

"Sure."

"Why is there so much mess?" Brennan asked.

"Grown up choices, honey, bad ones," He looked confused. "I'm not sure why the kitchen looks this way but at this point we need to help Hontie fix it."

Downstairs I rounded up Hontie and together we retrieved the crib from the flower bed, and shoved it fully assembled through the front door. Breathing heavily, we muscled the crib to the second floor. "Why did you set the crib up outside?" I asked Hontie.

"My friend is loaning it to me and her husband offered to put it together. Seemed like a good idea at the time,"

She blew her hair from her brow. "I didn't think I would have any time to assemble it myself."

Now that the crib was in place in the middle bedroom I gave it a shake to see if it was secure. The side rail flopped outward clearly not attached to the main rail. "Umm, Hontie? We need another bolt, I think."

"Oh dear, all the parts were here. Go check in the flower bed."

"Seriously?" *Did I say that out loud?*

"I'm sure it's right there. I need to get ready to go to the airport." Hontie left me staring after her as she descended the stairs.

Night had fallen and the next level of inside projects had begun. Heath was still seaming drywall working by large halogen style lamps. My evening goal was to find places to store all the things that inhabit the bowels of every kitchen. Since no cabinets would be going back in the kitchen I needed to 'find homes' as Hontie put it, in all the other large cupboards in the dining room, bathroom, etc. Sasha, resident canine beast, pleased that some pathways had been created, plodded through the kitchen. Heath cursed as she cut a little close to his work space and lamp cords.

"This house is run by animals and furniture!" He growled.

"Right now, I'm feeling the latter is a blessing." Every cupboard I had opened was barely half full. The upside, I was making progress. The downside, Hontie won't ever be able to find anything! I moved Sasha along to the living room and gently closed the pocket doors and effectively caged her in.

Sounds of footsteps on the stairs signaled Hontie was now dressed and ready to go fetch the family. "Heath, may I use your car to go to the airport?" she asked. "Mine hasn't returned from the minister meeting and it would be easier to pick up everyone in the Expedition."

"No problem. I don't think that I'll need to go anywhere. Plus, Georgia's Jeep is here."

"One question, Hontie," I gestured to the grand mess that was the dining room. "Anything in here that isn't staying? Like these odd sized Tupperware without lids?"

"Oh they stay," Hontie snatched them up protectively. "I only have three containers and there are lids here..." she glanced around befuddled, "somewhere."

"Fine, what about the moss green percolator from the 1960's with multiple inserting parts?"

"Doesn't Mom have one just like that?" Heath peered in from the kitchen.

"Oh yeah, that is hers," Hontie picked up the base. "We used that for the open house at the shop."

That was what... a year ago? I reached down for a few pieces. "Do you have all the parts?"

"I did." *Classic phrase, ranking right up there with 'Once upon a time'.*

"I don't think it worked properly even at the family functions we used it for," I said.

Glancing at Heath, I could see his thoughts were echoing mine. "Executive decision," he announced. "Trash!" *Officer Heath's in the house!*

"Oh... well," Hontie looked pained. "It's your mom's."

Heath and I locked eyes and nodded. "Trash!" We proclaimed in unison.

"Oh dear..." Hontie chewed her lower lip. "My Tupperware is **not** trash. I am certain the lids are here somewhere."

I gave Heath the 'yeah, right' look, and began moving piles. Hontie picked up Heath's keys and left for the airport. The good news was the cupboard condensing strategy of 'shove over add more stuff' was working. As long as the cupboard doors could close the system worked for me! Turning to address another pile of kitchen guts a quick blur whizzed by my eye.

"Waaaooooh! What the heck was that?"

"I'm sure it was the resident dining room mouse." Heath was eerily calm. He had been here too long and was beginning to accept way too much insanity as normalcy. "There is also a resident kitchen mouse, just in case you were wondering."

"Great." My tourette's syndrome was back fighting my value structured upbringing. I rubbed my forehead, as I just strung a sailor's curse streak in my head.

The quiet calm of systematic work fell over the house. The kids had accepted banishment to the upstairs. *Thank heaven for rechargeable batteries!* My big sister Clare and sister-in-law Catheryn should be arriving at any moment. My hip rapped into the Hoosier cupboard in the dining room. I had been working the best I could around the beautiful cupboard, but it was massive. "Heath… any chance this Hoosier can be moved back to the kitchen?" Heath stared at me. "Under the circumstances one room is really as bad as the next, but it would give some semblance if the furniture was in the room where it belonged."

With a shrug Heath agreed and we gingerly slid the large piece back to the kitchen. "I have a lot of sanding to do so keep it covered and it should be okay."

I pulled the sheet over the top and tucked it as best I could around the base. "Great, so tell me what I missed out on Monday and Tuesday."

Heath released the air slowly from his lungs, and took advantage of the break to mix himself a stiff JB and coke. "Want one?"

I held up my hand. "Not for me."

"Suit yourself. I'll give you the condensed version." He talked as he mixed. "I arrived with the impression that I was going to patch some dry wall and maybe paint some trim. When I pulled in Monday at lunch I was greeted by a 100-ton roll-off dumpster in the driveway. The gardens were and are still in various stages of the weeding and mulching process." He paused, took a punishing swallow of booze and leaned heavily against the sink. "I was informed by Hontie that the dumpster would be picked up the next morning and I asked her if the rest of the outside clean up was going to happen before it left. That's when I was told – the outside clean up **was** done."

My mouth dropped wide and he gave me the 'I know' look complete with a shake of his head.

"Then," he continued, "major mistake… I entered the house. Correction," he waved his finger at me. "I entered hell. The horse hair plastered ceiling and walls had been partially pulled down. The beams and wiring within the walls were all exposed. The kitchen sink was cocked in the remaining wooden base and water was dripping under and over the counter into multiple buckets and pans."

I was speechless. Heath rattled the ice in his cup. "Again, I turned to Hontie for some explanation for the internal combustion. She explained that on a rainy day two weeks ago Phil was unable to move forward with the outdoor painting projects. So after digging four large holes in the yard to expand the deck, he moved inside to remodel the kitchen."

With an expression of sheer horror I said, "This entire family is on crack."

"Yeah, but one hundred people are coming here in five, make that three days now," Heath released a weary breath. "So, doing what could only be done, I dug in."

"Madness," I muttered. "What did Phil say when you saw him?"

Heath's brows lowered in thought as he worked to pull back his conversation with Phil. "My ten second discussion with Phil revealed he had no kitchen reconstruction plans. *'Here's the thing… '* Phil said to me, 'Ella's family will be here tomorrow and I need to get the lake house party ready." Heath shook his head, "Party ready." He lifted his cocktail. "So," Heath continued, "I asked Hontie what her plan was for the kitchen. She told me she had an old farm house porcelain sink stored in a barn across town. We discussed her view for the new kitchen and made a Home Depot list. Phil agreed to give me a full work day. So, Tuesday morning, 7:00 A.M. I got up, entered the labyrinth of pipe hell in the basement, shut off the water, ripped out the sink and base cabinet and chucked both into the dumpster as the roll back truck was backing into the driveway to haul it away. Next, I drove across town and retrieved Hontie's sink. Having no lumber I dismantled a discarded futon and crafted a sink base from the salvaged lumber. Phil arrived about noon for his full work day and he and I drove forty miles to Home Depot. We loaded two carts of drywall, plaster, plumbing, and lighting necessities. At the register, after all the items were scanned, Phil stood with his hands jammed in his pockets and a lollipop in his cheek. I held out my hand and Phil pointed to the courtesy basket of pops by the register. I refrained from decking him and rubbed my fingers together to signal cash, not suckers."

"Oh Heath, you're *not* serious."

"'Here's the thing'… he said to me. 'My wallet is in my car at the lake house.'"

"Right." I snorted out a laugh.

"Luckily I had three Home Depot gift cards and a Discover card in my wallet." Heath drained the last of his cocktail and continued. "We drove back to Hontie's, stopping at the lake house for him to check his messages... " Heath lost himself for a moment –"another story." He waved a hand dismissing the memory, sat his cup on the sink and mixed himself another drink. "We got back here, and Phil helped me wire and hang five recessed spot lights. After that we started to hang the sheet rock for the ceiling."

I moved to the refridge and grabbed a bottle of water. The picture he was painting was unbelievable. He swirled the liquid in the glass and once again blistered his insides with a long drink of whiskey. "It wasn't all horrible," he chuckled. "I got to witness Ms. California operating a push mower in the open field." His laugh gurgled. "I'd be willing to bet that it was a virgin experience for her." I shared his amusement thinking back to Thea's grass stained pink high tops. "Later that night Hontie and I enjoyed a beer while surveying my accomplishments and formulating my next day's plan. We said good night and Hontie went upstairs. I was pleased enough for the day and I popped open my second beer while admiring my four ceiling lights..."

"Wait a minute... four?"

"Yeah, unfortunately four, not five. Phil had to leave to meet Ella for something and in our rush we covered a light by mistake. I jumped on a stool, ran my thumb across the freshly hung wall boarded ceiling, grabbed a hand saw, and unearthed number five. The wall board was only slightly charred."

"For cryin' out loud, Heath. The house could have burned to the ground! I can't believe you're still here. Most people would have slammed the truck in reverse and saved themselves."

"Considered it," he shrugged resigned to his fate. "But really Georgia, what else could I do? There are one hundred people coming here and this house will be presentable damn it."

"Crazy." Heath and I went back to silently working. At 9:15 pm, just as I felt I was making some mild progress, headlights entered the driveway.

Clare and Catheryn had arrived only two hours later than I had expected. I could only imagine their reactions, as the van's headlights swept across the property giving them a preview of the nuptial haven. My big sister Clare was a full time paralegal with three kids. She was the typical suburban super-mom complete with minivan, decorative cupcakes for birthdays, and immaculate flower gardens. Her only outward flaw as far as I was concerned was her tendency for immoderate cleaning. I looked at my grime encrusted hands and dust covered clothing.

This was not going to go over well.

The resounding slam of the van door was followed by Clare's "Good Grief!" *That about summed it up.* Clare's favorite expression for all situations was "Good Grief." She was capable of using a variety of tones making the phrase suitable for all occasions. Surprised, disgusted, exasperated, shocked, inspired; her creativity with inflection was remarkable.

Next I heard my sister-in-law Catheryn's comment. "Maybe it's not as bad as it looks." This was a clear representation of Catheryn's ability to always look for the good in every situation. Unbelievably tolerant, Catheryn had worked for the Department of Correction the last several years with juveniles. She counseled troubled kids through hard life situations. Recently she had decided to work part time, so she could raise her and Heath's three children.

Patience and optimism we were going to need.

I dropped the handful of cooking utensils I had been working to sort and prepared for Clare and Catheryn to come to me. They entered through the mudroom and into the kitchen where Heath stood amidst halogen lamps and whirling fans with spackle bucket in hand.

"No, it's not bad, it's worse." Disgust dripped from Clare's mouth. "And let me just put this out there before we go any further. I **am** going to Bouckville tomorrow."

Clare and Catheryn rounded the corner and discovered me in the dining room. There were no words. Caged behind the pocket doors, Sasha began to bark. I walked over and slid the door open enough for her to come and greet the girls. "I will take her outside." Catheryn said. She grabbed Sasha's collar and led her through Heath's obstacle course and safely out to the deck.

I watched as Clare's eyes panned the room. She suffered from a 'tidiness' illness, so I knew the scene in front of her was fighting with all the cleaning genes her body had to offer. She grabbed the closest rag and furiously began to dust. Residual puffs of dry wall dust floated every which way.

Wildly, Clare gestured with the filthy rag, "What on earth are Phil and Ella thinking?" She erupted. "Is there not a wedding being held at this home in three days?" Clare turned and bumped smack into the kitchen table. "Good grief, you can't even walk! It looks like a construction zone." She absently rubbed her hip. "What did Hontie say? Is she livid? She has to be livid. This is a nightmare!" Clare breathed heavily between questions but left no time for explanations. Knowing her, I waited her out. All she needed to do was vent her frustrations, and then compile a mental list of tasks in priority order. I watched as she closed her eyes and inhaled slowly... and exhaled. "I just need to take a moment."

Psycho. Sure enough her outrage was reigned in and oldest sibling containment mode began.

Heath had momentarily abandoned his spackling and stood in the doorway with Catheryn. "The improvements here are too great to detail." His voice, rough with fatigue had drawn a look of concern from Catheryn. "This remaining disaster zone, though to the two of you may seem insurmountable, we" he nodded to me, "actually can see pockets of progress."

Clare and Catheryn took a second to visualize a scene that could have looked worse than what they currently faced.

"Hard to picture it was worse, right?" I stretched my tightening muscles. "Be glad it's dark. You should have seen it in the daylight." The room erupted with countless questions and Heath quickly began to fill them in on the prior day's events.

Waving us off and making a "T" with her hands Catheryn said. "I need to hear everything but first I need to pee." She dashed to the bathroom. Five seconds later we heard a scream followed by a thud. The unattached toilet seat had given her an unexpected ride to the floor.

"Oh, sorry, forgot to mention that," I called out from the dining room. "Seat is not attached," I told Clare, "and the hot water will be turned on tomorrow, but there's no shower curtain anyway." These small details I realized would have any normal person leaving town, but really that was how far past normal we'd gone.

"There's no hot water?" Clare's eyebrows shot up as she turned to Heath.

"Yesterday I bathed in the lake," he said. "And to-night I'm going to duct tape painter's plastic to the wall and go polar shower."

"Good grief," Clare huffed.

Catheryn emerged, adjusting her shirt. "Well, that was fun."

"Let me just tell you about our trip," Clare said as she gently shook out her dust rag. "I have a feeling it is just a precursor to the days ahead."

Catheryn climbed on the nearby step ladder. I grabbed my water bottle and leaned against the wall as Clare's tale began to unfold.

"So, my babysitter meets me at the house, we load up the kids and their luggage and send them off. Catheryn arrived on schedule, we packed the van only to find my luggage had gone thirty minutes south with the children."

"You're kidding." I looked from Clare to Catheryn who shook her head.

"No, unfortunately, I'm not." Clare idly sifted through a drawer of kitchen utensils. "So Catheryn and I headed down to do some luggage retrieval. I pulled into the driveway, requested my bags, hurriedly loaded them and threw the van in reverse. **Whack!** I plowed into the pick-up truck at the end of the driveway."

"Imagine that," I said flippantly. *All females in my family have no ability to use vehicle mirrors and we chronically back into and over things.*

"I checked the damage and pressed on!" Clare pumped a rallying fist in the air. "We got on the interstate and the van started screeching and wouldn't shift out of second gear." Clare had taken the van to the mechanic seven times in the last six months complaining of a transmission ailment. Each time the mechanic reassured her that all was well. Still, you would think only one hour into the five hour trip thoughts of postponing or even aborting the trip might have entered into a rational mind. But, oh no! Nothing would interfere with Estrogen Weekend! Bouckville or Bust!

"So what did you do?" I asked and then took a swig from my water bottle.

"We drove." Clare said simply and Catheryn nodded in agreement. "I set the cruise at fifty-five and turned up the radio to drown out the unpleasant automotive serenade."

"Women," Heath muttered.

"My mechanic said there was no problem. We drove with the RPM needle thingy in the red and kept an eye on the temperature gauge."

"Needle thingy?" Heath said. "I repeat… women."

I was stunned. Even I think I would have had to re-think the trip at that point; potentially stranded on the highway hours from home certainly held no appeal for me. I shook my head and continued to work on my water bottle.

Catheryn picked up the story where Clare left off. "So three hours along we decided we'd better pull off to get some dinner and pray."

My mouthful of water sprayed across the room.

"Yes, we did!" Clare confirmed. "After devotions and dinner we set out again and here we are!"

"Yes, here you are," Heath said from the doorway. "Welcome to hell."

"Where is everyone?" Catheryn asked.

"Everyone who?" Heath answered. "We are it sweet-heart."

Catheryn's eyes darted to me and all I could offer was a raise of my shoulders. "Hontie went to the airport for Gavin, Jade, and Davis. Their flight from Indiana was due to arrive at 10:00 pm. She took Heath's Expedition because some other relatives were arriving tonight too." Clare's eyes bulged. "No, no," I read her mind. "Only Gavin, Jade, and Davis are staying here."

"Thank goodness." Refocusing energy on the state of affairs, Clare resumed dusting. The fury of attempted containment got the best of her. "Gavin and Jade cannot walk into this."

My thoughts exactly.

"Davis cannot safely be anywhere on this first floor."

Understatement of the century.

"What's our plan? We need to formulate a plan. Oh good grief, look at that." Hontie had a four foot custom made wall rack displaying thirty or so pieces of unique kids' pottery dating back to the 1900's. Each delicate dish had a muted picture of a nursery rhyme which encouraged the child using it to eat every bite. It hadn't been covered and was coated with dust. Clare tenderly removed a tiny bowl. "Filth! Why weren't these protected?" She blew the dust. "Peter Rabbit... who knew?" She mumbled to herself and wiped viciously.

"Clare," Heath said with quiet control, "put down the rag."

Clare shook her head from side to side. "Heath, it has to be done; we can't possibly..."

"Clare," Heath was slightly more authoritative. "Step away from the rag."

Puffs of dry wall dust floated about. "But surely we must... Ah Ah," she held up a finger, "Ah-Choo."

"Bless you." Heath, Catheryn and I said in unison.

"Thank you. We must try..."

"You're going to break something," Heath's voice was even.

"Just a minute," Clare rushed on. "I need to try to..." Her rag continued to race, as she stretched to wipe the grimy shelf. Smash! Crash! Crumble! "Oh no, I can't look." Clare covered her face with her hands. "No, no, no. Don't tell me I've broken one of the child plates!"

"No, actually a cup and saucer," Heath answered flatly.

Clare whimpered as she picked up the chips and shards. "Wait, I see old glue." She relaxed slightly. "This piece was broken before." She shrugged her shoulder, "That makes it a little better, right?"

Still sitting cross-legged on the step ladder, Catheryn repeated the earlier question. "What are Phil and Ella thinking?"

Clare piled the crumbled pottery carefully on the shelf. "This," she gestured broadly to the room, "well it is unspeakable. And the glimpse my head lights offered, as they swept over the side yard? Well let's just say it wasn't pretty either." Clare turned to Catheryn for agreement and then turned to me. "Have the outside preparations begun?"

"Why Clare, have they begun?" I jumped in dramatically. "They're complete."

"Yeah, as complete as the kitchen and plumbing," Heath muttered.

Brennan heard the commotion and had come to greet his aunts. "Mommy, are we going to play some cards?"

"Yes babe, I'm working my way there," I answered. "Where's Payton?"

"He fell asleep."

"OK," I glanced at the wall clock 9:55 P.M. "I'll be there in fifteen minutes Bren. Just let me do a little more here."

"Georgia go now," Clare waved me off. "We're fresher than you."

"Thanks Aunt Clare." Brennan grabbed my hand and started to pull me from the room.

"Alright honey, gimme one minute." I turned back to Clare, "let's set our game plan for tomorrow." After a brief discussion I climbed the steep back steps to my poorly inflated mattress for a well earned round of UNO.

Our plan for tomorrow: an early departure for Bouckville, preferably before 8:30 A.M., followed by a full day of flea marketing.

Chapter 5

The bounty awaits! Treasures to find!
Barter, barter, buy!

The early morning sun peeked through the curtainless window of the bedroom bringing the bright promise of a new day. *A little too bright, at the moment.* I shifted on my inflate-a-bed and sank immediately to the hard floor with a thunk. I twisted my head to survey my dorm style room. Between the suitcases, the television and the VCR I had dragged in for the boys, there was only a single exposed plank of flooring left for passage through the room. As for the occupants, more bodies than beds proved nearly accurate. Payton, Brennan, and I were balancing on the double-bed sized air mattress in the far corner of the room. Hontie was stretched out diagonally on the mattress with blankets drawn to her eyebrows. She breathed deeply and evenly, exhausted from her midnight shuttle service to the airport. There was a lump on an old army cot that resembled a human form which had to be Clare. The old cot was the type you would be afraid to turn over on for fear it would collapse.

A strange squeaking noise was coming from some-where nearby. Errreee, Errreee, Errreee. I listened more carefully. The sound was not in this room I realized. Errreee, Errreee, Errreee. It was coming from behind the closed door which led to the middle bedroom. Errreee, Erreee…

Rolling over gently, my behind sank fully to the floor. The air in the mattress shifted and Payton and Brennan rose up as if riding on an ocean wave. They both groaned but thankfully stayed asleep. Carefully I eased to standing and as quietly as possible on the old plank floor, I tiptoed past the slumbering bodies.

Beneath the blanket mound Clare appeared to be sound asleep. Having had grown up with her, however, I knew that she could be quite nocturnally active. Sleep walking and especially talking was not uncommon for Clare. Her episodes were amplified by stress and fatigue. Considering the current conditions of Hontie's home, a nocturnal event was highly probable.

Errreee, Errreee...

My foot settled on the plank by Clare's head. The board squeaked. I froze in place and held my breath. No movement. Errreee, Errreee... I heard muffled voices from the next room followed by silence. Gingerly I lifted my foot for another tentative step.

"What is that noise?" Clare's voice whispered from beneath her cocoon of blankets.

Startled, "Jeez, Clare." I caught my breath. "I assume it's Davis squeaking the crib springs."

"Hmmm, I guess Hontie made it back okay." Clare stretched bravely and the cot creaked in protest. "Oh dear," she yawned. "What time is it?"

"Time to move," I answered. "Thursday promises to be a beautiful day! Bouckville day one!" I cheerfully descended the steep back steps. My excitement was abruptly stunted as I hit the laundry room at the base of the stairs. Who knew a kitchen could hold so much stuff? Stacked on top of the clothes washer and dryer were large serving bowls and boxes of cups and mugs. On the floor more cabinet drawers filled with sharp knives, spatulas, wooden spoons, and small miracles, the tops to Hontie's three precious Tupperware containers. "Well what do you know?"

Traditionally, we tried to have breakfast before 7:00 and hit the road by 8:30. We were only beginning to stir. It was 9:00. I refused to get upset. I knew this trip was going to be different.

Kitchen noise was the best way to stir any family and set the day in motion, so I started there. Nosing a bit I found Catheryn had added fresh bagels and cream cheese to the mix. I rummaged a large pottery bowl from the laundry room and filled it with several bagels. I dug out some fruit and juice from the fridge and carried everything out to the deck. The heavy dew of morning had soaked the wooden benches and created a slick walking surface. Treading carefully on the mossy dew-drenched boards, I arranged our breakfast buffet. I turned my face toward the sun and breathed in the day. Perfect!

Time to start the coffee. Another one of the Bouck-ville famous traditions at Hontie's was camp coffee. A small four cup stainless steel perk pot and an open flame would produce pure morning nectar the life blood for the masses. The problem was 'camp coffee' took time, precious time, and yielded so little per pot. This year since there wasn't a working stove, the propane camp stove on the deck would have to do. *Now let's do the math, folks.* We have seven coffee seeking adults with a ten minute prep time yielding two and a half mugs of coffee per pot. *Ugly.* If your coffee required cream you were required to give Squeak, Hontie's cat, a splash of cream in the saucer provided on the counter. Trivet, another of Hontie's resident cats, had only three legs – *a story I had never heard.* Somehow Trivet didn't rate high enough for cream in the morning. *So much for equal feline treatment.*

Rustling sounds were coming from the dining room. I'm not the only one awake! I turned round the corner and ran into my very sleepy cousin Gavin. He was rummaging through some luggage outside the bathroom door. "Hey Gavin!" I said with all the excitement a whisper could offer. I hadn't seen Gavin for two years. Hooked on his hip was a beautiful Gerber baby. His full face was framed by curly wisps of blond, bordering on golden brown hair. He inspected me scrupulously, then grinned. "This must be Davis," I reached out to touch the angel.

Davis responded with a rumbling "Ahhhh harrr".

"Nice to meet you, too!"

"Harrr… issss…"

"Oh Gavin, he's beautiful!" We shared a hug. "How was your trip?"

"Long of course, but Davis traveled well despite an extra hour and a half wait for my uncle's plane to come in. We just took off his shoes and let him dash around the virtually vacant airport."

"I bet that made a great memory shot for Grammie."

"Yeah," Gavin smiled wearily. "We're beat. I'm going to feed this guy, find the diaper bag, and disappear again for a few hours."

"Do that, we'll catch up later." I strolled back into the kitchen to check on the coffee.

"Morning Mommy," Brennan walked toward me for a hug.

Clare followed with Payton on her hip. "That room," she said referring to the laundry, "It's like taking your life in your own hands."

I took Payton from her as he rubbed his sleepy eyes. "Morning sweetie, let's go sit on the deck and wake up a little."

"Cats!" Payton jittered with excitement.

"Okay, you are awake." I set him down and watched him gather Trivet, purring like a Ferrari, into his lap.

More clattering sounded behind me. More bodies were stirring! "Good morning, Hontie. I just saw Gavin and Davis. I was glad to hear the airport trip was uneventful."

"Yeah, Davis was so adorable!" Hontie's grin was filled with true Grammie pride. She ducked back into the laundry room. I heard boxes being shifted while she searched for who knew what. A moment later Hontie trudged through the kitchen hugging a cardboard box. She sat the box on the floor by the sink and began to unload juice cups and coffee mugs. "There was only a minor near miss with Heath's car."

"What kind of near miss?" Heath said gruffly. With Catheryn in tow they moved into the kitchen and right to the stack of coffee mugs on the sink.

Hontie giggled nervously. "Well Heath, I didn't realize until the way home that I had made the trip with your handgun in the glove box!"

"Whoops," Catheryn said lightly. "That certainly would not have pleased Airport security!"

"I was glad I didn't know it was in there. I hate weapons." Hontie shuttered.

"Never crossed my mind," Heath said with a grunt and followed his nose to the brewing camp coffee.

Hontie watched as Heath and Catheryn staked claim to the first pot of camp coffee. Caffeine on hold, she set her empty mug aside and went to the dining room to take over feeding Davis his breakfast. Without a fight, Gavin gratefully disappeared back upstairs to join Jade and catch some extra rest.

Slowly the family gathered on the dewy deck. Canvas lawn chairs were pulled from our vehicles as an alternative to wet deck benches. The peaceful rays of early sunshine masked the somewhat improved chaos which hovered all around us. A large stack of buckets Hontie didn't want carried to the barn were piled by the deck doors. Two saw horses and a sheet of plywood created a work table and held Heath's tools and extension cords off the damp deck surface. The remaining deck, thankfully, resembled a deck. We sat and enjoyed the breakfast which burdened the small aluminum table.

Muted conversations drifted in and out of earshot. Heath didn't feel comfortable leaving the kitchen at such a stage of disrepair, Hontie wanted to enjoy Gavin and Jade's first day, and Clare and Catheryn were figuring out what projects should be tackled next. Me? I just wanted to get to Bouckville.

"Let's go." I said to Clare in a tone which meant, NOW!

Clare nudged Catheryn. "Georgia is going to leave without us." Within minutes we had gathered all our flea market needs. Clare, Catheryn, the boys and I were set to depart for Bouckville day one. I climbed behind the wheel of the Jeep and eased off the lawn. On top of the mailbox sat the unopened bottle of water I had seen the day before. Untouched since the previous day, it was a tiny symbol of purity in our sweltering Hell.

The Jeep hugged the winding unblemished countryside. We had been driving for twenty-five minutes without so much as a stop sign. At home our community was experiencing urban explosion. My daily commute to work, six long miles, offered one stop sign and seven traffic signals. Not to mention hundreds of vehicles in a rush to nowhere... not exactly smooth sailing.

Suddenly a breathtaking scene filled my windshield. An enormous crystal clear lake stretched for several hundred yards. The shoreline was sprinkled with vivid flowers and small bungalow camps with boats tied securely to bobbing docks. The view as the sun danced across the water resembled an artist's masterpiece.

In the next small town several homes were undergoing restoration. It had been two years since I'd been here and the houses were still relatively at the same level of completion *or lack of.* Maybe long term renovation projects were a New York thing. "Brennan, have you ever seen a lighthouse where there isn't any ocean?"

"What?" He was a little confused, but interested.

"Up here on the right we are going to pass a post office that is a lighthouse," Aunt Clare explained. Sure enough the small building coming into view had a red and white striped lighthouse anchoring the right side.

"Cool. Payton, did you see that?" Brennan was impressed.

"I did! I see it! Where's the beach?" Payton craned his neck in search of water, as the lighthouse disappeared behind us.

I was lost in the scenery until Clare spoke. "Georgia, I think we turn right here."

Before me was a view any flea market connoisseur would love. Along Main Street the few small shops that called Bouckville home every day of the year opened their doors and merchandise freely overflowed down the steps and into the parking lots. People, more than the street edge could hold, bustled between the orange safety tapes the police had strung to protect the walkways. Vendors set up tents and tables practically on top of one another to compete for their next sale. Food merchants too juggled for a piece of the action offering an obscene variety; kettle pop corn, pit beef, cream puffs, ice cream, and believe it or not lobster! Grassy areas were converted to parking lots and at three-dollars per vehicle were a lucrative venture. Large circus style striped tents were erected and were filled with countless antique and flea market vendors.

We hurriedly parked and prepared to enter the fray! I sent Brennan off with Clare and Catheryn and kneeled in the newly mowed field to tie Payton's shoes. "Okay buddy, here are the rules." I waited for direct eye contact to assure he was hearing me. "Always have a grownup hand and you must only use your walking feet. No running. No skipping. NO touching, only looking." *Are we having fun yet?* "Many things here are BIG dollars."

"Okay mommy." Payton bounced up and down on his toes.

"No bouncing." *Cripes.* "Let's do it!" We entered the action.

Two hours into the day we're moving along well. Brennan was about to venture into his first flea market bartering session. I had allotted the boys each five dollars per day. They needed to decide whether to save for a prize find or whittle their bucks away. As expected the five-dollar pocket fire had begun. Bren **needed** to buy a real shot gun. The gun was missing major components making it a really authentic play gun. Price seven-dollars. The vendors were a grandparent type husband and wife who were probably in their late seventies.

Brennan picked up the gun and looked at me. I gave him the go-ahead nod. He cleared his throat and addressed the woman. "I'm interested in this gun." Pause, swallow, "What is your best?" Relieved that that part was over, Brennan sighed.

The old woman wandered over, took the gun, and looked at the tag. She stepped back and spoke in the direction of her husband. "He's interested in the gun."

"What?" The Henry Fonda-like gentleman toddled over.

"**He – wants – the – gun.**" She repeated in loud, distinct syllables.

"It's missing the chamber and barrel," he told me.

"That's alright," I put my hand on Brennan's shoulder. "He just wants it to play." Brennan's head followed the conversation like a ping-pong match.

"**It's broken.**" The man shouted toward me. *I guess I appeared to be hard of hearing.*

"He just wants it to play with," I smiled at him, greasing the wheels of a sale. Laying her hand on his arm, his wife said, "He wants it for play."

"He wants to play with it?"

"Yes," I nodded. "To play with."

"And then he'll bring it back?" Obviously bewildered, the man looked at his wife.

Now I was confused.

"George!" She was clearly frustrated. "He wants to **buy** it **for play.**"

"Oh," the light dawned, "For playing," his head bobbed, "alright."

Next problem, the price. I nudged Brennan. He cleared his throat and asked the woman, "Will you take five-dollars?"

"George, will you take five-dollars?" She held out the tag for him to see. "It's marked seven."

George dug in his pocket and handed her a five dollar bill. She rolled her pleading eyes to heaven and shook her head. "For pity's sake," she mumbled under her breath. She looked at me exasperated. "Five dollars is fine."

"Sold! Great job, Bren." He beamed as he handed the woman the money and accepted his first day purchase.

We had made it to mid-day and the boys were ready for fuel. We stopped at the shortest food line for some hot dogs and fries, while Clare and Catheryn went ahead to do one more acre.

"So boys, what do you think?" I sipped on my lemonade.

"Great, Mommy," Brennan answered. "Thanks for bringing us."

"How about you, Payton?"

69

"I like the trains," he said around the hot dog in his mouth. "Can I get a camoose? Or maybe a mocamotive?"

"Sure, honey, we'll look." Rubbing his head I smiled at both of them. "You both are doing great. Let's keep a watch for Aunt Clare and Aunt Catheryn."

"We should call them the two C's for short," Brennan giggled pleased with himself. "No, no, I've got it! C-squared!" he amended.

"Yeah, that's great," I agreed, "C-squared."

"See scared?" Payton questioned. "What's a see scared?"

Brennan and I just laughed.

Chapter 6

We now tune back to our regular scheduled program, Hades, the renovation, starring the unsuspecting visiting relatives from Pennsylvania.

Thursday, middle of the day: Back at Hellsville, a.k.a. Hontie's. The sight of the wedding reception still resembled more of a home renovation program gone wild. Heath was seaming drywall, and Gavin was prepping the ceiling.

"What time do you expect Phil?" Gavin asked Heath.

"I've stopped expecting Phil," he answered dryly

"Mmm… not much has changed there," was the response from Gavin. "Oh, I just heard a car."

A few minutes later Phil and Ella shuffled in, acknowledged no one, and plopped canvas totes overflowing with dirty clothing on the floor in the laundry room. Ella sorted the clothes and with a slam of the lid and a quick turn of the dial the washer jumped to life.

Phil leisurely leaned a hip on the stove and observed Heath and Gavin's efforts. "Looks great you guys," Phil said then stretched his long body. "Man, we had a late one."

Ella rounded the corner and wrapped herself around Phil. "Don't forget to get the coolers out of the car before you leave." She rose up on her toes and gave Phil a smacking kiss. "My sister should be here any minute." She sauntered through the kitchen and out on to the deck.

"Right-o sweet'ums," Phil stared dreamily after her.

"You two aren't staying to work?" Gavin pinned him with an older brother get-your-head-out-of-your-ass look.

"Oh... well..." Phil pulled his pack of cigarettes from his pocket and tapped it negligently on his palm. "Gavin, *here's the thing*... I've got to go pick up the glassware for the church. We are going to have a champagne toast on the lawn...," Phil got lost for a moment in his own visualization. "That will be so awesome." He slipped a cigarette between his lips, "So I need to move the champagne glasses to the lake house," his lighter fired and he sucked the toxins deeply into his lungs, "after I pick them up from the restaurant."

"Moving glasses you haven't picked up yet for a lawn toast two days from now?" Gavin muttered, as he took a moment to process the absurd explanation offered by his brother. "No Phil," Gavin said firmly. "You're needed here."

"Phil," Ella called impatiently from the deck, "Coolers!"

"Coolers, right." Phil disappeared. *Crack that whip!*

Hontie, filthy from weeding and mulching all morning, joined Ella on the deck. "I need to grab a bottle of water." She flopped down in a canvas deck chair and pried off her dirt covered garden clogs as the sweat dripped from her face.

"Oh Lottie, Phil and I brought some clothes over. I put them in the washer. We also brought over some of the food. Phil is fetching the coolers now, so we can load up your fridge."

The only point Hontie had been firm about was that no food was to arrive here for storage and/or assembly until Saturday. The continual process which usually worked well for Phil and Ella was to ask again and again for what they wanted like a couple of four-year-olds. They would wear Hontie into submission and when she'd finally grow weary of saying NO, she would say YES just to shut them up!

"Ella, we have discussed this," Hontie said. "There will be no food stored here or assembled here until Saturday." Hontie dangerously bare footed walked into the construction zone. "We are in the middle of a major, unplanned, renovation project. We have a day and a half deadline in which this kitchen must be ready for food preparations. There isn't any room in the fridge for any storage of wedding food until Saturday."

Undeterred Ella moved through the kitchen, opened the door of the refrigerator, and surveyed the contents. "Phil said there is plenty of room. Just toss out all this old food."

Smiling her certainly airbrushed smile, Hontie gently closed the refrigerator door. "That is not old food. Isabella sent food with Heath. Clare, Catheryn, and Georgia brought the rest. There are eleven people living here and eating here." Ella and Hontie locked gazes like bulls preparing to charge. The humming fans and construction sounds swirled around the intensity of the moment.

Thudding feet sounded in the mudroom behind them, followed by a crash as the double decked coolers Phil had retrieved from the car hit the floor. "Coolers, CHECK!" he bellowed then chuckled to himself. The rising tension between mother and fiancée unnoticed, Phil looked to Ella as he awaited further directions.

Ella's lips pulled back in a smile even though her eyes read fire. "We will be back for the laundry this afternoon. Phil, leave the food in the coolers; they'll make room in the fridge." She sauntered out leaving Hontie gawking open-mouthed after her.

Hontie stepped into the mudroom and flipped open the top cooler lid; salmon, shrimp, and no ice. "Don't eat the Salmon," she said and dropped the lid. Remembering she was thirsty, Hontie opened the fridge and decided a beer rather than water would be required.

Chapter 7

Bouckville bliss: Ice cream, bull horns, and ruby red slippers, Toto, we're not in Kansas anymore.

Clare, Catheryn, the boys, and I were enjoying a perfect first day at Bouckville. The sun's wattage had been softened by even cloud cover. Nothing dark and threatening, but extreme sunburn wasn't a worry. Brennan, Payton, and I stood with fresh squeezed lemonade in our hands.

"We ready to move?" Clare asked.

"Yes," I answered, cleaning up the trash. Brennan carried it off to multiple trash/recycle containers. *Novel idea.* "Payton are you still okay for walking?"

"Actually," his big blue eyes locked with mine. "My legs are a tiny bit tired."

"How about a ride in the piggy back chair, buddy?" I had purchased a child hiker backpack to help Payton's day last a little longer.

"Okay Mommy," he conceded.

After snapping the waist support and adjusting the straps, Catheryn helped me load up Payton and we were off again. "I can see all the flea market!" Payton excitedly tapped the top of my head.

"Wonderful," I answered. "Watch for cool trucks and trains."

"Beep! Beep!" He said delightfully.

"Look Mom!" something had caught Brennan's eye. I followed the direction of his gaze and I saw it. A beautiful toy top perched on a display. It was red and blue with a yellow spiral plunger. Better yet tons of nursery rhymes enveloped the body.

"It's fabulous! Good eye, Bren," quick high-five. "Don't show your excitement to the vendor or we lose the deal." We walked across the shaded grove. Payton was on my back which made getting into the vendor's display difficult. I reached up and grasped the beauty, but wisely wore an expression of disinterest.

The vendor shouted across the tent, "I can do better!" The tag said sixteen dollars which I felt was reasonable.

"What's your best?" I entered the barter dance.

"Thirteen."

I felt like a gamble and with Brennen looking on I reached up to place the top back on the display. Sensing the sale was slipping, the vendor quickly moved toward me. "It is in great condition," he pulled the top down to the table surface. "Beautiful when it spins." The plunger sank into the tin top and it twirled delightfully.

"Yes, it's nice." I was so proud that the boys didn't give my lust for the top away. "I was thinking, ten." Moments later Brennan and I danced from the tent with the top in hand!

"Excellent Mom, you got him to drop six bucks!"

"Yep," I couldn't help but grin. "Fun, huh? Hey look, here come C-squared."

"Beep, Beeper!" Payton chimed in again.

"See another truck buddy? Good eyes! Beep, Beep!"

I could see Clare had something tucked beneath her arm. She turned and the item appeared to jut out of the other side of her body as well. "What do you think Aunt Clare is holding that is long enough to stick out on both sides of her body?" I asked the boys.

"Looks like horns," Bren answered unconcerned.

"Horns?" I focused, "Oh my goodness you're right!" Bull horns were tucked securely in Clare's arms while she looked through another vendor's stash.

"Do you think she really bought them?" Brennan asked.

"No, I'm sure she just wants to show them to..." I couldn't believe my eyes, but sure enough Clare turned and headed, bull horns and all, our way.

"Cool," Brennan was clearly impressed with this latest treasure. He rushed off to meet her. I couldn't help but chuckle. When she finally was within hearing range, I asked her through my giggles, "You bought horns?"

"Yep, for the bedroom," Clare grinned thoroughly pleased with herself. *Alrighty then.*

"Beep! Beeper!" Payton said again from his perch.

"You see another truck honey?" I bounced him a little shifting the weight on my shoulders. "He's been spotting vehicles left and right from his sky box," I said to Clare.

"Beeper!" Payton was more insistent this time.

"Beeper?" Clare echoed.

Finally, I clued in. Not 'beep' as in vehicle, but 'beeper', as in peenie weenie. "Oh, honey I'm sorry," I grabbed his feet and gave him a stirrup to stand in. He stood up in the pack taking the weight off his private parts.

"Better," Payton announced with relief.

Clare cracked up. "You've castrated him! He'll never have children." She could barely contain herself. "Come here buddy," she lifted him from his torture chamber.

Catheryn joined up with us a moment later. "What did I miss?" She looked around at our amused faces.

Brennan filled his lungs and delivered the update in one spew of breath. "Mom bought a toy top, dealt it down six bucks, Aunt Clare bought bedroom horns, and Payton will never have children, whatever that means."

A renewed giggle fest ensued. Catheryn watched as Clare, whose bladder tended to threaten in moments like this, crouched to the ground, and told herself to focus as she took deep breaths in an effort not to pee.

"Breathe slower Clare, you'll hyperventilate." Catheryn couldn't help but laugh as Payton ran in circles around us like a puppy.

Hours later my butt was dragging. I knew hauling the piggy back chair would be tiring, but oh my. We had entered the last large area we expected to peruse today. The boys and I had found a shade tree and decided to rest while Clare and Catheryn worked the field. "Mom, you sure weren't kidding; this place is endless." Brennan snapped off a blade of grass, laid it between his thumbs and attempted the famed thumb whistle.

"Pretty amazing, huh?" Payton drove his five dollar purchase up and down my leg making appropriate automotive sounds. "Like your truck, sweetie?" He had found a mini-Hess truck collectible. It was an eighteen dollar, five dollar purchase. *Sue me.*

"Yeah, it's really fast," Payton answered clearly satisfied.

"When we find the aunts, we are going out this little alleyway back to the main drag. There is always a Hershey's ice cream stand there. How does a cone sound?" Both boys perked up and began the flavor debate.

"Mommy I see Aunt Squares," Payton pointed down the row. "Can we get some cream now?"

"Squared," Brennan rolled his eyes.

I bypassed the brother bickering and steered them back to ice cream. "Mint chocolate chip cream sounds good to me."

A few minutes later, armed with cones we began to back track in the direction of the car. "Did I just feel rain?" Brennan held out his free hand.

It had been overcast all day but no real ominous clouds were anywhere in view. "Maybe." I had adjusted the seat in the back pack and Payton was now riding comfortably.

"You're pretty brave letting him eat that cone that near to your hair," Clare noted.

"Lesser of the evils. I figured it was easier for him than walking and eating."

Clare's eyes grew large as she picked up speed. "Oh, I love this group." She ducked down an alley into another small vendor area anchored by a great old barn.

Resigned to another detour, I followed Clare and Catheryn down the pathway. "We'll work our way through and wait at the road." I shouted after C-squared. *Keep the troops moving without the appearance of being rushed.*

"Mom I just felt more drops," Brennan said again.

I glanced to the sky. "If we get a little wet, that's just part of the experience."

"Cool."

"I don't want to be experienced," the little monkey on my back said a bit concerned. "Done with my cone, Mommy," Payton reached forward and handed me the soggy stub.

Three minutes later Niagara Falls made an im-promptu visit to Main Street Bouckville. No warning. No gradual precipitation. The heavens exploded and a torrential bone soaking rain dumped down. Unbelievable wind gusts pushed everyone under very limited cover as unsecured items shattered all around us. A large cupboard caught in the wind's force toppled and destroyed a table of Depression glass. Vintage postcards swirled in the air while the owner of the valuable paper goods swatted in a futile attempt to save a few items. The boys and I ducked into a tent at the end of the alley. The merchants were trying to save some of their inventory, the majority of which unfortunately was glass. The boys and I tried to move out of their way and lend a hand at the same time. Maneuvering carefully we wedged farther into the tent.

"Don't touch anything," I whispered to Brennan.

"Holy cow! I've never seen rain like this!" He was fascinated.

Feeling slightly like Dorothy in preflight I wasn't so thrilled. Payton was quietly whimpering from his perch in the piggy back chair. A wind gust filled the tent and lifted it up to the maximum height the securing tethers would allow.

"Mommy!" Payton grabbed two fistfuls of my hair in fright.

"It's like a tornado!" Brennan squealed excitedly. More sounds of shattering glass and the helpless shouts of vendors trying to save what they could filled the air.

"It's all right Payton honey, just a little storm." The strangers who had also sought cover in the tent eyed me skeptically. "Where do you think C-squared ended up?" I tried to distract the boys. Digging into my tote I pulled out our rain gear. "Bren, put this poncho on."

"Awesome!" *Nothing fazed this kid.*

"Do I get a plastic coat too?" Payton made sure he wasn't left out.

"You sure do!" The boys donned their lovely dollar store multicolor ponchos. Payton's poncho covered my shoulders as well since he still sat in his perch. We were about fifteen minutes into the downpour and there seemed to be no indication that the rain was slowing. People had begun to leave their shelters resigned to the fact that the day had become a washout. We worked our way to the front of the tent. There was still no sign of Clare and Catheryn.

"Keep watch for Aunt Clare or Aunt Catheryn to pass the tent opening," I told Brennan. "We'll have to back track to find them if they don't show up." Ten minutes passed and the rain converted to a mild shower. "Forget the back tracking; we're going to head back to the Jeep." I tugged up Brennan's plastic hood and gave him an encouraging smile, "Let's go!"

One step out of the tent we crashed into C-squared. "Oh, we thought you washed away!" Catheryn playfully patted the boys' poncho covered heads.

"We tried to get you on the two-way radio," Clare waved her radio at me.

"Forgot I even had it, we haven't separated all day."

"Yeah, that's what we figured;" Clare took the lead with Bren. "Let's call it a day."

"Imagine what we've missed back at the house," Catheryn said.

I'd rather not.

Chapter 8

Blindfolded and strapped into a high speed roller coaster without any knowledge of the upcoming twists, loops, and turns would be fine if you were riding under your own free will and were in search of the next big thrill.

We returned back to home front hell at about 3:00, and were relieved to see it hadn't rained a drop. We had learned at breakfast there were several outside projects all awaiting able-bodied hands. Lawn mowing, flower planting, mulching... *Endless.* Another car parked on the lawn signaled that Mom had arrived at some point during the day from Pennsylvania. *Glad I hadn't been here to witness her arrival.*

My mother, Isabella at sixty-one had morphed from super mom into elite grandmom status. Raised by the war generation, a generation centered on values, Mom had a rock solid core of respect blended with compassion and an unyielding sense of right and wrong. After years of selfless parenting, she had turned her children loose as parents do, to become what we would in this world of ours. Then it was her turn. Mom's adventurous side, which was a fantastic surprise to me and my siblings, had been back seated long enough. She began to teach herself Spanish and vacations to the beach to enjoy leisurely bike rides were replaced with white water rafting, zip lining in Peru, and mission trips to the Dominican Republic, *for crying out loud*. She was reborn! Despite her random use of Spanish in an attempt to become fluent, Mom was a joy.

On top of the escalating stresses Mom would face preparing Hontie's house and grounds for one hundred wedding guests; the arrival of Uncle Nathan, Hontie's ex-husband, and his family, would add another dimension to the mounting dysfunction. Mom would always protect those she loved the most, even when they didn't need it. *A trait I hoped to inherit.*

Hontie's ability to set aside past issues and share the joy of her youngest child's wedding with his father was inspiring. She had told me once 'past is past', and any issues she had were hers alone. *Healthy.*

For me? I was with Mom. The idea of Uncle Nathan happily returning to the home where he and Hontie had begun a young marriage and family, made me twitch.

Call Dr Phil and schedule an appointment, cripes.

"Grandmom is here somewhere boys. Go find her." *Soften her up with grandchildren.*

Weary from our first day Bouckville escapade, Clare, Catheryn, and I climbed on the deck. Sasha was stretched out in the sunny corner flanked by Hontie's cactus collection. She raised her massive head and panted in acknowledgement. Catheryn and I lowered ourselves into canvas chairs while Clare ventured into the kitchen to grab drinks.

The kitchen had now reached another level of construction craziness. Clare weaved her way to the refrigerator and noticed that the new dry wall had been completely hung. The walls and ceiling had even been treated to the first coat of spackling. Definite progress. The work crew consisted of Heath, Gavin, and Phil. The men worked tensely without conversation and communicated with only an occasional grunt.

Clare retuned to the deck with an armful of bottled water and juice pouches for the boys. "No Corona?" I caught the bottle she tossed my way.

"Since we may have to operate power equipment this afternoon, I made a supervisory decision to hold off our consumption of alcohol." Clare said. *Responsibility sucks.*

The boys ran through the yard and bounded onto the deck. "Juicy!" Payton spotted the drink bags.

"Did you find Grandmom?" I asked.

"She is over by the barn spreading mulch." Brennan picked up a drink and then sat down next to Sasha.

Since we still had daylight, C-squared and I decided to tackle the long list of remaining outdoor chores. Already tired from the day, I grabbed my small bounty purchases from the Jeep and dashed up the steep back steps to the peace of the bedroom. I admired my first day's treasures, my top and my tiny red-metal-toy phone, then stretched out across the mattress. A few moments later, my peace was interrupted as Brennan's feet pounded up the steps.

"Hontie told me to put on some work clothes. I'm going to plant the new whiskey barrels." The excitement of doing real jobs visibly vibrated from him.

"New whiskey barrels?" I remained on the mattress, eyes closed.

"Yep, she had to buy three barrels to cover the holes in the yard."

"Holes?" I massaged my temples.

"Yep, you know those big dirt piles in the yard when we got here. Phil dug holes to make a bigger deck."

"And let me guess, he never made a bigger deck." *Thank God for small miracles.*

Brennan began to rummage through our suitcase. Opening an eye I watched as items of clothing took flight. "Babe, you didn't really bring 'work' clothes."

He straightened abruptly, his brow furrowed. "Well then what do I wear to plant?"

"What you are wearing."

He gave himself a quick once over, and shrugged his shoulders. "Alright", he tossed the items of clothes he was holding back on the pile, hurdled over me, and in a few quick steps he disappeared back down and outside to help.

I closed my eyes; I tried to will myself to a place of peace. Muffled voices drifted through the open window. Mom was working beside the barn sweeping the broken concrete slab. "Are we moving some tables over here? Will there be any lighting?" I heard her ask. I didn't hear anyone reply. Guilt cut my siesta short. I couldn't lie here and relax while everyone else pitched in. I hauled my behind up, pulled myself together, and prepared to head back downstairs to join in the mayhem. "Lottie?" I heard Mom's voice again through the window. "This barn is a mess. Should I straighten it up?' I flopped back down and sighed deeply; I needed another minute.

On the opposite side of the house, Hontie, Clare, and Brennan worked on the "new" whiskey barrels. Up to their elbows in dirt, Clare and Brennan sifted soil through their fingers while Hontie issued Martha Stewart style soil mixing instructions. "One part soil, one part manure, one part magic mixture ensures proper nutrient fertilization ratio."

Clare smiled and nodded. If only there were a visible cartoon bubble floating over her head it would surely say: "Hontie, you're a nut ball!"

Clare and Brennan continued working to fill the three barrels with the proper nutrient mixture and of course proper blend of colored flowers. Another car pulled on the lawn. Ella climbed out with three people in tow. A girl heaved a canvas tote from the trunk, skirted around the trash filled trailer, and followed Ella to the deck.

Clare looked up and prepared to greet Ella, whom she had yet to see. Ella blew past her, marched up the deck steps, and then casually over her shoulder said, "This is my sister and brother and his girlfriend."

Dumbfounded, Clare watched as Ella disappeared into the kitchen. Her sister offered a sympathetic smile; "I'm Anya." She jostled the heavy tote on her shoulder, and then she too was swallowed by the house.

The shock clear on her face, Clare turned toward the other pair. Ella's brother and girlfriend presented an interesting eyeful. The girlfriend looked Calvin Klein runway ready. Her ink black hair framed her face and hung lifelessly to her collarbone. A white gauze tunic draped from angular shoulders and fluttered at hip length. Linen pants, also white, were set off by a tailored cuff that flirted along her calf. She stood, posed with one foot angled in front of the other accenting her Jimmy Choo goddess sandals. The laces ended after numerous wrappings around her leg in a bow at her hem line. Stark white and spotless, she looked extremely out of place. Wearing her perfected runway sneer, she observed Clare with obvious disgust.

Ella's brother on the other hand attempted a 'gangsta' fashion statement. Black cargo pants hung low and offered four inches of boxer brief exposure. His multi-print dress shirt was unbuttoned and hung open over a wife beater tank. Around his neck multiple medallions and chains of varying lengths were draped. He held an open bag of chips and was at the moment enjoying snack time. Together they stared at Clare amid her planting process. *Well, she was elbow deep in shit.*

Clare plastered her 'I was raised with manners' smile in place. "I'm Clare," she cleared her throat, "Phil's cousin." With a tentative giggle, she held out her hands. "Can't really offer to shake your hand at the moment, but it's nice to meet you both."

The 'Artic queen' huffed, crossed her arms over her chest, and turned her back. 'Gangsta boy' shoved a fistful of BBQ chips into his mouth. "Roldf," he muttered and buried his hand once again into the bag. With his mouth over flowing he tossed his head toward his girlfriend, "Soola", he said with a spray of chips. No surprise she didn't even bother to pivot in her spotless Jimmy Choos.

Clare gaped at him, unsure if that was an introduction or some sort of spasm.

Phil burst from the house. "Rod! Somi! Great to see you! " Arms wide open, hugs, pats on the back, and a secret Best Friend Handshake. *Quite the greeting.* The girlfriend, Somi? *Gimmie a break,* lit like a Christmas tree at the appearance and attention of Phil. She batted her painted lashes, whispered something in Phil's ear, stepped back and shot a scathing look into Clare's direction. Phil followed Somi's gaze and glanced over at Clare and Brennan. "That looks great you two!"

Clare stepped back and looked at the whiskey barrels. "Well it's one more thing off the list, right?" She said cheerfully.

"I got to mix the dirt," Brennan said proudly, "Scoop of poop, scoop of soil, and scoop of magic mix."

"Yeah?" intrigued, Phil looked to Clare, with a grin, "Magic mix?"

"Your mom," Clare raised her soiled hands.

"Gotcha", he gave her a wink. Somi huffed loudly enough to be heard over Rod's chip munching and gained Phil's attention. "So guys, we a go for tonight?" Phil asked them. Somi's eyes darted in Clare's direction. The three promptly lowered their voices and walked around the front of the house.

Clare, thankful the meet and greet was over, curi-ously watched their retreating backs. "We're all done here

Brennan, great job!" They both looked at their magic mix stained-to-the- elbows arms.

"Yuck!" Brennan said.

"Yeah, let's find a hose."

Inside I waded through the laundry room and ran into Ella, who had just entered home improvement central. "Hey there," I said as she plunked down a canvas tote filled-to-bursting with dirty laundry.

"Hey there yourself," Ella motioned to a now visible woman behind her. "This is my sister, Anya.

There was enough resemblance between them I would have figured, but Anya's hair was long and the natural curl was softer. "Hi, it is nice to meet you." She smiled politely.

"We dropped off wash earlier. We're just here to grab what is clean, toss in some more and then we're off to the lake house." Ella shifted to the task of sorting the dirty laundry.

"Let me slide out of your way." I did my best to move through the even more crowded laundry area as Ella and Anya whispered quietly to each other about getting done quickly and moving on with their evening plans. Thankful someone knew how to make a plan, I stepped past them where I could see Heath now at work solo in the kitchen.

"You are really good at this." I said, as I ran my hand along the smooth wall. "Where did your work force take off to?"

He grunted. "Gavin went to help Jade with Davis, and Phil took off outside when Ella…" Heath trailed off as Anya's distressed voice reached the kitchen.

"Ella, the clothes we put in earlier didn't dry and the washer didn't spin out."

Heath looked over to me and wiggled his brows mischievously. I was pleased that stress and fatigue hadn't completely stolen his humor.

"We're going to have to take them wet and hang them at the lake house to dry." Ella consoled her sister.

"Are you serious?" Anya whimpered, "I need them for tonight."

"How inconvenient," Heath chuckled under his breath then shifted his attention to the ceiling.

The sounds of laundry being dumped on the floor had me turning. Sure enough, dirty clothing spread over the floor. Both totes were now hastily being filled with wet laundry. The sisters climbed over the piles of discarded dirty clothes to the kitchen. "Well, it looks great everyone," Ella hefted the heavy canvas tote to her shoulder. Anya stepped to her side, then the pair backed carefully out of the work zone to the deck.

I watched the exiting Ella and raised my hand, "See you later." And they were gone leaving Heath and me standing in their wake.

"What's with the chuckles there Mr. Fix-it?" I asked Heath. "What's the deal with the laundry?"

His eyes danced with delight, looking younger than he had since my arrival. "Oh, not much... my plaster wouldn't cure due to the extra humidity from the washer and dryer so I unplugged them."

"Classic."

An hour had passed and everyone was busy doing all kinds of things. Random items still littered the side and back yards, so I decided to work there.

My hands were full of potting and planting crocks when Hontie found me on the deck side of the house. She surveyed the yard then whispered covertly, "Where's your mom?"

"Don't know." I held the shards of pottery up for her to see. "These aren't being used for the reception, right? Some of them are broken."

"No, they're for a project. Take them to the side of the barn." She motioned for me to follow her. "I need to talk to you and Clare and Catheryn, but," checking over her shoulder, she lowered her voice, "not in front of your mom."

What on Earth could it be now. "Is everything OK?"

Hontie cast another wild look around the yard, "Not here, let's find the girls."

I followed her through the kitchen and out the mud-room door to the yard by the barn where C-squared were attacking lawn duty. Clare had dragged the mower over from the field and Catheryn was clearing the small crescent shaped grass area of sticks and stones, so Clare could mow the grass.

"Georgia just put those crocks and lids along the side of the barn with the others," Hontie said while doing a 007 style sweep of the perimeter. "I saw in a magazine how they nailed all sizes and colors of crocks and lids to a barn and sort of made a mosaic."

"That sounds cool," Clare caught the end of the conversation.

Sure enough I found a stack of pottery odds and ends by the barn. Turning to Hontie, "Is this project happening before the wedding?" *Why do I even ask?*

"Oh, I sure hope so! We just need to figure out how to nail them." Hontie smiled her had-one-too-many grins and focused on Clare. "Where's your mom?"

"Haven't seen her." Reading Hontie's expression, Clare walked over. "What's wrong?

"We need Catheryn." Spotting her, Hontie called out, "Hey Catheryn, could you come here please?"

Clare and I exchanged looks. "What's going on" she mouthed to me. I shrugged my shoulders as Catheryn jogged to us.

Hontie took a very deep breath. "I just want you to know I haven't said yes, but I told him I'd ask." *Never a good way to start.* "Your Uncle Nathan," she made quotations marks with her fingers, "says he'll buy the pizza if you three would go to the lake house tomorrow night during the rehearsal dinner to baby-sit all the children."

"Hell no." "Absolutely not." Clare and Catheryn replied simultaneously before the question had settled into my brain.

"Is he insane?" Clare gestured wildly. "We haven't seen him in countless years! And we have never even met the... how many kids?"

"Twelve," Hontie answered calmly.

Clare cleared her throat, "twelve West Coast darlings. He really wants us to plop down for the evening in a lake house with them?"

Catheryn jumped in, "We're not included in the rehearsal dinner, yet we're convenient enough to watch everyone's kids." The always calm Catheryn began to pace. "NO!"

Hontie held up both hands for peace. "I just told him I'd ask. You all have a long day at Bouckville planned again tomorrow," she rambled on nervously, "and I know you have some things to do yet here."

"Just a few," I muttered under my breath.

"Georgia?" Clare looked at me for some reaction.

"What?" I had no plans of adding child care for the masses to my weekend duties. Twelve children ages two through thirteen who had never set eyes on the folks from Pennsylvania in a rental home on the lake front until heaven knows what hour of the night. *Uncle Nathan must be on crack.* Hontie, Clare, and Catheryn watched me intently waiting for my reply. I raised a shoulder, "I've got two kids of my own to care for." Bone weary I lifted my hands in exasperation. "We do have plans for the day and more than enough work to do prior to Saturday, like a barn mosaic," I added flippantly.

Catheryn abruptly stopped pacing, "A what?"

"Forget it." I patted Catheryn's arm. "The point is, I have absolutely no time, energy, or inclination to be nanny for the night. In fact, I'd rather be pecked to death by chickens."

"Well said." Clare deliberately turned and headed back to the mower.

"Hontie?" I efficiently changed the subject. "I noticed some plants by the driveway. Where do they go?"

"Oh colored flowers are for the whiskey barrels here, along the drive." We walked along the gravel driveway. "All the white ones get planted in the moon garden. Just mix them in amongst the other perennials."

A station wagon whipped into drive as I grabbed the non-white flowers. "Who's this?" Through the windshield on the front seat was a tiny gray haired lady. Wearing a huge smile, she waved enthusiastically at me. The driver, a woman with wild curly hair hopped from behind the steering wheel and flew around the vehicle, as if on roller skates. A frenzy of movement, she opened doors and pulled out various things while speaking rapidly to her companion.

Hontie stood beside me, "Oh, that's Ella's mother, Sylvia, and her good friend, Jewel." Then in a whisper she added, "Sylvia is a little larger then life. Her accents softens the impact of her language, but be prepared the F-bomb is her word of choice."

Wonderful.

I had heard tales of Sylvia, a stage actress with a heavy British accent and a mouth like a trucker. *Should prove interesting.* She was a blur of color as she whipped in and out of the car. Sylvia's wild auburn hair had curls which rivaled my own. Every few seconds she'd pause to blow a stray curl from her eye. Fuchsia capris and a turquoise blouse billowed out as she moved. Arms loaded, she barreled toward us. Sylvia peered over the frame of her teal spectacles which clung to the tiniest tip of her nose. Another whirlwind introduction was headed my way. *There's nothing like meeting people when you are knee deep in frustration.* I plastered a smile on my face, as she stopped within inches of my flower laden arms.

"Hello all!" Sylvia glided across the drive. Hontie handled the intros like a pro. Sylvia leaned in and sniffed the blossoms in my arms. "Exquisite #//*-ing blooms, darling!"

"Thank you," I swallowed the laugh that pressed at my lips.

Sylvia raced top speed through the mudroom, as Ella and Anya stepped out. "My beloveds! There you are!" Mother and daughters exchanged quick air kisses and then the girls set off for Hontie's car. Ella and Anya weren't out of ear shot when Sylvia hit the kitchen. "Oh darling, what the #//* happened in here love?" Ella and Anya froze for a fraction of a second and then picked up their exiting pace. "Oh Christ… and in here! #//*! #//*- it darling!"

Where to begin. Hontie rushed after Sylvia for damage control.

Ella raised her voice to drown any further commentary from her mother. "Catch ya later Georgia." She shouted from the end of the drive. She wrenched open Hontie's car door, grinned, and gave thumbs up to the cousin lawn crew. "Looks great you guys!"

"Yep... later." I shoved another festive annual in an already overcrowded whiskey barrel. "Sounds like you've got a lot of cool stuff planned for tonight."

"Oh? Not much really." Ella sounded guarded. She shared a quick concealed look with Anya. "Just last minute odds and ends." They smiled at each other and hopped into the car and slammed the doors. That was odd, even under the circumstances. Ella gunned the engine and gravel sprayed, as the sisters backed from the drive.

Hanging from the passenger window, Anya hollered, "Just odds and ends... wedding stuff!" Tires squealed over what sounded like laughter, as they vanished down the road.

"Wackos." *Had these people lost all their brain cells to the California sunshine?* Finished with the barrels, I gathered up the white plants and headed toward the moon garden. The left border of the oversized flower bed was shaped in a crescent and planted with only white flowering plants. Beautiful! *A very Martha Stewart moment in a very non-Martha environment.*

Clare was viciously attacking the small courtyard beside the moon garden with the lawn mower. I placed the white plants safely among the established plants and went to the barn in search of a shovel. Shaking my head, "moon gardens, cripes."

"AAAAHHH!" Clare screamed taking years from my life. "Help!" The mower ground to a stop and a huge dirt cloud enclosed her. I ran back to Clare who sputtered and coughed, as she waved at the dust. "Georgia," she hacked again, "did you see that?"

Catheryn was next on the scene. "What happened? Are you hurt?"

Clare gestured wildly, "Parts are flying off and look," she pointed to the mower. "I've lost a wheel." She dropped to the ground and patted the grass in search of bolts.

Gavin and Heath rushed from the house to answer Clare's distress call. With his hands jammed into his pockets, Phil ambled behind. The testosterone trio observed Clare, as she crawled on the lawn.

"You all right?" Gavin asked Clare. Heath simply removed his hat for a thoughtful scratch.

"Oh… Clare, yeah, that mower…" Phil dragged his hand from his pocket and rubbed his chin. "*Here's the thing*… those bolts don't really fit that wheel set up. You have to, you know, tighten them a bit." With an expression which was a mixture of pity and bewilderment, Gavin gawked at his younger brother.

Clare glowered up at Phil from all fours. "Good information to know."

Afternoon quickly had become evening. Tonight's dinner consisted of pulled beef sandwiches, cheese, and crackers. Clare had toted the crock pot from PA and this morning she had situated it in the bedroom to avoid the dust and toddlers. After slow cooking all day the tender beef tasted like heaven. We fixed platters, sat on the deck, and discussed the various stages of insanity currently occupying our lives.

"So Heath, you headed out to the bachelor party?" Clare asked.

"Bachelor party?" Catheryn said.

Heath's response was a shrug and a grunt. He gestured over his shoulder to the kitchen. "No possible way I'd even consider it. Besides, I came here to do Bouckville with my wife. Tomorrow I am going with you guys, regardless."

Catheryn smiled at him, as only a wife could and then turned back to Clare. "A bachelor party?"

"Mmm," Clare nodded as she chewed her sandwich, "and Bachelorette."

I thought back to Ella's strange behavior and her tire screaming exit. "Wedding details, last minute odds and ends," I said softly.

"Huh?" Clare looked at me puzzled.

"This afternoon, Ella and Anya flew out of here when I mentioned their plans for tonight."

"Ha, she thought you were cruising for an invite." Clare took a bite of sandwich.

"They're having a party?" *Poor out of touch, Catheryn.*

"We are the work force, hon" Heath patted Catheryn's knee. "We hardly rate a party invite."

"Just slave labor," Clare sighed, "It's not like we'd go."

Mom sat in the corner of the deck surrounded by Hontie's house plants on steroids. She listened but offered no wisdom or comment. Actually she appeared on auto pilot quietly enjoying her sandwich.

"Clare these sandwiches really are terrific," I said. Echoing mmmms were heard around the deck. "Isn't it funny that we seem to be the only ones concerned about the house and grounds status?"

"What would happen if we stopped working?" Clare wondered out loud.

"They wouldn't even notice," I swallowed the sandwich in my mouth. "Cats," I nodded in agreement with myself. "That's what they are, gypsy cats. They always land on their feet."

"El gato!" Mom spat out, "El felino!" Her random use of Spanish startled us. Practicing for her next trip to the Dominican Republic, Mom used as many Spanish words each day in an effort to become fluent. The only problem was no one else spoke Spanish.

Through the glass deck door Hontie could be seen doing a dance in front of the newly hung kitchen sink. "She's on crack," I said.

"What?" Clare leaned toward me.

"Hontie," I motioned toward the door. "Dancing in the kitchen, she's on crack."

Mom perked up. "Qué?"

I pointed to the deck door and repeated, "Your sister is on crack."

"What?" Mom was clearly confused, "Qué haces? What did she crack?"

Clare and I snickered.

Hontie joined us on the deck, beaming. "I can't believe what that room looked like on Sunday. Heath you have transformed it in just three days!" She wrapped her arms around Heath from behind and kissed the top of his head. "I have a sink!" Hontie twirled, "and not just any sink, but my stored in a barn for five-years across town farm house salvaged sink!"

"Wow," Clare glanced into the kitchen with renewed appreciation as Hontie waltzed with herself.

"And I can't believe you're dancing knowing one hundred people will be coming here in two days." I said dryly.

Hontie pulled up the last remaining camp chair and sat with a huge sigh. "It will come together." *Toke. Toke.*

"We will bring it together is more like it," Clare quietly muttered under her breath. "Hontie?" Clare said seriously. "Don't Phil and Ella want it to be nice?" Clare paused as Hontie bit lustily into her sandwich. "Don't they?" Clare pleaded for an answer but none came. She sat back in her chair and muttered, "How can they not be here fixing this mess?"

Nudging Clare I stated the obvious, "They're on crack."

Mom was still perplexed. "What?"

"Oh Clare, they want it to be nice," Hontie consoled.

"They want it to be nice?" Clare's voice pitched high. She cleared her throat, "Then put the time in and make it nice."

I just couldn't get over how families could be so diverse. We would plan for weeks to host a Pampered Chef party. This crew invited one hundred without any formal planning. *For cryin' out loud.* I sensed the building fury and went for a little crowd control. "Hontie, what projects are left?"

Hontie lifted her drink to her lips, considering. "Let's see," she took a sip. "Oh, the sap buckets. They must be primed and then they all need two coats of green paint." She looked over her shoulder; "I have a sample here somewhere. We need to wrap the middle of each one with twine to make a band and hot glue the bows in place."

For the love of all things holy... *What have these people been doing all of these months*? I leaned forward in my chair, dinner forgotten. "How many buckets exactly?"

"Twelve." Hontie took a bite of sandwich, set her plate aside and hopped to her feet. She walked to a pile at the corner of the deck. Poked around, and then held out a ball of twine. "Isn't this hemp twine great?"

"Uh-huh... great." *Madness.* "Are the buckets galvanized?"

"Yeah," Hontie turned and pointed to the corner of the deck. "That's what is stacked over there."

Yes, the towering nested buckets I spied upon my arrival. "Why not leave them plain?" I scanned the faces of my family for support. No one was following our conversation.

"Oh Georgia, there's time." Hontie beamed that I'm-beginning-to-lose-my-sanity smile. I watched as she carried the twine back into the house.

Glancing skyward I searched for some divine intervention only to find myself being studied by a green eyed Jellicle cat. Skitz, who was lazily stretched on the roof top, peered at me with that feline mystical gaze. *Creepy really... a little too Steven King.*

At what point would this event move to a recovery process, not a rescue effort. Should we not have a list for "must do", "wouldn't it have been nice", and "screw it?"

We finished the evening working outside until, as Payton put it, "the sun went to bed". Jade put Davis down in the middle bedroom, then left in my Jeep with Gavin for the bachelor festivities at the lake.

Heath was determined to get the ceiling seams finished and the plaster repaired on the kitchen's long wall. He solicited C-squared to help him. Around 9:00 P.M. the boys and I went up to the mattress which now, thanks to Clare's portable pump, was firm. Brennan and I settled in for UNO while Payton snored quietly at our feet.

2 A.M., too exhausted to rest, I crept downstairs to investigate noises I thought were Heath under construction deadlines. Tiptoeing past the cot, Clare sat bolt upright. "Turn the light on! Hold the rail! Careful now!" My heart thudded in my throat as she proceeded to flop back down none the wiser. Nocturnal Clare had been known on several occasions to stand toe to toe with you, stomp her feet, and announce, "I am awake." While she looked every bit awake and alert, she was actually 100% asleep. Clare would never own up to her craziness the morning after. The behavior was relatively harmless but scared the crap out of you.

Downstairs the noise turned out to be Gavin and Jade making sandwiches.

"Hey guys, you have fun?" I squinted against the light.

"Yeah, great. We're just really hungry," Gavin said as he dove into a two-fisted turkey sandwich with all the trimmings. "Your mom's sliced turkey... hmmm heaven."

I stifled a yawn, "I just thought the noise was Heath and I came down to chase him off to bed."

"He was actually showering when we got here." Gavin said between munches.

"Ridiculous," I shook my head. "This whole thing is freakin' insane."

"You know it, right?" Jade finished putting the sandwich fixins away. "How was my babe?"

"Davis was great, no worries. Get some rest you two. I'll see you in a few hours."

Chapter 9

Some days you awake only to find you're still living yesterday's nightmare.

Friday morning 8:00 A.M. Traditionally, we would already be at Bouckville making that first purchase but no. I found myself just opening my eyes to the renewed horror that this was truly happening. Through the adjoining door I heard, "Awee, awee, awee." A giggle soon followed. Davis, I realized, was up and hanging on his crib doing the famed toddler I'm-ready-for-the-day dance. I'm sure Gavin and Jade didn't feel the same way following the bachelor party with the free-flowing beverages and assorted extras. I'd be willing to bet a well rested toddler with a full diaper and an empty belly were the last of the joys mom and dad were looking forward to at dawn. "Awee, awee, awee!" another gleeful giggle rang out again.

I extracted myself from the inflate-a-bed and slowly climbed to my feet. The room stayed silent, thankfully. I tiptoed toward the stairs. A flash of black and white rocketed past my legs. Before I had a chance to scream, it impacted the window of the bedroom. The body of Skitz fell in slow motion and landed, much to my surprise, flat on its back. "For cryin' out loud, cat." I slowly exhaled trying to regulate my racing heart. Skitz flipped to his feet and glared at me with feline ferocity. He gave a full body shake and restored his dignity, tossed his tail in the air and strutted from the room.

"Guess I shouldn't have shut the window."

"Cripes, Clare!" I jumped yet again. "Wiggle a toe or something." Davis's giggle sounded again from the other room. "He's an early riser."

"I guess I could go for him," Clare said peering out of one eye.

"Are you awake?" I eyed her skeptically.

"I'm talking to you aren't I?"

"You know as well as I do that doesn't always qualify as awake."

"Oh good grief," Clare pulled the sleeping bag over her head. "What did I do?"

"Nothing too horrible," I assured her. "I'll go start the camp coffee. We need to get moving."

"Gas is on," was her parting comment. At last, a real kitchen stove could be used to perk the camp coffee. *Small miracles.*

Rich coffee aroma filled the house and stirred the exhausted. Within the hour everyone sat on the various chairs and damp deck benches with coffee mugs in hand. While enjoying breakfast on the deck these past mornings, I had discovered you could learn a lot about people by observing their morning rituals, especially as it pertained to coffee. Some sat eyes closed, others talked quietly. If you forgot the circumstances which surrounded us, you would almost believe we were on a quiet family retreat. However, away from our work; our kids' sport schedules; and committee commitments, individual personality traits could not hide behind the first day's cup of java.

Clare was seated, legs crossed, mug perched on her knee with both hands wrapped securely around the warm mug. She merely hugged it, rarely drinking.

Mom held her mug handle with her left hand and created a saucer with the other. Lifting her mug, she repeatedly blew across the top of her coffee to cool it.

Heath, so desperately in need of caffeine clarity, insistently slurped the extremely hot liquid burning his mouth each and every time.

Hontie and Catheryn fell into the same category. They would make several trips to and from the house, sometimes taking their mug along for the ride. More often than not their mug would end up lonely and growing cold on a counter top. The morning multi-tasker's cup was usually recovered from the microwave mid-day, where after a reheating cycle; it had once again been forgotten.

My favorite coffee personality would have to be the stalker. No Mr. Coffee percolator was safe from the impatience of the java stalker. Fooling himself daily into thinking he could switch his mug for the pot and catch the espresso-like liquid from the unfinished perk process. Gavin at this very moment could be seen pacing in front of the now functioning stove with a mug in one hand and a toddler in the other. He would never venture farther then a few feet from the impossible to interrupt camp style perk pot. It was a humbling experience getting two and a half mugs per fifteen minute effort. Those next two and a half mugs were his!

Where does Georgia fit into the mix? Thankful to be a decaf girl who packed the Folgers singles.

Stories of the previous evening's escapades circu-lated, as we worked to become fully awake. A friend of Phil and Ella's had once again been a party concern.

"Oh Joe," Hontie shook her head. "He's so reliable and good hearted," she said. "He'd do anything for anyone, but he has a major drinking problem. It's just such a shame."

Jade, fresh from her shower, worked a wide tooth comb through her tangles. "Well last night it wasn't a shame; he nearly drowned," Jade said seriously. "He fell right out of the boat."

"There were boats?" I raised my brow at Clare.

"Mmm, and fireworks," Clare said over the rim of her cup.

"Booze, boats, water, explosives… you gotta love that."

Gavin with Davis on his hip carried his blessed mug of java onto the deck. "Joe nearly got himself tied up in the motor climbing back in." He passed Davis to Jade who leaned down and sat him where Bren and Payton were petting Sasha.

Catheryn walked quickly onto the deck. Suddenly she appeared as if on ice, her footing lost as she hit the deadly moss by the door. She caught herself on the arm of Heath's chair and saved half of her coffee and ended in a partial split. "Whew, I almost went down."

Despite the applause from Davis and Payton, Hontie rushed over concerned. "The sun just never hits strong enough on this side of the house to dry up that goop." She helped Catheryn to her feet, "Are you okay?"

"Never better," Catheryn straightened and brushed at her moss green knee cap. "Beautiful."

"Mom wiped out there last year," Clare said.

"Oh, I do that every visit, *deslizarsé*." Mom stood and waved a hand toward Catheryn. "Maybe I won't this year since you did. I'll go make another pot, *hacer grano de café*."

Hope that means coffee. "How is it you maneuver around it daily Hontie, without killing yourself?" I asked.

"Oh Georgia, I am a very talented woman."

"No doubt," I said dryly.

"It really should be power-washed." Clare's eyes were fixed on the slippery patch. *Have to clean!* "Is that something we can rent? A power washer, I mean."

"Clare," Heath's voice vibrated with warning.

"I'm just saying someone could get hurt." She considered a moment, "maybe just a good scrub with bleach and a brush."

"Those power sprayers are great," Catheryn joined in helpfully.

Heath's focus zeroed in on his lovely wife. He pinned her with stern eyes. *Could someone please get Heath some more coffee? This could get ugly.*

"Put a throw rug over it;" I added my two cents.

"It's dangerous." Clare stated again.

"I'm understanding that, Clare." Heath cleared his throat. "Ladies," his mind finally put the issue and words together. "Power washing the deck is one of several things that should have been taken care of." He took a deep breath, "If the bride and groom are not concerned with three foot deep holes dug and left in the yard for the deck expansion project; the fact that seventy-two hours ago there was no working plumbing in the kitchen; an unattached toilet seat in the only bathroom; and no hot water in the home, I seriously doubt they are concerned with a slippery deck. Oh, and let us not forget the gutted kitchen that still may not successfully pull off food prep for tomorrow's affair."

We all stared. When you heard the list, it truly was unbelievable.

"So…" Heath gave Clare a look that had her withering. "Your feedback has been accepted. The deck surface will remain as is." *Subject closed.*

"It was just a thought," Clare sulked.

"Girls," Jade leaned over. "Gavin and I are driving to Syracuse to pick up a few items from Target." Catheryn and Clare perked up. "Toilet seat, shower curtain, I'll add rugs to our list." She gave Clare a wink, then rose and gathered up Davis. "Hey Georgia, you mind if I wash up Payton?"

"Nope."

Mom stepped out of the house, holding a cup of mystery liquid and a curious expression. "What have we caught here?" She said as she walked to Hontie and passed her the glass. Hontie rolled her eyes and mumbled something under her breath. We watched as she stepped to the deck rail and tossed the cups contents over the rail.

"What was it?" Clare inquired.

Her excitement deflated, Mom said, "I thought it was an interesting moth, mariposa nocturna."

Hontie looked at Clare and mouthed 'a mouse'. *Like it was too inconceivable to say out loud.*

"Hmmm," Heath was unfazed. "Depending on the questionable liquid remaining in the bottom of the cup, I'd say he felt no pain."

"Sick," I said.

"What was in that cup?" Brennan asked, while he scratched Sasha's belly.

"Nothing honey, we'd better get ready to go to Bouckville." I clapped my hands quickly, "Time's a' wasting."

Brennan knew he had missed something. He grabbed my hands and I pulled him to his feet. "Yeah," Brennan smiled, "I got big bucks to spend today!"

"You do?" I was surprised. "Five dollars per day is all I'm doing."

"Uncle Heath gave me money for helping yesterday. Your five plus his five…" he grinned. "Aunt Clare gave me three for the barrels, so…"

"He's the thirteen dollar kid!" Heath chuckled.

"I have a cinco dólar bill with your name on it," his grandmom upped the ante.

"Eighteen dollar kid!" Heath enjoyed the moment.

"Awesome!" Brennan rushed inside to find Payton.

"Okay troops," I said to Heath, Catheryn, and Clare, "let's move."

"Good morning, all." Startled, we turned and found three new faces standing beside the deck steps.

"Hey," Hontie hopped up and greeted the newcomers. "Everyone? These are my good friends, Tom, Sueanne and their son, Drew. He's three." The adorable little red-headed boy hung on Sueanne's leg. "They live up the block."

"We know you are heading out, but really we were anxious to meet your family before Saturday." Sueanne said with a genuine smile. Tom stood on the ground yet seemed eye to eye with us. He was six foot plus with wavy black hair. He too met each of us with an easy smile and twinkling eyes.

Sueanne nudged an obviously shy Drew encouraging him to climb the three wooden steps to the deck. She leaned down and her long chestnut hair toppled over her shoulder shielding Drew's face. Tossing her hair to the side in a practical move, the power of Sueanne's face punched out. Her dimples winked and she too had something dancing behind her green eyes. She stayed crouched down beside her son, as the intros were made.

"Sueanne is preparing a brisket for the reception tomorrow," Hontie told us, as she pulled a canvas chair forward and offered it to Sueanne.

"Wow, that's great," Clare said. Sueanne settled into the chair and Drew climbed into her lap. I watched as Catheryn, Clare, Hontie, and Sueanne effortlessly chattered away. Precious Bouckville minutes were ticking away...

TICK, TICK. Having little interest in polite conversation, I went inside to find the boys and gather my flea market stuff.

Tom scaled the steps in two easy strides and accepted the out-stretched hand of Heath. Sensing women talk, Tom and Heath wandered into the kitchen. Tom let out a long low whistle, as he walked to the sink. "You're on the job what, three days?" Tom said to Heath who shrugged a shoulder in answer. "Remarkable what you've been able to do." Tom stopped and noticed the ceiling. "Recessed lighting, plumbing, plaster... man, Heath, what haven't you done?"

"Commit homicide." That earned a rumbling chuckle from Tom. Heath accepted the sincere appreciation and knew at once he had found a kindred soul. "Can't say it was expected or that it's been easy. But at this point I will get this room to a degree of completion that I'm comfortable leaving Hontie with," Heath said.

"Good man."

Chapter 10

Stepping outside of your situation may yield unexpected peace... for the moment.... savor that moment.

Finally we had made it to Bouckville, Day Two. Hooray! Now we needed to find the energy to enjoy it. Heath and Catheryn stumbled on a unique Hoosier cupboard early in the day priced $1800, but valued at $3000 easy. They were building a home in Pennsylvania that would be completed in a few months. They were looking for an old dresser to convert to a bathroom vanity not a fabulous kitchen piece, so they decided to mull it over.

The boys were again on a mission for weapons, so today I was packin' a machine gun styled BB gun and a play pistol. I had found a Fisher Price Teddy Bear pull toy and a few other small items.

"Georgia," Heath called from up ahead.

The boys and I crossed over to him. "What did you find?"

"This dresser. It's great and the price is right on."

I looked at the tag, seventy-five dollars, but I also looked at the piece. Solid wood, no nails, dovetailed corners, pegged drawers. "This dresser is **old** Heath."

"Yeah," he rubbed his weary face, "that's what I thought." He tipped his hat back on his head. "I figured you'd know." The vendor of this booth was probably in his late sixties. He levered himself from his lawn chair and began to slowly work his way toward us. He took his time, sizing us up, figuring what we knew, and most importantly, what we might pay.

Jogging over, Catheryn gushed, "Oh, Heath, that's perfect!"

"Price just went up," Brennan muttered quietly.

Catheryn stood in front of the dresser checking the height with her hips as she gently rubbed the top checking the condition of the wood. "Perfect," she said again.

"Perfect," I said carefully, "but not for what you want it for."

Catheryn looked baffled. "The height is right and we'll cut through the top for the plumbing." The vendor noticeably winced.

I looked to Heath. "I'll pay you seventy-five dollars not to buy it or I'll pay him," I motioned to the vendor, "a hundred and buy it out from under you." Heath just tipped his head and acknowledged me. The unspoken sibling understanding passed between us.

"What?" Catheryn watched us both yet missed the connection.

"We aren't interested," Heath said to the vendor and began to move away.

"What?" Catheryn hurried after him. "Heath it's perfect."

"Mom," Brennan tugged my arm. "What just happened?"

"Simple babe, this dresser is early 1800's," I stroked the top reverently. "You don't buy a beautiful handcrafted piece that's 200 years old and 'whack' the top for plumbing. That's what reproductions are for." I looked again at the unmistakable craftsmanship and sighed, "Hard to pass up at that price, but I have no room anywhere in our house to put it."

"Got it," Brennan answered and we moved down the road. After lunch we traveled to the faraway fields... long walk, little rewards. Heath was understandably tired and C-squared were pressing hard.

"Mommy," Payton asked from his perch. "Is there much more flea market?"

"Yes."

"Awww," he pouted.

"You're doing great, buddy," Uncle Heath patted his head, "and you're almost as big as me!" Payton giggled.

"Georgia, why don't I take him for a little?"

I looked at Heath and his void of energy body. *Yeah I'm going to add forty-five pounds to your back when your feet are barely clearing the ground.*

"I'm going to let him walk up here at this next set," I smiled wearily. "Thanks, though."

"I still need an anniversary gift for Catheryn," Heath lowered his voice. "This year is pottery. I like the bowls with the stripes."

"Yep, there are a lot of pretty ones. Have you been comparing prices?"

"They seem to go sixty and up," he said. "Size, color, and condition I guess."

"Sounds right." We crossed the road and entered the field. "These vendors are usually a little lower priced. Keep your eyes open." Heath lifted Payton out and took on my empty hiker pack. Two tents later, jackpot! A beauty of a bowl and a great deal. After stuffing cash in my hand Heath distracted Catheryn and I made the purchase for him. Well done! I gave Heath a thumbs up and crouched down to stash the bowl inside my tote. Suddenly I found myself tackled. Payton had leapt to my back and knocked me over and left me lying like a turtle on his shell. *Attractive.* I shoved Payton aside and got to my knees. The shocked vendor looked over me helplessly. Thoroughly embarrassed I made my way to my feet. "This is one of those times where I'm glad I don't know anyone," I said to the vendor.

"Gives you a story though," he replied.

"Sure does," we shared a mercy laugh. *Cripes!* I joined the rest of the crew at the end of the tent. "Hate to tell you folks, but we're done for today." Brennan appeared relieved. C-squared decided to press on to the final fields. Heath, having made his bowl purchase, happily joined me and the boys on the trek back to the car.

"Did you enjoy your day?" I asked Heath, as we pulled out of the field.

"Yeah, I wish I had more energy and more time."

"Time and energy are on the short list this trip, huh?"

Heath tilted his head back and closed his eyes. Sleepily replied, "I'm afraid to think of what's left to do."

"Oh... the long list..." I peeked in the back seat and saw the boys were already fast asleep. *Ah yes so many things left to do.*

Chapter 11

Miss Manners suggests: Out of town guests should be made to feel at home. Be sure to arrange transportation, accommodations and dining in advance.

It was mid-afternoon when Heath and I returned to the house. Astounded, we discovered the deck was being power washed! *Progress in our absence!* The stranger who was doing the labor turned out to be none other than the drunken bachelor party guest, Joe. He had spent hours at Hontie's. He had fixed some loose spouting and replaced the deck railing Phil had removed too! *Nifty!* Hontie, Mom, Gavin, and Jade had finished for the day and were getting ready for the rehearsal dinner.

Recharged from his power nap in the Jeep, Heath dove right back into the kitchen venture. I settled the kids with snacks and a movie upstairs, and then tromped through the plagued with disaster laundry room. I decided to focus my energy on rooms that might actually have guests in them tomorrow. I dodged Heath in the kitchen and entered the improved ruins of the dining room.

Half of the room still looked great. The dining room table was clear and even boasted a pottery bowl and a doily. The bathroom door was closed and I could hear the shower running. I shut my eyes for a quick prayer of gratitude. Hot water and a shower curtain and probably even an attached toilet seat.... *Amen.*

I heard a muttering behind me. Mom seated in a rattan armchair by the window was quietly monologuing to herself. She clutched her pocket book in her lap like a ninety-year old granny. "I'm not going." The ticking of clock over her head sounded impossibly loud in the silence that followed. I summoned my energy for the next crisis. Rehearsal dinner. I was actually relieved to not have been invited. It was a ritual, however, that Hontie and Mom couldn't skip.

"Mom of course you're going," I said knowingly entering a minefield. "Hontie needs you with her. You'll have a fabulous dinner in an equally fabulous restaurant." *Of course Uncle Nathan, Hontie's Ex., would be running this particular shindig.*

Mom huffed, "Lottie, fus pasarse sin. I'm not interested in fabulous anything. No festivaldo." She blurted in Spanish. I watched as she dug a tissue from her purse, removed her glasses, and began to buff the lenses.

I took a deep breath and turned my attention back to my current task of condensing clutter outside the bathroom. This was another of my favorite spots in Hontie's home. A windowed out-cove stretched between an under-the-stairs closet and the bathroom door. The barely five by eight foot space held a gorgeous zinc lined dry sink and usually millions of over sized house plants. Today, toiletry bags, suitcases, and shoes cluttered the floor around the dry sink. The doors were the only visual proof that the bulky sink actually existed under the piles of luggage. Wedding attire hung from the multiple plant hangers attached to the large window frame. Beside the bathroom door the microwave stand sat loaded with a mish mash of cooking spices, canned soups and cereals. I opened the double doors of the cabinet under the microwave and found it was blessedly half full. I shoved over the contents and started stacking the other supplies inside.

"All spices, hot cocoa, oatmeal, etc. are going under microwave cart," I announced for all who were within earshot.

Gavin emerged from the shower and snagged a freshly pressed dress shirt from a plant hanger. "Hey Georgia, any chance I can use your car tonight?"

I'm sure glad I drove myself. My extra unnecessary vehicle sure has come in handy.

Jade ran down the stairs. "Is that okay Georgia? You guys are staying here right?" *No invitation was issued.*

"Well, I guess if we need transportation we've got Heath's truck."

"Great," Jade scooped her bath bag. She moved past Gavin, "Davis is upstairs in the crib, honey." The bathroom door closed and the shower turned on again.

I glanced into the dining room at the black and white cabinet clock, 5:15 P.M. "Mom where's Hontie? What time is dinner?" Question ignored, "Mom, you guys really need to get going."

"I'm not sure I'm going anywhere. No vi salir." Her words were clipped with impatience. Mom pursed her lips tightly and resumed the granny position.

Alrighty. The dining room hummed with tension. Time to change topics.

"Do you know if Davis is going, too?"

Just then Clare and Catheryn returned from Bouckville and provided a much needed diversion. Stopping off at the fridge to pull drinks, they skirted Heath, as he worked solo on the ceiling.

"We missed the deal!" Exasperated, Catheryn pulled an oak ladder back chair away from the table and flopped. "Heath and I decided to get the fabulous Hoosier cupboard and of course when I returned to that vendor, it was sold." She popped open a bottle of water and drank deeply.

I raised my hands. "Of course, it should have been purchased right away." Catheryn bobbed her head in agreement. "There's always one treasure missed each year."

"Yep," Catheryn observed Mom's statuesque posture and passed me the 'what's up with that' look. "Isabella, you look nice." Catheryn said cautiously. No response. "What are the plans for the rehearsal?" No response. She looked back at me where I shook my head, subtly signaling for her to leave it alone.

Clare added a lime to a cold Corona, as she entered the Dining Room. She gestured toward the deck. "Who would have guessed High Functioning Joe would be the guy with enough brain cells to realize the deck needed a power wash one day prior to the event."

"Yeah, he arrived several hours ago, removed some loose spouting, repaired some deck banisters, and then broke out the sprayer." I took her beer for a much needed hit.

"Keep it; I'll grab another." Clare headed back through the kitchen ducking under Heath's outstretched arm, as he applied the textured ceiling. Mom, Catheryn, and I sat in comfortable silence until Clare returned and grabbed a seat on a step stool.

The bathroom door opened and Jade emerged. "Clare... hey, I put the dinner things for Davis on a plate in the fridge." Her mid-western unhurried dialect drawled. "He's not fussy but he will need a bath at some point."

I guess that answered my question. Davis would be staying here with us at home improvement central. Payton wandered in from the kitchen. "I'm done with my snack Mommy."

"Okay, do you want to play trucks?" He bounced happily. I picked up the cars and trucks Hontie had out for Davis and set Payton up in the living room behind the pocket doors. Footsteps down the front stair produced Hontie looking comfortable in mother-of-the-groom attire. We each made appropriate comments to bolster her ego prior to a sit down dinner with the Ex.

"You ready Isabella?" Hontie asked. Mom stood making comments under her breath that were best not translated and shuffled toward the door. "Well we're off," Hontie said with a rigid smile. "See you guys... in the morning, I guess." She disappeared with mom muttering on her heels. Gavin and Jade set Davis up with Payton in the living room. They passed through the dining room plucking up my car keys on their way. "See you later."

"And then there were three..." Catheryn said quietly.

"Enjoy the moment," Clare sighed. Catheryn and I echoed her.

We sat motionless for a few minutes. In the background the power sprayer hummed and sounds of Heath applying ceiling coating hypnotically soothed our ears.

Davis and Payton began to fight over the only three matchbox cars in the house. *Moment over.* Clare moved off to deal with them.

I glanced out to the kitchen and noticed Heath still standing in the same spot working out of the same bucket of ceiling putty. Swiping the brush into the bucket then back to the ceiling, swirling... back to the bucket... . repeating... repeating. As I watched, I realized the bucket was in fact empty. Heath seemed to be moving on automatic pilot.

High Functioning Joe entered from the deck. We exchanged casual introductions without getting to our feet. "It's going to need another going over in the morning." Joe said as he moved comfortably to the fridge and grabbed a brew.

"It's just so great you came to do it." Heath dropped his brush into the bucket and caught a tossed bottle of beer.

Joe twisted off the top of his beer as he walked toward Heath. "I'm not having a parade of Californians march through Lottie's home without doing the simple things."

"We appreciate that." Heath said sincerely, as they clinked their bottles together. They tipped their bottles back, virtually drained the contents and then completed their male bonding with resounding belches. *Cripes!* Not wanting to get sidetracked, Heath picked up his brush to work again.

"Heath I think you need to put that bucket down." I broke his rhythm long enough for Catheryn to join him. His hollow expression fixed on me.

"I need to finish the ceiling, Georgia."

"I've been watching you for fifteen minutes; I'm pretty sure that bucket's empty."

"Finish your beer, honey. Just take a minute." Catheryn spoke so quietly it was almost unheard. Gently she placed her hand on the brush and Heath glanced down and took in the very empty bucket.

"Well then we need to go get more." *Clearly he was delirious.*

"There are assorted leftovers," Clare said, "How about we all eat."

We fixed an impromptu meal. Clare, Catheryn, the boys, and I gathered around the oak table and enjoyed turkey sandwiches, wedges of fruit, and cheese. Heath and High Functioning Joe stood in the kitchen with sandwiches in hand and continued to discuss small projects.

"I'd like to finish the ceiling," I heard Heath say to Joe. "Where is the closest hardware store?"

"Home Depot, Syracuse," Joe answered popping the top on a fresh brew.

"Been to that one, nothing closer?"

"Nope."

Watching from the dining room, I was amazed that this conversation was serious. "You really want someone to go get more?"

"I'd appreciate it." Heath pinned me with an expression that could make a stone sweat, then turned his focus back to Joe. "How late do you think they're open?"

"Probably 9:00," Joe tipped back his beer.

Panic mode. "How far is Syracuse?" I asked.

Considering, Joe shrugged, "Oh, I'd say forty-five, fifty minutes."

I glanced outside to the rapidly fading sun. "Its 7:30, so if you seriously want someone to go we need to go now."

Heath held his hands out to either side and gave me a DUH look. Sensing a road trip was in my future, I dropped my eyes to the floor.

Tucked behind the wall out of sight, Clare mimicked the act of drinking and pointed to the kitchen. "Good point," I mouthed to her.

"Joe?" I waited a moment for his dilated pupils to connect with mine. "Can I reasonably find Home Depot, in the dark, the first time out of the shoot, on roads I've never navigated in forty-five minutes?"

"Probably not," he answered honestly. Joe looked at Heath and pointed to his bottle, "another buddy?"

Heath dismissed him with a quick shake of the head. "Georgia," Heath said, as he held tightly to the remaining shreds of his control. "Why don't you put Joe in the Jeep shotgun?"

Hail Mary! I prayed fiercely; "Just remembered something, I don't have a car." *Prayer answered.*

Heath stood statuesque, his gaze fixed. Catheryn removed the empty beer bottle from his hand. "I'll fix you a stiff drink honey," she whispered.

Clare put Davis on the floor to play cars with Payton. "Georgia, I'll clean up dinner; you start baths."

"All right."

The diversion seemed to be enough for Heath's fatigue to sink deeply in and for a small dose of reality to adhere to his brain. Resigned to the fact that a Home Depot run would not occur, he entered the dining room followed by Joe. Heath leaned against the wall, as Catheryn appeared with a much needed JB and Coke. The glass met his lips and he sipped a long, slow soothing half glass. As the alcohol began to settle into his belly, a calm expression crossed his face. He inhaled deeply, exhaled slowly, and drank again. He reached out and handed his empty glass to a wide-eyed wife.

"We've got a good hour and a half of daylight left. We're moving to paint." A distant rumbling of thunder groaned outside. *Perfect. Even the gods were acknowledging our predicament*

"Paint, super." I said. Translation – *Are you out of your mind?* At least I could busy myself with the boy's bath time. I planned to soak them until their toes got pruney.

"Okay," Catheryn hopped to it! "Let me see what kind of paint clothes I can come up with." She ran out of the room and up the stairs.

"Eager, isn't she" I muttered to no one in particular. Brennan, who had been under the table quietly petting the cats, stood up and scared the crap out of me. "Jeez, buddy, give me some warning."

"Mom can I help paint?" He inquired hopefully.

"If only you could, honey, small kitchen, four adults, two little guys. I'll need your help outside the kitchen keeping Payton and Davis occupied until bedtime."

"All right," Brennan scuffed his heel on the floor. "After they're asleep, can I help?"

"Yeah," *and with any luck you'll be asleep by then, too*. I ducked into the bathroom and noticed Jade's run to Target had been successful. We now had a new and attached toilet seat and the duct taped painters plastic had been replaced by a real shower curtain. I pulled the curtain aside to fill the tub only to realize it was a foot too long and three feet off in width. "What the heck?" Closer inspection revealed it was in fact a stall curtain not a tub curtain. "Why wouldn't it be?" I called the little ones and prepared to double soak them and let's be honest, *HIDE*, as long as possible.

Chapter 12

Funny how some projects could show 100% improvement, yet still remain 20% complete. Troops... fall in and sound off!

The soothing water and fresh jammies had done the trick. I passed Davis to Clare and she was settling him in for the night. In the kitchen, Heath pried open the cans of paint Hontie had selected. A barricade was erected to keep small children and large dogs out of the work area. Joe had wisely taken his leave and within thirty minutes Catheryn and I stood like assembled troops in front of Heath awaiting instructions.

I watched as Catheryn folded up the legs of penguin speckled pajama pants. "A little crazy," Catheryn said while flipping and flipping the waist band of the pajama bottoms. She caught my gaze. "Heath's pants," she explained.

"Don't want to sport your own PJ's?"

"I sleep in a tank top." *Enough said.*

"Heath do we know what walls get what color?" I asked doubtfully.

"Yes," color-blind Heath responded, "Red on these two and Banana Cream on these two."

I grabbed a paint tray and roller. I chose yellow and a short wall. My mistakes would be less noticeable and I could fool myself into thinking I was making great progress. Heath, Catheryn, and I dug in working in quiet, quick efficiency.

Brennan's head poked around the corner, "Mom, can I help now?" He sidestepped the barrier gate and carefully crossed the kitchen. Looking around at the small work space with multiple exposed wet surfaces and open cans of paint, I quickly deduced this was not a good idea.

"How about a movie, honey?" Brennan's hopes were yet again, shot down.

He rolled his eyes, "How many times can I watch Pirates of the Caribbean?"

"You're absolutely right." I laid my brush down defeated.

"Bren buddy, do you know how exceptional you are being?" Uncle Heath walked over and gave his shoulder a quick squeeze.

Brennan stared up at him baffled. "Exceptional at what?"

"At tolerating this whole situation, you're a great kid." Bren blinked in the face of praise. Smiling, Heath lightened his tone. "We know you know better but in twenty years when you are preparing to link your life with another, please remember this weekend. If you ever do this," Heath gestured to the room around him, "to your family, I will be first in line to personally beat you senseless." Giggling, Brennan disappeared back upstairs.

"Thanks for that," I said to Heath.

Clare, now also clad in PJ's joined the work force. "Payton is on the mattress playing his Gameboy and watching Scooby-Doo," she said to me.

"At least it's not Pirates of the Caribbean," Heath said with a snort.

"Huh?" Clare looked questioningly at him. "Davis lay right down," she sighed. "He seemed to be exhausted."

"Goes with the territory," Catheryn hummed while rolling a long stripe of red.

Clare grabbed a paint brush and looked to the General of Reconstruction, Heath. "Where do you want me?"

He directed her to trim edging and for the next hour we worked like a seasoned crew, limited talk and much labor. The storm outside seemed to be moving closer as frequent lightning flashes and rumblings of thunder became our new music.

"I think we're in for quite a storm;" Clare looked out the deck doors. The light was fading more rapidly due to the imminent storm. Heath's estimate on working daylight was fairly accurate. It was 8:45 pm and that pre-storm eerie greenish glow that the twilight sky held was encasing the house. A long growl of thunder sounded in the distance. "Hey Georgia, think I should check the kids?"

"We'll hear them if they get upset."

Clare looked at her wet brush and splattered forearms, "true," she agreed, "we'll hear them."

Knuckles rapped on the deck door. Startled, we turned and saw a woman standing like a deer in the headlights on the opposite side of the glass. She was dressed in a knee length flowered dress and sandals. Perched on the top of her head was a red hat with a wide brim and a fabric band that matched the dress. In her hand she held a sheet of paper which at the moment hung loosely at her hip. Her head dipped slightly as she looked over the edge of her glasses. She peered at us much like specimens on a slide. Heath strode to the door and swung it open. "Can I help you?" His gruff voice etched out.

Obviously unsure she glanced at the paper she held, then into the house, and finally back to Heath. "Ah...," she hesitated. "This Ridgeline Road?" Her voice was heavy with a French accent. "Is wedding?"

"Yes," Heath answered cautiously.

C-squared and I edged closer to the door which caused the woman to take a step in retreat. What a picture we must have made. Heath's huge body filled the door frame. He wielded his paint brush like a weapon. The rest of us stood surrounding him in various styles of bedroom attire like some kind of slave painting harem. *For cryin' out loud.* Based mainly on obvious family resemblance, I spoke over Heath's arm. "You must be Ella's family."

"Ella?" puzzled. The women warily glanced around at the deck and kitchen carnage. *Lady... this place looks good.* "Ella? Who is Ella?" She said clearly baffled.

"The bride," was Heath's dry response. Clare, Catheryn, and I shared a helpless look. How could we possibly explain that she was in exactly the right place?

After a moment light dawned, "Ohhhh," the woman said, "Gabrrrrriella," rolling her r's effectively. "I... HawHaw, Gabriella's aunt."

We skipped the 'HawHaw' for a moment and jumped right to 'Gabriella'. Although none of us had ever heard it, we assumed it must be Ella's full name. We accepted with another leap of faith.

Switching the paint brush to his left hand Heath extended a relatively paint free hand. "I'm Heath." Relieved to be making some headway, he said, "We're Phil's cousins."

The handshake was accepted, brave woman. She looked to Heath and cocked her head, "Who... is... Phil?" *Cripes!*

HawHaw, as bewildered as the rest of us, stared helplessly at her paper. A string of French followed. Then remembering herself she said, "Is wedding?" positive that there had been an error.

"Yes," Heath said again and took the paper she offered. The paper showed a map and directions to Hontie's home on Ridgeline Road. On the bottom of the page was clearly written "go to Ridgeline Road home and you will be taken to your accommodations." *You've got to be kidding me.* "Wedding…" Heath said on a whisper of breath. "Here," he paused for translation time. Calmly he raised his eyes to HawHaw's and waited for the facts to sink in. "Wedding, here," he repeated, "tomorrow." Their gazes held.

Her reply was an unmistakable moan. *Yeah, no punch line.* She looked unsure. "Accommodations?" HawHaw asked as she glanced to the street behind her.

Physically pushing Heath aside, Clare joined our French wedding guest on the deck. The sight on the street had Clare pulling up short which was only a problem for fast moving Catheryn who plowed right into her back. C-square forgot all about HawHaw and moved transfixed toward the deck steps. Their jaws dropped.

Clare observed a cluster of chattering French folks at the end of the drive. "Good grief."

I retreated into the kitchen and allowed Heath and C-squared to roll out the welcome wagon.

Thunder rumbled again, closer this time. I dashed upstairs quickly to check on the boys. Clare had made her way to the street where she discovered two full car loads of French speaking Canadians. Pulling out all pleasantries, Clare waded into a complete conversation with a heavy set older gentleman whose eyes were buried in her cleavage. Let's just say Clare wasn't dressed in "greet-the-relatives" PJ's. She struggled to follow his broken English and eventually learned that he was Ella's Uncle Julien. The entourage of French had traveled eight hours from Canada and were looking for the house they were to stay in for the weekend. *Nice, very nice.* Since none of us had answers to any of the issues and we were without a working phone, the decision was made to send them to the local bar.

"You will have food, bathroom, and phone," Heath reassured them still holding a paintbrush.

"Ask the bartender; it's a small town. Maybe they know where you're staying." Catheryn said.

I joined my family on the deck, as eight car doors closed with eight distinctive thunks. Tempers simmering, we waved them off in the direction of the bar.

Disgusted I dropped my waving hand. "Can you #//*-ing believe that?" Big sister Clare's eyes bugged out at the triggering of my emotional Tourette's syndrome. I paced the deck like a caged tiger. "There is disorganization and there is disrespect." I looked to the others for support. "Eight hours in a car and we've got no idea they are even headed this way!" Thunder boomed and big heavy drops of rain began to fall.

"Not to mention we have a minor language barrier," Heath put in.

"We should introduce them to your mother," Catheryn added, as we filed into the house.

Head in her hands, Clare collapsed to the floor. "This is so beyond any scope of reality." As the events of the last fifteen minutes settled, the shift from outrage to hysteria was swift. Clare's body started to tremble. She held up her hand, "do not make me laugh." Her notorious weakened bladder was threatening. Eyes closed Clare took deep Lamaze breaths, as she willed herself to focus. She wrapped her arms around her stomach and after one final cleansing breath she seemed to be back in control. "I'm out there standing on the street making small talk, shaking hands, and being friendly. Meanwhile Uncle Julien is grasping my hand and staring at my boobs!" Abruptly Clare squatted on her heel. "Oh good grief," she gave in fully to her laughter while tears streamed down her cheeks.

"I know. I ran upstairs to check on the kids and caught the conversation from the second floor window. Quite the view you were offering Clare."

"Cut me some slack, Georgia." Clare wiped her cheeks and tugged at the zipper on her sweatshirt. "We are all making do here." She tugged the zipper again and failed to reign in her chest and dropped her hands. "Oh, who am I kidding?"

"Insanity," I said, "layer after layer of insanity."

Heath, his feet planted firmly, stood at the deck doors mesmerized by the storm. "But... .we sent them to the bar." His head hung pathetically.

"Safest place for them," Catheryn walked over and gave his arm a reassuring pat.

"I don't know," I gazed at Heath "I'd have to say you are a bit Braveheart."

"Braveheart?" Heath turned fully into the room. The left side of his face was heavily streaked with yellow paint. He looked like Mel Gibson headed to battle. *Fitting.*

"Oh honey..." Catheryn couldn't help it. Laughter again filled the room and Clare collapsed to the floor repeating her 'focus' mantra.

"Okay everyone let's keep it together." Heath ordered and we returned to the tasks at hand, as if the situation had been resolved.

"Mommy can I help paint now?" Brennan appeared again. *Time to relent.*

"Sure let me clear a spot." After moving the ladder, I handed him a roller. "Did Payton fall asleep?"

"Yep," he answered while concentrating on the roller. "Can we play cards later?"

"You just want to cream me again!" I gave his head a playful rub and glanced out to the growing storm. A jagged bolt scorched the sky followed instantly by a blast of wicked thunder. Brennan stepped to the side and admired his two long red streaks. Pleased with himself he nodded his head, and handed the roller back to me. "Done?"

"yep."

"Great job buddy," Oblivious to the raging storm Brennan grabbed a juice box from the fridge and set out for the second floor. Settling back into the task at hand, darkness had truly found us. I was thankful the little guys were exhausted because the storm was fierce. "This really is a great color."

Heath grunted agreement.

"Do you even know what color it is?" I asked completely colorblind Heath.

He stared vacantly. He'd lost all humor, "I assume it's red 'cause it's darker than the other one."

"Touché."

We resumed our duties, as the storm swallowed us. Clare had begun to mutter to herself. "Come on up to the Bouckville weekend... relax on the deck... bond with family... it's a grand time."

"I've bonded alright... with you three." I said.

"Utterly ridiculous," Heath added.

"At least Hontie will have a wonderful kitchen," Catheryn said, always thinking of the positive.

A quiet giggle had begun to grow in my belly. It turned quickly to an uncontained chuckle. Heath's shoulders quivered in response. Now I knew I had lost my mind. Contagious unexplained laughter amongst siblings was truly classic.

"No Heath," Clare warned. Heath's weary eyes began to crinkle with amusement. Catheryn was the next to fall. "This is *so* not funny," she bent over and held her gut. "Not funny at all..." Clare squatted down to prevent bladder malfunction. "Not funny, not funny, come on guys really... enough... please." She closed her eyes. "F-O-C-U-S," she told herself intently.

"She's going to pee herself Georgia." Disbelieving, Heath shook his head. "Did you see her face? HawHaw was it? What kind of name is HawHaw?" Heath grabbed a ladder to steady himself. "Who's Ella? Who's Phil?" Snort.

"Only the flippin' bride and groom!" Clare wiped her cheek, as the tears fell again.

I walked to the center of the kitchen and raised my paint roller to all corners of the room. "If this is a prank show with a million dollar prize at the end, it's not been worth it."

"But we will take the money," Clare called out. "Oh that's it, I've got to pee!" She dashed to the bathroom.

"For heavens sake Clare," Heath called after her and dismounted the ladder.

"It's a medical condition!" Clare hollered back, punctuated by the slam of the bathroom door.

With our much needed trip to Happy Ville completed, Heath piped up, "Okay ladies," he took a deep breath and mimicked Clare. Eyes closed he exhaled slowly "let's f-o-c-u-s."

Clare returned from the bathroom and maturely stuck out her tongue.

Lightning blazed across the sky followed by an echoing roll of thunder. "Whoa," Catheryn said, "that was close."

"Let's hope we don't lose power," Clare worried.

"Worse things could happen." Something in Catheryn's tone drew our eyes to her. "You're not going to believe this…" Her gaze was filled with utter disbelief. We turned toward the deck doors, as a bolt of lightning streaked through the gloom, illuminating HawHaw.

They're back from the bar.

Heath whipped the door open to offer shelter from the raging storm. We must have been a terrifying sight because HawHaw actually retreated into the wicked weather. "Please," Heath pleaded, "step inside." Catheryn hurriedly pulled back the ladder as Clare scooped up the paint tray by the door.

"No tele-phona," HawHaw said as rain funneled from the brim of her hat. "No accommodation."

"Good grief," Clare muttered in disgust.

I leaned my elbow on the ladder dumbfounded. Julien, the boob man, crossed the deck and joined HawHaw on the threshold of the kitchen.

"Hallo once again." Julien's brow wiggled suggestively, as he eyed Clare's chest.

Julien's gaze snapped up, as Heath stepped into his line of sight. "What to do?" Julien said with a trivial chuckle.

About the phone, lodging, or the ogling of new acquaintance's breasts?

"I am so sorry for your inconvenience." Heath raised his palms with compassion. "So very sorry, you are welcome to wait here."

Julien's brows shot high. He had no trouble with that translation.

Language barrier forgotten, Heath continued, "I assure you that beyond this room I can make you quite comfortable." We, the harem, flanked him nodding our heads in agreement.

HawHaw clutched Julien's arm tightly; alarm apparent on her face. Julien mumbled something to her in French and gave her hand a reassuring squeeze. They turned to Heath as a united unit and Julien said, "We... no... renovate."

"Well then we are back to square one." Heath raked a hand over his weary face.

"How about the pizza shop?" Catheryn whispered to Clare. "They have to have a phone."

"Pizza?" Julien pointed down the road. "We sit pizza shop. No telaphona."

"No phone?" Clare and Catheryn were stunned. Indifferent, I just watched the continuous absurdity from across the room.

"We go," HawHaw tugged on Julien's arm encouraging him to leave.

Heath tossed his hands into the air. "Go where?" Exasperation caused his voice to spike, as the pair of French abandoned the deck.

Catheryn hurried to the laundry room and grabbed a poncho. She squeezed by Heath standing at the door and pulled the plastic over her head.

Heath snared her elbow, "Wait a minute. Where are you going?"

"To find a working phone." She lifted up on her toes and kissed Heath's painted cheek. "Farewell Mel." Catheryn attempted to lighten the mood an instant before she disappeared into the storm with the French.

Clare, Heath, and I stared at the open empty doorway. The rain had scaled down to a steady shower. A groan of thunder resonated in the distance.

"Storm's passing," Clare said.

"Yeah," Heath said dully.

"Your wife just left with strangers," I added absently.

"Yeah."

With my face buried in my hands, I replayed this last chain of events. "This is like some crazy novel or Ben Stiller movie."

"Yeah."

"You know," Clare turned. "Don't we have Hontie's shop key somewhere? Isn't there a phone there?"

"Yeah," Heath said again.

"That's four 'yeahs' in a row Heath; you sound like Rainman and you're starting to freak me out," I said. "Clare should we try to find it? The key I mean." A mild commotion on the deck produced Catheryn, as she ran back into the kitchen.

"Now what?" Clare said.

"I am running to Sal's; that's where the rest of the French are. HawHaw has Ella's cell number and they have to have a working phone."

"Do you want me to come?" Clare asked.

"Nope, I got it under control." She thrust a power to the people fist in the air, "Be back in a flash."

Once again we stared at an empty door. "Vince Vaughn," I said quietly, "or John Cusack."

"Huh?" Clare said.

"I'm casting the movie. Heath could be played by Vince Vaughn or John Cusack."

"Good grief Georgia." A split second later Clare added, "just as long as I'm played by Marisa Tomei."

One mad dash block away Catheryn stood in the rain outside Sal's Pizzeria. Assessing the situation, she observed a table of French Canadians through the window rambling over coffee. A sedan in the lot held an older gentleman in the front seat with the door ajar. Huddled beneath an umbrella, HawHaw and Julien stood by the car. Catheryn gathered her poncho close and went toward them. "HawHaw? Do you have Ella's number?" HawHaw looked questioningly at Catheryn, as she drew a square in the air with her fingers. "The paper?"

"No telaphona," HawHaw wobbled her head.

"Please... paper, yes telaphona, I am certain." Catheryn turned her pleading eyes to Julien, who pried the paper from HawHaw's clutches. Catheryn searched her lacking foreign language vocabulary and said, "Gratsi!" She tucked the paper inside the safety of her plastic poncho and ran inside Sal's. Catheryn slammed through the door and sent the welcome bells into a spectacular clanging spasm. Wide eyed stares from those within, as Catheryn rounded the corner of the ordering counter and approached the employee who was currently on... the **phone.**

"Phone." She demanded and would have appeared threatening if she weighed more than one hundred pounds. Stunned, the man froze and the receiver fell from his ear. Catheryn snagged the phone and slipped it between her shoulder and her ear and heard 'large loaded and a side of onion rings' "Huh?" Catheryn momentarily baffled, "Oh you'll need to call back," she promptly hit disconnect. The employee backed away with his palms in the air. Catheryn laughed at herself. "Sorry, pardona, excuse' moi. What ever language suits you." The room fell silent as she punched in Ella's number. Waiting for the line to connect, she looked up and found all eyes on her. "I'll just be a moment 'kay?" *Psycho.*

Muffled laughter filled her ear as Ella came on the line. "Hello..."

"Ella? It's Catheryn. I've got French Canadians and no housing." Full blown party noise was the response.

"What? Who is this?" Ella laughed at somebody's comment. "What?" Ella said again.

"It's Catheryn... the French have landed. Ring any bells?"

"Oh, take them to Honeysuckle's."

It was Catheryn's turn for a "What?"

"Two doors down from Sal's on the right." Ella said.

Catheryn was speechless. No concern or apologies. Nothing.

"Sal's," Ella continued, "You know where that is?"

"I am standing in Sal's."

"Great! Honeysuckle's house, it's..."

"For heaven sake, Honeysuckle?"

"Right here!" A woman sipping a soda at the counter moved toward Catheryn.

"Honeysuckle?" Catheryn said as the woman approached. "Ella's friend?"

"Yep," she jerked her head over her shoulder. "These my house guests?"

Catheryn stared at yet another bohemian. "You expecting carloads of French Canadians?"

"Sure, Ella said they'd be along at some point." Honeysuckle dug deep into her pant's pocket and produced a cheerful Winnie the Pooh key ring boasting one shiny key. "Here you go. Two doors down on the right," she slapped the key on the counter.

"Order's up Honey," the cashier began to total up her bill.

Realizing she still held the phone, Catheryn shook her head clear. "Ella? Ella?" Of course she had hung up. Miss Honey, food in hand, was preparing to exit. Catheryn quickly grabbed the key and dashed around the counter. "Wait! You need to take these guys with you!" She gestured frantically to the curious French.

"Oh sure... after I deliver this food to my friend and well, I'd like to eat too while it's hot. I can come back. Yeah... I'll be back for them in a little bit."

"You're kidding, right?" Catheryn looked to the French who were watching intently. "They have been driving all day and sitting around for the last hour and a half." Catheryn thrust the key at Honey, "You need to settle them in. Now!"

"Oh really... take the key and walk them down. I'll check in on them later. It's right around the corner." Honey looked at her houseguests, "Make yourselves at home." With a jingle of the bells on the door, she was gone.

Catheryn looked at the key in her hand and grimaced, as the ridiculously jolly Pooh Bear mocked her. "Crap." The ever positive Catheryn faltered for a moment. Across the room the French were gathering their possessions and helping each other with coats. She had no choice but to press on.

The ringing of the bells produced Julien who looked at Catheryn expectantly, "Accommodations?"

She merely held up the key and offered what she hoped was a friendly smile.

A few moments later the French were loaded into their respective vehicles. Slicker clad Catheryn stood before them like an air traffic controller. She waved at them through slapping wiper blades beckoning them to follow her. With fine rain falling, Catheryn held up two fingers, and pointed down the block, then jogged out of the lot ahead of them.

No sidewalks and no street lights proved exciting but hope bloomed when Catheryn saw a lighted front porch boasting gorgeous flower boxes with playful character garden stakes. Piglet, Tigger, and of course Pooh Bear himself offered Catheryn her first genuine sense of relief in hours. The respite was cut short, however, when she glanced over her shoulder to check on the caravan. Removing her eyes from the foot path proved nearly fatal. Her right leg disappeared to the knee in a rain water filled pot hole. "Well shit." Caught in the head lights of the French Catheryn could do nothing but wave them in to their blessed accommodations. She hauled herself from the muddy abyss and jogged the final steps to the front door. Dogging her heels were the hopeful house guests. Catheryn unlocked the door. "Who gets the key?" The herd stampeded past her. "Key... anyone?"

Alone on the porch, poncho dripping, her PJ pants saturated with muck, and Pooh Bear dangling from her finger tips, Catheryn closed her eyes. "Dear God," she prayed, "please let me be at rock bottom."

A blathering of French from the drive had Catheryn dropping devotions. She watched as a couple laden with baggage crossed the dark street. Astonished, Catheryn observed, as they boldly climbed the steps of the unfamiliar home and rapped on the front door. A moment later the front door swung open and Sueanne and Tom appeared on the other side.

"Bon jour, comment cava?" Sueanne rippled out flawless French. "S`il vous plait entr`ee, il pleut." The couple chattered effortlessly with Sueanne, as Tom carried their baggage and the foursome disappeared into the house.

Bewildered but too exhausted to try to figure out how the French knew their accommodations were across the street, Catheryn decided to fold. She looked at the car in the drive where Julien and HawHaw still stood. Since these two seemed to be the ring leaders, Catheryn dismounted the porch and prepared to drop the key and make haste. She navigated the unforgiving mud holes, as she approached the car. The older gentleman was still seated in the front seat. HawHaw's face was riddled with concern; she spoke intently with Julien.

Catheryn cleared her throat. "Excuse me, HawHaw? Sorry, here is the key. Make yourselves comfortable."

Julien's hand clasped the key but he also gripped Catheryn's hand firmly.

"Moment," he said as he listened intently to HawHaw's rant.

Not understanding a word of French didn't mask the desperate worry in her tone. Finally Julien and HawHaw faced Catheryn.

What! What now, Catheryn thought.

"Emergency?" HawHaw said followed by a string of French and rapid gestures to the man in the car.

"Emergency?" Catheryn parroted.

"Yes, yes emergency. Is near?"

"I don't live here!" Beyond frustration she rubbed her temples and gathered herself. "Syracuse?"

"Is near?" Julien inquired.

"About an hour."

"How to travel?"

Catheryn was puzzled, "Car?"

"No… no direction of travel. The north, the south?"

"I do not live here," Catheryn threw up her hands in surrender. "Call 911, that's nationwide, right?" She held Julien's gaze "9-1-1, Emergency."

"Telephona?"

"For the love of all things holy," Catheryn muttered and collapsed against the hood of the car.

* * * *

"Georgia, gimmie a hand with this refrigerator," Heath tugged the stainless steel beast away from the wall.

"What do you want me to do?"

"Catch anything that falls off the top and move those coolers." *Let me grab my other set of arms.* "I want the long wall painted." With one huge pull Heath parked the fridge beside the sink.

"Red?"

"Yeah," Heath unplugged the fridge and removed the outlet cover. "Red."

Clare filled a fresh tray of paint. "Hey Georgia why don't you pack it in, Brennan is waiting for you to play cards." She cut off my protest, "We're down to this wall, and none of the paint is dry enough to apply a second coat. You have held Brennan off long enough. Go."

"But…"

"Really Georgia, go." Heath said, "Two sets of hands on this wall are good."

"What about Catheryn?" I asked.

"She'll turn up." He said undaunted.

Chapter 13

When the world is spinning out of control, grasp a small task and focus on it. Carve out your own private 'happy place'.

The wedding day had finally arrived. The sun peeked through the trees and the birds were singing softly. The sky was an absolute perfect blue with a puff of the occasional white cotton ball cloud. The day could not have been more perfect. Ella looked like an angel and Phil couldn't have been more handsome. The couple stood beneath the canopy draped in fresh wisteria and ferns. The soft dripping sounds of the soothing waterfall tickled your ears, as the stream softly traveled though the valley...

Drip. Drip. Drip. Drip. *Stream? Valley?*

Slowly I awoke. The dripping was not a waterfall but in fact from the garden-hose-on-full-blast rain that was happening outside my bedroom window. *Now that made much more sense.*

It was in fact the day of the blessed union. I glanced around the room from my inflate-a-bed. Hontie was up and gone while all the others in our suite were bone-tired and still sound asleep. I dressed, navigated the chaos of laundry, and stepped into the kitchen. *Delight!* The kitchen was fully painted, except for the trim around the doorways. A small workbench was tucked perfectly into the nook next to the sink. I was amazed. The worker bees had outdone themselves and the impossible had happened. Not complete mind you, but a picture of 'nearly there'. I had thought it was impossible to accomplish in three days.

I opened the refrigerator to dig out some fruit and juice. It took a moment to register that the jug was warm in my hand and the light inside wasn't on. *Not good.* I closed the door and assessed. The microwave clock was on so we had power. Looking up I discovered the problem. The power cord which was unplugged last night for painting lay draped across the top of the massive stainless steel refrigerator. *Oops!* I restored power to our only source of refrigeration and got back to getting breakfast together.

Through the mudroom a hooded figure resembling a north Atlantic sea fisherman complete with yellow slicker to the thigh, peered through the window. I nearly startled out of my sandals. "Hontie! You scared me to death!"

Comfortable in her Gloucesterman attire she stepped inside. Drenched she extended her arms. "My kitchen," she spun around in delight, "is tremendous!"

Vanna White's got nothin' on you.

"I know hard to believe. What time did you guys wrap up with dinner?"

She sighed heavily, "Much later than expected. Your Mom and I got here about two in the morning."

Ouch, I bet Mom was beside herself with joy. I glanced past Hontie to the extremely wet world outside, "What's our rain plan?"

Without any hesitation, Hontie responded, "The rain will stop at noon." *Alrighty…* She continued, "I am on my way to Skinnyatlas to pick up the flowers."

These statements made sense in the deep dark world of crack. Dare I ask? Sure, "How far away is Skinnyapolis and why are we picking up flowers instead of having them delivered?"

Hontie laughed, "Skinny-Atlas. It's only about forty minutes. The florist is not actually a florist but is an acquaintance through a framing client. She and her family own ten acres of land where they grow cutting flowers. Their arrangements are spectacular." Hontie took a breath, "I am going to get the flowers and pick up the corn at the market. I'll be back in about three hours."

"Three... ?" With that... the mother of the groom was gone. Open mouthed I gaped after her. *For cryin' out loud.* I turned and found Clare had descended to the first floor.

"What's the rain plan?" she asked sleepily as she pulled the milk from the fridge.

"Who needs a rain plan when it's going to stop raining at noon?"

"What?"

"Exactly." Clare was too exhausted to decipher my sarcasm. "You might want to re-think the milk, Clare. The fridge was unplugged over night."

"Nice." She returned the milk and opted for water. Slowly she looked around the room. "I guess it is actually pulling together."

I followed her gaze and again took in the amount of work that had been accomplished, "You and Heath did good work. Catheryn make it back okay?"

"Yeah, but not without additional adventure," Clare filled me in on Catheryn's trip to the 'Hundred Acre Woods'. An escapade complete with Pooh Bear and a dying man in need of an ER.

"The movie will need a slew of extras," I said and we shared a mercy laugh.

Clare moved to the deck doors and stared out at the torrential conditions. "I am just so glad I left my kids at home."

"It would have given you an easy exit though." Muffled noises throughout the house signaled that the remaining inhabitants had begun to stir. Clare and I retrieved the toaster from the dining room and set up a mini indoor buffet. Camp coffee puffed out that oh-so-seductive aroma while folks engaged in quiet private talks amidst the ladders and paint cans that cluttered the kitchen floor. Davis and Payton settled in for some cereal in the dining room with Jade.

"Mommy?" Brennan stood by the toaster with a knife and the cream cheese. "Can you help me?"

"You bet." I carefully stepped over Sasha's furry body which was sprawled in front of the refrigerator. The pop of the toaster sounded, "Is it dark enough?" Brennan nodded.

"Georgia," Mom called from the corner of the room. "Would you please drop one in for me? Tostador." She had one leg hitched on the small ladder, as she blew across her coffee.

Heath bumped me not so gently from behind and handed me a bagel he had prepared to toast.

"Sorry, were you waiting?"

"I'll catch the next one." He lumbered away crossing Sasha's massive outstretched body with no stride adjustment.

I sent Bren to join Jade and the little guys around the dining room table and grabbed an apple on my way back to the safety of the far corner of the room. Mom's voice rose above the murmured conversations. "The sap buckets need twine and bows," she began, "and Sueanne will be bringing some mason jars over for the pinwheel favors." The toaster popped and she rose off the ladder to check her bagel. "Most important though," Mom continued, "Ella's mother is coming to assemble the cake, so we need to find her a nice work area."

"How about Cancun?" Heath suggested under his breath, then brutalized his tongue with a scorching slurp of coffee.

Mom pushed the bagel back into the toaster and rolled on. "There are a few things that need to be brought over from Lottie's shop for the reception and just a little more tidying up to do outside."

"Good grief, Mom. Have you looked outside?" Clare mumbled while she poured a cup of camp coffee. A splash of coffee escaped her mug. Clare looked down at the grime caked floor. "Floor needs washed; I will get to that after breakfast."

"Any more coffee in that pot?" Gavin asked Clare quietly.

"Yeah, just one, though. We need to reboot." Gavin and Clare worked to refresh the coffee, while Mom's verbal list of preparation projects continued in a steady flow, much like the rain outside. Perched on the small step ladder, she finally began to wind down. "...so once the tents are up we can work under them until the rain stops." Satisfied with her mental schedule, Mom got up to submerge the same bagel, forgotten during the discussion, back into the toaster to reheat.

I could see the stacks of sap buckets in the mudroom. *Choose a project or be assigned one.* I gathered the buckets and stacked them on the work bench. "Clare, where's the twine and glue gun?"

Hugging her mug, Clare walked over to the work bench. She blew across her coffee to cool it while she eyed me, as I stacked the final two buckets. "Georgia, Hontie explained that project to Catheryn and me yesterday. If you wait a minute, I will help you."

Translation: Youngest sibling couldn't possibly do this without a major screw up. I fixed my smile. "Well I'm ready; you're not. It doesn't really sound that difficult, so I'm going to dig in." *Well said! Good for you! I gave myself a pat on the back.*

Clare took her coffee and slid back to the middle of the room. Heath hovered over the toaster still waiting for his turn.

"I think if we move the small kitchen table to the corner that would be an excellent working spot for Sylvia," Mom spoke cheerfully. "Yes that should do nicely, Amablemente." *The delusions were endless.*

Heath cleared his throat and the room became hushed. "We still have painting and picture hanging to finish. Cake assembly? No." He spoke quietly yet he commanded the complete attention of everyone in the room. Mom watched, as her plans for wedding cake assembly went up in smoke. "Priorities?" Heath gestured in frustration toward the toaster; "You're killing me here." He snarled with an edge that bordered on disrespect. Mom's audible inhale had all eyes centered on her. I ducked under the pressure as the weight of the air in the room tripled. *Awe..Heath's in trouble.* I stepped away from sap bucket central to watch the action first hand.

Mom focused on a far, faraway place. Her face frozen in sheer disgust; her lips pursed rigidly. Everyone in the room held their breath as the tension mounted to an all time high. I shuddered; grateful I wasn't the child in her sights. Heath raised his palms; "Mom..." he spoke more gently this time. "If you want the bagel, please eat it. If not, I am ready for one and this one has been doing the toaster see-saw for the last twenty minutes."

"Good grief, the man just needs some food." Clare released her breath. "The bagel's killing him, not a table for Sylvia's nice working area."

Cripes!

The tension in the room deflated like a balloon and much needed laughter filled the air. The rain continued falling steadily, so everyone settled in to do what needed to be done inside.

Fueled by bagel and feeling overly ambitious, Heath decided to complete the trim painting in the kitchen. C-squared thought helping him was a good 'dry' choice. Mom, however, forged on to outside jobs. Despite the rain she began field preparation. *Insanity.*

"Externo de aventura," Mom said, as she pulled on her rain jacket. "Send Brennan out with me; there are several small projects he can help me with."

Pausing, glue gun mid-stream, I chose my tone carefully, as to not repeat the bagel/table incident. "Mom, Brennan is out of extra clothes. He is wearing the only dry long sleeve shirt he has left. I will send him out when it stops raining."

"Okay, around noon then, mediodía," Mom answered without missing a beat as she disappeared into the monsoon.

Crack, I tell you.

Not much later, paint brush in hand, Clare walked over in a poorly conceived camouflaged effort to look over my bucket progress. I glanced over my shoulder fully expecting a lesson on Twine Wrapping 101. She didn't disappoint. Sucking in a huge breath Clare spewed. "How about I hold the twine while you wrap it tightly applying a droplet of hot glue to the back side of the bucket being sure to stay perfectly parallel with the previous strand." I bared my teeth. "Ooo-kay, I guess I'd just be in the way, you seem to have it under control." Clare adjusted a bucket slightly and walked away to rejoin the trim painting.

Mid-morning

Fans hummed loudly in the kitchen. Heath, Clare and Catheryn worked from small buckets of paint, touching up the woodwork trim throughout the room. The race was on to finish the paint and have it dry before the reception. The wet weather was as much a hurdle as the ticking clock.

Phil bounded up the deck steps and burst into the kitchen. Drenched and dripping, he promptly shook like a dog. "Morning all," he all but sang as rain droplets splattered the freshly painted room. With a muttered oath Clare settled her paint brush on the lip of the open paint can. Ella's brother, Rod, who had followed too closely bumped into Phil and spilled today's morning munchie bag across the floor.

"Good grief," With an irritated sigh Clare crossed the room, damp rag in hand. Phil and Rod remained ignorant as Clare dropped to her knees, gathered up the crumbs, and mopped up the spritz.

Oblivious to the painters-three, not to mention my hot glue gun singed fingers, Phil rubbed his hands together excitedly. "The priority of the morning is music!" He announced grandly. "Any extension cords you are finished using, Heath?" The sound of the spinning fans filled the room as Phil looked expectedly at Heath.

The muscle pulsed along Heath's jaw. *The lyrics of Pink Floyd's 'Comfortably Numb' played in my mind.*

"No? Okay," Phil disappeared into the laundry room in search of extension cords with Rod on his heels. *Good luck with that.*

Finally, the last bucket was dressed with twine! *Small miracles.* I walked through the mudroom to look outside. The soaking rain had shifted to a steady soft shower, but it was only 11:00. Phil and Rod's cord search had taken them to the barn. They disappeared inside as Hontie, her car loaded with exquisite fresh cut bouquets, backed into the drive. Through the rear window I could see the back seat stuffed with fresh corn for the reception.

Hontie got out of the car and pulled her hood over her head. Wellies protecting her feet, she sloshed through the standing water. "From what I can see, the flowers are beautiful, Hontie." I said as I steered across the puddle filled driveway.

While we stood, the rain changed again, slowing to a fine drizzle. Phil joined us with Rod at his side. I watched as Rod slowly worked at winding up a thirty foot bright orange extension cord. Slung over his shoulder, the cord trailed through the muck during the walk from the barn and had wound itself around the lower half of his body. *Hmm... rain... electricity... Might be fun to watch.*

"Awesome Mom," Phil beamed at Hontie. He tossed his head toward Rod, "We're working on music."

Hontie lifted the hatch of the Subaru and the full beauty of the flowers struck me. "Wow!" I took in the riot of color and flawless blooms and each bouquet bundled in its very own purple plastic water bucket.

"Great aren't they?" Hontie touched a burgundy sunflower's friendly face. "Worth the trip," a smile tickled her lips.

More worth the cost of delivery. "They are striking, Hontie. What's the plan?"

"Phil lift that corn out," Hontie ordered startling the music minded. "Somewhere there are two galvanized tubs to put it in to soak;" she was speaking in the direction of Rod, but his extension cord project was requiring his full concentration.

"Rod?" Hontie said and then shrugged at his non-response. I, on the other hand, continued watching his bumbled attempts to wind the cord. *Rocket science.* Come to think of it I was fairly certain he's a mute. All I'd witnessed him doing since I'd arrived was eat, drink, smoke, and shadow Phil like a conjoined twin. "Georgia, where's your Mom?"

"She's working in the field."

"Good, the flowers will need to be transferred to the sap buckets but let's wait until noon... that's when the rain will stop." Hontie walked toward the field to check in with Mom.

"Mmmm," I accepted the madness and found myself nodding at her retreating back. Rod and Phil disappeared around the back of the house in search of the galvanized tubs.

Another car arrived with Ella and her sister, Anya. Ella had her sweatshirt pulled tightly up over her head and face in an effort to not be seen by the groom. *Traditions? Are you flippin' kidding me?*

"I just need to get the cocktail glasses and hors d'oeuvres tumblers out of the laundry room." Ella whispered to me as she passed by.

The sisters ducked into the mudroom just as Phil reappeared from the back of the house. *Without corn soaking tubs.* He had his hat pulled down to the bridge of his nose and looked like a celebrity avoiding the paparazzi. "Mom, I'm going to get some ice for the beer." *Now there's a priority.*

"No Phil, you need to be here," Hontie insisted.

"But it will only take a minute."

"No Phil," she repeated with an uncharacteristic-like edge. Hontie paused and took a cleansing breath. "I need you to go to the shop and bring some things here, and then I need you to get the tents up and arrange the field for the reception. Also, decide who is picking up the grill." Hontie's foot was finally down. "Send someone else for the ice." *Halleluiah!*

"Tents?" Phil looked baffled.

"Yeah, tents," Hontie continued. "We've got the one Isabella brought from home set up by the deck. Carry it to the field and get the rest put up wherever you feel is best." Hontie strolled confidently into the house.

"Tents, huh?" Phil muttered under his breath. He scratched his head and looked at Rod the mute. "Hmmm, tents."

Dare I ask? "Phil?" I asked slowly. "There are tents, right?"

"Well Georgia," he adjusted his hat and rammed his hands deep into his pockets. *"Here's the thing..."* he paused assuming that sounded like a reasonable beginning to a solid explanation. "The two tents I asked to borrow from the mother of a childhood friend are at her house." He sighed, "and she's on vacation."

Warning sirens rebounded inside my skull. *Okay, vacation, no biggie.* "So... .the tents?"

"Yeah," his answer just hovered, like a big ol' hot air balloon.

Next question... .*I knew better.* "Tables? Chairs?"

"Yeah," Phil recovered quickly. "I can have as many tables and chairs as I need from the Historical Society in Colinotia. I just need to pick them up Friday by 3:00." He smiled proudly, clearly pleased with himself.

*Do I have the strength to tell him it is 11:00 in the morning on **Saturday**?* Why bother. Dropping my head, I probed my throbbing temples certain my devil horns were protruding. Nope, just the beginning of what promised to be a perfectly vicious headache.

I watched in horror as Phil and Rod his man-shadow wandered off toward the tableless, chairless, and potentially tentless reception field. Hontie re-emerged from the mudroom holding a string of dragon fly garden lights. My face must have been a give away to my building inner hurricane. "Smile, Georgia!" Her ever jovial voice called out. "Look at these cheerful twinkle lights I found for the courtyard."

Even the unique and admittedly cute lights left me unmoved. My first genuine non-sugar-coated reaction since I arrived leapt from my mouth. "I am struggling to find a single reason to smile. Sincerely struggling."

Hontie stared at me blindly. She only fumbled for a second and then regained her composure. "Georgia how

153

about you cut some fresh flowers for the milk carrier and the porcelain pitcher for inside the house? The cutting shears and the gathering basket are inside the door." She motioned over her shoulder to the house. "I am going to work at hanging my lights by the moon garden."

Finally, a life preserver, flower cutting. That I could do. I went inside to grab the shears and set out to lose myself in this job. *A solo mission that would provide me with the much needed buffer between my living nightmare, and my insane blood relatives.* Lost in my thoughts I trudged into the house and bumped solidly into hooded Ella.

"Oops, sorry Georgia, is Phil this way?" Ella whispered, as though we were sharing some sort of conspiracy.

Unable to join her in the charade I gave a snort of impatience. "Couldn't tell you."

"Oh! Oh!" Ella backed up quickly and tugged her sweatshirt completely over her face. Impressively, Ella hurdled Clare who was scrubbing the floor and ran to the laundry room. I glanced over my shoulder and sure enough, Celebrity Phil was headed our way.

"I am entering the house," Phil shouted dramatically, **"and I am heading for the laundry room."**

"Oh! Oh!" Ella squealed from the laundry room. Phil chuckled to himself and swiftly spun into the dining room.

Idiots. I watched with no joy as Phil and Ella's theatrics hit new heights. "Enough you two!" *Cripes.* "You love her; she loves you. The wedding is in four hours. **Hours!** Say hello, good morning, and move on with the day." They were both clueless, as to how *not* cute the act was to the current work force. Ella spared no one a second glance. She held a crate of glassware in front of her face and strode though the kitchen. Anya met her at the mudroom and the sisters departed to prepare for the wedding. Safe passage granted, Phil and Rod wandered to the deck. Their conversation shifted from music to beer... then back to music. A white work van with its diesel engine rumbling pulled alongside Heath's trash laden metal trailer.

The window lowered and High Functioning Joe leaned out. "Phil buddy," he shouted. Phil passed on a few last bits of advice to Rod and gave him an encouraging thump on the back. Joe hollered again, "Let's motor dude." Phil dashed off the deck and climbed aboard. The engine roared into reverse and the pair set out to who knows where.

Rod stood like a sad puppy watching his master leave him alone. He wandered to the deck steps and then backed off unsure. Bewildered, Rod turned and looked into the kitchen for guidance. Heath and Catheryn were busy painting while Clare viciously scoured the floor. Everyone was busy... except me. *Move!* Desperate for flower harvest therapy, I hurried to the laundry room for a basket and cutting shears. I came back into the kitchen and glanced at the deck. Rod had left the deck to brave the task Phil had left him with, alone.

Hontie set up a ladder on the concrete slab beside the barn. Draped across the picnic table were her twinkle lights waiting to be hung. I started toward her and faltered at the sight of Rod's girlfriend, Somi. *The woman must own stock in Clorox.* Her hands were fisted on hips; her lips peeled back in a snarl. The recipient of Somi's wrath was the love of her life Rod. He toed the mud in the driveway with his boot while she continued to rant about setting up the music, so they could leave to pick up the beer. Rod stared expressionless. The long extension cord was threaded over his shoulder and a bag of corn chips in his hands. "If the music is going to be over there," Somi pointed boldly to the open field, "then your power cord obviously will need to be, over there." Rod's head jiggled like a bobble-head on a dirt road. He shifted toward the field and then he paused to shove a handful of snack into his mouth.

"Rod?" Hontie called from the top of a ladder. "I am ready for that extension cord."

When Rod turned to obey Hontie's request, Somi slapped a hand on his chest, merely held up a finger, and he froze like a well trained schnauzer. Tiptoeing over the wet driveway in her white Burberry rain boots, Somi reached Hontie's ladder. "The cord he is holding is for the music." Her words spat like venom. "It is not for your Christmas lights by a barn where no one will even be."

Hontie just smiled, "I thought this would be a quiet spot for those who want to sit and chat after the sun goes down."

With a huge eye roll Somi said flippantly, "The party... is over there. Got it?" Somi glared at Hontie out of the top of her eye sockets. "Rod?" She pivoted on her heel and snapped her fingers, "With me." The mute lap dog eyed Hontie for a millisecond then a small almost wicked smile twisted his face. Snickering, Rod trotted off behind the Canine Queen.

Unfazed Hontie climbed down the teetering ladder and ducked in the barn. A moment later she emerged with a long extension cord and she continued to power her twinkle lights.

I crossed the driveway to the garden, my sanctuary, and got lost among the sun flowers, bee balm, and globe thistle. The therapeutic snip, snip, snip filled my mind. Minutes later, my basket held a bounty of gorgeous colorful blooms.

Chapter 14

**"I can see clearly now the rain has gone...
I can see all obstacles in my way."
I wish I were blind.**

NOON, as promised, the sky faucet turned off. Not exactly sunny and the ground had definitely become soup. Inside the house, thanks to Clare, the floor sparkled. She had organized all areas viewable from the kitchen and decided that a partition curtain would be needed to conceal the remaining construction mess in and around the laundry area. *Brilliant.*

Catheryn was on deck washing out paintbrushes when the sound of female voices had her looking across the lawn. Somi and another woman Catheryn recognized as Honeysuckle from the previous night were carrying two dinner platters each and appeared to be on a fast track for the deck. Somi, the colorless, had ditched her rain attire for yet another solid white ensemble. White mini skirt, white sheer blouse layered over a white camisole, and one and a half inch wedge heeled white leather sandals. The duo marched up the steps, wordlessly passed Catheryn and headed for the kitchen. "That kitchen is not ready for food quite yet." Catheryn called after them.

Somi flipped her jet black hair over her shoulder and pinned Catheryn with her demon eyes. "We are putting them in the refrigerator." Miss Honey watched the exchange between Somi and Catheryn with wide eyes and then followed the staccato clipping of Somi's heels into the kitchen.

"Good luck with that," Catheryn huffed.

Fifteen seconds passed and the women were back on the deck. Somi and Honey's eyes were filled with alarm; their noses were inches from a wet red paint brush wielded by Heath.

"No refrigeration!" Heath gestured with his red paintbrush. Each flick caused paint to spritz near the Abominable Snow Bitch's shoes. "I don't know what to tell you." Heath bared enough teeth to be threatening. The women appeared like a Cirque du Soleil act; platters teetered in hand as they dodged erratic splatters of red paint as Heath waved his brush. "Find a cooler. Take it back to wherever you came from. We can't help you here." His voice rose with each sentence. "There have been no arrangements made for food."

Not that there have been many preparations for much else, mind you.

Catheryn barely contained a smile as Heath, not so gently shut the screen door in their faces. The subject was closed.

Smoke poured from Somi's ears. She strutted across the deck in her *Blanc* mini skirt and plunked the platters filled with hors d'oeuvres on the deck benches. With a flick of her head her partner in delivery, Miss Honey, to follow suit. She whirled around and again pinned Catheryn with her glare. Catheryn looked at the hors d'oeuvres. Plum tomatoes sliced with a sliver of mozzarella and a basil sprig, wedges of brie and clusters grapes, all artfully arranged. The uncovered platters sat on the only deck bench that the sun shine had successfully reached.

Somi threw back her shoulders, adjusted her hemline, and tossed her hair *again*. "Honey, lets bolt." She addressed her counterpart. "They will only sit out for an hour or so." Miss Honey nodded in agreement.

Somi and Honey dismounted the deck and trekked through the grass without the slightest pause. Catheryn's fog filled brain took a moment too long to process that they were seriously leaving.

Catheryn twisted around and rubbed her eyes as if to assure herself this was not an illusion. Nope. The bench, full of colorful appealing hors d' oeuvres, sat proudly in the sunshine. Whipping back around, Catheryn saw Somi pass the trailer full of trash and step onto the side walk. Only then did she realize the platters were staying exactly where they were. Horrified, Catheryn yelled, "Hey! You can't leave these here! It will be more like six hours until the reception." Honey and Somi didn't break stride. "**SIX!**" Catheryn helplessly shouted again.

Pivoting on her heel Somi, Queen of the Canine, leveled her gaze to Catheryn. "Deal with it." With a final whiplash hair toss, she and Honey were gone.

Exasperated and on the verge of tears, Catheryn rushed inside. She bumped into Gavin then handed the paint brushes to Clare. "Nice job, Heath," Catheryn said softly as she bristled back out the side door and jogged down the deck steps.

Heath shared a concerned look with his big sis then raised his shoulders. "I thought I handled it okay." Clare shrugged and continued working. Concerned, Heath took a moment to step outside to look for Catheryn. She was nowhere to be found. Resigned to whatever spousal repercussion would come, he returned inside and moved to the next task. Heath stepped into the dining room to retrieve eight brown paper wrapped pieces of custom framed artwork. Gently he sat them on the table where Jade and Davis were finishing lunch.

Gavin walked in behind Heath. "You find Catheryn?" He handed a wet cloth to Jade to wipe off Davis's messy fingers.

"Nope." Heath's single word spoke volumes. Frustration, exhaustion, and acquiescence.

"It is what it is," Gavin exhaled noisily.

"And what it is... ain't good," Jade replied.

Heath carried the art to the kitchen table and gently blew the drywall dust from the wrapping. "Within the hour we'll be ready to hang artwork," he said to no one in particular, as he loosened the masking taped edges.

A loud clank of metal sounded from the driveway outside the mudroom. "Phil?" Hontie's weary voice called. "This corn needs to be soaked... today." She moved through the mudroom, "Has any one seen Phil?"

Gavin walked to the sink, "We've stopped looking for Phil," he muttered dryly and winked at Clare.

Hontie grabbed a bottle of water from the fridge. "The corn was supposed to be soaking an hour ago. I dragged the tubs over and they are sitting in the driveway."

Gavin turned on the faucet to wash his hands. "Jade's giving Davis a bath and hopefully a nap before we have to leave for the wedding. I'll handle the corn, Mom. Is the hose still hooked up in the laundry room?"

"Yep, run it out the window, the tubs are right there."

"Got it," Gavin moved across the room and the disaster laundry room swallowed him.

"Thanks Gavin," Hontie sighed and turned slowly absorbing the ever changing kitchen. "It just keeps getting better and better."

"Or worse depending on your vantage point," Clare whispered under radar.

* * * *

A block and a half away and out of breath, Catheryn climbed the steps and knocked on the front door of Tom and Sueanne's home. The door opened and ever friendly Sueanne

160

looked at Catheryn and was immediately concerned. "What's wrong, Catheryn?"

Running on less than empty Catheryn promptly burst into tears. Caught by surprise Sueanne quickly wrapped her in the comfort of a warm hug. "Do you have any coolers?" Catheryn's voice was muffled into Sueanne's shoulder.

Tom appeared from the other room. "Like for drinks? Ice chests?"

"Yes," Catheryn stepped back and regained her composure. She inhaled deeply, counted to three... and released. "The wicked witch, Somi and associate just deposited appetizers on the deck. Food, uncovered, unrefrigerated, and told me to deal with it! As if I haven't been 'dealing with it' for the last three days."

Sueanne reached out and offered Catheryn a freshly squeezed glass of lemonade. "Here, sweetie, drink this."

Confused, Catheryn accepted the glass, not quite sure where it had materialized from, and savored a long drink. "Tom honey, please grab the ice chests and deliver them to Lottie's." Sueanne smiled at Catheryn, "On the deck?" Catheryn could simply nod. "To the deck please, Tom." She patted Catheryn's arm, "See? All better now."

"Thanks." Catheryn, overwhelmed by the normalcy, indulged in a few more tears.

* * * *

Back at chaos central, Gavin and Brennen worked tag team to haul the forgotten, not yet soaking corn from the end of the driveway, to the tubs. Brennen laughed at something Gavin said and the pair disappeared into the mudroom. I stood amongst the towering sunflowers and looked down at my overflowing basket of blooms. Unfortunately for me, my flower harvesting was complete. I couldn't hide in the garden much longer. *Damn it.*

I exited my short lived haven just in time to watch a garden hose be shoved out of the laundry room window at the rear of the house. Below the window sat two galvanized wash tubs next to the two bushels of corn. Brennan dashed out of the mudroom and put the end of the hose into one of the empty tubs. Gavin leaned out the opened window directing Brennan. I watched Brennan give Gavin a quick thumbs up and started to toss ears of corn into the tubs. Thrilled with the current project, Brennen turned toward me. His face illuminated with childhood joy, as he brushed his filthy hands on his pants. *Oh my, the simple things.*

"Bren, when you are finished helping Gavin with the corn, Grandmom has some projects for you. Please do your best to stay as mud-free and dry as possible."

Yeah, right.

"Sure, Mommy," he pitched in the final ears of corn and then bounded off to the big field to find his Grandmom. As he raced by me I noticed odd smears across the legs and rear of his black sweats. Paint... wet, not drying due to the humidity, woodwork kitchen paint. *Why not?*

I shook my head and sighed as my attention was drawn to the road. A fully assembled tent was traveling approximately 30 mph courtesy of High Functioning Joe's work van. With Phil seated shotgun, Joe drove right into the neighbor's yard through the lawn around the back of Hontie's barn and pulled into the field. Joe and Phil hopped out of the van leaving the doors ajar and motor running. Together they grabbed the aluminum tent legs and slid the tent off the van's roof, walked a few feet and plunked the tent onto the grassy field. Seconds later the pair hopped back into the van and drove off again. *Well, it is a tent.*

Time to arrange my fresh flowers. I stopped on the mudroom step. From this vantage I was able to observe all of the other reception preparations. Brennan was gathering rocks and tossing them into old fence post holes, along the border of Hontie's property and the field. Since this would be the major walkway for the evening and at some point the sun would set, it would be nice if guests wouldn't risk breaking their legs. Mom had retrieved the old quilts which were to be nailed to the barn in lieu of a door. Crouched beside the barn she was currently sifting through the pile of tools in search of a hammer. The barn served as storage for Hontie. Her kayak hung across old hay ladders and her other large item adventure gear, snow shoes, skis, were stowed with the utmost of care. When I had arrived Wednesday, the barn's interior still held some sense of order. After three days of urgent clean up, it had become a 'catch everything'. The closer we were getting to the wedding, the more the deposits into the barn had become careless tosses into the void.

In the courtyard next to the barn, a picnic table had been carried and placed under Hontie's cheerful twinkle lights. At dusk with the white flower filled moon garden, it would, as Hontie envisioned, be a lovely spot to enjoy the evening. Piled on top of the picnic table were a whopping six card tables, one craft table and leaning against the barn were eight metal folding chairs.

"Georgia," Mom caught me standing still and appearing unproductive. "When you're finished with the flowers, why don't you and Brennan set up the tables and chairs I brought from home in the field?" I watched as she stretched a beautiful quilt to the top of a ragged plank of barn siding. With a hammer pinched between her knees and a nail tightly in her lip. *Impressive.*

"Alright, Mom." I had stretched the flower harvesting task to the maximum. "I just need to arrange the flowers, and then we'll be over." She nodded and then whacked away at a nail in the corner of the quilt.

"Coming through!" Gavin whizzed by me nearly knocking me from the step and spilling my basket of blooms. He grabbed the hose which was spurting water to switch it to the other tub and dropped it just as quickly. "OUCH!" He

163

danced around the hose as it weaved like a serpent, "Damn it... . OUCH!"

I looked closer and could see steam rising into the air from scalding hot water puddles in the drive. Hot water? *Nothing at this point would surprise me.* I left Gavin to fend for himself and walked into the kitchen. At the sink Clare dumped filthy water from her scrub bucket and the floor shined like a show room. I took an extra moment to wipe my muddy shoes.

"Flowers are pretty," she commented.

"Floor is just as pretty." Gavin's curses exploded from behind me.

"What's up outside?" Clare asked.

"You really want to know?"

"No."

Gavin flew past us and disappeared into the laundry room leaving a ripple of colorful language in his wake. With a raised brow Clare gave me a questioning look. *Of course she wants to know.*

"Hot, very hot, only hot, water to soak the corn."

"And why wouldn't it be." Clare's eyes dropped to the floor. A look of sheer frustration transformed her face as she took in the perfect trail of mud caked foot prints left by Gavin. I turned to console her and found she had already begun to refill the bucket with new soapy water.

With a huff Gavin drifted back into the kitchen and went to the fridge to pull a beer. "The hose is hooked to the hot water valve. Since there hasn't been hot water in the house for several weeks, I can understand the oversight." The beer hissed as he removed the top and guzzled heartily. "God Almighty himself could not fix this disaster. "

"On the contrary," Heath responded as he examined a gorgeous framed watercolor. "I'm counting heavily on the Almighty to pull us through."

"What is that?" Gavin eyed the artwork, "Vegetables?"

"Artichoke," Heath tossed a half hearted shoulder shrug, "and some fruit."

"Hmm..." Gavin said.

On her knees again, Clare scrubbed at Gavin's trail of muddy foot prints. I tiptoed around her and went to find the milk bottle carrier to finish my flower arrangements. In a blur of motion Catheryn jogged up the deck steps and ran straight into the kitchen. She went directly to Heath and wrapped her arms around him and sank in. Heath looked to heaven. He tipped his head at Gavin. One disaster at a time, he thought, one disaster at a time.

"Well, the hot water..." Gavin drank deeply as he measured this latest obstacle. "The tools on the deck have vanished so I can't switch the hose to cold. There is one scalding bucket of water soaking the corn in the drive." Dumbfounded Gavin raised his hands in submission. "I'm running to Mom's shop for the stuff she wants." He tossed his empty bottle into the trash and noticed Clare, on her knees, yet again, scrubbing the floor. Gavin lifted his foot and discovered his mud crusted shoes. "Well shit Clare, I'm sorry."

She waved him off. "Just go out that way please." Gavin followed the tracks she had yet to clean and departed for Hontie's shop.

Mom came into the kitchen. Thankfully she noticed Clare in scrub mode and stopped at the threshold in her muddy sneakers. "Where has Gavin gone?"

"He's fetching the needed antiques from the shop," Catheryn said.

"He only filled one cubeta with agua. Solamente uno and the water is HOT!"

"Yep," Heath responded while holding up another framed vegetable.

"Is he going to fix it?"

"No," Clare said as she dumped the bucket of dirty water into the sink.

Mom's head ping-ponged following the comments. Clearly displeased at the lack of concern from her offspring, she huffed impressively. She unearthed a blanket from the mudroom and tossed it on the floor by the sink. Next she grabbed two scrub buckets, stepped carefully on the blanket, and took command of the sink. "Hervir agua," she muttered as she twisted the cold faucet on. "Not mucho calor agua. Hervir!" She placed another bucket under the faucet while she dumped the other into the tubs of corn. "Demencia. Idiota," she muttered. The cold water bucket relay took twenty minutes of her life. *Minutes she would never get back.*

My flower arrangements were complete and I moved on to field prep. I tracked Mom down by the barn contemplating a barn mosaic. "What's the field plan?"

Mom tossed the pottery pieces back on the pile. "Good Georgia, alright, the tablecloths are still in the car in case it showers again." She moved to the minute pile of tables and chairs. "We need areas for cake, bar, music and dancing, and also a place for the head table and guest seating."

I tallied the tables on top of the picnic table, six. Seven if you counted the craft table. *Well, that's one table for each area. Be done in a jiffy!* "Mom, you are aware that there are no more tables and chairs coming."

"None?" she appeared baffled.

"No tables, no chairs."

The emotions that swam across her face were price-less. Shocked, disoriented, confused, irritated... at a complete loss she said, "Well, I have all the tablecloths in the back seat of my car when they do." I watched as she bustled off.

Where's the crack house? Will somebody please take me to the crack house? Resigned to my task of creating a reception area out of nothing, I looked for my helper. "Bren," I shouted.

He raced over, "Yep, right here Mom."

"You're with me and we need to work some magic."

"Cool!"

We made our way to the field to make some deci-sions. The full acre grass field was nestled behind Hontie's barn and was bordered by two of her neighbor's properties. There were no fences to mark actual property lines and it seemed that everyone just mowed what they felt was necessary and let the rest grow wild. Back home the start of one lawn mower would trigger a chain reaction and cause every home owner down the street to hop on his John Deere and ride his property line in an effort maintain an even grass height. *Crazy... but true.*

Brennan and I observed the lone tent that had been deposited in the middle of the field. One tent, seven tables, eight chairs... one hundred guests. *Madness.* Where should we even start? I was sure I looked as lost as I felt when I spotted Sueanne and Tom. Hand in hand they crossed the field with Drew skipping happily behind them. "Bren, I am feeling better already."

"Huh?" He looked up at me.

"Hi, Georgia, hey, Brennan," Sueanne's eyes swept the area. "Where's Payton?"

"He's inside playing with Davis," Brennan answered and knelt down to Drew. "Wanna go inside?" Drew looked to Sueanne and waited for the go ahead nod. Giggling the two boys raced from the field to the house.

"To have their energy," Tom said with a smile.

I moaned in agreement, and then gestured to the field and started to tell Sueanne and Tom the plight we're faced with today. "I'm trying to choose the best cake, food, dancing, and guest areas."

"Can we help?" Tom asked.

"Sure, but really, *decide* is all we need to do as you can see we have a tent… **one,** and there are only a handful of card tables and folding chairs at our disposal."

"Ahhh," Sueanne dipped her head compassionately. "We've known Phil and Ella long enough to not be surprised by that."

"Yeah well we live far enough away to be staggered by it." Sueanne draped her arm over my shoulder, and we both sighed deeply.

* * * *

Gavin returned from Hontie's shop. Leaning casually on the hood, he scanned the property. "Mom," he called when he spotted Hontie, "where am I going with this stuff?" He pointed to the car loaded with the various pieces she had requested. Hontie waved him to the field. Gavin slid back behind the wheel and drove through the neighbor's yard and into the field to unload.

Slowly the field was accented with vintage wares. A custom crafted room divider was to provide a unique back drop for the cake. It was made from twelve architectural harvested tin ceiling tiles. A carpenter friend of Hontie's had encased the tiles in cherry wood creating a double sided room divider measuring six by nine feet. It was a remarkable piece of craftsmanship which carried with it a price tag of $800.00. Beside the barn the unsightly port-o-potty was now shielded for privacy. An aluminum framers display draped with vintage linens was placed and together with an enamel table, fresh flower filled antique pitcher and bowl, scented hand sanitizer, and towelettes the port-o-potty suite was complete. *Lovely. People might not be able to find it, but lovely.*

Chapter 15

Countdowns are exciting and expected at New Years, twenty-first birthdays, or championship football games, but for weddings?

SATURDAY, 1:00 PM

I found myself back at sap bucket central wielding the hot glue gun yet again. A good friend of Hontie's had crafted bows for each bucket. Yes, they just arrived, but hey, yesterday the buckets weren't painted. So bows two hours before the music starts? *Why not.*

"Brennan buddy?"

"Yeah, Mommy."

"Could you please carry these finished buckets to the driveway."

"Sure thing," he grabbed two and headed outside. As I glanced around the fully painted, though not quite dry kitchen, it glimmered with hope. The inspiration for Hontie's kitchen, the antique grocery store sign, "Bananas for Sale" leaned against the sink. Heath and Hontie were by the table determining the placement of the vintage sign and framed art work for the final touches.

With the final bow in place, I followed Brennan outside. The sun was working hard to dry up the puddles the saturated ground couldn't absorb. I passed by the beautifully accented port-a-potty and joined Brennan at the edge of the field. Together we transferred the flowers from the water buckets. The dazzling bundles of blooms transformed the painted sap buckets in front of our eyes. Each one now brimmed over with outrageously beautiful fresh-cut flowers. Indeed an incredible touch. Well done, Hontie!

The fully assembled tent retrieval project had yielded three tents which bordered the field. Phil, Rod, and High Functioning Joe stood by the barn admiring their handiwork. Phil called to me, "Isn't it beautiful Georgia!" His voice resonated with sheer joy.

"It sure is." I joined them and Phil slung his arm companionably around my shoulder.

"It is just how I pictured it in my head," he said dreamily.

Don't comment. "Phil before you go pick up the grill, would you carry the other tent around from the side yard?"

"What tent?" He looked at Rod, "you see a tent?" Rod replied by shoving a handful of peanuts in his mouth.

"The tent Mom brought from home." Phil appeared confused. "You know, the tent that has been set up in the side yard since Monday."

Light dawned, "Oh, yeah right, the white one." Phil grinned at High Functioning Joe. "Get the van Bud; we got another transport."

"Actually Phil," Joe said, "I am going to hook up that trailer and haul all that trash out of here." *First the power washer and now this?* Once again the last person you'd expect to be on top of things. *Maybe I should have a beer for clarity.*

Phil turned to Rod and dug a handful of peanuts from the bag he held. "Let the trash go," he waved at Joe. "Seriously man, we'll handle the trash later."

Panic crept up my back. ***Intervention!*** I fervently sprang into action while the munching twosome was peanut distracted. I took Joe by the elbow and ushered him toward his van at the end of the drive. "You can handle the trailer Joe? Great, super, huge help!" I opened his van door and encouraged him to climb aboard. I will help Phil carry the tent to the field." The diesel engine roared to life and the beep, beep, beep, reverse safety alarm sounded in the air. Relieved I walked back to the peanut pair who in two minutes time had littered the area where they stood with discarded shells. *Cripes.* "Hey, Phil?"

"Huh?"

"The tent is in the side yard." I beckoned him to follow me. "Bren!" I shouted across the field careful not to allow time for distraction. "We need your help." Brennan dashed in our direction. The sound of Joe's van's engine revved as he pulled from the drive to the opposite side of the home to hitch the trailer. *Thank you, High Functioning Joe.* Rod and Phil were still rooted in the same spot. "Phil?" His eyes swung to me, "Grab the Mute, and we'll carry the tent to the field." The deliberate slap sailed clearly over their collective heads. Phil and Rod walked along the muddy trail behind the house to the side yard. I released the breath I'd been unaware I held, slung my arm over Brennan's shoulder, and followed them. *Another minor crisis averted.*

Heath had come out of the house, summoned by Joe's back-up alarm. He meandered across the deck and observed Joe who had leapt from the cab and was kneeling in the grass. "Need a hand there, Joe?" Heath asked.

"No, you've got work yet," Joe stood and brushed filthy hands on filthier jeans.

"Work..." Heath lifted his ball cap and raked his fingers through his hair, as he descended the deck steps. "More work than time, I'm afraid."

"Ain't that the God's honest," Joe said as he hoisted himself into the cab of the still running work van. Heath tapped the hood and walked to the street assisting Joe in an accident free exit from the yard.

"Well what do you know?" Phil chuckled, "A tent." The small bit of satisfaction that had filled my heart escaped. *My blood relative. Cripes.* Rod rammed the bag of peanuts deep inside his cargo pants. It was only fifty feet from the side yard to the field edge but Hontie's property was lined with trees. We needed to maneuver carefully. Carefully was an unfamiliar concept to these two. Gnawing away like squirrel, Rod wrapped his hands around an aluminum tent leg and hoisted it into the air. Without thought Phil grabbed the opposite corner and together they began to drag the tent toward the trees.

"Wait!" I watched in horror as the tent pitched and low hanging branches scraped roughly across the fabric top. "Phil, hang on a minute!" *Morons.* I took hold of a leg and directed Brennan to the opposite corner. "Lift together, so we can even it out." *Good plan.* However, as soon as Brennan and I lifted, Rod and Phil were off to the races. The tent slammed into another tree with larger branches. I slowed but Rod and Phil had other plans. They shoved harder and the fabric threatened to split. "Wait!" I shouted again.

"It will go," Phil insisted and pushed harder.

"Stop! Stop now!" Gently I continued, "Please put the tent down." They obediently sat the tent down. Happy for a break, Rod reached in his pocket and a split second later fired up a cigarette. "The legs adjust. If we shorten them the tent will slip right under the branches."

"It lowers?" Phil examined the hardware and gave the latch a flick. The tent sank three feet. "Well how about that." With the legs successfully lowered we made it to the field without any casualties. "Let's carry it over next to the grill for the bar," Phil said. Rod bobbed his head in agreement while puffing on a cigarette. Brennan and I just walked along, unsure where the invisible grill and equally invisible bar were located.

With the tent re-elevated to maximum height, Phil reached into the rafters and pulled the canvas carrying case from the aluminum supports. He tossed it over his shoulder and walked with Rod toward the barn. "About the grill,

Phil…" I boldly, *or foolishly,* decided to tackle yet another crisis. "What is the plan there?"

"Oh yeah, the grill, ***Here's the thing***…" Phil stopped walking and grappled at his pocket for a cigarette. "There aren't any vehicles large enough to pick it up and the rental place is on the way to the chapel." With a flick of his lighter he inhaled deeply. "We'll use Heath's trailer, yeah," he reasoned with himself. "That should do the trick."

Translation: The grill to cook the food for one hundred people will not be picked up until after the ceremony. *SUPER.* I watched Phil and Rod saunter away, blissfully carefree. Mere hours until the event would be in full swing. *Amazing.*

Brennan lifted my hand and wrapped himself into my arms. "Oh Buddy…" I sighed.

"No grill?"

"Another grown-up decision honey… a bad one."

"One question Mommy," he turned his face to mine.

"Just one?" I teased.

"What is that thing over there?" I looked where he pointed. An intriguing accent piece sat at the far edge of the field.

"Hontie has so many unusual lawn accents, but…" I squinted then rolled my eyes to heaven… a keg. An untapped and not iced keg of beer parked proudly in the field. "That would be the beer."

"Beer?"

"It's for later at the reception." *I so need to get out of here.* I rubbed Brennan's head, "You hungry?" He bounced up and down. "Go find your brother."

SATURDAY 2:00 P.M.
One hour until the bride would walk down the aisle

I walked through the mudroom and into the virtually perfect kitchen. The vintage grocery store sign, 'Bananas for Sale', now hung over the sink. Five feet long, the painted tin sign had been the inspiration for the paint selection. Large twelve inch cardboard numbers could be interchanged to reflect the price per pound! Fabulous!

I stepped over Clare, who was again on her knees scrubbing the floor. *Sick.* "I am taking the boys for lunch."

"What?" Clare sat up abruptly sloshing water over the rim of her bucket. "Georgia the wedding is in one hour!"

Time for reality run down. "Yeah well, Mom and Hontie are to be there **now** and they are showering. The groom is still here *as is* the best man, and neither of them have showered. The wedding is at 3:00 which puts the reception at about 5:30 or 6:00? Currently there is no grill to cook the food for the one hundred guests, so I am walking the boys to the pizza shop for some lunch."

Clare looked pained. "But... you're leaving?" She clutched her scrub bucket like a life line.

"Yep, for lunch and if I don't get to the blessed event that's fine, out of my control. But in my control?" I watched as Brennan led Payton from the dining room. "Feeding my kids and respecting them enough to take care of the basics." That received wide eyed stares from all within earshot.

"Grown up choice, Mommy?" Brennan joined me.

"Yep, a good one." I lifted Payton to my hip. "So, I will ask again, anybody want anything from the pizza shop?"

Clare blinked owl-like, then shook her head. "No, I'm good." She dropped her bucket and scrubbed with renewed zest.

"Don't worry about me, I'm fine," Catheryn answered from atop a ladder where she wielded a staple gun. I watched, as she worked to secure a bed sheet to a rafter. The gun shot again, as she worked to conceal the construction mess in the laundry room.

"I'll take a sub Georgia, any kind," Heath salivated. "Large, no onions."

"You guys sure?" I asked Clare and Catheryn again. No response. "Okay boys; let's hike to the pizza shop. On second thought…" I scooped up my keys and whispered to Brennan, "Better yet, let's take the Jeep before someone else does."

He gave me the giggle I needed.

We drove all of one hundred and fifty yards to the pizza shop, ordered a large cheeseburger sub for Heath and some slices with sausage for Brennan, and plain for Payton and me.

"Hey Bren, you want to run this sub to Uncle Heath?"

"You mean like a delivery guy?" He asked excitedly.

"Yeah, but without the wheels," I grinned at him.

"Cool!" *Simple joys.*

He grabbed the sub, dashed out the door, carefully crossed the lot and disappeared down the street. A few minutes later he reappeared, checked for traffic, and burst back through the door to the dining area of Sal's.

"Well done, sir," I teased.

"I never saw anyone so excited about a sub before," he said. He collapsed into our booth and slurped his soda pop.

"Really?"

"Yeah, I think it was gone before I even got out of the kitchen," he giggled. "Uncle Heath may have even eaten the wrapper!"

"We don't eat wrappers," Payton announced seriously.

"That's right, buddy, we don't eat wrappers." I turned to Brennan; "I wonder if we should get Heath another one." The counter help called our number and we forgot about the sub discussion and ravenously devoured our pizza.

"Are we going to get to the wedding, Mom?" Brennan asked with a mouthful of pizza.

"Not sure," I answered honestly. I softened at his sad expression. "Listen, the chapel is at least a half hour away from here. We are doing our best to get there," *True,* "and of course we want to be there," *Gray area,* "but we are the last people who **need** to be there." Brennan listened intently. "Hontie, Grandmom, Phil of course, and Gavin must be there. There is very little time left to actually get there on time, but we will try to get there."

He seemed to accept this and looked out the window. "That's one less for the shower Mom."

I followed Brennan's gaze and spotted Phil in the not street legal car speeding down Main Street. I shook my head in disbelief. We are forty-five minutes away from the wedding ceremony site and the groom is seemingly unfazed. *Pass the pipe; I need a hit.* "Are we all done here, boys?" I gathered up the plates and napkins.

"Yep!" was their unison reply.

SATURDAY 2:25 P.M.
Thirty-five minutes and counting

One hundred and fifty yards later we pulled onto the lawn. Mom and Hontie stood on the deck dressed and ready to go to the chapel. Gavin emerged from the house also decked out in wedding garb. He crossed to Hontie and their collective body language screamed tension. *Maybe I should have chewed more slowly.*

"...if I take your car you can come with Heath." Gavin pleaded with his mother.

"No Gavin, that won't work. Heath needs to pick up the grill." Mom walked on the deck, Hontie gave her a directional head jerk. "Isabella, let's go. We are already late."

"El tardio," Mom muttered and they disappeared into the house leaving Gavin standing visibly frustrated.

I climbed from the Jeep and unloaded Payton, as Brennan slammed the rear door. The resounding slam drew Gavin's attention to me and my, oh so empty, Jeep. *Damn it.*

"Hey Georgia," he jogged down the deck steps wearing a let's-make-a-deal grin. "I need to pick up Phil at the lake house and get to the church. Can I take your car?"

Surprised? "I guess the groom needs to get to his own wedding." I dangled the keys. *Snatch.*

SATURDAY 2:35 P.M.

"Bren shower, we gotta move!" I dug a bath towel out of the dry sink and shoved him into the bathroom, just vacated by Catheryn. Wrapped in a bath sheet, she jogged to the stairs as Heath descended.

"Who's in?" He asked Catheryn.

"Brennan," she said without so much as a pause in her step.

Heath walked through the narrow hallway and paused next to me at the dry sink. I looked into his weary eyes. With a shave kit in one hand and a towel in the other he asked, "Georgia is he up for locker room style bathing?"

Confused I asked, "Is who up for what?"

"Can I shave at the sink while Brennan showers?" He nodded at me encouraging approval.

I raised my brow and shoulders. "I'm sure that's okay; just tell him to hurry up."

Heath pulled open the door and disappeared into the bathroom. I checked for Payton who was lying on the floor under the dining room table gently running a matchbox car up and down the oak claw foot table legs. I listened to his impressive automotive sounds and wondered for a moment how little boys were so good at it. On a sigh, I dashed from the room and up the back steps to gather our wedding clothes. In the bedroom I found Clare rummaging in her luggage. "Nice time line, huh? Good grief, this is insane."

"Yep."

"Is the shower available?"

"Should be in about ten minutes, Bren and Heath are locker room bathing, what ever that means."

Clare looked equally puzzled then shrugged, "guy thing."

"I guess." I laid out Brennan's dress clothes on the bed then tossed Payton's and mine over my arm. My gift bag which still was under the window caught my eye. With a quick move I added it to my laden arms.

"What's that... your gift?"

"Yeah, I never got time to put it together. It's just bath towels, practical, and domestic. I am being hopeful I realize." My sarcasm wasn't subtle. The idea that Phil and Ella would create anything close to the resemblance of a normal family home was absurd.

Clare chuckled quietly, "I made a deposit in the hardware store account. Don't talk to me about hopeful." We gathered what we needed and carefully went down stairs.

"Payton?" I heard, rather then saw him and knew he was still playing with the car. "Time for a pit stop buddy, its tubby time."

"Awww," he whined.

"Let's do your tubby in the kitchen." I ignored his protest, laid our clothes on the table, and shoved my gift bag underneath. I crossed the room and flipped the latch on the dry sink and grabbed a wash cloth and towel. "Come on buddy, bring your car along," I reached for his small hand and we walked to the kitchen.

"How do you tubby in the kitchen?" He inquired curiously.

"Well, it's a spot tubby," I explained.

"I get spots?"

"No silly, we only wash the spots on your body that show." I risked a look at the clock on the microwave, **2:42 P.M.** *Cripes.* I wrung out the wash cloth, "That way you look and smell clean but really you're only just-enough clean."

"Okay," was Payton's trusting reply, as I started to wash his face.

Brennan appeared wrapped in a towel. "Mom, where are my clothes?"

"Upstairs on the mattress." Gavin stepped into the kitchen with Davis on his hip dressed and ready. "You guys headed out?"

"Ten minutes yet. Phil was headed to the lake house to swim and dress." *Swim? Leave it alone.* "We're going to swing by and pick him up then get him to the chapel." Gavin grinned, as Jade walked in the kitchen. He let out a low approving whistle at her flirty strapless sundress.

"Oh look at my handsome men," Jade nuzzled Davis's cheek and gave Gavin a quick peck.

"I'll go get the car seat ready;" Gavin shifted Davis to Jade's arms.

"Sure… good," she answered. As he left, she looked at me and said what I had thought, "Swim and dress… catch that?"

I just raised my hands; there were no words. "Can Bren ride with you guys? It would be nice if he, at least, made it to the service."

"Yeah… crazy, right? Sure, I'll go settle Davis in." She looked at towel clad Brennan. "Come on out when you're dressed." She carried Davis out onto the deck.

"Fast! Fast!" I hurried Brennan to the back steps. "Dress fast so you can ride with Gavin and Jade. I'll see you at the chapel." Quick kisses for Bren then I turned my attention back to Payton. I laughed as he stood with a towel draped over his head. "All done, buddy, now let's get you dressed."

SATURDAY 2:45 P.M. tick, tick

Payton sat on the edge of the dining room table, his tiny sock clad feet swinging gaily. I tugged his shirt over his head; "push your arm in." He thrust his left hand through and then attempted to shove the right when his toy car got stuck in the material.

"Mommy, I'm stuck."

"Back it out buddy," I said. With all the appropriate automotive sounds, he effectively reversed the toy car's engine then shifted the match box car to his other hand and successfully slipped his arm into the sleeve. Clare flew by us with her bath towel in hand. "Georgia, I'm in," she called, "be out in five." So glad we grew up on well water and camp showers. There was nothing like water conservation in drought or the thrill of a small hot water tank in a camper to teach you how to shower quickly and efficiently.

True to her word, Clare reappeared as I pulled Payton's second shoe on. Wrapped in a towel and turban she hurried into the kitchen, only to run into Tom and Sueanne who stood in the doorway. Clare stood frozen. Tom cleared his throat and muttered an apology. The breath Clare held whimpered out. She clutched the towel around her body then straightened her shoulders. "Meeting and conversing with people in various stages of undress is becoming quite common for me." She laughed self-consciously, "how can I help you guys?"

Tom averted his eyes respectfully. Sueanne just smiled then crossed to Clare. "I think it will be, we, that help you. Knowing Phil and Ella as we do, we expect there is still much to pull together."

"You would be correct," Clare replied. Embarrassment forgotten, she launched into the list of remaining things which needed attention,` then added the list of things we hoped for. To their credit, Sueanne and Tom didn't flinch once as Clare rattled on, and on and on.

I placed Payton on the lone carpet in the living room, handed him his plane from Bouckville, and begged him to remain clean for five minutes. *Tall order.* I prayed the dry sink held just one more dry towel. *What fantasy side trip was I on...* of course the towels were gone. I picked up Payton's damp one and shut the bathroom door behind me. I hopped in the shower to find the water tepid and chilling fast. As my goose bumps grew goose bumps, I decided to skip shampooing and settled for 'spot' cleaning as well.

SATURDAY 2:57
Wedding bells will be ringing in three minutes

Dressed and as ready to leave as I would get, I folded another bath sheet and stuffed it inside the deep floral printed gift bag. I rammed the co-coordinated tissue paper in along side the towels without finesse, then wondered why I was making the effort. The paned glass pocket doors from the living room opened and Catheryn stepped carefully across the planked floor in her nearly stiletto heels. "Don't we clean up well," she said.

"Speak for yourself. I know that I look pretty damn close to how I feel."

"Clare almost ready?"

"Should be."

Catheryn picked up a piece of tissue paper and folded it with the flair I lacked and handed it to me. "Gift... hadn't thought of that." She turned to Heath who was playing with Payton in the living room. "Do we have a gift?" she asked him. Heath walked past Catheryn into the kitchen, as if she had not spoken.

I looked at the gift bag and decided to quit, then I rummaged for the card. "Really Catheryn, I think you guys have gifted in sweat."

"True," she answered. I heard Heath mumble something left un-deciphered from the kitchen.

I laid the card on the table and dug a pen out of my bag. "You guys want to sign in on this?"

Catheryn waved me off; "I'm over it." Heath leaned heavily in the doorway adjusting his tie. "Let me do that honey;" Catheryn stepped over and fixed it for him. "Perfect." She stepped back to the table and scooped up her purse.

"Have you thought of what you're saying?" I asked Heath.

"You're speaking?" Catheryn turned, surprised. "At the ceremony?"

"Phil asked if I would say a few words on behalf of our family." Heath turned and walked into the kitchen leaving Catheryn and I to stare after him.

"When did that happen?" Catheryn's high heels clipped after him. I sat the gift bag on the floor and followed them into the kitchen. "You're speaking?" Catheryn repeated. "What are you going to say?" Heath looked intently at her. The moment of silence stretched on and on, until finally he answered with a shrug. *Well said.* "Are we ready?" Catheryn asked Heath... another shrug. "Mercy," she said and rolled her eyes.

Clare raced down the main stair case. "What, you didn't want to brave the back stairs in heels?"

"You got it." She buzzed by me, dropped her purse on the dry sink, and stepped into the bathroom. With a flurry of movement she spun out again. "Are we ready? How's my hair?"

"Yes we're ready and your hair is good," I answered.

"It's big, isn't it?" She said as she patted her head.

"It's good." I rolled my eyes, as Clare ducked back into the bathroom for one last check in the mirror.

"This is nuts." She grabbed her purse and after a quick check of the contents she headed for the truck.

I gently rolled the pocket doors open to the living room. The pace of Payton's playing had wound down considerably. He had stretched out across the chair and ottoman and was on the verge of sleep. "It's time Payton; let's go." I said with quiet enthusiasm. He stirred enough for me to lift him up.

"Can I take my plane, Mommy?" He asked through a yawn.

"Sure, buddy," he'd be snoozing in minutes.

Chapter 16

Enduring this event will require much, much, more alcohol. Waiter?

SATURDAY 3:05 P.M.

We're late

"All in?" Heath adjusted his mirrors and pulled out slowly due to the trailer in tow.

"Well, do you think after all this madness we'll miss the big event?" Catheryn asked from the front seat, while using the visor mirror to fix her lip color.

"They probably won't even realize we aren't there," Clare answered dryly from the back seat.

"It takes thirty minutes to get there, right?" I inquired.

"It might be over before we even arrive." Clare's voice dripped irritation.

The truck was flying over the unfamiliar back roads. The trailer pitched on every turn and made loud screeching and banging noises with every bump.

"Whoa!" A still awake Payton exclaimed from the back seat. "This is like a roller coaster!"

"Honey," Catheryn prepared to offer Heath some driving advice. With a swift look from Heath, she quickly swallowed her words.

We stewed in our silence. Distance from the house provided time for our minds to begin to process what we had survived. In my wildest imaginative moment I never would have predicted the events of the last three days. Construction, landscaping, painting, plumbing, concierge services, family counseling… We were invited guests. *Cripes!*

The trailer wheels shrieked in protest, as the truck hugged the next tight turn. I gripped the seat in front of me to the point of pain. *For cryin out loud, who drags a metal trailer to a wedding?* "You know who I'm annoyed with?" I said to no one in particular. "Hontie. How in the world can she continue to swallow this garbage? I don't mean the literal garbage, which is bad enough. I mean Phil and Ella and the cavalier way they live their daily lives."

Clare grumbled in agreement. "It seems to be constant. No money, no vehicle, no housing… .How can anyone raise a family without stable employment?"

"You surround yourself with suckers." Catheryn said under her breath.

"They sure do have big plans though, and even bigger dreams," I said. "It must be exhausting for Hontie on a daily basis even without an invasion of wedding guests."

Heath used the rear view mirror to make eye contact with me. "You know what Hontie is?" I stared back at him. "She's a well-dressed volcano."

I visualized Hontie dressed in her mother-of-the-groom attire, purse in hand, and corsage pinned in place. Her brow furrowed in frustration, as she watched Phil sledge hammer the walls from her quaint kitchen. She observed him, as he dug halfway to China in the side yard and then stole her car for the hundredth time. The blood rushed to her head and exploded with the force of a volcanic eruption. "Do you think?" *Despite Hontie losing her head, I felt slightly better.*

"Yep and as far as the wedding goes, we will make it," Heath said confidently. "Not a doubt in my mind and I'll tell you why. The groom and best man only have a ten minute lead on us."

"I guess," I answered doubtfully.

"Do you really think Hontie is upset?" Clare asked unsure.

"I'm not sure if she's upset or in shock," Catheryn answered. "I know she's used to Phil's erratic behavior, but this was just too much, too many weeks in a row."

"Do you think 'Nanny 911' does thirty-year-old children?" I asked.

"Nanny 911," Heath snorted. "Call it what it is, corrective parenting. Missed my turn," Heath gave little warning before swinging the truck into a wicked U-turn.

"Trailer!" Clare squealed. "We've got a trailer hooked on the back!" Heath's head whipped around, partial-exorcist, and pinned her to her seat. "Just thought you might have forgotten," she laughed tightly.

Heath backed up successfully and completed the turn. On the correct road we wound higher and higher toward the crest of the mountain.

"Gosh, it's beautiful here," I observed. "Too bad we're all too worn out to appreciate it." Up ahead a lovely chapel came into view. Multiple cars lined the lawn.

"Looks like a full house," Catheryn said.

Heath slowed slightly and we pulled on the grass, trailer and all.

"We missed it," Clare pouted and pulled off her seat belt.

"We missed nothing," Heath grumbled as he set the emergency brake.

"But look," Clare pointed, "Those people are leaving." Sure enough, two cars were pulling out of the parking area.

Just then Brennan raced over to the truck. "Did we miss it?" I asked.

"Miss what?" He answered.

"The wedding, silly," I tucked his shirt in.

"No, we just got here." He wiggled uncomfortably and tugged his shirt to loosen it. "Gavin and Phil are right over there."

"Told you," Heath grumbled. Only Phil would be standing outside the chapel more then a half hour after the wedding should have begun and not yet be married. I unloaded a sound asleep Payton from the back seat and we made our way to the chapel entrance.

"Phil and Ella take the Plunge 3:00 Saturday

Saturday, yes. 3:00? *Well no,* 3:45.

Forty-five minutes after the bells should have chimed, Heath, Catheryn, Clare, the boys, and I climbed the concrete steps to enter the chapel. We were met by a man with Whoopi Goldberg dreadlocks gathered into a high ponytail on top of his head. He looked at each of us with a huge smile and offered a hand shake to Heath.

"Welcome," his booming voice met our ears as another car flew up the gravel road toward the chapel. There was no time to digest this man's genuine friendliness. "Please, find a seat," he said in a deep hypnotic tone. Then he excused himself and stepped around us. Silently he moved outside to greet the other guests, who were later than we were!

"Wow," Clare whispered to Catheryn. "He had manners."

"I am sure he's with the church," Catheryn said, as she linked her arm through Heath's and filed into the chapel.

My eyes were stuck on the still dispersing dust cloud that had arrived with the late guest vehicle. From the dust ball emerged none other than the… BRIDE! "Nothing like being fifty minutes late to your own wedding," I muttered under my breath. I hoisted Payton up higher on my hip and nudged Brennan toward the sanctuary.

Once inside, the pure countryside chapel image was complete. Six stained glass windows lined the outside walls of the single room. An elevated platform stretched across the front of the chapel. The front wall of the chapel was an enormous stained glass window. Nearly ceiling to floor, the window depicted Jesus in a shepherding scene. The vibrant colors and detail were breathtaking. Below the striking colored glass, two small flower arrangements had been placed around a pink pillar candle on top of the altar. The ornately carved altar was draped with a cream colored cloth embroidered with a cross. Spaced evenly across the platform, four chairs had been placed. Each dark wooden chair was uniquely carved and upholstered in rich scarlet fabric. Beautiful!

Three sections of standard wooden pews divided the modest sanctuary. Two aisles separated the smaller side sections from the main seating area. The chapel was filled with guests, but there didn't seem to be any designated bride or groom sectors. Shuffling as quietly as a group of six could in dress shoes on a wooden floor, Heath located Mom. She was seated in the middle section about six rows from the back with enough room for three. He stood aside and motioned to Clare and Catheryn to slide in the pew. I spied Hontie seated in the row behind Mom with room for me and the boys. Brennan slid next to Hontie only to realize he couldn't see the action, *which had yet to begin.* Of course we juggled and I flopped with the grace of an eighty year old into the pew, with the boys on either side of me. Hontie smiled wearily at me. "We made it," I said. "Why aren't you up front?" I whispered.

Hontie shook her head discreetly, "I'm fine."

Translation – no arrangements made for mother-of-the-groom.

Mom turned in her seat. "It is **not** fine;" she said over her shoulder.

"Isabella, please... " Hontie said tightly "It's fine."

"Es mucho intolerable-o," Mom said. *Okay.*

Unaware of the exchange Clare fluffed her hair then leaned toward Mom. "Why is Hontie in the back?"

Mom rolled her eyes skyward and pursed her lips impressively. Hontie touched Clare's shoulder. "It's fine. I am fine," she insisted.

Mom shook her head again fiercely and her Spanish Tourette's was triggered once more. "Es mucho disrespect-o."

"Isabella," Hontie pleaded. Clare gave Hontie a concerned look, then spun back around. Organ music filled the small chapel. *Away we go!*

Father of the groom, Uncle Nathan entered down the left aisle with his mother, Great Grammy on his arm. *Some traditions were in place.* Led by the pastor, Gavin and Phil walked down the right side aisle. Phil's choice of wedding garb consisted of a crisp white shirt, unbuttoned at the collar. The shirt hung loosely untucked against his dark pants. His hands were comfortably buried in his pockets and he wore loafers on his feet. When the men reached the front of the chapel, the Pastor walked across on floor level while Gavin and Phil climbed the four steps to the platform. Phil grinned out at the seated guests, relaxed as ever, as the bridal party began to process. A boy about three-years old walked nervously along the aisle. The guests responded with appropriate "Ooos and Ahhhs", as he made his way to the front. Following the little boy was Ella's daughter, Meg. I hadn't seen her for two years; my how she had grown. Next

Ella's sister, Anya, the matron of honor, walked down the aisle and joined a grinning Phil on the platform. The congregation spun in their seats then stood in an attempt to get a glimpse of Ella, as she stepped into the aisle.

Next to me Brennan bounced on his toes, "I can't see, Mom."

"Shh, honey, no one can see."

Ella climbed the steps to join Phil, and everyone finally got a look at the couple of the hour. She wore a winter white camisole with a long sleeved sheer blouse over top. Her slate colored skirt ended about two inches above her knee. Her wild curly hair had been contained in a basic up sweep showing simple dangling earrings at her ears. A half inch wide black ribbon had been tied around her throat like a vintage choker. The rest of her adornments were surrounding her ankles. Multiple bracelets, hemp, beaded and leather, topped off her black wedge heeled sandals.

Taking Phil's hand, Ella was escorted to her spot. She sat in the high backed chair atop the platform. A moment later the bridal party took their seats as well.

Looking around at the gathered family and friends, I couldn't help but chuckle when I thought of how we had arrived at this moment. Everyone else looked on to the couple in front of us with the typical expression of bliss. No one seemed to mind that we were one hour behind schedule or that the six latest guests to arrive, *besides the bride,* were wet-headed, hurriedly dressed, and sprinkled with long dried paint droplets.

The minister asked us to take our seats, as he rattled off his greeting and stated all the typical pleasantries. "I was beginning to be concerned when I had guests but no groom." He smiled out at the full chapel, "But no one else seemed concerned," he laughed warmly. "A member of Ella's family informed me that the bride was not here yet either and assured me that this was quite common for our lovely couple." More rumbles of laughter filled the room with the exception of our two pews. *We had no humor.*

"Anyway… once again, welcome to the union of Phillip and Gabriella. Please stand together and join me now for a brief word of prayer." He proceeded to pray without any mention of true gospel foundation. *Another modern society miracle - faith without faith.* I am continually astounded by the "new age" faith systems which host services in churches complete with stained glass and pipe organs yet seem to forget to open the bible. It was true art to be able to offer a prayer without mentioning God, or Jesus at all. *Heavenly Father? Holy Spirit? Give me something!* The pastor asked us to be seated. Sitting still was torture; I found myself drifting easily toward sleep. As I fought to stay awake, I glanced over Catheryn's shoulder and watched her flick yellow paint from her leg. Clare, a mere six inches from Catheryn worked to chip red from her finger nails. *Aren't we the classy ones?*

Payton stretched out across my lap and blinked at me with big sleepy blue eyes. "Is it my turn to get married?" he asked.

"No sir," I whispered playfully.

"Aww," he pouted. "I want to be on stage and marry with somebody."

I leaned down to his ear, "Who sir, do you want to marry with?"

"Ashley," he answered wistfully.

I couldn't help but smile, "Ashley?"

"Yes," he sighed. "She blows kisses at me at school and I blush bright red."

Oh dear. My attention was drawn back to the front as Sylvia made her way to the front of the sanctuary. *An actress, this should be good.* True to form Sylvia shared some sappy memories, shed three point six tears, and heaved a huge pull-it-back-together sigh. *For cryin' out loud.* All that was missing was a spot light to illuminate her as she floated back to her pew.

After that a man moved forward. I looked at Hontie who mouthed, 'Ella's father'. He read a beautiful poem. Sentiment snuck up on me; it was a truly lovely moment. Next Heath stood and made his way to the front. The sight of him kicked sentiment through the picturesque stained glass window and made my blood boil. I had never seen such walking exhaustion, except on Survivor. *Somewhat accurate.*

Heath acknowledged the bridal party and then smiled wearily across the congregation. "It's quite fitting that Jesus' first miracle was a wedding. In the time of Jesus, weddings were celebrations that lasted seven days, which..." glanced at his watch, "I'm within 24 hours of reaching." Our two pews quietly moaned in agreement but the remaining bulk of the guests just didn't get it. "Frankly," Heath continued, "we may indeed, require a miracle."

"Or two," Catheryn whispered to Clare.

Heath continued on with his very eloquent, impromptu spiel. He remarked about Phil as a child and the man Phil had become. Then he wished God's blessing on Phil and Ella, as they began their married life. *Lovely, just lovely.* Finally Heath finished and led the congregation in prayer and lumbered back to his pew.

As he sat, Clare leaned across Catheryn's lap. "Right off the top of your head," she said with a lift of her brow.

Heath just raised a shoulder in response. The rest of the ceremony was a blur, reciting of promises, an emotional exchange of rings. *Sorry unmoved, empty... just plain empty.* Brennan, however, sat poised on the edge of his seat absorbing every moment of his first nuptial experience.

Finally it was over. The bridal party exited leaving the guests waiting to be released from their seats. Everyone waited and began to get a little restless. A few guests stood and peered down the aisle. Realizing no one was coming back, we released ourselves. Our family felt no rush to get outside. We stood and allowed the guests from the front of the chapel to file past us.

Mom moved into the aisle and set off for the front of the chapel. I watched, as she fought the oncoming guest traffic headed who knew where.

I looked at Clare, "That was good; I guess."

"Yeah, I suppose this crew is used to a start time of whenever." She turned to Hontie, "There were guests leaving when we pulled up. I was positive we had missed the whole show."

Hontie smiled and laid her hand on Clare's arm and leaned in, "Oh, they weren't guests." Her voice was barely audible. "The chapel," she whispered, "had been accidentally double-booked for a memorial service."

"What?" Clare gasped.

"They printed a change of time in the local newspaper but not everyone saw it." Hontie frowned, "It's a shame really, a terrible shame."

"You just can't make this stuff up," I muttered.

"Yeah, and considering the tardiness track record for these two, they could have bumped the wedding by an hour and not told anyone." Catheryn said from the aisle.

"Well at least it's over. There's nothing more we have to do." Clare said. "But…," she pondered a thought, "What will they do for the reception?"

"Not our deal Clare," I said.

"If it involves music, food, and booze, they'll have it covered," Heath stated flatly.

And he was right. Notoriously Phil had no money for real needs like groceries, housing, and utility service. But mention a party or a need for a stiff drink and Phil would get it for you, pronto. He would take up a quick cash collection from prospective guests and dash off to the food and liquor stores. Impromptu festivities would quickly follow. Music, fine food, and drink would be enjoyed so swiftly that no one would ever consider the actual costs incurred or change they had not received.

Brennan pulled on my arm and gained my attention. "What's next?"

Heaven only knows. "We head out to the lawn, buddy."

Half of the guests had filed out, so we joined the flow. Mom hustled up the aisle carrying the flowers from the altar. "Georgia these are to be on the vino de mesa."

"The what?"

"The champagne table, put the flowers on the table."

"Champagne table?" Catheryn said in a horrified whisper. "Here, at the church?"

"Why wouldn't there be a booze table at the church," Heath said just low enough for her to hear.

"Georgia?" Mom insistently shoved the flowers at me.

Guess I had more to do after all. Disgruntled I took the arrangements from Mom. "Champagne table, I'll get them there." I positioned the boys in front of me and leaned down to Brennan, "Hold your brother's hand, use good manners, and cut us a path out of here."

"Got it Mommy," Brennan pressed ahead. "Excuse me please... excuse me, thanks." As I expected, the crowd responded better to a juvenile's request and we popped out the chapel doors in no time.

Chapter 17

Respected doctors say "If you are drinking to anesthetize your life you have a problem." We have a problem.

On the front lawn sat a table draped with a beautiful white linen cloth. The table top was covered with champagne glasses filled to the rim with bubbly. In the center of the table multiple bottles of champagne sat popped waiting to be poured. I scanned the lawn looking for the bridal party, anticipating a toast would begin the celebration.

What did I know about the order of things when it pertained to a gypsy wedding?

Most of the guests in my view had a glass of champagne in hand but no one was waiting for a toast. Consume away! I walked down the chapel steps to the table. I rearranged the bottles, condensed the glasses and set the flower centerpieces in place. Job completed, I selected a lovely glass of champagne. I paused a moment to inhale the fragrance. Bouquet enjoyed, I hoisted it in the air to toast the non-traditional, savored the first sip... and slugged the rest. I sat my empty glass back on the table, *tacky*, and grabbed two more. *Lush.* "Let's go boys," I said and walked to the farthest property line the chapel had to offer.

The boys raced in circles in front of me, as I took a moment to absorb the view. The gravel road which led to the chapel was the only road in sight. The chapel itself appeared painted into the hills. Lush green trees provided the back drop for the basic white chapel. Narrow wooden slats sided the building and framed the colorful stained glass windows. On the left side of the chapel was a gravel parking lot. I wondered how many folks wandered this way on a Sunday morning and if extra parking spaces on the grass were needed like today. On the opposite side of the chapel a small cemetery was tucked under the shade of the tall trees. I could see a few memorial markers from where I stood, all of which appeared very old and weather worn. Between the cemetery and the chapel, much to my delight, sat an outhouse. The same white wooden siding had been meticulously cared for which said that this outhouse was not for show but was ready for use. I giggled ridiculously. I turned my back to the chapel and could see for miles, and miles. *Beautiful.* The land was marked in different tones where the fields changed from wheat to hay. Pockets of wild flowers sprinkled colorful bursts throughout the pastures and fields. Cattle grazed without a care alongside the only building in sight, an old threshing barn. The barn's roof sagged heavily from age and having endured beam breaking winter snowfalls. The air was crisp and clean. The sky a brilliant blue dotted with puffs of cotton clouds. *Extraordinary.*

Lost in my vision, Clare appeared beside me, "Thirsty?"

Startled, I sloshed my champagne across my wrist. "No," I licked my hand. "Therapy."

"Nice Georgia," Clare said with a laugh, then waved to Catheryn who was headed our way. "Check her out." I watched as Catheryn tiptoed gingerly across the soft grass.

"Wrong shoe choice," Catheryn said as she pulled even with Clare. Using Clare's shoulder for balance, Catheryn lifted her foot and plucked a hunk of soil from her high heel. Righting herself she glanced across the mingling guests, "Flowing freely, huh?"

"Yeah," Clare answered. "Georgia's way ahead and I'm joining." Catheryn and I watched as Clare stalked toward the champagne table to grab a glass or two.

"Where's Heath?" I asked Catheryn.

"He got waylaid by the pastor," she replied. "There sure are a lot of people."

"It was supposed to be one hundred. Inside the chapel I would have guessed less, but spread out…"

"Yeah," Catheryn agreed. "There's Heath. I'm going to get him and some champagne." She rose to her toes and treaded cautiously away. I once again slipped into the picturesque surroundings.

An overly loud burst of laughter drew my attention across the lawn. I saw Uncle Nathan, champagne in hand, spinning an elaborate tale for a small group of guests. I could hear the appropriate "Ooos" and "Ahhs", as he gestured grandly and gave the story an extra entertaining punch. I knew just how they felt. As a child I remembered Uncle Nathan to be mesmerizing. He would entertain us with grand stories of the exotic places he had traveled as a renowned photo journalist. It was clear to me even as a young child that Uncle Nathan loved what he did. He was never outwardly boastful yet exuded a charm and confidence that was destined to make him very successful. And it had. His career choice, however, required eight months a year globe trotting which would prove back breaking to a family unit.

Looking across the lawn as his story wound down, I sized him up, adult to adult. Time had treated him kindly. His hair was silver sprinkled with a high recession, which being male only made him appear more handsome. The California sun had given his skin a healthy bronze glow. He was dressed in style, very George Clooney, as if he were torn from the cover of Esquire. He wore a deep green tailored dinner jacket, a crisp open collared dress shirt in pale yellow, and creased oatmeal trousers. From his head to loafers the dollars dripped.

I sucked in a bolstering breath. *Next hurdle of the day – reintroduce yourself to the uncle whom you haven't seen for twenty-four years.* No easy way around it, and it needed to be done and discreetly. I did not want to upset Mom or Hontie by interacting with the Ex. I scanned the lawn; Mom and Hontie were nowhere in view. No time like the present. I snagged Brennan and Payton, postponed their game of tag, and crossed the lawn in the direction of Uncle Nathan. "Let's do this," I encouraged myself. "Hi Uncle Nathan," I put a hands on both boys and positioned them in front of me. "These are my boys, Brennan and Payton."

Uncle Nathan turned and upped the wattage on his smile. "Georgia," a hug for me, "Pleasure to meet you boys," and hand shakes for them. "I have heard about both of you from Gavin and Phil. Are you enjoying yourselves?"

"Yes, it's my first wedding." Brennan said.

"Mom wouldn't let me have a marrying turn." Payton pouted.

"Oh," Uncle Nathan leaned down playfully; "your turn will come sooner than your Mom can imagine." He stood and faced me; "Oh Georgia, you're all grown up!" *Tends to happen over twenty-four years.*

"Yep, I'm a mom and a business owner. Things are good," awkward silence. "Nice service."

"Yes, they finally pulled it off," he answered. I watched him search the grounds for the wife and children that I'd rather not meet. I looked over the lawn myself and much to my horror Mom and Hontie were only ten yards away chatting by the chapel steps. *Exit time!*

"Good to see you, Uncle Nathan." I corralled the boys, "See you at the reception."

"Sounds good, it was good to meet your boys," he called after us. I gripped the boys' hands firmly and hurried back to the safety of 'my people'. Payton tugged free and raced across the lawn taunting Brennan to chase after him.

With thirty feet separating me from family disloyalty, I chanced a glance toward Mom. My covert exchange had been a success! I released the breath I was unaware I held.

"So Mom, Uncle Nathan is Phil's dad;" Brennan lined up the ducks.

"Yeah and Gavin's," I answered. "He's a photographer and he travels to different continents taking pictures for National Geographic and the Discovery Channel."

"That's cool, I guess," Brennan said quietly. "But he left his family?" Honest feelings, honest questions, honest answers.

"Yep, he made a new one." I dropped my arm over his shoulder.

"Not so cool."

I pulled him close and kissed the top of his head. "No, not cool." *Time for a subject change.*

"What did you think of the wedding?"

"All right." Brennan smiled sheepishly. "The ride over was a little wild."

"Wild? Wild how?" Visions of pre-wedding champagne and nerve settling shots of whiskey, *in my Jeep*, filled my head.

"We picked up Phil at the lake and Jade sat on his lap in the front seat."

"On his lap? Wasn't there room in the back seat?" I interrupted.

"Yeah, just me and Davis but..." Brennan thought for a second, "I think there was a reason." He shrugged his shoulders and dismissed the question. "Anyway, they got to talking about the foosball game last night and how Gavin and Jade beat Ella's brother and his girlfriend, Somi, you know the mean one?" *He had been following along.* "Jade said they kicked their asses, but Somi said they could 'take 'em anytime' and Gavin said it was 'wicked cool'." Brennan had become so caught up in telling the story that I had no choice but to enjoy the tale and leave the profanity alone for the moment. He hurried on, "Jade said the greatest part of the night other than beating their sorry asses was when Somi got mad and walked outside. The rain had left massive puddles, and a truck went by and hit one, splashing her new white designer dress and looney baton hand bag."

"Louis Vüitton," I said under my breath. *There is a God.* "Well, that certainly was a colorful trip for you." *Although I still didn't know why Jade rode on Phil's lap in the front seat.* I gave Brennan a hug, "Oh honey, great story but," I whispered, "If you retell it, drop the A-word."

"Got it! I'm thirsty. Where are the kids' drinks anyway?" He looked around.

"Aren't any, buddy. Sorry."

"Then what are the other kids having?" He pointed and I followed his direction. Sure enough, the kids were drinking… **champagne.** *Why wouldn't they be?*

"That, my love, is another shining example of a grown up decision Bren." I leaned down and looked him square in the face. "A bad one." *What do you do?* "I'm not in charge of those kids, but I am in charge of you. No grown up drinks. Not even a sip." I watched as the pack of kids huddled around a car in the parking lot and passed the champagne glass around to share. I rolled my eyes skyward, "They will be so sick." *Unless of course this wasn't a new thing.* "You know what Bren?" I steered his attention away from the champagne consuming delinquents. "I have juice boxes in the Jeep." His eyes lit with delight. "Let's find Gavin and get my keys." Clare was standing in the center of the lawn with her back to the chapel. Holding a single glass of bubbly, she spotted us and jerked her head in the direction of the delinquents. "You see that?"

"I see it alright. Nobody seems concerned," I answered.

"Nobody even watches them," she remarked. "They're like extras in some high society motion picture."

Clare spun back around and sipped her champagne. "Oh, Georgia look, there's Uncle Nathan. We should go say hello."

"Yeah, I did my meet and greet while Mom and Hontie were out of sight."

Clare swept a glance over the lawn, "Good idea, you see them?"

"Not at the moment, you're clear."

Clare walked off in the direction of Nathan, leaving me once again alone with this tremendous view. The pockets of feisty flowers which held their own in the high grass that separated field from stone road made me smile. Bright purple spiked loose strife mixed with wild daisies and flowering weeds. I wondered if anyone would notice if I wandered away to harvest a fresh bouquet. I wanted nothing more then to get lost once again amongst the friendly blooms. *Nice thought.*

I looked over the guests on the lawn in search of Gavin and the keys to my ride. It was quite the varied group really; pockets of friends and family, children to seniors, sporting casual to contemporary styles of fashion. As I studied, I could make a few associations; Sylvia was jabbering in fluent French with HawHaw. The women spoke as much with their hands as their lips. Our pleasant Whoopi styled chapel greeter had a child about three years old planted securely on his hip. The little boy was sporting a Jr. sized dread-lock pony tail hairdo and enough facial resemblance to assure me that these two were together. Anya joined them and slid affectionately under the free arm of the man who hugged her close. The little one, not wanting to be left out, reached for her. Anya handed off her champagne glass to the man and kissed the little boy's cheek, as he wrapped his arms tightly around her neck. These three were an obvious family unit.

A brisk mountain top breeze swirled and sent skirts rippling. "Whoa Dearie, it's kicking up!" I heard Sylvia's friend Jewel say. She stood tucked in between the steps and the building with Great Grammy in the senior corner. I was sure these gals were both in their eighties, but you would have never guessed it. Great Grammy was decked from head to toe in a practical blue gray pant suit complete with the latest fashion jewelry and moderately heeled dress shoes. Jewel, befitting her name, wore a striking emerald colored blazer over a printed blouse with coordinating slacks and flat shining gold dress slippers. The wind fought against their firm hold hair spray in a futile attempt to unthread their perfect silver haired upsweeps! *Toss 'em some red hats and they'd be set!* Each lady elegantly held a glass of still full champagne. They were much too vivacious to truly be labeled seniors; they clutched their colorful crocheted wraps around their shoulders in an attempt to ward off the chill.

On the opposite side of the steps I saw Hontie. A full blown genuine smile in place, as she chattered animatedly with her friend Lila. Mom was there too and I now recognized more of the yakking pack of females. These were Hontie's dearest group of friends. Their conservative attire offered no hint of the true free spirits that had united them over the last few years. A fearless thrill seeking ensemble consisted of nine women whose ages ranged from forty to a generous seventy plus. Each woman had tackled the snafus of life; illness, divorce, career instability, and had re-emerged stronger, better human beings. In recent years they had become a club of sorts and celebrated surviving life by embarking on adventure trips. They had strapped bicycles to the deck of flat bottom boats and piloted them through the channel locks of the Erie Canal. They had shot the rapids of the Colorado River on a two week no amenities trip through the Grand Canyon. Their latest excursion had taken the adventure junkies to Peru. Each woman had zip-lined above the lush canopy of the rain forest dangling over one hundred feet in the air. They followed their vertical tour with hiking along the waters of the anaconda filled Amazon River.

I looked at the women and reveled at their fearless nature in direct opposition with their individual outward appearances. Their next planned event was a windjammer cruise where together they would tackle the open sea while trimming the jib. *Whatever that means.*

Spotting Jade with a weary Davis on her hip, I nudged Brennan. "Over there, cut us a path to Jade." He rushed forward and sliced through the crowd like lightning.

Jade's brows winged up, as we approached. "So…," her exaggerated Indiana accent drawled. "Interesting… right?"

"I guess interesting is one adjective we could use." We clinked our glasses in a private toast to the idiots and emptied the contents.

She eyed me over the rim of her glass, "Some ceremony… Hmm?"

"You can say that again." I rolled my shoulders in an effort to relax my tense neck and shoulders. "I was glad to see Great Grammy ushered down the aisle. Nice classy touch."

"Oh Georgia you silly, silly girl," Jade laughed richly. "Classy? It sure would have been…" she leaned down and set Davis on the ground to play with Brennan. "…if it hadn't been a mistake."

"Mistake?"

"Catch this…" She stepped closer and lowered her voice. "Bride, fifty minutes late, nice… .Great Grammy, her age and all, needed a bathroom…" She gestured to our location, "…middle of the mountain… upstate New York… Got me?'

"Oh this is going to be bad," I muttered.

"No indoor plumbing," Jade exaggerated the drama.

"Really… really bad."

Jade motioned with her glass to the small white building at the rear of the church, "Out house."

"Cripes Jade, your serious."

"Dead." She held up her hand as if to attest to the truth. "So Nathan walked with his mother, so she doesn't ya know, break a hip crossing the lawn." I closed my eyes and visualized the scene, as Jade continued, "So, the bride flies in the gravel road and Great Grammy isn't finished. Ella dashed up the chapel steps; you know she **can't** wait. Like five more minutes would make a lick of difference." I covered my mouth in shock knowing there would be more. "Nathan had to cradle carry Great Grammy, literally." Jade held her hands in front of her and mock jogged in place. "They had to run across the lawn into the chapel to beat Ella down the aisle!" Jade raised her brows with a look of 'can you believe that' while downing the last of her champagne. Those were the most consecutive words Jade had strung together since her plane touched down three days ago.

Fatigue + Family + Frustration + Alcohol = Clarity? More champagne please.

"Speaking of Nathan," Jade's voice took on a mischievous tone, "have you seen your ex-uncle?"

"Yep, the wife wasn't with him, but I got the hello-haven't-seen-you-in-twenty-five years conversation over with."

"Classic," Jade nodded slowly. "Modern family."

We're modern alright.

"Hey Jade, who was the greeter? We assumed he was with the church because he seemed so normal, but I saw him standing with Anya."

Jade nodded, "Warren, her husband. He is a great guy. A big time advertising executive."

"Huh, who knew?" I glanced over to where he stood with his family. "We were just caught off guard by his manners."

"Understandable," Davis tugged on Jade's dress. "Hi-ya Mister Man," she lifted him to her hip. "Mommy needs more booze," she nuzzled his wind blown cheek, "much more booze."

Despite the generously filled champagne table, there couldn't possibly be enough booze in the state to right this apple cart. "Hey Jade where's Gavin? I need my jeep keys."

"Oh?" Jade appeared surprised. "What's up?"

"Other than I've had enough nuptial bliss to last me for… oh, let's say at least ten years," she nodded knowingly. "Gavin needs to ride with Heath to the rental place to pick up the grill. Bren and Payton need juice boxes from the back seat, since we're serving champagne to children as well as grownups."

That earned a heartfelt eye roll, "I know it … right?" She adjusted Davis more securely on her hip. "There," she pointed across the lawn with her glass as Gavin made his way toward us.

"So cool to see all these people from the old days," Gavin said as he tickled Davis's cheek. Since he and Jade had settled in Indiana, they rarely made the trip across the country for visits. Not quite as nostalgic as Gavin, Jade offered him a half hearted "Hmm…"

"Hey Gavin, I need my keys."

"Yeah?" He patted over his pockets. "What's up?"

"Nothing, except the guests are already headed to the house for a reception where food is to be included. Food which can't be prepared because the grill your hapless brother reserved to cook it is still at the rental store."

"Good point." Gavin appeared pained, "but Georgia, I need your car."

"No," I responded patiently, "you need to ride with Heath to the rental place." *Whatever post ceremony joy ride that had been planned, just lost its wheels.*

"Oh," Gavin scrubbed his hand over his face, "yeah, that works." He burrowed into his pocket and handed over my keys.

Jade hoisted a sleepy Davis a little higher on her hip. "Georgia, can we come with you? He's desperate for a little nap."

"Of course, give me five, ten minutes tops. I will meet you at the car."

Etiquette required I at least acknowledge the bride and groom following the bonding first kiss. Phil and Ella were currently tangled around each other beside the table of booze. I propelled myself in the direction of the newly joined. Smile in place, I cleared my throat and disturbed the little 'moment' they were sharing.

"Hey Georgia," Phil said and slung an arm around Ella. "Meet my wife!" Ella giggled. I gagged.

"Congratulations guys," I leaned in for a little half-hearted air kiss. "Just wanted you both to know Jade and I are heading out."

"You're leaving?" Phil said and slugged back another glass of champagne.

I resisted the urge to grab him and give him a firm shake. Instead I decided to try the tactics that work on Payton. I held his eyes to the point of discomfort and willed him to FOCUS. "Your guests will be arriving at the reception any moment now." Phil stared vacantly at me.

"The reception immediately follows the ceremony." I spoke slowly hoping he was hearing me. "There is no one at the house to meet your guests."

Phil mulled that information for a moment, "Oh yeah... good thought." He nodded in agreement and lifted a bottle of champagne from the table. He refilled his glass and then Ella's while smiling adoringly into her eyes. They intertwined their arms and savored a long slow drink. I watched as they lowered their glasses, murmured sappy love talk, and shared a gentle kiss.

For cryin' out loud. I noisily cleared my throat. *It was either that or slug Phil upside his head to regain his attention.* "Phil? Reception..."

"Right Georgia.... reception," he nodded.

"I will head back to the house with Jade. Gavin needs to take Heath to the rental place for the grill." I paused and waited for his brain to catch up. "The grill Phil, you know to cook the food at the reception... which is, um, **now**!" Ella reached for a fresh glass of sparkly, hesitated a micro-second, and then grabbed a full bottle of champagne. I gawked, as she strolled away unconcerned over the details of the grill lacking reception. Phil, wearing a perpetually goofy grin, watched Ella until the crowd swallowed her. I waited until finally his gaze returned to me. "Grill," I said firmly.

He lifted the bottle of champagne, "Yeah well, *here's the thing...,*" he topped off his glass once again then drank the final swig from the bottle. "I reserved the grill, but I need $60.00 to pick it up. Do you have any money along?"

"No I don't," not a moment of hesitation, "Didn't even grab my purse.*" I was telling lies on the lawn of the church. How can one branch of the family tree be so stunted?* In a tone reserved for the weary I said, "You need to come up with a plan, Phil." *Cripes, it was endless.*

I made a beeline for Clare, Catheryn, and Heath who stood together on the outskirts of the lawn. Casually I approached Clare and whispered, "Just giving you a heads up – the grill is reserved but not paid for. The groom needs $60.00"

"Not a chance," Clare said on reflex. I shuddered as her face contorted for a fraction of a second into an expression that I have seen Mom wear in times of utmost disgust. *Frightening really.*

"Umm, you're scaring me Clare."

"I just did a Mom face didn't I?"

I watched her warily and nodded.

"Good grief," Clare visibly shook. "I know what I just looked like. Sorry," she said sincerely and stepped away from me. In a discreet undertone she informed Heath that the grill was not paid for.

"Humph," Heath offered. *We were all fresh out of tolerance.* "Guess we'll all be a little hungry," was his flat response.

"Yep," Clare crossed her arms over her chest and grimaced. I tell you, the hair on my neck was standing at full attention. I shuddered harshly and drew Clare's attention. She caught my expression and softened, "Sorry Georgia."

The milling of guests continued. I had never seen wedding guests so content to stand on a church lawn and not be in any hurry to move on to the reception. Uncle Nathan and wife had completed a full circle and were approaching our group.

Meet-the-woman-I-replaced-your-aunt-with intros, comin' up!

I certainly had not consumed enough alcohol to pull this off. I made an attempt to busy myself with the boys who were engrossed in a game of tag. Over my shoulder I observed the wife. Ironically she looked a lot like Hontie-natural, earthy, wearing a no muss no fuss navy blue dress which hung to her ankles. The dress had simple lines, smock styled, and with it she wore basic flat leather sandals. She appeared to be the kind of woman I'd like under different circumstances. Her nervous smile and hesitant handshake won her more points, as she clearly understood her role at today's wedding. Some honors, regardless of where the cards ended up, belonged to the mother, not the wife. Willing to cut her a little slack I surveyed the lawn for Mom and Hontie. I found them both deeply involved in other conversations and at a relatively safe distance. I stepped toward Uncle Nathan and wife keeping myself two feet out of 'friendly and inviting conversation' territory. Her name was Barb. I nodded a polite hello, nice to meet you and then promptly returned my attention to Brennan and Payton running in the grass behind me.

Heath engaged Barb in appropriate conversation and masked any awkwardness well. He then turned his focus on Uncle Nathan which left Clare alone with Barb. Dangerous ground with Mom and Hontie just a few yards across the lawn. I chuckled, as I watched Clare step even closer to Barb. Led by nervous energy combined with the comfort of flanking family, Clare leaned in, admired Barb's dress and asked her about her occupation. Barb responded to Clare's kindness and quickly the two of them were chatting away.

Classic Clare, I settled in for the show. I could read the uneasiness lurking in her eyes, as manners led her quickly in way over her head with Barb. Clare didn't need or want this much information. Her body temperature had spiked causing her cheeks to pink slightly. No one else would have picked up on the inner turmoil Clare was battling. I, however, watched closely as she kept one eye on Mom and Hontie still busy with their buddies by the steps while nodding politely at Barb. If Mom glanced this way even for a millisecond, Clare would be in big time hot water. *Yes the younger sibling in me secretly anticipated that moment.*

A cool breeze rustled, reminding me we were definitely in upstate New York. Everyone clutched their arms to stay off the chill and from the corner of my eye, I watched in slow motion horror as Uncle Nathan turned toward Clare. "You're cold," I read his lips to say.

Clare smiled as she rubbed her arms, "No, I'm fine."

"Take my jacket," Uncle Nathan gallantly shrugged out of his coat.

Clare held up both hands, "No really," her wild eyes darted in the direction of Mom, "I'm fine." I turned my attention fully on Clare knowing manners would not help her wiggle out of this predicament.

"Oh Clare, just take it for a moment." Uncle Nathan slipped the jacket over Clare's shoulders, as Barb looked on proudly, "Just warm up a bit."

"Oh dear," Clare gave a nervous giggle followed by a defeated, "Really, I'm good."

"There," Uncle Nathan squeezed Clare's shoulders oblivious to her discomfort. "That's better." He turned his attention to his wife who was observing the distant hill side intently. Barb pointed something out and together they walked a few feet away and chatted about the distinguishing characteristics of the landscape. Head hanging like a whipped dog, Clare stood silently. Her expression said it all – I'm so dead.

I had to work hard to swallow the laughter that bubbled up inside of me. I could hardly contain myself. This was a Hall of Fame moment for every youngest sister. You wait years to find your older sibling in a tangle of trouble that only you can help resolve. Finally... you have all the power. *Do you help?* I walked toward Clare grinning.

"Georgia," she whimpered to me behind the painted smile. "Help me."

I noticed Uncle Nathan and Barb returning. "Sorry I'm enjoying the moment much too much." I passed her and sidled up to Heath and Catheryn. Gavin joined the group and placed his hand on Heath's shoulder.

"Hey Heath I hear we need to make a road trip." Gavin said.

"Yeah and I hear we've got no funds," Heath answered.

"What?" Gavin scanned our faces in hopes of an explanation. None came.

I turned to look over my shoulder and watched Clare extract herself from Uncle Nathan's jacket under the pretense of leaving for the reception. She thanked him as he reached out for the jacket and visibly relaxed, as he gently took his wife by the elbow and led her off for more social time. Dabbing the sweat from her forehead, Clare flicked one last glance toward Mom and crossed to me.

"Very slick," I laughed.

"Yeah funny," She rolled her eyes. "Much too close for comfort," she shuddered. "What's the status on the grill?"

"Same... no money, no grill."

"Won't the one hundred guests be surprised?" Clare said flippantly.

High functioning Joe lumbered across the lawn with a bottle of champagne in his hand. He slapped Gavin companionably on the arm and held out the bottle. In the true spirit of party *on dude,* Gavin lifted the bottle and swallowed deeply. "Hey Hheatthh," Joe slurred, "yall mind it if I ride to the rental place wit cha?" Our eyes fixed on Joe as he garbled on, "I got $180 bucks wit me and figures we should see if any tables and chairs 'vailable to rent while we at it."

We stood collectively slack jawed staring at Joe. Once again, the last person you would expect on the bride and groom's personal friend list to come through, and he was about to come through **big.**

"Joe," Clare stepped up, "that is not your responsibility." She said in hushed voice.

"Yeah, but I been Phil's bud long enough." Joe shook his head with understanding. "These details 'scape him," he lifted his shoulders in a negligent shrug then slugged from the champagne bottle.

"You do realize you'll never be paid back," Catheryn laid a consoling hand on Joe's arm.

Joe looked at her and gave her a firm nod and accepted his fate like a captain going down with his ship. I was amazed once again at the length people would go to ensure this event was a success. "Cats," I said more to myself then anyone else. "They always land on their feet." *Enough!* I turned and watched my boys, as they laughed and rolled over the grass. No permanent scarring evident from these last three days. "Hey boys," I called, "Saddle up."

"Mommy," Payton's delighted voice shouted, "I tackled Bren again and again!" The grass stains over his pant legs were proof of that. "I am the most powerful of all little brothers!"

"Wonderful honey," I smiled down at him and tossed a wink to Brennan. "Most powerful huh?" Brennan raised his shoulders in an absent gesture. "We're out of here." Their chorus of hoorays rang out. I made eye contact with Clare and Catheryn and I tossed them a hitchhiker thumb.

"Right behind you," Clare said. I trailed the boys to the Jeep where Jade and Davis stood waiting.

With the kids secured in the back seat, Jade and I climbed up front. Jade buckled in then started to punch straws into the juice boxes for the boys. "Exhausting… right?"

"Total understatement," I started the car then realized my feet wouldn't reach the pedals. I pulled the lever to slide my seat forward and something rolled and bumped my heels. I leaned forward and swiped my hand under the seat. My fingers touched the smooth cool surface of a glass bottle. With a final stretch I unearthed a very large, very empty bottle of wine. "Nice." I handed it to Jade who tucked it securely under her feet.

"Heath and Gavin headed to the rental place?" she asked while handing the boys their drinks.

"Yep, thanks to Joe." I adjusted the rearview mirror. "Payton, stop touching Davis, please. Let him drink his juice."

"Joe?" Jade asked with surprise.

"Yep, wallet attached to friend to the rescue. Phil had no money – surprise of the century – and the grill hasn't been pre-paid."

"Not pre-paid? What? Was cooking the salmon optional?"

"Well refrigerating it was."

"What?" Alarm packed Jade's whisper.

"Phil brought it over yesterday in a cooler, no ice, and left it sitting on the porch for the entire day. When it finally was squeezed into the fridge late yesterday afternoon, all was well, until Heath unplugged and moved the fridge last night to paint the wall."

"Oh no," Jade said.

"Yep you guessed it. He forgot to plug it back in. I found the plug draped across the top of the fridge this morning when I got up."

"Classic," Jade said.

"Yep. Don't eat the salmon."

"On that."

"Finished mommy," Brennan handed up the empty juice boxes.

"Good. Now all of you close your eyes and take a nice rest until we get back to Hontie's." Jade and I exchanged the 'yeah right' mom look.

Jade closed her eyes and took a deep breath, "So what if there was no Joe?" she said wistfully.

"There's always a Joe. They've built their lives around and on Joes," I realized.

A long moment of silence passed, when Jade muttered, "We're all Joes."

"Yep, in one form or another, we are all Joes."

Chapter 18

It turned out the straw that broke the camel's back, was worth about $800.00.

I pulled the Jeep on the lawn and as predicted, guests had begun to arrive and were wandering around the driveway. I prayed Jade and I didn't look like we were the event planners.

"Now what do we do?" Jade watched, as more guests pulled up to the house.

"We take the kids and go through the deck."

"Hide... good plan." Jade lifted a sleepy Davis from his car seat, as more cars pulled in to the property.

Brennan climbed out of the car. "Okay boys," I deliberately kept my voice down, "inside." We moved stealth-like toward the deck. Once inside I whispered to Brennan, "The ground is still way too muddy from the rain, so we are going to go upstairs and change out of your good clothes."

"Why are you whispering, Mom?" Brennan asked.

"Because I don't want the guests to think that I am in charge?"

"In charge of what?" His voice rose innocently.

"Shh... honey," Jade giggled, as she and Davis headed for the front stair case. I ducked into the laundry room bound for the back steps. Well out of the earshot of meandering guests I said, "Okay Brennan, the reception is the big party with food, drinks, and music to celebrate Phil and Ella's marriage." We hurried up the stairs and into the back bedroom. "Usually the events of the day are planned with precise detail. **Usually**, the bride and groom take extra steps to assure their guests are comfortable, while everyone celebrates together."

I heard the voices from the guests in the driveway trickling through the open second floor window. Confusion was clear as they discussed where to go and what to do. One lady remarked about how lovely the adjacent field looked, so she felt confident that they were at least at the right home. "Oh it doesn't matter Brennan, let's just change our clothes and go down to the deck and try to salvage some moment worth remembering that doesn't involve remodeling." *Cripes!*

I looked over to where Payton was struggling to remove his shirt. It needed to be unbuttoned first, but he had tugged over his head and pulled one arm free. The shirt had become lodged tightly around his throat. Brennan and I stood silently and watched him struggle. Payton led himself in endless circles like a dog chasing his tail. Finally he stepped on the edge of the air mattress and toppled face first with a splat. That snapped me out of my trance, "Oh Payton!" I kneeled on the mattress nearly ejecting him from the inflate-a-bed. "Let me help you," I started to laugh, as I unbuttoned his collar and wrestled him free.

"Whew Mommy, I was stuck!" Payton said.

"You sure were! Let's get your warm clothes on." I dug through the suitcase. "Here Bren," I tossed him pants and a long sleeve shirt. "Payton honey, hop up here on the big bed, so I can help you."

Jade knocked lightly on the adjoining door, "You decent?" She called.

"Yep, come in. Brennan hand me those wedding clothes, and please put your sweat shirt on too."

"Mom," he whined, "it's not even cold."

"Just take it down to the deck for later." He huffed but picked up the sweatshirt. "Thanks honey. Hold Payton's hand on those steps. Better yet, have him sit and slide down a step at a time." I pulled on my denim shirt, as Jade poked her head in the bedroom.

"I guess we can't hide out forever," she said with a smile.

"Can't we?" I flopped down on the mattress. "Someone who knows what's going on should be along soon."

"From your lips," Jade said, as she shifted Davis on her hip. She crossed to the window overlooking the driveway. "Looks like a few more car loads of guests have arrived." She turned to me and shrugged her shoulders, "We better go down."

I resigned myself to be a joiner and followed Jade downstairs. The kitchen was empty, so I went out to the field to check to make sure everything was okay.

Perhaps I had spent the morning viewing the field through jaundice eyes or the post-nuptial champagne had rewarded me with rose colored glasses. The field was stunning. Absolutely breathtaking. The simple acre field had become a fairy tale vision effortless in its simplicity, yet surprisingly bold and nearly sophisticated. The trees on the property border appeared expertly manicured creating a foliage frame around the walkway to the field. I walked carefully remembering how slick the mud had become before we had left for the ceremony, only to discover large nugget mulch now lined the path and the morning rain mud had vanished. White tent canopies in various sizes and heights dotted the acres edge and added to the casual elegance of the scene. A few picnic tables had been draped with the colorful cloths Mom had sewn and a line of small card tables were set up for food. Beneath one small tent a four gallon glass jar rested on a card table. Four inches of dark red liquid sat in the bottom of the jar along with countless slices of oranges, lemons and limes. The beginning of a fine Sangria.

The antique room divider from Hontie's shop stood proudly under the smallest canopy along with a small table. Crafted from metal ceiling tiles, the divider was incredibly beautiful. A good working space for Sylvia had never presented itself this morning, so no cake sat on the table. In the far corner of the field under the largest canopy I could see my Grandmother's china elegantly placed in a service for six. Two red tapered candles stood in the center of the table in anticipation of the new Mr. and Mrs.

The oversized sap bucket bouquets provided an eruption of riotous color throughout the field. Mom and Clare's mid-night assembly project, the twelve inch pinwheels, were grouped by threes and fours inside glass mason jars. Each pinwheel was made of colorful scrapbook paper and mounted on a wooden dowel rod with hardware that allowed it to spin freely. Calligraphy tags were attached to the center of each pinwheel lettered with Phil and Ella's names and the ceremony date and time. The unique handmade favors were the perfect touch and when added to the whole, they helped to create a snap shot worthy of any bridal magazine.

The tall trees failed to provide enough wind protection, as a rushing breeze blew across the field. Pinwheels whirled rapidly threatening to become airborne, as tablecloths fiercely fluttered tipping mason jars over. Fortunately alert guests grabbed them before they rolled and shattered on the ground. I sat the jar closest to me upright and replaced the trio of pin wheels back inside. As the wind settled, I released my breath, tragedy avoided. As I turned, my heart sank. *Disaster.*

The room divider had fallen and had flattened the small table. I rushed across the grass quickly and kneeled beside it. Despite the screen's size and weight, I struggled to stand it up. I had made no progress when an unknown guest hurried over to lend me a hand. "Thanks," I told him when we reached upright position. "OH NO!" The metal ceiling tiles pulled apart.

"I think the fall damaged it," he reached down to straighten it. "Will it stand on its own?" Lifting the last panel we did our best to prop it in a secure position. *Yes, the wind was not controlled by the tornadic force that seemed to surround Ella and Phil, but I was staring at an $800.00 price tag for cryin' out loud.* **$800.00.** My heart was in my throat.

For some reason, even though it was a single loss in an extremely long list of casualties, for me it was the final straw. My patience went from simmer to boil in an instant. It really had little to do with the divider and more the culmination of events over the last three days. I was so done... off duty. I would not stand around and wait to see what possibly could happen next. I left the field in search of the sanctuary that was my direct blood line. When I reached the field entrance, I found myself face to face with Sylvia's friend, Jewel. Still dressed in her wedding attire, her tiny frame bustled toward me. Jewel had that grandmotherly air of comfort surrounding her and I needed a fix. She quickly closed the distance between us, and I took a moment to allow her peace to seep into me.

"Hello Georgia dear," she said.

"Hi there yourself, Jewel. Are you enjoying the day?"

"Oh very much," she smiled warmly and linked her arm through mine. Together we stood looking over the reception field. "It is a picture, isn't it? You've all outdone yourselves."

"As my brother says, that's what families do," sarcasm tainted my weary words.

"Not all," Jewel turned and placed her hand on my cheek. "Not all." Her gaze moved back to the field. "Lovely."

"Well here's an insider's tip;" I threaded my arm through hers and we stepped into the field. "See the handful of tables and chairs?" I turned my attention back to Jewel, "Not enough for everyone. Tell whomever you know who needs a seat to snatch one while they can." *It was like the flippin' Titanic. Not enough lifeboats and we were sinking fast!* "And Jewel, one last thing… stick with the beef."

I left Jewel to fend for herself and walked around the back of the house to the safety of the deck. As I walked up the winding path, I found that this once mud slicked path now too had been covered with a layer of fresh mulch. Where had it come from? *Fairy dust? Sprinkle! Sprinkle!* On the deck I found Clare, Catheryn, and Heath seated comfortably. They had changed clothes and sat in tight ranks with expressions of varied disinterest. "You guys having a sit-in?" I asked.

"More like sit-out," Clare crossed her arms defiantly.

"Yeah, I can get behind that idea. In fact I arrived at that point just a moment ago when I picked up Hontie's $800.00 very broken room divider in the field."

"No," Clare gasped, "the ceiling tile one?"

"The very one." My butt had barely touched the bench when Tom appeared in front of me. He balanced a tray holding four lovely frosty beers.

"I decided to begin your flow of alcohol and continue it for as long as you need it." He said with a twinkling smile.

"Could be a long night for you," I accepted the drink. "Thank you," I took a long, refreshing sip. "I need to find my boys."

"Beverages are under control," Tom said as he handed glasses to Heath, Clare, and Catheryn. "Georgia?" Tom turned back to me, "Sueanne has Payton over there with Drew, and Brennan has the soccer ball over there with Meg."

Amazed and speechless, I just stared at him. "Thanks Tom and I mean for it all." I made an encompassing gesture. "The bathroom cleanup, pin wheels, our family china, you and Sueanne were busy while we were out." Remembering the mud-less walking paths, I raised my brow, "Mulch?" Tom nodded. "Great thinking."

"Don't mention it," he clinked his glass to mine then vanished off the deck.

Clare sipped her beer, slowly wrinkling her nose. "If only this were a margarita." She sipped again. "You know if Tom and Sueanne weren't here... I'd be nuts."

"Yeah you're sane." I enjoyed the peacefulness of our little deck haven. It appeared as if the guests had all arrived from the chapel. The buzz of conversations and party atmosphere filled the air. The crowd was nicely dispersed in and around the home and gardens. The deck was just enough out of the mainstream and suited us just fine. Through the glass doors I could see Ella in the kitchen managing the food crew. *Odd, the bride prepping food?* Like a gourmet production I watched ten or more friends of the bride and groom swarm like little worker bees within the newly finished kitchen. Plating fresh grapes and berries surrounded by a trio of cheeses and thin slices of bread. Filling tumblers of pickles and olives. *Where were these able bodied devoted-to-the-cause friends the last several days?*

As if reading my mind, Clare muttered, "They were attending lake front bachelor parties and rehearsal dinners."

"Humph, Right you are." I tried to return my attention to my beer when I spotted Mom, as she wove her way through the maze of bodies in the kitchen. Clearly on a mission she stopped and stood at the deck door inspecting each of us in turn. I tried not to make eye contact. I knew our collective relaxed postures complete with frosty beverages in hand would not please her. I felt her eyes bore down on me.

"Georgia I could use your hands a minute. En la casa, rapido!" Mom said then she turned and disappeared into the kitchen.

Sucks being the youngest.

"Why me?" I looked at Heath who negligently shrugged his shoulders. "I mean there are four of us sitting here." Resigned, I rose to follow Mom into bedlam.

Clare smiled over the rim of her cup, "good luck with that." I resisted the urge to stick out my tongue at her but did take a second to envision her stuck in Uncle Nathan's jacket. My soul immediately brightened.

I joined Mom in the dining room where the oak table had become the gift table. A tasteful basket sporting hemp twine and bow like the ones on the sap buckets sat off to one side with a few envelopes inside. Fingering the bow on one of the wrapped packages, I spoke to Mom. "Okay I am in the *'casa'* Mom, what do you need?" She ignored my flippant shot at Spanish, as she busied herself with the pile of tablecloths stacked on the rattan chair by the window. "Those cloths are really beautiful, Mom."

"..dos, tres, muy Bonita si, quatro…" In moments of extreme stress Mom had a tendency to grasp firmly to small tasks in an effort to maintain a morsel of control. Usually the tension would result in a nervous energy that would cause her voice to raise a few decibels. She could become so intently focused that it was difficult to break into her zone. Currently the task of choice seemed to be tablecloths. Mom had been raised attending formal affairs both small and large. A proper etiquette upbringing had yielded far more social nuances than using forks from the outside in. And even though I appreciate that the smallest accent can make an occasion spectacular, it seemed obvious to everyone except Mom that the gypsy/bohemian handbook clearly skipped over etiquette. Tablecloths really, an hour ago there were only a handful of tables. *Cripes.*

"No lujo por time-o!" Mom yelled in my direction.

"Mom," I gentled my voice, "English, please."

"Pardona," she smiled tightly. "Heath and Gavin rented tables. I have no idea at what expense or who footed the bill." With a shake of her head she dismissed any possible discussion. "Sueanne was to empty a few factory bins from the bathroom to serve the bread. I guess Clare forgot to tell her." A tsk tsk followed. "You will take care of that," she paused and deliberately lowered her voice. "We need to bring the table around for 'torta' assembly and then help put out the last of the rented tables and chairs." She turned and lifted an armful of tablecloths from the dining room chair, "Once arranged, we'll put out the 'serville-tas'..."

I hadn't a clue what a torta was, let alone a serville-tas! When Mom stopped for a breath of air I waved my hands in the universal 'cut'. I proceeded cautiously, "Mom, I'm done. You're done. Clare, Heath, Catheryn... all done." She looked pained. "Grab a glass of wine," I told her, "find a seat, and enjoy the show."

Mom looked at me as if **I** were speaking a foreign language. So I tried it. "El Done-o, consum-o some wine-o." *Not funny.*

"Oh... just a few last minute details," Mom said then flopped the cloths back on the table and began to count them again. *Hello! The whole wedding was a last minute detail.*

Still, the youngest child always wanted to please, so I relented. "Okay Mom, I'll get the bins for the bread, but that's it; I'm finished."

"Muchas gracias Georgia. I'll work on tables and tablecloths. Muy Bien," she hustled back through the kitchen, arms loaded with table linen.

In the bathroom I admired the factory bins Hontie had stacked along side the tub. I remembered when she bought them at Bouckville a few years ago. The bins were probably used to sort items along an assembly line. They were a lovely shade of robin's egg green and were impressively heavy. Stacked on top of one another the bins were used to hold towels, shampoo and other bathroom necessities. I attempted to condense the bath essentials into the bottom bin and still have the room look nice. I successfully emptied the top two bins and lifted them to carry them into the kitchen. It was only then that I noticed the spilled shampoo and loose hair lying in the bottom of the bins. *Yuk.* Out to the kitchen I traipsed with the filthy bins. Sylvia saw me coming, "Oh Georgia darling, been looking for those love," she took them from me and moved to the far corner of the kitchen.

I stood amazed at the amount of bodies in the kitchen. They moved like a seasoned staff in a world class restaurant. Glass tumblers were being filled with olives and pickles at one station, and at another station stacks of stark white luncheon plates sat awaiting fruit and cheese. Carefully I weaved my way through the workers and followed Sylvia to the small table which overflowed with dozens of straight-from-the-bakery rolls. White bakery paper bags mounded on the verge of spilling to the floor. Hard crusted, multi-grain, poppy seed were just a few of the varieties I recognized.

"Sylvia?" I whispered since we were in the company of multiple food goddesses. "The bins really needed to be washed." I reached past her arm and pointed to the shampoo and gunk in the bottom of the bin.

Sylvia flipped the tub over and gave it a solid whack on the bottom and grabbed the roll of paper towels. "#//*- it darling, this will have to do."

Frankly I agreed 100%... with the #//*-it part anyway.

I watched in horror as she proceeded to line the tubs with paper and without pause tossed in the fresh rolls.

Taking a cue from the resident stage actress, I exited stage left. My crew of blood relatives sat right where I had left them on the deck with fresh brews in hand

"How's it going in there?" Clare asked me, as she gestured to the house with her full glass of beer.

"Mom is spewing mucho Spanish-o and counting tablecloths." Groans sounded from the group. "Oh and a serious health alert, don't eat the bread in the factory bins folks. The bins needed to be washed out, hair, shampoo, use your imagination."

"Gross," Clare said. "No bread from the factory bins... got it."

"Add it to the list," Catheryn itemized, "salmon, bread, shrimp..."

"...and raspberries," Clare finished.

"Here you go." Startled I turned to find a fresh brew for me and a smile from Tom. *Heaven.* I looked out into the garden and saw Payton and Drew having the time of their lives like long-lost-little buddies. Brennan however, was out of sight.

Heath caught the concern in my eyes. "Other side of the house," he said.

"Okay thanks," I relaxed a little.

Just then a chill swept over the deck, followed by the staccato clipping of stiletto heels. Goose bumps decorated my arms and the air temperature dropped enough, so I could see my breath puff out. I willed my body to turn. Sure enough Somi, the Abominable Snow Bitch, had joined us. She passed an equally divided look of disgust at all of us and then strutted to the ice chests. She flipped open both lids, peered inside, then slammed them closed again. As she whirled around, her inky black hair appeared Medusa-like and her eyes narrowed to evil slits. "I guess it crossed no one's mind here today to actually put the sodas in the coolers, so they would be cold and ready for the reception," she seethed through her teeth.

Momentarily stunned, Clare and Catheryn sat gaping at her. Heath calmly lifted his beer to his lips, but his penetrating stare spoke volumes. For a moment he was Officer Heath quietly waiting for the tantrum of some half crazed lunatic to pass.

Lacking Heath's control, I sucked in a huge breath and prepared to blast the frost queen back to Arctic Hell. "You know what Somi…" That was all I got out before Heath stood. His body rapidly unfolded from the chair and all eyes moved to him.

"I'll help you carry the coolers to the field." He handed his beer to Catheryn, stacked one cooler on top of the other, and hoisted them effortlessly.

I watched Somi morph into an object of male attention. Her eyes batted playfully and her voice answered breathlessly, "Oh thanks, Heath." Her body language added, 'you're so big and strong.' *Bitch*. Heath moved off the deck with Somi trailing. We watched until they were out of view.

"Can you believe her?" Catheryn stood and paced. "The coolers would not be here if I hadn't gotten them or the ice for that matter, which Tom got to prevent food poison."

"Never in my life," Clare broke in, "have I ever encountered another person who matches the rudeness and disrespect of that woman."

"Woman?" I said, "Call her what she is, please, a bitch."

"Maybe we should offer her the unrefrigerated salmon," Catheryn said quietly.

Heath stalked back to the deck without a word. We watched, intimidated by his militant posture and fierce expression. He grabbed his beer, tipped it to his mouth. He sighed heavily, "That's the closest I've ever come to actually punching a woman in the face."

He was so serious that I couldn't suppress the laugh that burst past my lips. Clare, Catheryn and I howled like the looneys we were becoming. Catheryn even added a very lady like snort to the first round of beer buzz giggles.

"Mommy?" Brennan approached us warily.

"Yes Honey," I reached my hand out to him, "You have fun playing with Meg?"

"Yeah, but I really got a headache."

"You do?" I motioned him over and felt his head. "I think you're a little warm. Let Aunt Clare feel your head."

He stepped over to Clare, "Yep, I think you're right."

"All I have is Advil," I looked at him, "pills." His eyes went large. "Do you think you can swallow a grown-up pill?"

"I'll try," he sounded a little unsure.

"I'll get the water;" Catheryn hopped to action. "You sit with Aunt Clare 'til your mom gets back.

"Heath," Clare whispered, "you don't think he drank anything do you?" Heath stared at her blankly. "You know, A-L-C-O-H-O-L."

"Brennan," Heath said, firmly causing Clare to jump as well as Brennan. "Did you consume any alcohol today?"

Startled Brennan looked from Uncle Heath to Aunt Clare with a combination of fear and confusion on his face.

Clare rolled her eyes at Heath's attempted interrogation. Softly she leaned toward Brennan and clarified, "Drink any drinks that weren't for kids."

"There aren't any drinks for kids," he said honestly.

"Which is why we are asking, sweetie. Did you drink **anything**?"

"No."

"That is probably the problem then," Heath said. "He's dehydrated."

I fetched my purse and dug out the Advil, just as Catheryn returned with the water. "Just one, right?" I asked Clare. She nodded. "Okay buddy, it's just like swallowing food. Just put it on your tongue and drink normally and it will go right down."

Brennan followed my instructions, swallowing, swallowing... He started shaking his head and looked at me as he extended his tongue. Pill.

"Tip your head back," Catheryn suggested.

"Fill your mouth with water first," Clare advised, "then lean forward."

We all circled him offering wisdom and encouragement watching him, as he followed all our suggestions. Brow furrowed, and head shaking, he extended his tongue. **Pill.** Eight minutes and countless suggestions later, success... No pill!

"Well done honey," I gave Brennan a hug. "Now it will take twenty minutes for it to affect the headache. Try to take it easy, okay? We'll get you some food shortly."

"Okay Mom," he slid off the bench to the decking where Sasha had stretched out, as if one hundred people dropped in to visit every day.

Two pre-teen female wedding guests sauntered out onto the deck. *What was it with teen fashion these days?* One girl had on a micro mini-skirt which hung off her non-too-mini derriere, while a-three-sizes-too small t-shirt stretched to the maximum around her upper half. The other girl wore low-rise pants with jeweled edged bell bottoms. Multiple chain styled belts wrapped from her hips upward to where the strapless halter top ended about three inches above her pierced belly button. She reached up to adjust her sequined beret, as her jaw moved like a bovine working her gum. The girls clomped over to pet the dog and cats, the only give away to their true age. Together they stood teetering on their four inch trend-setter sling backs. They blew a pair of huge pink bubbles and dismounted the deck. "Where are the parents?" Clare wondered out loud, and shook her head in judgment.

"They're just trying to find themselves," Catheryn said. She had worked in youth advisory facilities after college and always was the champion of teens discovering themselves. "Youth to adult is a long bumpy trail of personal discovery and growth."

I cleared my throat, "Well, I discovered some upper thigh leading to butt cheek and a whole lot of shoulder and soon to be cleavage."

Brennan looked up from petting Sasha, "what's beeclevage?"

Heath masked his chuckle in a cough. *Time to change the subject*, "Are you hungry Bren? Want to go get something to eat? How's your head?" *Pick one, just skip the beeclevage, I prayed.*

"I'm not hungry yet, Mommy." Brennan stood and stretched. Sasha lifted her massive head, and he obliged her by leaning down for one final scratch. "I'm going to walk out and see if I can find the other kids."

"Alright," I watched him go. "Is anybody going for appetizers?"

"Thinking about it." Catheryn grabbed Heath's knee, "We need to get some food and soak up some of this alcohol, honey." Heath turned his expressionless face towards his wife, nodded then linked his fingers with hers.

"I'm starved," Clare answered honestly, "but I'm afraid if we go to the field there will be things that need to be done."

The hip-hop girls returned to the deck and announced, "Anyone who wants to watch Ella and Phil get married should go over to the barn now." Strutting their stuff, the girls vanished into the house.

I shared a baffled look with my family, as a group of guests moved across the deck in route to the barn.

"Fairly certain I've already done that." Heath said.

Catheryn's brow quirked; "I'm not too sure." We watched, as more guests passed through the kitchen and out the mudroom door. Bringing up the rear of the conga line were Jade and Gavin. Gavin pulled Jade toward the deck bench and sat next to Clare.

"Detour with the normal people," Jade said, as she sat on Gavin's lap. She smiled weakly, but her expression said it all. This day had no end to its absurdity.

"Dare we ask?" Clare said.

"Yeah what's the deal?" Catheryn asked them.

"J.P. is here to make it official," Gavin said. *Of course he was.*

"Why wasn't the chapel official enough?" I inquired.

"Something about the minister not having valid credentials," Jade said with a shrug. *Of course he didn't.*

"Oh and P.S., the groom needs sixty bucks to pay the J.P.", Jade added dryly. *Of course he does.*

We sat in united silence, resigned to the fact that this bohemian lifestyle and all that entails will never be decipherable by mainstreamers.

"Where's Davis?" Clare asked.

"There are so many people here that haven't seen him in awhile and want to hold him that we are actually getting a break." Jade stood and pulled Gavin to his feet. "We have a wedding to attend." Gavin shrugged but dutifully followed Jade through the kitchen. Heath, Clare, Catheryn, and I watched them go but made no effort to follow. Heath sighed hugely and settled more deeply into his canvas camp chair.

"You know this probably would be the ideal time to hit the appetizers," Clare said.

"Might be the only safe thing to eat all night," I reminded them.

"True," Catheryn said, and then she reached out and took both of Heath's hands. "Ready?"

"You go ahead. I'll be right behind you." Heath said. I noted that alcohol added to his exhaustion was causing him to take on the form of the chair.

Clare stood and straightened her tipsy self and followed Catheryn to the steps. "Whew, if Tom keeps up the beverage service, we may be tanked before sundown." Clare giggled.

I smiled as I noted Clare's sway, "Which is happening quickly." *The sunset and the tanked.* "Coming?" I asked Heath. "You really need to eat something."

Heath motioned to the dining room window; "Check that out."

Turning, I could see into the dining room where gifts covered the oak table surface and the basket sat overflowing with cards for the happy couple. Phil was hunched over the table ripping open envelope after envelope in search of fast cash. I watched, as he peeked in each card, removed money, and rammed it into his pants pocket. *Classic. Even unsuspecting guests were footing the bill for the events of the day.*

"Groom needs sixty bucks," Heath muttered, as he unfolded himself from the chair.

"Yeah, well he better hurry or he'll be late for his second ceremony too." *Cripes.*

Chapter 19

I have learned from much practice that Lamaze breathing and prayer will see you through nearly everything.

My trip to the field proved more magical than the last. Tables of varying sizes and shapes now dotted the center of the lawn and were draped with colorful cloths. Guests were enticed with tumblers filled with pickles and olives and plates of cheeses and sliced breads. People conversed in clusters throughout the field while they enjoyed the food and drinks.

Heath, Catheryn, Clare, and I worked the length of food tables adjacent to the field's edge. Large platters of sliced tomatoes dressed with olive oil, mozzarella, and basil sprigs; stainless steel bowls of large shrimp with cocktail sauce; and trays piled with fresh fruit were just a handful of the choices offered. *The food goddesses really knew what they were doing.* Farther down the line the questionably sanitary factory bins sat loaded with rolls awaiting the beef brisket. In the corner of the field an enormous grill loomed. Ominous, the stainless steel giant looked like it could handle food for one hundred no problem. *So glad it got picked up!* More men than could possibly be productive were layering charcoal in the belly of the beast in preparation for cooking. I saw High Functioning Joe at the forefront leading the lighter fluid brigade. *Safe.* Fumes filled the air, prompting me to quickly grab a second bunch of grapes and encourage my siblings to high tail it back to the deck.

"If you had just arrived, you'd think you had entered a well planned affair," Clare said with her plate balanced on her lap. She lifted a pineapple wedge to her lips, "Tents and tables plopped down as if some high dollar wedding co-coordinator had arranged every last detail."

I chuckled as Clare tore the pale flesh from the pineapple rind a little more aggressively than necessary.

"Mmm hmm," Catheryn agreed. "It is beautiful... those pinwheels Clare," Catheryn said with awe, "and the tablecloths your Mom made... striking." She held up a slice of plum tomato and slid it into her mouth. "Mmm... delicious."

"Not earned," Heath mumbled around a mouthful of cheese.

He was right.

"But you did have one thing dead-on Heath," I swallowed a grape. "If it involves booze and food, Phil and Ella do it up well." Laughter drew my attention to the lawn where Payton and Drew were playing under Sueanne's watchful eyes. I sat my plate aside and picked up my beer. "I'm going to give Sueanne a break." I stood and could see Mom working in the reception field. Her arms were loaded with something, as she worked in fast forward to accomplish yet another task. "When will Mom realize the effort is over?" I said to Clare.

"She's in the zone," Clare said.

And breaking into the 'zone' is an invitation only event and even if I were to be invited, I wouldn't RSVP.

A few of Phil and Ella's friends hustled past me on the steps. I overheard their rumblings about there being no lights in the field. *Oh, the details.* Seemed tedious at 1:00 to decide where the power supply would need to be in the evening. *The sun had the nerve to set.* **What to do!**

"Freakin' idiots," I muttered under my breath.

"I heard that," Sueanne stepped up to me chuckling. "Georgia, how about I take Payton to my house for a sleep over?"

Well, I certainly hadn't seen that coming. "That's okay. Thanks, though – you've already done more than enough."

"It's really no trouble," she nodded toward the boys. "They are really enjoying each other."

"Yeah, but Payton's never done a sleep over even for relatives. I think I will let them just play it out."

"Alright," she seemed disappointed.

"Why don't you grab some food, Sueanne? I'll watch the little guys."

"That's okay." Her face crooked with humor. "Over the years Tom and I have witnessed the food handling standards of this crew first hand," Sueanne laughed warmly. "Other than the brisket and the brew," she lifted her wine glass, "I'll just say NO."

"How did you get roped into the brisket?" I leaned my hip on a whiskey barrel, "I've been dying to ask."

"I used to run a catering business and I had done this particular brisket recipe for other large affairs," she wiggled her brows; "I sort of have a reputation." Suanne sipped her wine. "When Phil and Ella asked me to prepare the beef, I said sure. My only requirement was that they meet me at the market on a set day and time."

"And they did?" I was amazed. "Punctuality and planning? That was a tall order for the two of them."

Sueanne looked over at our boys wistfully. "They really are children in a lot of ways, our Phil and Ella. They are hungry for boundaries with firm sides." She was full of compassion. "But..." she smiled sheepishly. " I also said if they were even five minutes late, the brisket was a no go."

"Obviously it worked." I was impressed.

"They were actually early." Very impressed.

I eyed Sueanne curiously. A moment later my beer loosened tongue rebelled. "Are you a Fairy?" I snapped my disobedient mouth closed. "I… mean…"

Sueanne's eyes twinkled brightly and a rumble of laughter passed her lips.

I rushed on, "It is just you seem to have this subtle power … " *Shut your mouth Georgia.* "…and you and Tom just fix things and cover details like a wave of a wand." *Cripes Georgia, shut it!*

Sueanne was delighted with the idea. "That would be wonderful; don't you think!" I bit my lips tightly together to avoid further embarrassment and dragged myself back to the deck.

Perfect timing, Tom was handing out another round of beverages. "Thanks." Catheryn and Clare and Heath were still holding down the fort along with Sasha and the cat crew – Trivot, Squeak, and Skitz. "Sasha," Clare patted her head. "You just lie there and watch the traffic pass by."

"I think she's just waiting for a plate to drop," Catheryn commented.

The 'Nuptials-Take-Two' had wrapped up and a few of the round two well wishers were filtering onto the deck. Through the dining room window I viewed Uncle Nathan as he led people through Hontie's home. As if he still lived there, he pointed out antiques and family heirlooms as he conducted the tour. He really seemed quite at ease, as the new wife and perfect children strolled about the ex-wife's property. *Very healthy… not.*

"Has anybody seen Brennan since he took his Advil?" I searched the faces of my siblings. Heads shook all around; "Maybe I should go look for him."

"Just keep still Georgia; he's fine," Catheryn said then wickedly added, "He probably joined the delinquents behind the barn and is toking on his first joint."

"Nice," Heath stared at his wife. A muscle jumped in his cheek and for a moment he nearly smiled.

I tried to relax but couldn't. "I'll be back." I took a lap around the grounds in search of my first born. Dusk was coming quickly. I was having trouble picking out people that I knew let alone people who might know Brennan. Ella's daughter, Meg, walked toward me with a faction of delinquents. "Hey Meg, have you seen Brennan?"

"Nope," Meg stopped in front of me. Before I had a chance to ask her something else...

"Who's she want?" A medium sized kid with white blond hair blurted out, as if I wasn't standing there.

"Her kid," Meg explained, "you know Brennan."

"Never heard of him." He spewed out the words laced with adult-like arrogance. He nudged Meg roughly, "Come on let's go. This is so, not our deal."

My mouth fell open as he started to strut away. I was unable to tolerate anymore rudeness especially from a possibly inebriated eleven year old. "Hey!" I called after him, "Whose kid are you?"

As he spun around, he thrust his hands on his hips, "Somi's." He snottily shot back.

"Cripes she's breeding" I dismissed him and his horrid DNA. "Meg please keep an eye out for Brennan will you? He wasn't feeling well earlier."

"Sure Georgia," Meg smiled, "I will."

Music now pumped from the field. An elaborate sound system had been erected under the largest canopy. White twinkle lights hung in the eaves illuminating space for after dinner dancing. The air was chock-full of delicious scents. Salmon sizzled alongside the roasting corn. Dinner might actually be happening in the near future. The casual time line didn't seem to bother the guests. Everyone appeared to be having a splendid time. I followed the mulch path around the back of the house.

The deck was bursting with bodies. Uncle Nathan, his wife and many others stood enjoying the night. In the middle of the crowded deck Clare stood deep in conversation with our midnight French Canadian arrival, Haw-Haw. Amazingly Haw-Haw's English had become fluent overnight. *Miraculous.* Not feeling social, I opted to stay on the lawn where Payton and Drew had begun a fierce rendition of King of the Mountain on Hontie's garden boulders. Still full of energy the boys were being monitored efficiently by Sueanne and Tom. Some of the delinquents were beneath the trees juggling a hacky –sac.

Out of the corner of my eye, I caught a blur of Mom headed my way. To my horror I saw she had a fully assembled table clutched to her chest. The table legs jutted from the front of her body like an obscure fork lift. *This could not be good.* Quietly I crossed the few steps of lawn separating me from my siblings. Clare's chat with Haw-Haw ended just as I reached the deck railing. "Umm… Clare? We may have a situation." The tone of my voice must have been enough as she turned warily toward me.

"Oh good grief what now," Clare said.

"I'm not quite sure what mission Mom's on, but she's headed this way in a hurry, carrying a table." Heath merely lifted his frothy beverage without comment. A shriek rang out from the back of the house. Catheryn joined Clare to watch helplessly as guests scrambled off the path in fear for their lives.

"Desocupar! Avanzar! Alejarse!" Mom's Spanish Tourette's was in full swing. *Cripes.* I heard Clare and Catheryn giggle at the absurdity as Mom bulldozed up the path. Knowing I was on my own, I braced my feet across the mulch path and prepared to reason with Mom.

"What's up?" I asked casually.

"Step aside Georgia." I had little choice, as the pronged table legs invaded my safety zone. "Sylvia needs to asamblea los tarta," Mom said in a hurry. At my baffled look she translated, "assemble the cake." *Oh, we were back to this again. A nice work area was still needed for Sylvia.*

"You're going to have the cake on the deck?"

"No Georgia," she chastised. "We're going to assemble the cake here and then take it to the field for serving. Now scoot!"

Step aside or be impaled... tough choice. As Mom whizzed by I asked, "So you're going to carry an assembled cake to the field?"

Mom ignored me and swiftly made her way toward the deck. Seconds later she screeched to a halt, as she realized Uncle Nathan and wife were socializing at the top of the steps. Warning sirens were nearly audible, as she spun on her heel and nearly decapitated a random guest. Rapidly Mom retreated and returned to my side, as if the last fifteen seconds hadn't occurred. *Yeah, no one noticed you and the four foot table jutting out the front of your body. For cryin' out loud.*

Mom spotted her first born. "Clare," she called a bit too loudly. Her voice had tightened with the taxing state of affairs. "Take this table."

"What?" Clare's eyes widened, as she took in the full view of the protruding table legs. "Mom come over to the steps," Clare quietly coaxed. "Georgia what's going on?"

"Sylvia needs to assemble the cake." I was a touch flippant. I inclined my head subtly to point out the unmentionables currently standing by the stairs. Clare saw Uncle Nathan and understood that Mom would get this mission accomplished anyway she had to, with the exception of accepting assistance from Uncle Nathan.

Without warning Mom hoisted the entire table up over her head. "For the love of all things...," I muttered in a hushed voice and turned away unable to watch.

"Grab it Clare! **Grab it!**" Mom bellowed.

"Good grief Mom put the table down." Clare's concerned whisper did not have the desired effect. "Heath?" She said persuading him to help.

"You're on your own." Heath said from his chair where he and Catheryn seemed to watch the exchange like a drive-in-movie.

Mom was in the zone!

"**Clare**," Mom yelped out again. "**Reach for it!**" She bounced the inverted table in the air drawing attention of others on the deck.

The need to rescue her overwhelmed me. I put my hand on her arm, "Mom, please."

Uncle Nathan moved across the deck to Clare, his coat wearing ally. "Can I help?" Clare stammered knowing Uncle Nathan's assistance was the absolute last thing Mom would accept. "Isabella, let me help you," Uncle Nathan said, as he stretched over the railing to grasp the table. Mom nimbly lowered the table out of reach. I watched as her eyes darted toward the now unblocked steps. She readjusted the table and scattered guests once again, as she made her break toward them.

Uncle Nathan anticipated her move and met her there. "Here we go Isabella," he said helpfully.

I watched in wide-eyed horror not sure what would happen next. No prediction could even come close to the actuality. As if Uncle Nathan hadn't spoken, Mom clutched the table, spun around, and began to back up the steps.

"I've got it!" she shouted. Undeterred Uncle Nathan was still brave enough to attempt intervention. "**I've got it!**" Mom hopped backwards up the steps clearing the way with her hip and booty. The guests on the deck gave her a wide berth as she cleared the steps, bowled right past Uncle Nathan, and successfully plunked the table down on the deck. "There." Mom straightened and dusted off her hands. Wearing a smile that bordered on institutional, Mom's stress laced voice squealed, "Now to find a cloth and Sylvia." And with that she disappeared into the house leaving us all in shock staring after her.

My gene pool... Lovely.

Conversations amongst the guests resumed, as they filtered off the deck and back to the reception field. I climbed the steps and stood with Clare who shook her head at Mom's actions. *There were no words.* Sasha moved her massive body into the center of the cleared deck. She flopped down, tongue dangling from the side of her mouth. Trivet hopped over and rubbed his head beneath Sasha's huge chin.

In an attempt to cover the peculiar previous events, Uncle Nathan's wife moved toward the canine-feline duo. "Oh, Sandy, you're just such a good girl," Barb cooed as she stroked Sasha's huge head. The three legged cat twined between her legs. "And Tripod still as friendly as ever."

Sandy? Tripod? *Yeah, you're tight with the family.* Note to self: when situations are already understandably, uncomfortable don't speak factually unless 100% certain of the facts. *Tripod, really.*

Gavin and Jade emerged from the house again. Gavin pulled over a chair and flopped down. Jade sat down on his lap with a glass of wine and sighed deeply. "Endless... right?"

"Yep," Heath answered.

"How was the renewing of the vows ceremony?" I asked. "Ever hear of that within four hours of leaving the chapel?"

"I know," Jade drew out. "Classic."

"Why did we even go to the church?" Clare wondered out loud.

"Especially when the minister was asked not to reference Jesus at all during the ceremony," Heath spoke quietly. Whiplash! All eyes on Heath.

"Excuse me?" Clare spoke directly to Heath.

"Phil and Ella asked the minister to perform the marriage but not to bring Jesus into the service. They didn't want to offend anyone."

"That sounds just like Phil and Ella," Gavin and Jade nodded in agreement.

"What?" Clare's exasperation shot out of her. "Wait I am confused." She leaned in closer awaiting further explanation.

"There seems to be a variety of religious practices represented in today's guests," Heath began. "In an effort to be non-denominational as well as staying away from all religious fundamentals as a whole, the bride and groom hoped guests wouldn't be offended and would enjoy the ceremony."

"Clearly, offending us was not a priority," Clare breathed.

Why the concern? This group seemed to just go with it, whatever the situation. Was it possible to even upset them? Clearly another bohemian mentality: Drift to the ideals of the faction you are standing with and have no firm convictions of your own.

We sat in silence and allowed Heath's account to saturate our fatigue and now partially inebriated brains. This was an interesting piece of information really. I thought back over the service at the chapel. There was prayer wasn't there? I admit I didn't follow with great intent. As I remembered, a smile bloomed across my face. My eyes lit with amusement that had just become crystal clear to me and a hysterical laugh burst from my lips.

"Funny?" Jade questioned.

Tears started to roll down my cheeks. "Georgia?" Clare started to giggle now too joining in my unexplained behavior. I held my hand up so Clare and the rest of my curious family understood I would let them in on the joke just as soon as I could catch my breath.

"Funny? Oh yes!" I wiped the tears from my eyes and regained control. "Do not bring Jesus into the chapel right?" I looked at Heath who nodded. "Well I must admit the majority of the service is a blurr, but think back. Does anyone recall Heath's first sentence on behalf of the groom's family?" They searched their memory banks. Clare was the first to get there. Her eyes locked on mine as I said, "Isn't it fitting that *Jesus'* first miracle was a wedding... ," laughter took over again and this time the others joined me. I walked to Heath and gripped his shoulder. "Don't bring Jesus to the chapel and you manage to do just that in the first sentence! Oh my... Well done, bro."

"Guess Phil didn't think I needed religious guidelines," Heath chuckled.

"Chalk it up to another blunder from the groom's family," Clare said. "You do realize that everyone, non-blood-related, thinks that we thought it would be a great idea to come to New York and gut and reconstruct a kitchen the week of the wedding." Clare raised her finger and made her next point, "**And** to make sure that refrigeration needs were never met making it as difficult as possible for Ella's food crew to do their part." That set off another round of much needed laughter.

"You're probably right," Heath sighed. "So I guess my speech was perfect."

"Merely icing on the cake of the day," I giggled.

"The cake that has yet to be assembled..." Gavin quipped. "I think the guests who truly know Phil recognize he had a hand in the chaos. I'm sure everyone is sympathetic for what went on here." Gavin gave Jade's hand a squeeze and she nodded in agreement.

"Yeah," Jade said going for a little crowd control. "I'm sure Phil and Ella both appreciate all you've done."

We looked intently at Gavin and Jade. Their sincere expressions appeared just a little too forced. Heath threw his head back and roared, "No they don't!" The eruption of laughter once again filled the night air.

Chapter 20

Some nights you wish would last forever, but some nights... just never end.

I stepped into the cool damp grass field and hugged my denim shirt tightly around my body for insulation. Along with the setting sun, the natural warmth of the day had dissipated. A full moon thankfully had blessed us, and the reception field was bathed in pale yellow light. Tiny votive candles blinked like fire flies on a handful of tables which combined with the moonbeams provided a mysterious atmosphere. *Not quite cozy since you had no view of who was standing next to you,* yet very pretty. Amidst the fairy tale setting, pockets of wedding guests were scattered with their cocktail or wine glass in hand.

Many guests had reached that point in the evening where alcohol and darkness no longer suppressed their need to dance. I smiled as I watched a woman tip her head back and release a very inebriated hyena-like tequila giggle. *Someone was having fun.* Strings of white and colored Christmas lights flickered above the elaborate stereo system which pumped out a unique blend of melody and rhythm. The poorly accessorized teens stood beneath the festive lights and performed a rather unique combination of body contortions. *Whether or not on purpose, I wasn't sure.*

Beneath the largest tent, the bridal posse had set up camp. Tall tapered candles had been shoved into the necks of multiple empty wine bottles and grouped in the center of the table. Flames leapt wildly in the wind and the melting wax dribbled down like lava encasing the bottles long glass necks. Illuminated within the quaint glow was Phil, with Ella on his lap, surrounded by the solid circle of bodies. An obvious private party. Finished with the bridal meal, the heirloom china had been piled precariously off to the side, in the manner that this group assumed was acceptable.

My patience for the evening was waning. I had found Brennan still plagued with a headache and had convinced him to lie down. I needed only to retrieve Payton from Sueanne and I could end this seemingly infinite evening. Wishing for night vision goggles, I squinted and surveyed the dimly lit field.

Strolling into the cool grass, I moved along to the ravaged food tables to where the grill, long finished preparing food, was surrounded by guests seeking heat. The bar and cake canopies were lighted with glimmering pillar candles. Sylvia's cake, interestingly enough, turned out to be three levels of cupcakes strategically placed on top of one another to form an actual cake shape. Each individual cupcake was frosted with yellow icing and drizzled with toxic, un-refrigerated, raspberries. *Tasty.* Alongside the towering cupcake, was a three tiered tray filled with cookies and candies. Catheryn was a novice baker with extraordinary skill. Ella had asked Catheryn to provide the specialty treats as an alternative to cake. The cookies were shaped like tiny flowers, hearts, and wedding bells each iced with pastel frosting and decorated with care. The candies were luscious spheres of white and dark chocolate covered nut clusters, and sinful melt in your mouth pink and white butter mints.

A cackling laugh drew my attention to a group of people seated between the bar and cake canopies. *Success.* Heath and Clare sat in the faintly lit field with an ally I had been waiting to talk to, Lila. One of our favorites, Lila was a member of Hontie's loyal travel group. With renewed energy, I moved through the damp grass to join them.

Heath sat stone still in his canvas chair. He appeared to have shrunk three inches and had become molded to his chair. His cocktail glass dangled from the tips of his fingers threatening to plummet to the ground on the next stiff breeze.

Clare, with a beverage of her own, wiggled to the music where she stood next to Lila. If I had to guess, *and I despise guessing*, I'd put Lila in her late sixties. A fire hydrant at less than five feet tall, Lila was known for her explosive wit and taste for quality booze. As a regular adventure travel partner of Hontie's, Lila was generally up for anything.

"Hey guys," I said as I reached them. "Hi Lila," I bent down and gave her a hug. "Having fun?" Her answer was a friendly grunt. I slipped Clare's glass from her hand and sniffed the dark red fruit-filled concoction. I felt the lining of my nose eroding, "Whoa!" *Lethal?* I handed it back to Clare without braving a taste. "What is that?"

"Not really sure," Clare said, and then drank again in search of the answer. "You know; I really can't taste it anymore."

I rolled my eyes. "Heath, Lila, do you guys know what's being served?"

"Besides my booze? Ha!" Lila's voice boomed, startling me. Heath and Clare chuckled companionably. Although Lila's humor was legendary, I got the impression that this was not a joke.

"Your booze?" I asked Lila, who merely lifted her hands in explanation.

"Her booze, her booze, her booze," Clare panted excitedly.

I cast a quick look in Clare's direction and found her grinning shamelessly. "Geeorgia really... lissten to thiss one," she slurred.

Grab another glass of woo-woo juice.

"Most affairs young Georgia," Lila's voice bellowed, "you bring your bottle of choice. For me an aged whiskey fits the bill just fine. You give your bottle to the bartender

251

and he stashes it behind the bar and serves you **and only you**, I might add, from it."

"But this affair," Heath gestured loosely with his glass, "is like none before it."

"Truer words," Lila said with a cackling laugh, as she reached toward Heath and the clink of their glasses rang long and pure.

I leaned toward Clare and whispered, "I'm not inebriated enough for this conversation."

"I AM!" she shouted.

Cripes, Clare.

"Nut shell!" Lila barked at me and motioned me to her side. Confused, I stepped closer. "Nut shell girl, here it is." Lila cleared her throat. "I travel with my own booze. I like what I like," she affirmed with a curt nod. "Most places take, hold, and care for your bottle. They serve you, as you need. Here," she gestured broadly over the field. "I sat my bottle down and it became part of the mystery punch."

"No," I gasped, "really?"

Lila motioned to the three gallon glass jug on the table. A beautiful burgundy punch sat with slices of oranges, limes, and lemons floating within it. "I placed my bottle on the table, along with several other bottles of liquor I might add, and a man I assumed to be the tender stood behind the table. He smiled… I smiled… and then he pointed me in the direction of glasses. When I returned with my glass I watched as the tender emptied every last bottle on the table into the jug with the fruit."

"So what's this we're drinkin' anyway?" Clare peered wide-eyed into her cup.

"Ha!" Lila's laugh exploded loudly. "Kick your ass cocktail!"

"Hmm…" Clare said thoughtfully then sipped at her drink again.

"Well, it's living up to its name," Heath said as he gestured to the dance area where the movement challenged were strutting their stuff.

"Those girls," Lila said as she took in the gauche boogie girls, "should be old enough to have that punch for an excuse."

"It's painful to watch," Heath said as he stifled a belch.

"Umm, Lila?" Clare wore a pained expression, "D'you come with that lady?"

Turning in her chair, Lila scanned across the field. Her friend, Kristen, was beneath the twinkle lights in the dance tent. Her soft body posture caused her to lean heavily on the arm of the man next to her. A tumbler of crimson brew sloshed gently over the edge of the glass as she spoke.

Clare squinted against the dark. "Did her skirt look like that when you got here?" I focused more intently in the dark. Sure enough the woman's skirt had double tucked itself, probably on a trip to the bathroom. Every inch of her upper thigh was revealed along with full panty exposure in the rear. *Beauty.*

"Oh! Well now," Lila tried to hoist herself from her chair.

"I got it," Clare handed Lila her cup and set off in the direction of rescue. As Clare reached her, Kristen threw her head back and the high pitched hyena giggle I heard earlier rippled through the air once again. Clare back peddled a step but was undeterred. We watched as Kristen twisted as only a drunk could and looked down while she simultaneously felt her butt. Her head tipped back like a PEZ dispenser and another ear piercing giggle rippled out.

"That always happens to me!"

That's the type of thing a person should only need to have happen once.

Kristen looked at Clare with the most peaceful expression, then embraced her fiercely, and uttered the top three words said by drunks. "I love you!"

"Oh... well... yes," Clare replied awkwardly. She patted Kristen on the back. "Me too." Her job completed, Clare returned to our group.

"Covered her ass you did!" Lila roared her approval and handed Clare her cocktail glass. Clare scrutinized the remaining fluid and fruit swimming in her cup. Thinking better of it, she emptied the contents into the grass under Lila's chair.

Entertainment over, I needed to move on. "Anyone see Sueanne? I need to get Payton to bed."

Clare gestured across the field where Sueanne sat at a table with the boys playing beneath it on a soft blanket. I joined her and we enjoyed some quiet conversation and some tawdry people watching.

Payton and Drew were growing quieter. "They're getting tired," I said. "Thank you so much for watching Payton tonight."

"No trouble at all. They occupied each other. It isn't often Drew has an opportunity to play with boys this close to his age."

I leaned down and urged Payton to climb onto my lap. "We need to check on Brennan, little man." I nuzzled Payton's cold cheek. "Tomorrow we have one final day to take in Bouckville."

"I wish I could go along," Sueanne smiled. "Last year I found the greatest walnut table for our sitting room. It's perfect for playing cards or anything, really."

"We have been so distracted with... everything..."

"I know. You and you family salvage the day and maybe Tom and I will wander up for a beer on the deck about sundown," Sueanne said.

"That sounds great." I hoisted a sleepy Payton to my hip and happily left the field.

"I'm not tired at all Mommy," the not-moving-body-except-for-the-mouth said from my shoulder.

"Okay honey, we'll just check on your brother." I knew Payton was teetering on the edge of unconsciousness. I stopped in the kitchen and pocketed an apple, some animal crackers, and a juice box for Brennan. To my horror I encountered an added twist to the already bizarre obstacle course in the catch-all laundry room. Extension cords were strewn everywhere. They zigzagged from all viewable outlets much like the snakes from Indiana Jones and the Temple of Doom.

Fitting.

"Okay Payton, this could get tricky." I was talking more to myself than to him. I hoisted him higher on my shoulder, as I raised my left leg and stepped over the first power cord. I leaned and reached forward to grab for the washer. *Victory.* Only four visible cords to go as my personal game of twister-plus-child continued. My attempt to clear the next cord with my right leg had become more complicated. My free hand reached out grasping for security and the what-I-thought-was-solid dryer turned out to be yet another drawer full of kitchen guts. *Cripes!* The drawer shifted and began to slowly slide off the edge of the dryer threatening to dump its contents. "No... no... no," I said and the momentum of the drawer miraculously stopped. I put weight firmly on both feet and counted my blessings. "Whew, let's not try that again. Okay, half way there Payton buddy." I took a deep breath, followed by a step toward the servant stairs. *The coast might be clear.* Just then I got caught at the knees with one final cord and my luck expired. I held Payton firmly and waited, as the cord pulled from its unseen power source and whipped through the debris like a popped helium balloon. I froze, held my breath and listened. No one screamed from outside, so the music and Christmas lights must have still been on. "Well, I don't know what we de-powered buddy, but we're moving on."

I readjusted Payton. His body molded to my shoulder like play dough, and by some miracle we arrived on the second floor unscathed. Brennan stirred, as the air shifted beneath him, as I lowered Payton gently to the air mattress.

"Huh? What?" Brennan blinked at me.

"How's your headache? Do you think you could eat?" I dug out the apple, animal crackers, and juice pouch I had carried up for him.

Brennan shifted and sat up. The air mattress bubbled into a little mountain under Payton this time.

"Isses, zzaiye" Payton said.

Brennan gave me a curious look. "Did he just say 'this is crazy'?"

"Sure sounded like it to me." We giggled.

"Well he's right," Brennan muttered.

I was well over this affair and was anxious to put the entire event to bed. Tomorrow a final hurrah at Bouckville for much needed therapeutic spending; followed by hopefully one evening of uneventful, unwinding family time on the deck.

Brennan popped a cookie into his mouth. "UNO, Mommy?"

"You're on."

Chapter 21

School bells are ringing; let's move!

Light dawned on the glorious morning after. I peeked around the room and saw all beds were still full. *Time to raise the troops and salvage the final Bouckville day.* Not too quietly I lifted myself off the mattress which shifted Brennan and Payton enough to cause them to stir.

"Oh... what time is it Mom?" Brennan stretched.

"Time to go to Bouckville!" I whispered excitedly.

"Last day, right?" He carefully rolled on his side.

"Last day," I said mournfully. "Today we are on the infield where all of the professional dealers set up. Big prices with a few deals mixed in."

A yawn came from across the room. Clare moved gingerly on her ancient cot. "What time is it?"

"Time to move!" came Brennan's cheerful response.

"Oh my," she said with a sigh.

"Bren get dressed and come down to the bathroom." I tossed him his clothes as Payton sat up. "Payton?" Dazed, Payton's unfocused eyes scanned the room. Clearly not awake I coaxed him, "Lie back down honey." He flopped on the mattress and pulled the blanket up and over his little head earning a giggle from his big brother. "Shh," I stifled my own laugh. "I doubt Hontie and Grandmom want to be awake this early." Their motionless forms agreed with me. I crossed quietly to Clare, "When you, Catheryn, and Heath are ready, we'll go."

"Not sure they're going," Clare stretched.

"Huh?"

"They have had enough," Clare sat up. "Last night Heath and I discussed them driving my van back home today. Catheryn said she didn't mind and that way if they get stranded, Heath will be able to handle it."

"But Heath won't get to see the infield," I said disappointed.

"They are truly out of energy."

"Aren't we all? Heath is right, though. Better for them to handle the van together than us on Monday with the boys."

Clare wrung her hands, "I don't feel right; the van is my problem." *Ms. Independent.*

"Clare please," I whispered quietly. "Just say thanks, smile, and wave them off." She appeared pained. I took a cleansing breath and tempered my voice. "If you haven't accepted that families pull together and help after this fiasco..." Payton groaned as he sat up. I held my finger to my lips and pointed at the unmoving lumps that were Grandmom and Hontie. I grabbed his clothes for the day and lifted him to Koala my waist. "Morning angel," I murmured. I tiptoed through the bedroom maze and mouthed to Clare 'get moving.' She nodded.

Bren led us down the steep steps. "Mommy where are we going," A heavy-eyed Payton asked.

"Flea market."

"Aww, I don't want to flea market."

"I know, last day, I promise." The labyrinth of a laundry room was even more daunting in the daylight. "Go carefully Bren." I lowered Payton to the floor and began to guide him through the web.

"What a mess!" Payton exclaimed. *Coming from a four-year old that's saying a lot.*

"Yep crazy." I held up some cords for him to walk under then I tried to step over without losing my balance.

"Crazy," Payton mimicked.

I walked into the kitchen and found Heath making camp coffee. "Hey," he muttered.

"I thought you'd be sleeping in." He shrugged a shoulder. "Clare says you're heading home today."

"As soon as the trailer is loaded."

I observed him as he willed the pot to perk and recognized this escape for what it truly was, a last ditch effort of survival. "What needs to go?"

"Card tables and chairs Mom brought from church, and the tent," he sat a mug down on the stove. "You want some of this?" I waved him off. "I'll take the tables you brought too if you want."

"Okay. You're taking Clare's van?"

"Yep," he poured the scalding hot coffee into the mug and true to form lifted it immediately to his lips and attempted to sip the blistering brew. I shook my head in amazement. Boiling equals hot... *HELLO!* Heath muffled a curse and dabbed his lip with the back of his hand. "Catheryn can follow in the truck, that way if we have any mechanical trouble..."

"Good plan. And now that I'm thinking it through, I will slide some of my Bouckville purchases in the van. That will free up some space in the Jeep in case I find something great today."

Catheryn burst in from the mudroom. "Georgia you can't put 'Bounty' in the van," She took Heath's coffee from his hand and blew across the top. "Great, thanks hon."

With a raised brow Heath simply walked across the room and opened the microwave. He pointed to Catheryn's forgotten mug, "Yours." With a mild huff he slapped the door closed again. I hid my smile, as Heath pushed a few buttons and the microwave hummed to life.

"Why can't I put stuff in the van?" I asked Catheryn.

The beep of the microwave rang and as Catheryn prepared to sip Heath's coffee again. Heath reached around her and took the mug she held, "Mine," he said, offered her the mug she had forgotten in the microwave.

Catheryn shrugged apologetically. "Georgia, you can't take a bounty shot without all the bounty."

"I guess that's true, but the whole feeling of excitement from the traditional weekend really has been lost. What difference would an accurate picture make?" The boys returned from teeth brushing, I hoisted Payton to my hip and snuggled.

Catheryn chuckled, "You know maybe we should put the ladders, tools and empty paint cans on the deck and snap that for this year's photo."

"That would certainly be more appropriate." I said dryly.

Giggling, Brennan added, "but Uncle Heath should stretch out in front of all of it."

"With 'RIP' written across his chest," Catheryn continued the fun. Heath stared at us unsmiling.

"And his Discover card in his mouth," I added another detail. "And some un-refrigerated salmon."

"Don't eat the salmon," Payton chimed in and finally pulled an honest chuckle from Heath.

Clare, Mom and Hontie were moving through the laundry room mid-conversation which had obviously begun upstairs. "...I just don't want to waste anymore of the morning, Isabella," Hontie said.

"But she's already gone to so much trouble," Mom answered.

Clare joined in. "Did anyone actually say yes?"

"Say yes to what?" I cringed.

"Sueanne and Tom are putting together a morning-after-breakfast for the members of the family staying here," Mom began. "We are to walk to their house when we're all up."

"When did this all get planned?" I looked to those who stayed up past my bed time.

"Sometime last evening," Catheryn blew over her coffee. "Sueanne is trying to do something nice for us since not much nice has gone on for us these past few days." She winced a little realizing Hontie was present.

Delay the day further? Was there no end?

"I know we are being selfish and ungrateful..." Clare stated dramatically, "wanting to start the infield before noon." She whined, "Do we really have to go?"

Lips pursed, Mom moved forward to reply.

"I think we just head to Bouckville," Hontie declared decisively. "Sueanne and Tom will understand."

"Whoo hoo," Clare hopped to life. "Let's rally!" She pumped her fist in the air.

"...or maybe not." Catheryn said as movement on the deck caught her eye.

"Morning all," Tom stepped into the kitchen with Drew in tow. "Hope you're all hungry." He peered around and addressed all of us equally.

"We were just headed your way," Mom said too cheerfully and pegged us all with a patent-pending eye stare to remind us of our 'grateful' manners.

Tom stepped onto the deck and easily lifted Drew to his shoulders. "Sueanne and I realize you're going to eat and run, but I know you'll enjoy the buffet she's thrown together."

Buffet... Cripes.

Down the road we trudged like the elephants in the Jungle Book. *Minus the happy marching song.* "Oh my," I said breathlessly as I entered Sueanne and Tom's haven. I drifted through the front room of the old Victorian home and tried to absorb each detail. The rich detail of original woodwork stripped of paint and naturally oiled was stunning throughout the small quaint rooms. An oak drafters table nearly seven-feet long graced the wall of the study. Beneath a window, hand- rolled bee's wax candles were sorted by color and stacked in an old letter sorting box. Bookcases filled with an eclectic selection stretched from the floor to the high ceiling.

I wandered through the choppy format, pushed open paned French doors, and entered the dining room. A five-legged-oak table was the focal point here. Suspended above it hung a wrought iron candelabra, draped with drying hops. A solid wall cabinet offered storage for serving essentials and at one time would have provided as a pass through for food from the kitchen. *Cool.*

A short hall connected the dining room to a fully modernized kitchen. Completely in her element here, Sueanne was milling about effortlessly beside the yards of counter space and a double sink that stretched along the long wall. Over the sink a large window offered a view of the side yard gardens and vegetable patch. Along the opposite wall a door stood ajar, revealing a set of servant steps leading to the second floor. Kitchen appliances and canisters of dry goods were stowed in plain view at the back of the room on custom-designed deep shelves. The back door was propped open to allow the breeze to circulate.

I stood on the back steps and was treated to a view of the backyard. Raised flower beds, bird houses, climbing trellises, a restored carriage house, and a courtyard with Adirondack chairs surrounding a potbelly stove... *Stunning.* I felt as though I had stepped into a <u>Better Homes and Gardens</u> kitchen and garden issue. I turned back taking in Sueanne, apron tied at her waist and a full-blown smile in place, as if having six people over for breakfast was a snap. In front of us a buffet, accurately described was presented on a floating butcher-block island; fresh juices and coffee cake, assorted muffins, egg casserole, and French toast teased our senses.

"Wow," and with that Bouckville was effectively placed on the back burner. We gathered around the eight foot farm table. A wooden high chair had been pulled up to the end where Drew sat and eyed Clare curiously.

"This table is great," Clare stroked the wood longingly. "Each year I look for one but getting it home always presents a problem."

"We looked a long time," Tom said, as he settled himself at the opposite end. "We really wanted to be able to seat fourteen comfortably."

"We carried our measurements around for more than a year," Sueanne picked up easily.

"And you got exactly what you wanted," Catheryn said around the muffin she'd stuffed in her mouth.

"Beautiful," Heath added and pulled a chair in next to Tom.

We enjoyed our breakfast immensely. More than the delicious food, the quiet ease in which it was offered. Some noise from the servant steps had us all turning. I was surprised to see the French speaking Canadians descend from the second floor. *Hmm... imagine that. Who knew?*

"Hello again," Catheryn said. *Catheryn knew.*

Sueanne walked to the base of the stairs, "Bon jour, dormez-vous tres bien?" *Impressive.*

Where was Sueanne a few nights ago when we were desperately language impaired?

The French did their best to mutter good mornings in English and joined us around the table. Conversation drifted to the night before and being in mixed family company we filtered our remarks. *Manners suck.*

One hour later with full bellies we were speed walking back to the house to grab our gear. Bouckville, the final day! We packed what we could in Clare's van and loaded the trailer with wedding things that went back to PA.

"See you tomorrow," I hugged Heath. "Drive safe, I know you're tired."

"Feeling better each step I take out of here." He climbed into Clare's limping family unit and Catheryn hopped in the truck with loaded trailer in tow.

"I still feel awkward about having them do this," Clare said chewing on her fingernail.

"Smile and wave," I patted her shoulder. "I know it's hard to accept help being a modern day multi-tasking mother and all. But this truly is just one of those times when you say thanks and leave it at that." The vehicles disappeared from view. I nudged Clare not too lightly. "Snap out of it! Bouckville! Boys load up, we're outta' here!"

Chapter 22

We become our Mothers...
Some days that's a scarier thought than others.

Mom and Hontie pulled out of the drive ahead of us. We had traveled a mile when Mom pulled into the local bank. "I need to hit the ATM," she said to us, as she grabbed her purse and hurried to the bank door.

"Last day, got enough cash?" I asked Clare.

"I have all I am taking. When it's gone, it's gone."

"So disciplined," I teased. "I always overdraw my checking account. It's tradition."

"Good grief, Georgia."

"Mom, what's grandmom doing?" Brennan asked. I looked over and saw Mom fiddling with the door to the ATM.

"I'm not sure Honey."

"She can't get in the bank." Clare lowered her window and called out, "Mom use your card to unlock the door."

Confused, Mom tried some minor breaking and entering by attempting a lock pick. "No, no," Clare called again. "Run it through the slide. It will unlock the door." Mom figured it out and entered the bank.

"Doesn't she use an ATM often?" Brennan inquired.

"Nope," I answered him, "Does her best to never use them."

"Generational thing," Clare said. "We can't function without them."

"Look now she can't get out," Brennan giggled.

"Grandmom's stuck," Payton sniggered. Sure enough like a mime, Mom was palm walking the glass door. We read her lips as she mouthed, 'I can't get out'. Helpless laughter filled our car and Hontie hopped out and used her card to disengage the lock and release her sister.

"Alright, boys," I made eye contact in the rearview mirror, "Last day. What are we looking for?"

"Army guys," Payton answered first. "Army tanks too."

"I'm not sure because this is a new place, right?" Brennan asked.

"Yep, the infield is dealers, big bucks stuff. You can find good values, though, if you look and if they didn't sell much yesterday." I looked to Clare. "What about you?"

"I'm still looking for retro bar stools."

"You should find them today."

Bouckville infield parking consisted of endless grassy acres. Each field was divided into sections by ropes and lettered, so you knew where to find your car following a long day of treasure hunting. Tractors pulled trolleys in the morning to move people to the entrance gates. Later on the tractors would pull wagons and haul large purchased items from the infield for easier pick up. What seemed overwhelmingly disorganized in fact was a fine science of people in motion. We pulled into the field and found ourselves separated from Mom and Hontie. "Where did they go?" Clare said.

"They were right in front of us." I was baffled. We parked and walked a hundred yards and paid our admission fee. We stood on the threshold of the infield, itching to get started.

"They will turn up." Clare shrugged and we decided to press on.

Thirty minutes into our day Brennan found a metal toy backhoe loader for $10.00. Now a seasoned barterer, I watched proudly as he walked away with it for $7.00. The lesson he failed to learn, however, was heavy items should be purchased on exit. Fifteen minutes after his proud purchase, he asked, "Mom can we put this in your tote?"

I kneeled down and rearranged my tote to accommodate the awkward toy. As I threaded my arm through the strap, Payton tugged on my pants. "Mommy, can I be in the piggy back chair?" *This day was going to last forever.*

Two hours later I had found some Fisher Price pull toys: 1961 Pelican and a 1959 Bouncy Racer, both in great shape. I hailed the vendor to barter when I heard Hontie laugh. Clare heard it too. "Two aisles over, maybe one," I said. She and Brennan walked off to see if they could locate them. "I'll catch up in a minute."

It was nice to finally have the entire force together. Clare and Brennan stood with Mom and Hontie who were visibly relaxed and enjoying their day.

"Payton," I said to the monkey on my back, "look what Hontie's holding." Tucked under each arm were two chalk-ware bull dogs. One was painted very close to actual breed coloring and the other was down right silly. Black with red accents, the pup had a cigar dangling from his lower lip and a derby cap fixed on top of his head. That was one of the many joys of Bouckville. You'd never know what would strike someone's fancy. *My motto was to never judge anyone else's purchases.* Payton and I joined the group. "Hontie your dogs are great!"

"I know, don't you just love their faces?" Hontie asked with delight. "And they are banks!"

"If you're happy, we're happy," Clare responded, "How about you, mom?"

"I've got a few needle packs." Old needles for hand sewing still in their original packages had become one of

Moms favorite collectibles. "I also found a lady with 1930's paper Halloween decorations: masks and jointed-light-weight card board cats, witches, and jack-o-lanterns. They are incredible," she said. "I had to walk away and think about them a little bit."

I laughed, "Mom you're always so practical." *That gene skipped me.*

"How about you guys?" Hontie asked the boys.

"I've got a metal loader and I got the price down three bucks!" Brennan said proudly.

"I'm looking for tanks," Payton called from his shoulder seat.

Glancing from him to me, "How are you doing that?" Hontie asked concerned.

"Is what it is," I responded. "We're heading to mid-grounds for some lunch."

"Okay, we're going to take it slow. Maybe we'll catch up to you about 3:00 at the Boy Scout food tent," Hontie said and received a nod from Mom. "If we don't meet you though, we'll see you at home."

Good thing some of the vendors were always in the same location. The Boy Scouts made a traditional fare consisting of salt potatoes and roast beef sandwiches, along with hot dogs and hamburgers. Each time a customer paid and tossed some spare change in the donation box they would ring a bell, and shout ".50 cent donation" and everyone would cheer. Quirky, but traditions sometimes are. We loved it!

The day dragged forward. Payton held my hand and had been walking the last hour. We turned for a brief shaded rest and shining like a beacon two aisles down were metal retro bar stools.

"There they are!" Clare took off rapidly.

"Who?" Payton asked.

"Not a who, a what. Aunt Clare wants barstools for her kitchen."

"Oh," he said without excitement. "...can I ride again?"

"After we're done at the stools, okay?"

"Aww," he whimpered.

"Hang in there honey." We caught up to Clare who was knee deep in negotiations. Game face in place, Clare looked at me with an expression of 'I'm not sure if these are exactly what I'm looking for, especially at this price'.

Playing along, I attempted to look stern. "What are you thinking?" I asked Clare.

"Hmmm... not sure. I wish there were six, not four." *Soooo not true...* but the vendor was listening intently. "And the color is... well... unique," Clare pouted.

"They are easily covered," the vendor woman stepped forward.

Tugging on my sleeve, Brennan asked me "Aren't these the kind she wants?"

"Shhh," I gave him the hairy eye.

Bending over, Clare fingered the price tag, stepped back, and pursed her lips.

"How much?" I asked propelling the game.

"Thirty for the set," Clare responded in her best 'too high' tone, then addressed the vendor, "What's your best."

Mirroring her, the vendor studied the tag. Her hard lined face gave nothing away. She sized up Clare, "Twenty-two."

"Done," Clare beamed at me, placed her sunglasses in the V of her shirt, and got out her checkbook. "Would've given thirty," she whispered to me with a wink.

"Twenty-two is better. Ask her to hold them until the end of the day." Transaction completed, Clare helped me secure Payton in the piggy back chair.

"Mommy!" Brennan called from a few booths up.

We made our way to him. "What did you find?"

"Look at these military pieces!" Delighted, he bounced and pointed to a well arranged display of exquisite toys. Everything from 1920-1965, submarines, airplanes and military men in various poses; the display was incredible. *Many, many, dollars.*

"Oh, they're fabulous!"

"Tank! Tank!" Payton exclaimed wriggling in his perch. I was glad for once that he was strapped in and couldn't reach any of the items. "Tank!" he repeated.

"That tank is $650 and is not a toy," a grumpy voice announced. Startled, I turned and looked at a dehydrated, over sun-exposed man, seated in a lawn chair amongst the toys.

Annoyed, I stared him down. Through a painted on smile I said, "As we are all, except the four-year-old, aware Sir."

"Just trying to protect my merchandise," he grumbled.

I turned to Brennan, "Although it is a wonderful piece and well within your budget, we'll keep looking." I took Brennan's hand and steered him away leaving Mr. Grumpy ogling after us.

"What did you mean 'within my budget'?" Brennan asked me quietly.

"I can appreciate the man's concern for a valuable piece. He's probably had horrible experiences with kids who touch and break, but you weren't doing either of those things." I smiled at him, "The budget comment was a stretch but after his rudeness, I wasn't going to give him a cent."

"Oh," Brennan was clearly disappointed, as he watched his dream of a $650 budget fade quickly.

The four of us headed for a huge tent and a much needed break. Inside the tent countless tables and chairs were spaced and at the far end a group of Boy Scouts were selling drinks. I backed up to the table and shrugged out of the back pack, leaving Payton standing trapped like a partially hatched egg.

"Mommy?" Payton asked concerned.

"What," I teased him, "You don't want to stay in your pack?" His head shook vigorously, and I extracted him from the piggy back chair.

Clare asked as she gently rolled the Pelican across the table top. "This one is really cute. Does he have a name?"

"Big Bill Pelican, I think." He was cute, as his wheels rolled over the table, his huge bill opened and closed to reveal a smiling fish inside."

"Pretty happy fish for being eaten," Brennan said.

"I agree," Aunt Clare smiled. "What else did you find?"

"I found a great old clip board, Brennan found a Boy Scout derby car from the 1950's, and Payton found army guys and a troop carrier truck."

"Wow, you guys were shopping hard!" Clare picked up the derby car, "Very cool, Bren."

About 4:00 Clare and I decided to end our day. Sadly we walked out of the grounds. Another year of Bouckville under our belts, another family ritual successfully completed.

On the ride back to Hontie's, the boys snoozed in the back seat and Clare had begun to nod off. I thought over past trips to Bouckville. Each year had very different highs and lows. But with the madness we endured this year: wedding, home improvement, guest relations…, this trip definitely ranked on a scale all its own.

Clare startled herself awake, "What? Was I sleeping?"

"Yeah."

"Good grief, I'm tired."

"I'm sorry Catheryn and Heath had to miss a relaxed day at Bouckville." I said as we pulled into Hontie's. "Maybe a beer on the deck when Hontie and Mom get back will start our healing process."

"Well," Clare yawned, "I can't say I'm glad it's over, but I really am glad it's over."

Coming out of his nap zone, Payton muttered, "Some days I don't remember what I did on days before this…"

Right there with you buddy.

Chapter 23

'Bouckville bliss' a mirage dangling at the tips of your fingers... perpetually unattainable.

Clare went to the fridge and pulled out two bottles of Corona and a lime. She stood in the center of the kitchen and rotated slowly. "This room really is stunning," she observed.

"Yep."

"At least Hontie got a beautiful kitchen."

"Hell of a way to get one." I said under my breath. I crossed to the kitchen table and found a scrap of paper with a quickly scrawled message:

'At the lake house.

Phil and Ella are coming back around 6:00 to open gifts and have a cook out.

Gavin & Jade'.

I gave Clare a speculative look. "That sounds... almost good."

"You know," she said quietly, "If we get just one night of quiet family time celebrating with Phil and Ella, I may just be able to put some of this nightmare aside."

"One night won't do it for me;" I tossed the note on the counter. A car pulled in, "Mom and Hontie are back, grab two more." Bren and Payton raced through the kitchen to the deck to see what other treasures they had found.

I picked up the cutting board and a knife and followed Clare to the deck. The tops popped from the evening's first Coronas... *Ahhh.*

Mom and Hontie sat comfortably in canvas chairs. At their feet the boys were enjoying the chalk-ware bulldogs. Sasha lumbered up the steps. She ambled toward Mom and Hontie, gave the inanimate bulldogs a passing sniff, and wedged herself in-between them, hopeful for a vigorous rub down.

"Hmm..." Clare sat with her eyes closed and head tipped up to the afternoon sun.

"How much time do we have to enjoy this moment?" I asked.

"Tiempo? Tiempo por qué?" Mom looked alarmed.

"Phil and Ella are coming for a cookout and gift opening around 6:00," Clare said, unmoving from her chair.

Hontie glanced through the deck door to the kitchen wall clock. "Well, it's 5:15 now, so I guess we need to pull some things together..." She settled back into her chair and tipped up her beer. Following a long pull she continued, "...but I'm not feeling like pulling anything together."

Nods of agreement all around. Everyone relaxed and absorbed the serene moment. Wrapping an arm around Brennan, I tugged him to my lap. "This is what each night of Bouckville is about. This is what Mommy looks forward to every year. Exhaustion from endless vendors, bartering, buying, and hauling... it all leads back to quiet family time on the deck as the sun fades."

"Yeah, I get it," he answered soulfully.

"But you know," I snuggled him a little closer, "I promised you and Payton a lake swim and so far haven't delivered."

"Really?" He turned a little too quickly and bumped my bottle. "Oops, sorry!"

"No worries." I brushed at the drip running down my arm, "Yeah, let's do it!"

"Cool!" He hopped to his feet. "Payton, we are going to the lake!" They rushed off to grab swim gear.

I smiled after them. The weekend hadn't scarred them as much as I had feared. "Hontie, how do I get to the lake house?"

Chapter 24

Serenades... cocktails... bungee jumping... Gypsy living.

Armed with vague verbal directions, we were in route to the lake house.

"I see a lake," Payton exclaimed.

"Well, we're on the right track." I glanced across to the shoreline speckled with a combination of bungalows, cottages, and modest family homes. "This is where Hontie's directions were a little sketchy, so keep an eye out." The road seemed as if carved into the hillside. To our right a mere twenty-five to fifty yards separated the road from the water's edge. On our left the two lane road was met by a steep rocky incline hugged by a thick line of trees. We wound our way along the scenic water's edge enjoying another absolutely breath taking panoramic view. Afternoon sun glittered across the lake highlighting boats tied to docks adjacent to practical homes. Barely blemished, the lakeside purity was refreshing to see in a world where the trend tended to build as many homes as possible in a small area to maximize profits.

"There!" Brennan shouted. "I see Hontie's car."

My tug of envy was knee jerk at the sight of the quaint stone cottage beside the road. I was reminded again of the different lifestyle I was immersed in. To think an owner of such a property would hand over the keys to an acquaintance in exchange for so little. *A rent free stone cottage on the water, sign me up.* From the road the charming dwelling appeared to be a single floor, but it had been built on the slope to the water which allowed for two stories. Parking was going to be a trick, as each property had a pad for about one and a half vehicles. Phil's pad was currently holding three cars and a motorcycle. The tight two-lane road had little to no shoulder and both sides of the road were parked solidly with cars and trucks.

"Gang's all here," I muttered to myself, as I moved slowly to the center of the road. I drove past the cottage only to realize there was nowhere to turn around. I swung the Jeep into the first open area and negotiated a tight three point turn. On my second pass I saw a small grass patch just long enough to slip into. Carefully I pulled the Jeep tight against the hill's edge. "Grab your shark jacket, Payton." (a life jacket decorated with sharks) You guys are both going to have to crawl out the driver's side."

"Cool!" Payton scrambled over the console.

"Don't forget the towels Bren." We followed the sounds of laughter and guitar playing to the side of the property. As I opened the gate, the boys and I stumbled into a back yard party that obviously had been going strong for days.

Tables topped with umbrellas had been placed on a fieldstone patio. The party goers were grouped in small clusters on the lawn and patio. Most held a glass of wine and a cigarette in hand. *So this is how the other 90% have spent their wedding weekend.*

At the far edge of the property, a giant oak tree towered. Its massive aged trunk leaned ever so slightly toward the immense body of deep lake water. I watched as the delinquents took turns swinging from a rope tied bungee-style, to an aloft branch. No lifeguard or otherwise responsible non-alcohol-consuming grown-up within reach, the kids took turns catapulting each other out over the open water. Twenty feet of free bird flying until the tethered rope returned them to the shore.

Another handful of adults were grouped around Phil. Casually he sat cross legged on a tree stump strumming his guitar and singing. Raw God-graced talent, his rich voice flowed out and mesmerized the group. He noticed me and the boys and dropped his lyrics but continued to play. "Georgia! Hey boys." Astonished, Brennan watched as Phil's fingers slid effortlessly over the guitar's strings. "How are your lessons coming, Bren?"

"Good," he answered.

Payton clutched my hand and eyed the water and the crowd with equal wariness. Phil smiled, as he noted the towels and playful life jacket. "Cool jacket Payton."

"They were hoping for a lake swim," I explained.

"Have at it," Phil inclined his head toward the dock. No more invitation was needed for Brennan. Stripping as he went, Brennan raced past the seated grown-ups. Payton just squeezed my fingers a little tighter and burrowed into my legs.

Phil's audience didn't seem upset at the interruption, so I quietly asked, "You and Ella are coming over to do your gifts later?"

He changed cords effortlessly. "Yeah and barbeque, that work for you?"

"We're looking forward to it. Remember Phil, we just got back from Bouckville; there isn't any food at the house."

"We've got it covered," he hummed a harmony. "We'll head over shortly. Ella was shooting for 'bout 6:30 I think."

A glanced at my watch... *6:45. Of course it was.* The sun was disappearing quickly and the water was just short of freezing but that didn't stop Brennan. He dove from the dock, treaded briefly, and climbed out to do it again. I hoisted Payton to my hip, "What do you think bud, you want to give it a try?" He gripped me tighter. I walked toward the dock as Brennan once again went airborne. I lowered Payton to the ground and he bear-hugged my thighs. I stroked his head in comfort, as one of the unsupervised children went sailing out over the water on the rope swing.

Brennan climbed from the water and watched as the kid recoiled toward us. Face lit with delight, Bren turned to me expectantly. "NO." I said. His face slacked in disappointment. "Not open for discussion." He shrugged his shoulders and leapt off the dock again.

"Hey there Georgia," Jade joined me by the water. "Pretty amazing party happening here..." She trailed off as another child soared across the dark water. "very safe... right?"

"Where are Gavin and Davis?" As if on cue I saw Gavin striding toward us with Davis perched atop his shoulders.

"There they are... my handsome men." Jade grinned. Gavin lifted Davis from his shoulders and passed him to Jade.

"Hey Georgia, Payton," Gavin said as he leaned down to the visibly nervous Payton. "Are you going to get wet little man?" Payton looked uneasily from Gavin to the water, as Brennan shot off the dock with a banshee holler. Laughing Gavin called, "Good one Bren. Are we going?" Gavin asked Jade.

"Yeah, going to try for a quick bath before bed," she told me. "You guys saw the note?" Jade asked. "Gifts and barbeque? Starting what... twenty minutes ago?" She chuckled and patted my shoulder with a sigh, "Casual living."

"We will be right behind you. I had promised the boys lake swimming, but it is getting cold fast."

I kneeled next to Payton. "Let's get your shark jacket on Bud." I zipped it up tight, "all set." He walked tentatively toward the dock but was content to keep both feet on dry land. He watched Brennan swim to shore and climb the concrete steps beside the dock. Shaking his hair from his eyes cold droplets of water sprinkled over us. Brennan jumped up and down on the floating dock.

"Come on Payton, stand out here with me," Brennan encouraged, "it's fun!" Payton stepped out onto the wet wooden surface and watched Brennan fly!

The cannonball showered Payton and me with water. "Whew, that's chilly!"

"Jump in! Jump in!" Brennan called from the water.

The dock bounced up and down on the water's choppy surface. "What do you want to do?" I asked Payton. His blue eyes were huge on mine, clearly unsure of what he was getting into. From this vantage I could appreciate his concern. The depth of the water made it appear black. Even as an adult, I needed no help for my imagination to run wild. Not wanting to impress my fears on Payton, I tugged his float a little tighter. Here we go," I held his tiny hand and walked to the edge. "You won't sink, buddy."

His eyes studied me. "There are big swimming fish in there," he stated seriously.

"No." *Lying like only a mother can.* "No fish in this lake."

"None?"

"Nope." We walked to the opposite edge of the jostling dock, as Brennan hurled his body again into the water. I crouched down, "Payton, it's just like swimming lessons honey, but you've got to get in now because it's getting cold." We left the shifting dock and returned to solid ground. Standing on the edge, I gripped Payton's hands in mine and dipped his toes in the cold water. He squealed with delight, so I repeated the process a few times.

"You want to try to get in?" I asked him.

"No fish?"

"None," I lied again.

"No fish," he stated to someone behind me. "No fish in this lake."

Smiling I turned around. "That's right," I said, hoping whoever was behind me would go along with the plan. Unfortunately, it was Queen Frostine wearing her white bikini and beaded sarong. *No day off for Vogue.* "He's concerned since the water is so dark." I explained. She stared at Payton for a moment expressionless. *Mustn't want to risk botox.* Somi shifted her steely gaze to me. Saying nothing, she bent to pick up a discarded towel.

"Were you guys in the water today? It's so cold." *Why do I continue to speak? It's like nervous energy meets Ms. Manners. Must be polite... kill the queen bitch with kindness.* Somi wasted not a breath not even to huff, as she dismissed me and strutted back to the house.

My focus switched to Payton, who seemed encouraged that nothing had eaten Brennan. "In we go buddy." He held the dock and stepped down to the top concrete step. The water sloshed over his ankles. He looked up at me nervously. Brennan cheered and Payton grew more confident. He lowered himself two more steps until he was able to tread water. His giggles weren't far behind.

I took a memory shot, painting the image in my brain. The simple joys of a first time lake swim.

Childhood perfection... *Soak it in Mom. Here is the good stuff.*

Two minutes later Payton turned blue, and lake swimming was officially completed. I dragged Brennan out of the glacial water, bundled him up and hopped back in the Jeep.

It was now 7:10 P.M.

Chapter 25

**The gypsy handbook defines 'fashionably late',
as 'chronically tardy'.
Just so we are all on the same page.**

Sasha lifted her head to acknowledge our arrival, as we pulled back into Hontie's. No one had moved since we had left. Mom and Hontie were still soaking in the peace of the ending day. Clare sat head reclined; eyes closed, and empty Corona dangling from her finger tips.

"You find the lake?" Hontie called, as we unloaded from the Jeep.

"Yep and the boys had a quick polar bear swim. Phil said they'll be heading this way soon." We climbed on the deck, "Right inside guys for dry clothes. Bren? Bring me everything that's wet. Everything."

"Got it," he took two steps and spun around and enveloped me in a rib crushing hug, "Thanks Mommy."

"You bet." I watched as the boys dashed into the house leaving me with renewed balance.

"You did tell them we have no food," Clare said without opening her eyes.

"Phil said they had it covered." I collapsed next to her in a vacant chair.

"Good." She said still unmoving. "So tell me, just how does the other half live?"

"For squatters? The other half appears to be doing just fine." I shot a quick glance to Hontie who was thankfully absorbed in her conversation with Mom and missed my comment. I filled Clare in on the beautiful lake property and the pertinent party details. "Did Gavin and Jade get back?"

"Yeah, they are giving Davis a quick bath. They wanted to get him to sleep before Phil and Ella get here." Clare sat forward and stretched. "I have no energy to clean up."

"Me either. I'll stay skuzzy."

"Here's the stuff Mom." Brennan held a pile of suits and towels. I took the sopping heap and tucked it next to my chair. "Payton and I are going to lie on the mattress and play with our Gameboys, if that's okay."

"Oh my non-delinquent child!" I grabbed him for a smacking kiss.

"*MOM*," he tried for the 'I'm nine years old' embarrassed look, but thankfully didn't quite pull it off.

"Grab some snacks on your way up."

"Awesome," he gave me a smooch and dashed into the house.

"I'm going to run down to the shop and call home before they get here."

I let myself into Hontie's shop for one last look at all the cool stuff she had for sale. It was a store that would thrive in a bigger town but hopefully with a few more successful seasons the shop would stand on its own. I coveted the buggy seat, the huge *not* for sale wardrobe and the major huge apothecary table. *Okay, I want everything!*

Sighing, I went into the office and dialed home... answering machine. "Hey babe, we survived the wedding and have had an exhausting last day at Bouckville. We should be on the road by lunch tomorrow. Clare's riding with me since her van broke down. I'll call when I get cell service. Talk to you tomorrow. Ready to be home. See ya."

I stepped onto the front steps and slid the key into the lock and bid farewell to Hontie's shop. On the sidewalk I glanced down the block to the town bar/restaurant. The deck was filled with people. A riotous burst of laughter had me smiling. *At least someone was having fun.* A closer look proved the deck dwellers to be none other than folks from the lake house. I watched as they clinked their raised glasses and tossed back a group shot. Phil stood and waved the waitress over for yet another round. *Very nice.* I climbed into the Jeep and started the engine. The dash board clock mocked me as it flashed 7:40 P.M. Apparently time was not really an issue... ever. The boys needed to eat. On the ride back I decided to round them up and go to the pizza shop.

I found Clare still planted in a lawn chair absently stroking Trivet in her lap. "I'm going to the pizza shop, you interested?"

That got her eyes open. "What? Phil and Ella should be here any minute... family time... gifts... barbeque?"

"Yeah, close your eyes and go back to your happy place. They're at the bar."

"What?"

"The bar and I mean THEY, the entire entourage." I spoke slowly for comprehension. "Shocked? Clare..." I shook my head. "I'm taking the boys for food." I went in the deck doors leaving Clare gawking at my back. "Brennan?" I called out.

"Yeah Mom in here," I found him helping to entertain Davis while Jade wrestled him into PJ's. "Go find your brother; we're going for dinner."

"Thought we were cooking out," Brennan said.

"We're eating out. Now scoot and find Payton." I turned my attention to Jade. "How's it going?"

"Perfect," she playfully blew a strawberry on his belly. "We had ourselves a long hot bath, didn't we Davis."

Jade tugged his shirt on, "Let me guess… lake party ran long right?"

"Long yes, but it appears that they're coming here by way of the downtown bar. Three miles without a celebratory shot may spoil the flow of the party."

"I know it… right?"

Hontie strolled into the room and picked up Davis. "Jade may I put him down?" she asked nuzzling his chunky neck. Davis erupted into giggles.

"Sure Grammie," Jade answered happy to pass on the chore.

I watched as they disappeared out of the room and up the steps. "Hontie is enjoying this time with Davis so much," I smiled at Jade. "Indiana is so far away."

"Yeah and this visit… well… chaos," she huffed. "It almost makes me appreciate the distance. I'd go mad living this way day in and day out." I nodded in agreement. "You know Georgia… we took the week as vacation for family. This has been a total disaster."

I could only imagine the compounded frustration Jade was dealing with. Being a daughter-in-law flying half-way across the country to arrive in a construction zone with a toddler, the expense of the wedding, and the loose schedule of obligatory events that went with it? It had to be grueling. "I'm really trying not to lose my patience," Jade said, "but there really has been no quality time between Grammie and Davis."

I heard the frustration and her need to vent was clear. I tried for damage control. "Keep in mind 100% of the chaos could have been avoided with some minor pre-planning." I gave her hand a pat. "Phil is Phil, but don't forget for a second that Davis is Hontie's light right now." I paused while Jade absorbed this, not sure if she believed me. "He was all she was focused on when I arrived. Getting to the airport for your arrival. This flippin' house was inside out and all she could talk about was Davis in his bare feet running around the terminal."

Jade smiled at the thought. "Yeah, I'm glad we have three more days," she said quietly. "We'll make them count!"

Brennan and Payton padded in from the kitchen. "Grandmom says the people are here now and we should not go for pizza." *Whoopee.*

"Can we play with the inquints?" Payton asked.

"Inquints?" Jade looked to me.

I swallowed a chuckle and whispered to her, "Delinquents. The uncontrolled, un-parented offspring that travel with this horde."

"Oh... yeah... right?" Jade giggled on her way to the deck.

Time to suck it up and find some manners.

"Hey Brennan," I said as I stepped on the deck, "Keep an eye on Payton. It's getting dark and those kids play a little rough."

"Got it," and off they ran to join the delinquents.

Chapter 26

**They say if life knocks you down, get back up...
but if you are going to allow yourself to be
treated like a door mat... then for heaven's sake,
lie down.**

The assault had begun. The serenity of the deck was
instantly shattered. I grabbed a chair in the corner of the deck
beside the steps. Across from me in a row like ducks sat,
Clare, Mom, Gavin, and Jade. In fast forward, Sylvia hopped
out of a car chirping directions to the unseen. "Grab the
blankets darling; we'll have a lovely #//*-ing picnic."

"I feel I'll be chilled," Jewel said as she unfolded
herself from the backseat. "I'd rather not sit on the ground."

"#//*- it darling, we'll toss some logs together and set
them ablaze." Sylvia waved a hand dismissing Jewel and
hooted a greeting to the next car load. "Rod darling," she
called to her son, "be a dear and string up the volleyball."

"Equipped, aren't we," Clare muttered to Jade.

"I know it... right?"

"Just how equipped remains to be seen," Gavin
commented quietly but rose to be a gentleman to lend a hand
to Jewel. "Why don't you come in and we'll start a fire in the
living room."

Jewel patted his arm and smiled at him coyly. "In my
day Dearie, we'd have done just that." She tossed a wink to
Jade and allowed Gavin to escort her to the living room.

Sylvia pulled a cane from the trunk. She whipped
open the passenger door and said, "Here you are darling, get
yourself inside and I'll fetch the wine." I watched Ella's

father maneuver himself from the car, as his wife bustled off to begin the party. Slowly, Art worked his way though the grass toward the deck steps. Mom sprang into action, "The living room is probably a good place for Arthur, too."

"We can't help but organize, can we?" I commented under my breath, as more cars pulled onto the lawn adding force to the invasion.

"I'm not doing anything," Clare stated from her chair. Queen Frostine mounted the deck. "Not a damn thing," Clare repeated with a little more heat.

Pantaloons this time and some sort of sheer draping blouse accented by multiple necklaces in varying lengths all with an absence of color. Somi's presence alone made Hell several degrees hotter. Manolo's marching; the fashion goddess passed me and went into the house. A moment later she'd dragged chairs to the deck. She stood in front of me, with her hand posed on her hip as she counted the empty chairs. After a quick tally she left the deck to join her people in the yard.

"Miss Manners has nothing on her," Jade remarked.

"Is she really this rude to everyone?" Clare asked Jade. "You've known her longer."

"It helps that you're from Pennsylvania," Jade said wryly.

Sylvia climbed the deck step, "Hello all! We are going to have us a little party, aren't we." *Joy.*

"Mom," Rod yelled from the yard. "Where are the poles?"

Sylvia spun around, "Poles for what?" She hollered back.

"The volleyball net."

"There are no poles," Sylvia looked at him as if he was the brainless twit we've all discovered him to be.

Gesturing broadly with both hands, she added, "#//*it darling. Find two trees and string it up!" She shook her head and disappeared back into the house.

Phil and Ella and about fifteen extras from the lake were huddled in the yard next to a car. Backed onto the lawn, the trunk was open and a full mobile bar seemed to unfold like an elaborate Broadway set. A cooler held multiple bottles of wine buried in ice, along with another jug of mystery juice. Beside the cooler a tower of cocktail and wine glasses was neatly stacked. Heath's words echoed in my head, *"If it involves food and booze, they do it up right."*

The kids rushed off to play football in the twilight. Judging by the level of exhaustion of all parties, I predicted there would be tears and/or injuries forthcoming.

Hontie offered greetings to all, as she joined us on the deck. Wearing a nervous but accommodating smile, she surveyed the party that had manifested in less than ten minutes. "My oh my," she said collapsing next to Jade. "Davis is down; he was so sleepy."

The car bar crew erupted with laughter. Jade frowned, "I am afraid with the noise level out here it won't be for long." As if on queue, a cry rang out from an upstairs window.

"Oh dear," Hontie started to push from the chair.

"I got it," Jade assured her. "See you guys tomorrow... right?" We gave her the comforting been there before 'hmmm'. We knew the reality of a tired mom settling a toddler. Lying down along side them usually ended like a heavy weight boxer in a title match. Mom knocked out cold long before the child.

Hontie glanced around at the activity the invasion had brought. I guess years of being forced to roll with the free spirited lifestyle that traveled with Phil and Ella, left her unfazed. "What did I miss?" she asked Clare.

"Mom is settling Art and Jewel in the living room and Gavin is starting a fire," Clare filled her in. "I believe they are planning to string up a volleyball net, and so far I've seen lots of people and booze, but no food."

"Oh," she sighed deeply and settled into her chair. "Where are they putting the volleyball net?"

Happy that the focus was not caring for the locust, I followed Hontie's lead and sat back to enjoy the show. Anya and the lawn mowing virgin, Thea, stood off the deck where various men had begun to fiddle with the grill. Ella, wine bottle in hand, joined them.

"Where do you want us?" Anya asked Ella as the trio climbed onto the deck.

Ella looked at the small table. "Here's as good a place as any." She plopped the wine on the table, and disappeared into the house. We watched as the troop settled in. Food, drinks, they had even brought their own ash trays. Anya called to her husband and the clan, Thea, Somi, and Honeysuckle climbed onto the deck. They tossed some bagged snacks and a few bottles of uncorked wine in the middle of the table.

"We need three more chairs," Anya said to Somi.

Shocked, Clare and I observed the Cur Queen as she bustled back into the house and emerged a few moments later with the chairs. *Amazing.* Running short on square footage, Somi placed the chairs legs within inches of my toes and the backs nearly against my knees. I looked across to Clare whose eyes had narrowed to dangerous slits. I shrugged my shoulders; "I must be invisible."

Clare snorted, "Super powers, cool."

Rod leaned casually on the railing by the steps. Somi turned and offered him a bag of snacks. "Are we set up for volleyball?" she asked him.

Sign me up for this game. How long would it take to transform Frostine into the Jolly Grass-stained Giant.

Rod greedily snagged the snack bag she offered and grabbed a handful of chips. "The only trees I found are over by the barn and one team will have to play in the flowerbed."

"Doable. Have a beverage then go put the net up." Somi turned back to her peers. She lifted a bottle of red wine. "If I've started with red do I stay with red?"

Warren, our greeter from the chapel answered her. His rich warm voice softly rolled over the deck. "Always move darker as the night moves on. Never go lighter until daybreak." *This must go along the lines of 'beer before liquor, never sicker'. Whackos.*

The wails of the first football casualty reached the deck. The little boy belonging to Warren and Anya screamed his way up the steps. Anya gathered him into the safety of her lap and his wailing calmed to a whimper.

"What's wrong darling?" Anya asked.

"I-I-I... b-b-ball... d-d-d-ark... f-f-fell," the boy sputtered between tears.

"I think Ella said there are movies to watch." *Nurture him momentarily.* Anya passed him to his father's arms, and moved inside to find Ella and the video babysitter before the wine went bad.

And I thought this train wreck had ended after the wedding reception.

The group at the table huddled together in hushed private conversation. They nodded to one another as they topped off their wine glasses. With a broad smile Somi peered over the deck, making sure to include Hontie and Clare in the sweep. "Do you think that there will be any food?"

Clare's hand slowly moved to Hontie's knee, "Don't you move," she whispered fiercely like a mother tiger protecting her young. The table of the elite snickered which only fueled Queen Frostine.

Draping her arm on the chair back, long white clad legs crossed at the knees, Somi turned the wattage up on her charm, "Phil?"

Phil sauntered to the steps with a cigar clamped between his teeth, "Yeah Somi sweetheart, what can I do for you?"

"Do we need to go to the store?" She batted her eyes innocently. "There doesn't seem to be any food." *Pout, pout.*

"Food... yeah," he looked at his watch. "Grocery closes at about 9:00, burgers sound good?"

"Anything would be great," she spoke dramatically. "We all haven't eaten since noon. We're ravenous."

"Alright, burgers." He scanned the hopefuls, "anybody want to ride along?" Rod nodded. "Cool buddy... can you drive 'cause *here's the thing*. My car's back at the house." Rod's head bobbled again and they moved toward the cars. "Damn," Phil stopped short patting his pockets, "My wallet's at the house, too." *Of course it was.* Phil looked to Rod who was already shaking his head. Those pockets were empty. "Hang on buddy," Phil puffed on his cigar thoughtfully. Striding back to the deck, "Wifey!" he boomed. "God I just love the sound of that!" Chuckles from the posse encouraged him. "Oh wifey." *Gag.* "I need some money for the grocery."

"What sweet'ums," Ella emerged out of the kitchen. "Money?" Patting her obviously pocketless skirt, she feigned surprise. "I didn't think to grab my bag."

Shock... Awe... Really? Do you own a bag?

Hontie and Clare sat statuesque and watched the Oscar caliber performance. *Masterful. I should tell you,*

Hanks, Cruise, Selleck, all the Hollywood 'Toms' couldn't have gotten it better. Who would tonight's sucker be? High Functioning Joe hadn't arrived yet. The suspense built.

Warren slid his son from his lap and told him to find his mama. He dug deeply into his pockets, and then scrutinized the cash in hand. I smiled as I watched him tuck the bills safely back into his pocket. "I'll drive you," his mellow voice rippled out.

Couldn't help but wonder what other impromptu expenses he'd covered.

Warren moved to where Rod was still standing. "Get back on that volleyball net, Rod," he gave his shoulder a pat. Rod's head jiggled yet again, and he headed off toward the barn.

Clare nudged Hontie. The brief exchange of words ended with looks of concern on both of their faces. Hontie exited the deck and followed Rod toward the barn. I gave Clare a questioning look. She mouthed 'moon garden'.

"Huh?"

"Volleyball, trees by the barn... one team in the flower bed."

"Oh," understanding, **"OH!** You don't really think they'd... " *Of course they would.*

Now that the food crisis was being handled and we knew what order to drink our wine... What's left? Oh yes, video-sitter. As the crowd shifted around the table, I moved out of my corner to sit with Clare. "Can you freakin' believe this?" she said as I sat. "They are like a plague. Move in, take over, and destroy."

"And to think I used to long for their carefree life-style. I am starting to view it for what is, leeching. Really skilled leeching."

"Well how long can it take to make burgers? Maybe they will decide we are lame and move on."

"Do you really think it's over?" I laughed tightly, "The night is young my friend."

Jade reappeared, looking a little haggard herself. "Davis is finally down," she crossed her fingers. "Impossible... right?" She sank into the chair on the other side of Clare. "What have I missed, or don't I want to know."

"The invaders brought no food, so Phil rounded up a willing wallet and went to the store for burger stuff," Clare said.

"They are setting up volley ball in the moon garden and since the sun is going down, they are discussing indoor videos for the delinquents," I added.

"Burgers and volleyball I can skip," Jade said, "but just where will the multitude of wild children be viewing videos?" her temper ignited.

"We were going to suggest hell," I told her flippantly, "But we're invisible."

"Super powers," Clare said with quick double raise of her brow. Jade's eyes lightened momentarily, grateful for the attempt at levity.

"Don't get too concerned about the videos," I tried to soothe her. "The TV is in the back bedroom. Ella's in a mini skirt and heels, so it's probably a non-issue."

"I just got Davis to sleep... you know?" Through the wide open deck doors, Jade watched in horror as high heeled Ella chugged through the kitchen, TV in hand.

Ella passed through the kitchen and called out just loud enough for us to hear "Anya, just give me a minute to hook this up in the bedroom, then send the kids up."

Jade was instantly enraged. "Did she say bedroom?" Clare and I nodded. "No way," Jade seethed and was on her feet and through the door after her.

Meanwhile, out at the barn Rod was trying his inebriated best to secure the volleyball net to the trees beside the moon garden. He had secured the first side and was moving to the second.

"Rod," Hontie interrupted his progress. "This is not an okay spot for a volleyball game."

Ankle deep in white blossoms he said "Looks good to me."

Flabbergasted, but only momentarily stunned Hontie tried again. "Not in my moon garden," she said a little more firmly.

He stopped, confusion riddled his face. "Moon what?"

"You will need to find another spot for your game." Hontie said firmly.

Rod scratched his head and repeated "moon what?" Satisfied she had made her point, Hontie crossed the drive. She bumped into Anya on her way through the mudroom.

"Rod out there?" Anya asked.

"Yes, he's moving the volleyball net," Hontie replied and stepped into the kitchen in time to see Jade burst in from the deck.

"If she wakes up Davis, I'll have to kill her," Jade growled.

"What?" Hontie rebounded to the next crisis.

"Movies for the mass of uncontrolled children in your bedroom," Jade clipped after Ella with Hontie on her heels.

Anya found her brother, Rod, on pause by the tree with the volleyball net in his hands. "What's doing, Bro? Need a hand?"

"I'm not sure. Lottie said not to play here, but there isn't a second choice." Rod looked at his sister for guidance. "I'm not sure..." *Being half drunk only added to his keen mind.*

"Why not here? Two trees, lights and lawn," she looked at the flowers. "Well, half a lawn."

"Something about a moon garden, I mean, come on, they're plants, they grow."

"Yeah, just put it up. Lottie just needs to deal with it." Anya clapped her hands, "Come on Bro, let's get it hung; it's getting dark."

Clare and I sat and watched as the swarm got more settled. Somi rose and greeted her man, as he and Anya rejoined the group. I listened as she inquired about the volleyball net. "It's up by the barn," Rod told her. Somi handed him a glass of wine, as Anya murmured something to her about Hontie's request for there to be another location for the game. Somi just threw her head back and released a wicked laugh.

"At least the damn twinkle lights will be good for something," Somi clinked her wine glass together with Anya and Rod.

"That's it," Clare seethed and stood abruptly. "I'm done. Good night, Georgia." She moved into the house, leaving me alone on the deck with the idiot troop. *Thanks Clare.*

Phil and Warren returned from the store with bags of groceries. The food goddesses sprung into action. I watched Somi, Ella, and Anya in the kitchen forming huge burger patties, washing and chopping colorful veggies. Sylvia appeared with a large pottery bowl and began to hand toss what would soon be an incredible salad. Outside Phil, Gavin, and Rod stood puffing on cigars around the grill as it heated. Brennan and Payton were off somewhere playing in the field with the delinquents. I sat in the comfort of my Harry Potter invisibility cloak, as the obscure conversations trickled in and out of my hearing range.

Warren filled his wine glass, then shocked me when he turned and offered me a glass. *Not so invisible after all.* Holding up my hands I shook my head. "No, thanks though."

"Sure thing," He lifted a pack of thin cigars from the table and opened them. Seated across from him was Thea, the Californian artist I had met on the first day. "Thea, what is your full name?" Warren focused on her intently, as he struck a match and ignited his cigar.

"Theadora, Theadora Norton," she answered.

"Theadora," he said slowly, savoring each syllable. "Theadora Norton, Theadora Norton," he quietly repeated her name. **"NI-ICE,"** Warren's rich voice bellowed. I swallowed a chuckle, as he swirled his wine and took a sip. He switched his attention to Honeysuckle and asked her the same. "Honey, what is your full name?"

"Honeysuckle Dawn." *For crying out loud.*

"Honeysuckle Dawn, Honeysuckle Dawn…" he drew out the name once again, **NI-ICE!"** I had stopped listening as Ella returned to the deck. "Georgia? You out here?"

"Yep."

"What movies do you have along for kids?"

"Depends on where they are watching them," I answered flatly, drawing more attention than I wanted.

"What?" Ella was confused by my sarcasm.

Pleased with my small victory, I stood my ground. "If the TV is upstairs near Davis who has just fallen asleep, then

I have none. If the TV is downstairs in the dining room, then I have three."

A slight flicker of annoyance touched Ella's expression. "Oh, I set the TV up downstairs where it's more manageable."

Reasonable of you. "The movies were on the floor in the bedroom where the TV was."

"Thanks," Ella said tightly.

I'm over it.

Dark was now upon us. The time to round up my kids had come. "Brennan," I called out into the night.

"Yeah," his response floated from the field to my ears.

"Time to come in, and bring your brother please."

"Alright."

"Brennan," Warren's focus was now 100% on me. "Brennan, your son?" I nodded. "What is his full name?"

"Brennan Kyle," I answered.

"Brennan Kyle, Brennan Kyle," Warren chanted then inhaled deeply on his narrow cigar. On a long slow exhale, **"NI-ICE,"** his approval again rang out. *I was glad it was dark because this moment was well, ridiculous.* "And your young one?"

"Payton," I told him stifling a giggle, "Payton Logan." He swirled the wine in his glass.

"Payton Logan, Payton Logan," he blew a steady stream of smoke. **"NI-ICE,"** he bellowed again. *Crack, I tell you. No other reasonable explanation.*

Brennan bounded up the steps followed by Payton. "Can I have a snack Mommy?" Payton asked.

"Aunt Catheryn's cookies are in on the table." He dashed inside in search of sugar. Brennan plopped down in my lap. "I'm hungry too Mom, but not for cookies."

"Phil is fixing burgers."

"Great," Brennan said "I'm starving."

"In fact, you can walk over to the grill and make sure he knows you want one," I encouraged him.

"Alright," I watched him cross the lawn where Phil and Rod and a few others surrounded the sizzling grill. Brennan made his request.

Phil playfully hooked him in a gentle headlock. "Five minutes Bud." Phil pointed to the smoking grill, "This one's got your name on it. Why don't you get a roll ready?"

Bren rushed into the house to do just that. I followed him to lend a hand but also to check on Payton. In the dining room Scooby Doo blared from the TV which sat on the plank floor. Five delinquents were sprawled across an heirloom quilt munching on leftover wedding cookies and slurping juice boxes. Payton had stretched out on his belly under the table playing his Gameboy.

I moved to the front sitting room where Jewel and Arthur were seated comfortably while Mom tended the fire. "This looks cozy;" I touched Jewel's shoulder.

"It is, quite." Jewel nodded toward Mom. "Your mother's got a hand with the fire."

"She should," I answered. "She's a pioneer woman." At Jewel's raised brow I explained, "Mom's home is wood heated." Notably impressed, Jewel inclined her head.

"When is the gift opening?" Art asked curtly.

"Sorry, I'm not running this shindig," I looked at him and shrugged.

"Well, I'm ready to be done," he said. "I've been sitting at the lake all day and now I'm sitting here. I'm cold, hungry, and tired. I'm ready to get a move on."

"Here, here," Jewel agreed.

Sylvia zipped into the room, "Great company, great fire, how are we doing in here?" she all but sang.

"Oh, I think 'we' are about done," Mom said quietly.

"That's a lovely fire," Sylvia said, as if Mom hadn't spoken. She tucked the blanket around Art's legs and delivered a quick peck to his cheek. "This is such a lovely spot." She turned to Jewel and patted her quilt covered legs, punctuating each word. "A lovely, lovely spot." And with that Sylvia was gone. Mom and I stared unbelieving after her. It was clear to me Sylvia was having a grand time and wasn't about to have her evening cut short.

Delinquents began to argue in the dining room, a moment later Davis began to cry from an upstairs bedroom. *Unbelievable.* Disgusted I went into the dining room and hitched Payton up to my hip. "Hey, he's not sharing that game," one of the delinquents whined at me.

I shot him a look I generally reserved for adult jack-asses. "He doesn't need to share it."

"Where are we going Mommy?" a weary Payton asked as he laid his head on my shoulder.

"Home buddy." I needed to get out of here.

"But I'm **starming**," he protested weakly. I grabbed him another handful of wedding cookies. "Thanks, Mommy." *More cookies? Why not?* I bumped into Jade in the kitchen, and mentioned that I heard Davis crying upstairs.

"Yeah, I sent Gavin up… enough, right." She checked out Payton's hand full of cookies. "Nice… give up on real food?"

"I've given up on a lot. Hey I know you're not looking to baby-sit, but could you watch Payton for ten minutes? I need to go upstairs."

"Sure... we're good, right little man?" Jade said as I transferred Payton. I walked slowly to navigate the laundry room maze. Clare should be asleep by now so I walked quietly as I formulated my escape plan. Standing on the threshold of the bedroom I could see the aftermath of the TV removal. Playing cards were strewn across the floor, video tapes tossed carelessly across the air mattress. Disgusted, I knelt down and started gathering the UNO cards.

"Have you been fed?"

I practically jumped out of my skin. "For cryin' out loud, Clare, I thought you were asleep."

"I'm too pissed to sleep," fury vibrated in every word.

I took a good look at her. She was lying on her side with her arms crossed over her chest, glaring at a fixed point across the room. *Scary.* "Clare, can you get all your stuff together?"

"What?" Clare sat up abruptly.

I shoved the deck of cards into the box and spoke slowly for clarity. "Can you get your things into the Jeep? Now. I'm ready to leave."

Clare clutched her blanket to her chest as hope swam brightly into her eye. A moment later, hope was bumped aside by rational thinking. "Georgia," she said sadly shaking her head. "We can't do that to Hontie." *Damn it... Manners.* "Not to mention we'd look like idiots running off in the night." Clare searched her mind for a viable alternative. She raised her hands in defeat and flopped back down on the cot and softly whimpered. "We're trapped." In frustration she grabbed her pillow, covered her face and screamed.

"You're right, I know it. Shit." I walked to the window and looked down on Hontie's cheerful twinkle lights glowing over the moon garden. "From up here it all looks so tranquil and lovely." Maybe Clare had the right idea hiding upstairs until morning. I noticed the two parallel trees without the volleyball net, "at least they listened about the volleyball net. I don't see it out there, anyway."

"It's behind the barn," Clare's voice was muted in her pillow.

"Oh, that's a better place, but there aren't any lights back there."

"No," she lowered the pillow, "I mean I threw it there, after I untied it from the trees."

I raised my eyebrows, not able to stop the giggle that pushed from my lips. "Clare, I'm surprised at you."

"I have my moments." She said trembling with laughter. "Mom wouldn't be pleased with me."

"On the contrary, under these circumstances I bet she would be very proud. Well done." Resigned to my fate, I descended the steps. I would finish the evening with the idiots comforted by the fact that I would never have to share the same air space with the majority of these people again. I entered into round two of midnight madness.

On the deck the aroma of sizzling burgers teased my nose. Payton was curled on Jade's lap munching sleepily on cookies. Beside them sat Sasha, watching as only a canine could for any crumb to drop. "Thanks for hanging onto this guy," I lifted him to my shoulder.

"No sweat... right?" Jade stood and stretched. "Sit here Georgia; I need booze... and food... in that order."

I plopped into the chair and snuggled Payton into my lap where he handed off his cookies to Sasha. Brennan joined us a moment later with a hot-off-the-grill burger. "That looks good, honey."

"I'm so hungry." He sank his teeth in. "Mmmm... ."

"Well, enjoy it then we'll head up and I'll kick your butt at UNO."

"Awww, you said butt!" Payton scolded me. "We don't say butt," he looked to Brennan for confirmation and then took my face into both of his tiny hands. "Mommy," he said firmly, "we don't say butt."

I snickered.

"You just said it three times," Brennan pointed out.

"Shh," I gentled Payton's head to my shoulder, "eat Bren, so we can go to bed."

Across from us Frostine and her posse had lit candles and were huddled around the small table enjoying burgers and fresh salad. Much like last night, it was a private little party. Why had they felt the need to move here from the lake house? Why relocate? They were oblivious to those who were calling this residence home and they certainly didn't come over to include any of us. Frostine led the conversation. She was describing a friend who was a designer in New York City. She had just her presented her first line. "...did you know how she struggled with that?" Frostine said laying the drama on thick. "She wore the slip dress and the pale green Prada's; Somi fanned herself for effect. "She looked incredible." The other women at the table hummed in agreement "It was just sooo not like her to step out of her level of comfort to wear such an extraordinary ensemble." Somi clasped her hands to her chest, "She was so brave."

It took effort for me not to snort. It's no wonder this group struggled to mingle with those such as us. Fashion bravery? *Cripes, let's hop back on the reality train.*

Phil plunked into the seat next to me. I pulled out my best manners. *I had to dig really, really deep.*

"Great night," Phil said holding up his huge burger. "Great eats, huh Bren," and sunk his teeth in.

"Yeah," Brennan agreed.

"Georgia," Phil swallowed hastily, "did you get one?"

"No, I'm good."

"Oh, just look at this night," he said breathlessly, and not just a little starry eyed. "It's just like Christmas." *None that I could remember, but seeing as the past several days had been an endless party on someone else's dime, I could understand his confusion.*

More than ready to wrap up my holiday celebration, I turned to Brennan, "Buddy, you about done?"

"Yep," He brushed off his hands and swallowed the last bite.

Payton was sound asleep in my lap. "You head in, hit the bathroom, and I'll meet you upstairs."

One hour of butt-kicking UNO, and Brennan, the champion joined Payton in dreamland. Clare was still trying to sleep. As I turned over to settle in, guitar music began to float up and into our window from the moon garden below.

"What now?" Clare grumbled from her cot.

"Could be the 4th of July seeing as we've already had Christmas."

"Huh?" She pushed to an upright position.

I extracted myself from the inflate-a bed and peeked out the window. Below Phil sat cross legged on top of the picnic table, guitar cradled in his lap. Gavin and Jade relaxed in chairs beside him while the twinkle lights flickered overhead. "Well Clare, the weekend we counted on, is happening now."

"What do you mean?" she asked quietly.

"Have a beer, relax on the deck with family... Phil is sitting with Gavin and Jade by the moon garden, serenading them."

"Eleventh hour."

"Should we go down? I feel like we should..." At that moment a distant echoing sound met my ears.

"Forget it?" Clare cursed and flopped back down. A rumbling grew louder as the posse moved through the kitchen beneath us. With the grace of a stampeding herd of buffalo, they rolled from the mudroom below. "Yeah, Frostine and friends just arrived." I turned my back to the window as the group settled in. Second wind gone, I lay back down. "Good night, Clare."

"Night."

Several hours, many solos, duets and group choruses of a varying array of talent later, I finally fell asleep.

Chapter 27

"We're outta here like a boner in sweatpants."

Departure day had finally arrived. Never in all my years had I ever been so happy to see the end of a trip come. I got up, got dressed, and quietly went downstairs to organize my belongings.

I backed the Jeep up to the deck steps and adjusted the seats to create a larger cargo area. We had a lot of bounty to transport home. Clare found me about an hour later, "Wow, you've been busy." Hugging her coffee mug, she leaned on the deck rail.

"Done is done," I wrapped in another parcel, "I'm ready to leave."

"I can see that," rubbing a hand over her face, she yawned deeply. "What's the plan?"

"Departure ASAP." Clare glanced over the piles I had organized on the lawn by the Jeep. I began to drag her barstools across to the deck and could feel the disapproval in her gaze boring into the back of my head. "You didn't wrap up all the purchases, did you?" she spoke gently, "We need the Bouckville Bounty shot."

I shot her a not so friendly look, "You *are* kidding?"

Setting her mug aside Clare wrung her hands. "We don't want to disappoint Hontie," she said.

"Heavens no," I said dramatically. "Why are *we* so concerned with others?"

"Because you were raised properly," Clare snipped, a little too mom-like, then disappeared back inside.

I watched her go, counted to ten then decided to postpone my personal pity party. Disappoint others? *Cripes!*

I stopped condensing the bounty and decided to pack the luggage. In the process I unearthed yet another empty container of booze and a full 6-pack of Bud in the back seat of the Jeep. *Finders keepers.*

Satisfied with my pre-pack, I moved on to the positioning of loot for the traditional photograph. By the time I finished carrying the stools and various other purchases back to the deck, the rest of the house was awake. Gavin and Jade were examining the bounty and we filled them in on the stories behind each treasure. This year was as eclectic as ever. Chalk-ware bulldogs, classic toys, retro bar stools, bull horns, smuggled pottery, and because the boys were along, a few toy trucks and guns.

Hontie hauled out her professional camera and took several shots while checking lighting and shadows. She had just completed a professional class in photography and the attention to detail was killing me. Every moment the process was extended, just added to my impatience. Finally… Hontie finished and I began to load up the car.

I heard mutterings and humor attempts about 'Georgia being full of energy' and 'I'm not sure why Georgia is rushing'. *For the love of all things holy... These had been the longest 120 hours of my life. Hours, mind you, that have been lost forever.*

"You guys heading right out?" Hontie asked while she put the camera away.

"Yes," I grabbed a stool and passed her on the way to the Jeep.

"Phil and Ella are coming by to open their gifts in a little bit," she offered.

I promptly bit the inside of my cheek. *'Find a happy place' I schooled myself.*

"Do you want to stay for that?"

She must have added crack to her coffee. "No."

"Well alright," she sounded a little sad and put off.

Well, imagine that. I was too tired for emotional blackmail. Clare came out to help load the Jeep, and saw I was deep in puzzle pack mode. She lifted a small bag and held it out, "Will it all go in?"

"Yes." I took the small bundle of breakables from her.

Looking over my shoulder, Clare examined my pack job. I knew she couldn't help herself, so I waited. It didn't take her long. "Maybe the stool should go over there, and if you shift the suitcases to the..." catching my expression, "...oh you've got it under control."

"I do," I pointed to the small pile of packages by the rear tire, "put those behind the seat." I placed the last large item in and closed the hatch firmly. "Twenty minutes Clare."

"Oh... well."

I stared at Clare assuring her that I was *not* open for a debate.

"Girls?" Mom called as she stepped on the deck. "I'm missing the canvas bag that my tent was in. Have either of you seen it?"

"Black right?" I asked her. She nodded hopefully. "Phil carried it back from the field on set up day, check the barn."

"Good thought." She began to leave and then noticed the fully packed Jeep. "You guys going now?"

"Yep," I prepared for Mom's get-you-to-my-way-of-thinking tactic.

"I'll be right behind you." Caught off guard, Clare and I gaped at Mom. Must have been a survivor's instinct, run away as fast as you can!

"You may want to check the barn too, Georgia. A lot of things got tossed in there by a lot of different people," Clare commented.

"Casualties of war at this point as far as I'm concerned." She handed me the last bag of small items which fit in the last available spot, on the floor by the front seat. "If I leave here with my kids and what remains of my sanity, I'll consider myself lucky." I shut the passenger door, "We're a go, time for good-byes."

We walked into the kitchen. Gavin and Jade were tidying up breakfast. "We're heading out," Clare said.

"Get out while you can… right," Jade gave us each a hug. "Travel safe."

"You too, enjoy your one on one with Hontie," I said, "and keep us in pictures so we can watch Davis grow."

"Yeah… fast changes… right?"

"Are the boys all playing together?" I gestured to the living room. I had barely seen them all morning. Jade smiled, "that's cool," I told her.

Clearly upset, Mom came through the mudroom. "Oh I'm just sick, sick about it," she muttered.

She was trailed by Hontie who kept repeating, "It will turn up, Isabella, it will."

Mom whirled on her. "It will have to be replaced, Charlotte. It belongs to the church. Poco serio!" Mom's voice spiked.

Hontie's head hung. Even she was showing signs of weariness. "Going?" Hontie said to Clare and me.

"Yes," we answered in unison.

Inhaling deeply, Hontie's head popped up with a huge smile in place as she said, "Thanks for the kitchen."

She was shooting for cheerful but her smile screamed insanity.

"No tent case, I gather," I said as I looked to Mom.

"No. No tent case." Disgusted, she began to tidy the barbeque mess the transient takers had left piled in the kitchen sink. Mumbling and she rinsed and stacked, "Mareado... I'm just sick about it."

"It will turn up," Hontie repeated wearily.

Say it a third time, and click your heels Dorothy, and maybe it will come true. Or maybe just hitch a ride over that rainbow and then onto the half-way house. Cripes.

I hollered for the kids to potty. Brennan listened, of course. Payton walked to the kitchen and began to debate. "Mommy," he furrowed his brow and placed his tiny hands on hips, "my wiener's not full."

Clare's mouth fell open visibly unhappy with my parenting methods. "His wiener is not full?" Clare shook her head and with a shocked whisper she muttered, "Georgia, good grief."

Ignoring her, I focused on Payton. "Try to empty your body anyway."

"But my wiener **IS** empty," he insisted.

"Please try." He conceded and with a final round of hugs we were ready to load up. "Seat belts boys," I climbed behind the wheel. "Ready?" I turned to Clare.

"Oh, soooo ready."

We waved a last good-bye and eased out of the drive. Out of the corner of my eye, my vision caught the one constant from the entire trip. Still standing tall, strong, and with seal yet unbroken, the lone bottle of water on top of the mailbox pole.

"Well, would you look at that," Clare said. Wordlessly we drove back to the interstate. Within a few miles the boys were snoring in the backseat surrounded by this year's Bouckville bounty.

EPILOGUE

Seated in the living room surrounded by a pile of torn gift wrap, Phil and Ella fussed over some bath towels. "Look at the colors!" she exclaimed. "They're so domestic."

"They aren't for the lake," Hontie called out from the dining room, and the remaining posse chuckled respectfully.

"They are just lovely, darling," Sylvia said perched on her husband's knee. Wine glass in hand, she looked on as her daughter proceeded with the next gift. "Simply, lovely."

Eventually Phil and Ella were down to cards. The eagerness for fast cash could be felt in the air. Several checks, gift certificates and hardware store vouchers later, they were on to 'The Big One'. Ella handed Phil the last remaining card for him to do the honors. "This one is from your Dad…" she drifted off in expectation.

Uncle Nathan's generous wedding check had been much anticipated. But most likely, knowing Phil and Ella, every penny was already spent. As Phil opened the card, a quick flicker of surprise crossed his face.

"Wow, what a gift." Phil handed Ella the opened card. Ella glanced down a neatly written column of figures listing the unexpected expenses Uncle Nathan had covered over the last few days:

$5,000.00

$ - 250.00 for Bride and Groom attire

$ - 300.00 for alcohol

$ - 400.00 for extra rehearsal dinner guests

$ - 450.00 for accommodations

$ - 550.00 for reception expenses

And a check in the amount of $3050.00

Well done Uncle Nathan!

PS: The canvas tent carrying case turned up the following week, in guest's car, in Massachusetts.

"Here's the thing..." Phil said to Hontie, "the trunk was, ya' know... open, so I tossed it in."